HER
KIND
OF CASE

A Lee Isaacs, Esq. Novel

JEANNE WINER

**bancroft
press**

Interior design: Tracy Copes

Cover: J.L. Herchenroeder

Author Photo: Joanna B Pinneo

HC: 978-1-61088-228-6

PB: 978-1-61088-229-3

Kindle/Mobi: 978-1-61088-230-9

Ebook: 978-1-61088-238-5

Audio: 978-1-61088-232-3

Published by Bancroft Press "Books that Enlighten"

410-358-0658

P.O. Box 65360, Baltimore, MD 21209

www.bancroftpress.com

Printed in the United States of America

For my parents

Milton Winer (August 27, 1920 – February 20, 2009) and

Bernice Winer (October 15, 1923 – June 6, 2012)

And my friend

Jean Thompson (January 19, 1951 – November 4, 2015)

I couldn't have loved you all more

CHAPTER ONE

Someone was knocking on her office door, but Lee didn't move or call out. It was much too early to deal with other people's problems. Her first appointment wasn't scheduled until nine, an hour and a half away, so whoever was knocking so insistently wasn't one of her regular, semi-normal clients.

Her regular clients may have broken the law, perhaps even a very serious law, but they knew about etiquette. You called, made an appointment, and waited downstairs in the beautifully appointed lobby until the receptionist phoned the lawyer and she came down to meet you. So, more likely than not, it was her new court appointment, a client suffering from borderline personality disorder in the first phase of her relationship with Lee: I love you; you're my savior; I have to spend all my time at your feet. Later, in about a month, the second phase would begin: I hate you; you're about to fuck me over; I want a new lawyer.

The knocking stopped and Lee could hear footsteps retreating across the tiled hallway. Good. Although she was often grumpy, today was worse than usual. Partly it was the new pain in her neck—she tilted her head sideways and immediately regretted it—but mostly it was the fact that in exactly eight months she would turn sixty.

Sixty?

How distant and improbable it once sounded. The age when people were officially on the downhill side of their lives. They might still live another twenty or even thirty years, but never with the same physical ease and belief, whether true or not, that any disability could be overcome, that every trauma would eventually heal. When they were young, the Rolling Stones sang, "Time is on My Side." Well, not anymore.

Lee had woken up at home a few hours earlier with the new ache in the upper left side of her neck. When she'd pressed her finger on the exact spot where it hurt the most, she could hear a slight cracking sound. She'd made it crack about fifteen times and then given up. The ache was here to stay. She could tell. It had that certain quality she'd come to recognize: Hi, I'm your latest physical discomfort and I'll be with you for the rest of your life; get used to me.

She would try. In the meantime, she got dressed, ate breakfast and drove here, stopping on the way for a cappuccino, which briefly consoled her.

Now, instead of working, she was staring at the fake silk tree that took up a corner of the office. She'd bought the tree twenty-four years ago when she'd quit the Public Defender and gone into private practice. After looking at more than a dozen spaces, she'd picked this expensive one in the Highland building and been here ever since. The office was large and she'd needed to fill it up fast with appropriately classy furnishings so that her future clients, defendants in various criminal actions brought by the District Attorney in counties all over Colorado, would feel relaxed and reassured that they were hiring someone substantial, someone who wouldn't take their money under false pretenses and leave town in the middle of the night. Like they would.

Lee didn't think of herself as a fake-tree kind of woman, but the reality of watering and maintaining a real tree that would eventually lose its leaves or catch some kind of incurable disease convinced her. As she continued studying it, the tree struck her as a kind of minor miracle. After twenty-four years of benign neglect, it still looked good. No, it looked great. Real. Almost everyone who entered her office commented on how lovely it was and how did she keep it so healthy et cetera. She never responded, merely shrugged. Unless you actually walked over and fingered one of the perfect green leaves, you'd never know they were silk.

Maybe when her cat Charlie finally died—he had to be at least seventeen—she'd replace him with a fake silk cat, and position it near his favorite red ceramic food bowl. No more brushing, no more feeding, no more contemplating his eventual demise. She shook her head and frowned. Morbid reflections on a fake potted plant that was only doing what it was supposed to: look real, stay lovely, never age.

Her enormous oak desk was covered with stacks of paper, each one clamoring for attention. The number of them was reassuring. Unlike many of the lawyers that had been practicing as long as Lee, thirty-four years, she wasn't at all tired of the work, wasn't longing for the day she could shut her office door, hand in her keys, and pursue a lifelong dream of sailing around the world, volunteering at an orphanage in Mumbai, or whatever it was people thought they had to do before they got too old. Lee was doing it right now. She'd had two stable passions since law school: lawyering and karate, defending people and kicking them.

After years of practice, she'd become one of the preeminent criminal defense attorneys in the Boulder–Denver area and had attained the rank of a master in Tae Kwon Do when she was awarded her fifth-degree black belt. There was nothing more she aspired to do, except to keep on doing what she loved. Which meant doing it well or not at all, and no matter how much it cost, concealing any signs of effort. Someday her mind or body might betray her, but for now she was the consummate professional flashing that easy, what-me-worry smile as the sweat dripped or poured down the sides of her expensive silk blouse. Look real, stay lovely, never age.

For no good reason—it was 7:36—the wooden clock on her desk emitted one of its gentle gong-like sounds that miraculously failed to annoy her. A present from Paul who somehow always knew what she'd like and what she'd dump into the nearest wastebasket. The sound was supposed to wake her up to the present moment. Mostly it just reminded her of Paul and the past. Like half the people in Boulder (well, maybe not half), Paul had been a Buddhist. When he meditated, it was quiet and peaceful so Lee could get lots of work done and they could still be in the same room—unless he was gone for a few months on one of his high-altitude mountaineering trips, which was also fine.

Unlike most couples, there had been a profound lack of noise in their relationship. Neither of them was afraid of fighting. There simply wasn't much to fight about. When she missed Paul, it was often just that silent harmony, the unexpected happiness of two self-contained people living together and doing exactly as they pleased. Had she taken that happiness for granted? No, she thought, never. Then caught herself and blew out an exasperated breath. The myriad ways a self-employed professional could procrastinate.

Time to get serious or she'd end up working till midnight. With the barest of sighs, she picked up a new yellow highlighter, grabbed a sheaf of papers from the top of the nearest stack and settled into reviewing the contents: a warrant signed by a district court judge to search her client's home computer for evidence of child pornography. The client, a real estate broker, had been busted a few weeks ago after arranging to meet an undercover officer whom he believed was a twelve-year old girl named Candy.

Candy? The name alone screamed, "I am a trap and you are the stupidest mark on the planet if you actually think I'm real."

As was often the case, the client had a sweet clueless wife who, at least so far, was standing by her man. When Lee mentioned the possibility of probation, his wife cried, "But that's for guilty people!" Which is why you ought to ditch him, Lee thought, but of course kept her mouth shut, her face impassive. Dissemble or find another profession.

But it was impossible to concentrate. Her usual self-discipline had gone rogue. She rubbed her eyes and pushed the papers away from her. Too many distractions: the new pain in her neck, her upcoming sixtieth birthday, inconvenient memories, the fact that the police were using smaller and smaller fonts in their arrest reports.

She heard footsteps outside her door again and decided to chance it. If it was the new borderline, she could always pretend she was late, that she was on her way to the airport for a last-minute vacation in Patagonia— sorry for the earlier-than-expected betrayal. As she rose from her chair, Lee could see a white business card slide under the door. A salesperson, she guessed, wanting her to switch malpractice carriers or add some new eye-catching links to her admittedly barebones website.

"Can I help you?" Lee asked, yanking the door open.

"Oh, you're there."

An attractive middle-aged woman with auburn hair stood up looking appropriately embarrassed. She was wearing a simple but expensive pantsuit, much like Lee's in fact, and carried an elegant green leather handbag on her arm. Her smile was warm and open. Not a potential client unless she had a secret addiction to painkillers or was one of those lonely affluent women who couldn't stop stealing things they didn't need.

"I know it's early," the woman said, still embarrassed, "but I have to be at work at nine and so I thought I'd just pop over and see if perhaps you were an early bird like me."

Lee nodded in the polite noncommittal way she'd perfected for meetings such as this. Only fools rush in. Lee never rushed, and she rarely misjudged.

"May I come in?" the woman asked, peeking over Lee's shoulder in case someone else, an even earlier bird, was already there. "You're Lee Isaacs, aren't you?"

"That's me. What can I do for you?"

"You look exactly the way I imagined, except you're taller. And your silver hair is gorgeous. Lucky you. I started dyeing mine a year ago and I'm already sick of it."

"Pardon?"

"God, listen to me. I sound like a housewife at the gym. In fact, I have an MBA and I'm the head of human resources at The Boulder Tea Company. People fear me." She grinned. "That was a joke, the fear part." She stopped and took a deep breath. "Okay, I'm going to start again. Hi, my name is Peggy O'Neill and I think I want to hire you."

Within the wide acceptable range of normal, Lee decided, and finally smiled.

"Nice to meet you, Ms. O'Neill. Why might you want to hire me?"

"Please call me Peggy. And forgive me. I rarely say the first thing that pops into my head. Well, sometimes I do but only when I'm nervous or upset, which isn't often. My nephew is in trouble. Big trouble."

"Sounds serious." Lee stepped aside and pointed to a large oak chair that faced her desk. "Come on in and let's see if I can help him."

"Thank you. Thank you very much."

As Lee sat down, she brushed the pile of papers to the side and grabbed a blank legal pad off the small credenza behind her.

"So right now," Peggy was saying, "he has a public defender, a young man who seems quite competent but very busy. I have only one nephew. I want to help him and I want him to have the best." She blushed a little, which made her even more likeable. "Anyway, I've called around and the lawyers I spoke to thought this was your kind of case."

Lee knew what they meant: difficult, seemingly hopeless, emotionally draining cases that turn your hair silver. A paranoid schizophrenic stalking the same frightened woman for more than twenty years, a distraught mother suffocating her newborn while her husband was out of town on business, an abused runaway stabbing a social worker who threatened to call her parents—just a few of the many cases where she'd managed to pull the proverbial rabbit out of a hat.

"What's your nephew charged with?"

"Murder," Peggy said, as if she still couldn't quite believe it. "His name's Jeremiah Matthews, but everyone except his parents call him Jeremy. He'll be seventeen in a couple of months, on December 25th actually, which never seemed fair to me. When he was younger and my sister Mary still let me see him, I would always buy him two sets of presents, one for his birthday and one for the holiday." She sat back and glanced around the room. "This is very nice." She pointed at Lee's favorite picture, a print of an odd, curiously compelling purple horse, hanging near the door. "That's a Fritz Scholder, isn't it? I love his paintings."

"I do too," Lee said. "What did you mean by 'still let you see him'?"

"Okay, before she met Leonard, my sister Mary was a smart independent woman who made her living as a graphic designer. She was her own person, a feminist like me. I don't know what happened to her, but I think she was lonelier than she let on. Leonard was this good-looking charismatic man who talked like he had all the answers. He was a serious Christian but not yet a zealot." She shuddered with distaste. "From the moment I met him, I thought he was a creep. I couldn't understand why Mary went for him. Married him! But I love my sister, so I tried as hard as I could to get along with him, never argued when he pontificated about religion or politics." She rolled her eyes, reached into her pocket and pulled out a stick of sugar-free gum. "Would you like one? It's a pathetic substitute for Marlboros."

"No, and thanks for not smoking."

"You're welcome. Anyway, when Jeremy was eight or nine, they moved to Colorado Springs and joined some kind of fundamentalist Christian group that was against everything. No singing, no dancing, no socializing with anyone who doesn't accept Jesus as their savior . . ." Her face clouded over. "I can't believe my sister went along with it. But she did. After that, I was lucky if I got to see them once a year."

"That must have been tough," Lee said, scribbling down the information. Over the years, her notes had become illegible to everyone but her. After the first thirty or forty trials, she'd learned never to write anything that some curious bystander could easily decipher.

"Tell me about it. Mary and Jeremy are my only living relatives. I was married once, for just a couple of years in my thirties. And I thought *he* was a chauvinist pig. Compared to Leonard, he was a doll. Anyway, I never got pregnant. When Jeremy was little, I did a lot of babysitting and we got very close. I always figured I'd be his Auntie Mame, show him the world." She shook her head and sighed. "Instead, I'm hiring him a lawyer."

"Well, a trip to Marrakech would be fun, but you're getting him what he needs."

"Exactly. Too bad about Marrakech though."

"So, whom did your nephew allegedly murder?"

Peggy grunted as if she'd been punched in the solar plexus, a pain no martial artist ever got used to.

"Some poor guy named Sam Donnelly. That's all I know. According to the Daily Camera, he was killed by a group of skinheads and somehow or another Jeremy was with them. He must have met them in Denver after his parents threw him out. I can't imagine—"

"Whoa, hold on," Lee interrupted. "When did his parents throw him out?"

"About eight months ago, around the beginning of February. Jeremy came to see me a few days later and he was so cold he was shivering. I begged him to stay, told him he could live with me and go to school in Boulder. He thanked me but said he couldn't, that he had to make his own way. I gave him a down sleeping bag, all the cash I had, which was about four hundred dollars, and a check for another thousand that he either lost or threw away. I told him he was always welcome. He slept on the couch that night and was gone by the time I woke up." She shrugged helplessly. "I don't know what else I could have done. He was sixteen. I didn't want to call the police. Finally, I phoned my sister but she refused to discuss it. I think Leonard was standing next to her, like he always does. Anyway, all she said was that Jeremy wouldn't follow their rules anymore."

"Any ideas what those rules were?"

"Oh God," Peggy snorted. "Leonard had a million stupid rules. Let's see, no alcohol of course, no swearing, no card playing, no television except for Christian shows, no dating girls outside the church, that kind of thing. Last time I was there, they were dragging him to services almost every night."

"So Jeremy finally had enough."

"I guess so. But I can't imagine how he ended up associating with skinheads. He wasn't like that. Leonard was full of hate, but Jeremy wasn't."

"That's easy. He was on the street. Kids on the street need protection. They need a 'family.' If they're desperate, they can't afford to be choosy." Suddenly, the clock on Lee's desk gonged again, reminding her—as if she didn't know—that time was passing. She closed her notepad, set it down, and then placed her pen beside it. "I'm sorry, but I've got a number of appointments this morning, and you'll be late for work if you don't leave soon." She drummed her fingers while she thought. "I have to meet your nephew before deciding whether to take his case. Sometimes there isn't a fit, and with a murder case, there has to be. Ultimately, Jeremy has to trust me enough to do what I tell him."

"Makes perfect sense," Peggy said, handing Lee the white card she'd tried to slide under the door.

"Thanks." Lee pocketed the card, then pulled a slim black book out of her briefcase and began scanning the day's appointments. She was booked solid until six that evening, not even an hour for lunch. She'd have to run over to Alfalfas and order a sandwich to go. "I'll get to the jail this evening and call you afterward. If it's a fit, we can discuss a retainer. It'll be expensive."

"Yes, I know. The other lawyers warned me. Jeremy's my only heir, so I guess it'll be an early inheritance." She picked her handbag off the floor and stood up. "Oh, one more thing. The police wouldn't tell me much, but one of the detectives I spoke with hinted that it was a pretty gruesome death. I'm not trying to dissuade you. To the contrary, but I think it's only fair—"

"Thank you," Lee said, trying to stifle a smile. "I've handled dozens of murders and every one of them was gruesome. It doesn't upset me." Except when I lose, she thought.

"Well, I don't know how you do it."

Lee didn't know how she *couldn't* do it. After her first homicide case, a routine stabbing outside a bar in Longmont, she was hooked. Handling it took everything she had: her wits, her skills, her experience all coming together in service of her client. As soon as it was over, she couldn't wait till the next one. In between, she got by through representing clients on the usual thefts, assaults, and burglaries. Nothing wrong with garden-variety felonies; they paid the bills and often challenged her. But not enough. She couldn't *live* on them. For as long as she could remember,

Lee had always thrived on fierce competition. When she was twelve, she considered becoming a professional downhill ski racer, but then came the sixties, and the idea of her life's work consisting of getting down a mountain as fast as possible without killing herself seemed a bit shallow. Finally, during her third year of college, after watching a Perry Mason rerun where Perry trounced the DA for the millionth time and saved his client, Lee decided to become a criminal defense attorney.

"In any event," Peggy was saying, "it was a pleasure to meet you."

"Likewise." Lee stood up and reached out a hand.

"You're not a hugger, are you?"

"A hugger?" Lee took a small step backward.

"No, I didn't think so. Well then, I'll take a handshake and wait to hear from you."

As soon as Peggy left, Lee slumped back into her chair. A hugger? She shook her head and picked up the phone. Paul was a hugger; he hugged people he hardly knew, people he met in line at the movies, or at the bank. And he never minded that she wasn't. Superficially, they were very different, but deep down where it mattered, they were as close as identical twins. Sometimes when he read her mind, she pretended he was wrong, but he never was.

Lee frowned. Why all this reminiscing? Paul had died five years ago. She was fine now. Content. Except for this aging crap, which she would fight against and refuse to acknowledge for as long as possible. Jack Benny's older sister, forever fifty-nine.

Finally, she straightened up and dialed the public defender's office whose number, *mirabile dictu*, hadn't changed in the twenty-four years since she'd left.

"Boulder-public-defender's-office-can-you-hold?"

The greeting, as always, sounded like a long single word followed by a click. Lee simply waited. Carol, the receptionist, fielded over two hundred calls a day. After a few minutes, when the pain in her neck got bad enough, Lee remembered the loudspeaker button on the side of her phone, pressed it, and dropped the receiver onto her desk. Two or three minutes later, Carol's voice came on again.

"Can I help you?"

"Hey Carol, it's me, Lee Isaacs."

"Oh hi, Lee. How are you?"

"I'm great. Listen, could you find out who represents a juvenile named Jeremy Mathews? He's charged with murder."

"Sure hon, just give me a second. It's only eight-thirty and it's already a madhouse. Are you going to make one of my lawyers happy?"

"I'm thinking about it."

A public defender's caseload was ridiculously high. Because she was a perfectionist, it had taken Lee more than seventy hours a week to handle so many cases. After ten years of it, she'd had enough and quit. But when she was young and juggling over a hundred active felonies, it was always good news when one of her clients managed to hire someone from the private bar.

"Okay Lee, I've got it. It's Phil Hartman's case."

"Is he there?"

"For you he is. Hold on."

It took another few minutes, but eventually Phil picked up.

"Hey Lee, are you going to make my day?"

"Maybe." She leaned back in her chair and placed her feet carefully on her desk. She was wearing a pair of black leather boots with a silver chain around the ankle. The boots were at least fifteen years old but like most of Lee's possessions, they looked brand new—the upside of being a perfectionist.

"Oh happy day," he sang.

"I said maybe."

"Come on, Lee. I've got five ugly sex assaults, a three-time loser cooking meth next door to an elementary school, and a burglar caught in the victim's backyard carrying the victim's forty-two inch TV who says it's all just a big mistake and wants the charges dismissed."

The image made her smile. Like all criminal defense attorneys, she loved hearing about other people's hopeless cases. It was a lawyer thing. The more pathetic the case, the more terrible the facts, the funnier it was. An outsider listening in might think the stories were being exaggerated for effect, but in fact they weren't. Luckily for the DA, the vast majority of criminal cases were obvious and utter losers.

"But wait," Phil said. "Matthews is a street kid. Who's paying?"

"His aunt."

"Great, you'd be the perfect advocate for him. He's exactly your kind of client."

"That bad?"

She could hear Phil opening his file drawer, rummaging through it, and pulling out Jeremy's case.

"Okay," he said. "For starters, he's an asshole."

"Ooh."

"Yeah, and not only that, he confessed."

"He confessed? Shit. His aunt didn't know that." She slid to a sitting position and grabbed her notepad. "All right, read me what he said."

"Christ, why do juvies always confess? It's no fun. Wait, I'm still looking. Okay, here it is: 'After being advised, Mr. Matthews told us he acted as the lookout while the others kicked Mr. Donnelly to death. According to Mr. Matthews, the victim was quote just a faggot who deserved to die unquote. Mr. Matthews also admitted kicking the victim a few times, but wasn't sure whether the victim was already dead. After these admissions, Mr. Matthews refused to answer any more questions and told us he needed to lie down and go to sleep. Detective Armstrong then escorted him to the juvenile detention center. On the ride over, Mr. Matthews became belligerent when he learned he was being separated from his co-defendants and demanded that he be housed at the Boulder County Jail. Because of his age and other security issues, his request was denied.'" Phil paused. "So, there you go. Not so bad really."

"Not so bad?"

"Well, I mean it could be worse. Let's see, they could have pushed the victim off a cliff."

Lee stared at her purple horse, which was almost but not quite faceless.

"I don't know about you," she said, still trying after twenty years to make out the horse's expression, "but personally, I'd rather be pushed off a cliff and be done with it than be kicked to death which would have taken much longer."

"You know what? You're absolutely right. I'd pick the quick death off a cliff too. No question about it. So, yeah, your client's an asshole."

"My client?"

"Oh come on, Lee. I know you're going to take it. You're dying on the vine. I haven't seen your name in the papers for months. You need something to keep you up at night."

"I have my cat," she muttered, drumming her fingers on her desk. He was right, though. She *was* dying on the vine. But was she ready to risk losing something big again? She was still licking her wounds from the last one, a self-defense case the jury didn't buy. Was it time? She'd been careful not to promise Peggy anything, had left open the possibility that she and the kid might not make a good team. But that wasn't really it, the reason for her hesitation—it was fear. Fear that she might no longer be at the very top of her game. And anything less than the top was below it and therefore unacceptable.

"Hello? Lee? You haven't hung up on me, have you?"

"Is there anything else particularly terrible besides the confession?"

"You mean besides the way the victim died?"

"Yes."

"How much time do you have?"

She glanced at the clock on her desk. It was a quarter to nine.

"Not much. How did they get caught?"

"Let's see. The report says that the three older skinheads were bragging about a 'boot party' a few nights later at a place called The Sapphire Lounge in Denver—"

"The Sapphire Lounge on Colfax?" Lee asked. "I used to eat Mexican food there. Probably thirty years ago."

"When you were ten?"

"You must be truly desperate to resort to flattery."

"It's not flattery," Phil protested. "You look great. I've had a crush on you for years. I'd ask you out in a second if I thought you'd say yes."

"Cut it out, Phil. It's one thing to beg, but now you're groveling."

"Ah Lee, you've forgotten what it's like to be a public defender. Groveling is one of the most important skills we practice on behalf of our clients. But FYI, I meant it about asking you out."

"I'm sure you didn't, but FYI, I never date men who are more than five years younger than me." As a matter of fact, since Paul's death, she hadn't dated anyone, but it would certainly be true if she ever started. "Did any of the co-defendants talk to the police?"

"No, ma'am, just your client. The others are *much* older, in their mid to late twenties. And they all have prior felonies."

"What about Mr. Matthews?"

"Nope. He's squeaky clean. This is his first boot party."

"All right. Thanks for your time, Phil. I'll let you know."

"Oh happy—"

She hung up the phone.

Lee finished her last appointment at six-thirty. Of the five people she interviewed, she'd agreed to represent two of them. The others clearly couldn't afford her, but she took the time to answer their questions and advise them how to convince the court they were eligible for representation by the public defender. She also told them to request Phil Hartman as their attorney.

The two cases she ended up taking weren't particularly serious or complicated: a run-of-the-mill domestic violence charge where the client, who'd just been fired, shoved his wife and then pitched her cell phone into the neighbor's yard, and a second-degree assault where the client, who'd taken too much Ecstasy, attacked a stranger on the Pearl Street Mall for staring at him. She could easily resolve the first case with a deferred judgment and counseling. The assault would be a bit more difficult, but eventually she would wrangle it down to a misdemeanor with a couple of months in the Boulder County jail.

As she turned off the lights in her office and locked the door, Lee still hadn't decided whether she'd take the Matthews case. Earlier in the day, she'd called the juvenile detention center and set up an interview with her prospective client for seven-fifteen. Outside her building, the evening was warm and surprisingly quiet, the traffic on Ninth Street almost nonexistent. The leaves on the trees were just beginning to turn, the only sign it was the beginning of October. It was a few minutes past seven. Most commuters were home now, eating dinner and doing all the things that regular people did.

Lee had never been regular. Nor had Paul. The only time they ate together was by accident or when they were on vacation, usually in the fall, which was their favorite season. Most years around Halloween, they drove to Glenwood Springs, where they spent four or five days hiking from dawn to dusk and then swimming in the enormous hot springs pool the town was famous for. Afterward, they ate dinner at one of the local restaurants and then strolled back to their room, where they made love until their hands lost their grip on each other and they drifted off to sleep. There was an unspoken rule that neither of them could bring any work on vacation, an agreement that made Lee cranky at the beginning of a trip and grateful toward the end.

Time to get moving. Lee took off her suit jacket, folded it carefully over her arm, and started walking. As she headed down Ninth, she saw a small red fox dart into the bushes next to the bike path. A black dog, off its leash, was following close behind. A second or two later, she heard someone on the path, presumably the owner, shouting at the dog.

"Gussie! Gussie, get back here!"

We're all being chased by something, Lee thought. At the corner, she turned left onto Canyon Boulevard, heading west. In front of her, the foothills at the mouth of Boulder Canyon looked beautiful and imposing against the evening sky. The detention facility was in the back of the Justice Center located at Sixth and Canyon.

Unless her destination was more than an hour away or she was in a hurry, Lee never drove. It had nothing to do with exercise; she got more than enough from her martial arts, which she practiced as often as possible. And it wasn't because she was so committed to reducing her carbon footprint, although of course she recycled and, at her friends' rather shrill insistence, reused her plastic bags. No, she walked for the same reason Paul might have meditated: to slow the movie down, to see how one thought followed another. It was how she recognized and cleared up fallacies in her thinking. How she refined her legal arguments.

But no matter how many times she considered her last major trial, where she'd defended a client named Lenny Hall for murder, she'd come to the same conclusion: Her formerly rock-solid instincts had failed her. It didn't matter why. It only mattered whether it was an aberration or the beginning of a trend. If it was the latter, she was through. And even if it was the former, she still had Lenny's ghost tagging along behind her. Not haunting her exactly, more like stepping on the backs of her shoes, breathing on her hair, falling down and reaching for her ankles.

Before his arrest, Lenny was a forty-year old bartender, a father of three, and an occasional drug dealer when his family needed additional funds. A few days before Christmas, he brought a gun to a meeting with a customer he didn't trust. Things got out of hand—the universal felon's lament—and the gun went off, killing the customer. In a panic, Lenny fled to his brother's home in Arizona. Two months later, at the urging of his family, he turned himself in and was charged with first-degree murder. After waiving his rights, Lenny told the police he'd pulled the gun in self-defense and that during a struggle with the customer, the gun accidentally went off. It might have even been the truth.

Toward the end of Lenny's trial, Lee had to make a tough decision. Did she put her client on the stand or simply rely on his statement? Her instincts told her to put the client on, that you don't win a self-defense case without the defendant's testimony. Anticipating this, she'd spent hours preparing Lenny, cautioning him not to let the DA make him angry, that if he lost his temper, he would lose the trial. Eventually, she called him to the stand, her last witness, confident he would hold his own. But he didn't.

Halfway through the cross, Lenny started shouting when the DA insinuated he was a lousy father. After deliberating less than three hours, the jury convicted him of first-degree murder. Did Lenny have himself to blame? Of course, but he also had Lee; she was the lawyer, the professional fortune-teller, the one who should have known.

When she reached the Justice Center, Lee walked around to the back and pressed the buzzer to be let in. The detention center was a small locked facility built to house a maximum of twenty kids. It was used to hold only the most serious juvenile offenders until their charges were resolved.

A few seconds later, the door unlocked and Lee walked down a corridor toward another, thicker door. Eventually, she was led into a windowless room and told to make herself at home. The room was furnished with a sad-looking purple couch, two metal chairs, a dying plant (thank God for silk) and a cheap floor lamp. A male employee in street clothes who looked like a bodybuilder promised to bring Jeremy in as soon as he could.

Lee tried the couch first and then moved to one of the metal chairs. She placed her briefcase on the floor with no intention of opening it or taking any notes. The only thing she held was her card, which she might or might not give to Jeremy.

Ten minutes later, the same guard reappeared with her prospective client.

"You can have him for as long as you want," he told her, backing out of the room. "He won't give you any trouble. When you're done, just knock."

"Thanks," she said.

"Who are you?" Jeremy asked as soon as the door closed. His tone was hostile and suspicious.

"Hi Jeremy. My name is Lee Isaacs. I'm a private defense attorney in Boulder." She smiled pleasantly and motioned to the other metal chair. "Have a seat. The chairs are a lot more comfortable than the couch. Your aunt Peggy would like to hire me to represent you."

"I already have a lawyer." Jeremy was probably six feet tall, the same as Lee, but his posture was so bad it was hard to tell. His head was shaved and he was much too thin, as if he hadn't eaten well for a long time.

"I know. Phil Hartman. I spoke with him this morning. He's an excellent lawyer but, like all public defenders, he's very busy. I'm an excellent lawyer too, but since I'm private, I have much more time than he does. I also have an investigator who can work full time on your case." She paused. "If you don't feel like sitting down, I guess we could both stand." She started to get up, but he shook his head and then sank into the other metal chair. "Great," she said. "So, I need to know what you think before deciding whether or not to work for you."

"I don't care." He shrugged and crossed his arms, which were covered with various tattoos: a skull and crossbones on his left bicep, an iron cross on his right, a small homemade swastika on one forearm, and the words—in case anyone missed his drift—"born to hate" across the other.

Lee nodded but didn't respond. It was a stock lawyer trick. Most people couldn't stand more than a few seconds of silence.

"Actually," he said, "I think it's a waste of money."

"Probably not. I'm very good at what I do."

Jeremy stared at her. His eyes looked feral. Don't come any closer, they warned, or I'll bite you.

"I don't need a good lawyer."

"Everyone charged with a crime needs a good lawyer."

He continued to stare at her, as if she might lunge at any moment.

"I-I won't take a deal if it means testifying against my brothers. We're all standing together." He took a ragged breath. "I mean it."

"Okay," she said, resisting the urge to put her hands in the air. "I hear you."

She tried silence again, but guessed it wouldn't work a second time. It didn't. The kid just kept staring at her, his body language warning her to stay put, that he would fight to the death if he had to. She countered by dropping her shoulders and sinking into the chair. After a long moment, he relaxed a notch. Which meant he knew nothing about physical combat. Good thing she meant him no harm; he'd be a pushover in a real brawl, and the breakfast of champions in prison.

"Can I ask you a couple of questions, Jeremy? I know almost nothing about your case except that you made certain statements to the police."

"So?"

"So they seem to indicate you were a willing participant. Is that true? By the way, anything you tell me is strictly confidential. I'm sure Mr. Hartman has already explained that." She'd stopped looking directly at him. Any further eye contact was useless, maybe even counterproductive.

Jeremy shrugged again, shifting his gaze to his feet. He was wearing black high-top sneakers with no laces.

"Whatever I told the police is true. Can I go now? I'm kind of tired."

"Hey, you can go whenever you want, Jeremy. I don't have any power over you. I'm not your jailer. I'm not your father. I'm not even one of your so-called brothers."

His head jerked up and his knees began bouncing up and down.

"What the fuck does that mean?"

Addressing the space above his head, she said, "It means that if I decide to represent you, I would work only for you. That I wouldn't take into account anyone else's interests but yours. And I would never make you do anything you didn't want to."

His anger subsided almost immediately. With a pleasant expression and some hair, he'd actually be nice-looking.

"Okay, fine. Whatever."

"Great," Lee said. "Can we go back to your statements?"

"Why? I-I already said they were true."

"Jeremy, I don't have much time. I need to know what I might be getting myself into." She thought for a moment. "Tell me about the victim, the man who was killed."

"What difference does it make? He's dead."

"Did you know him?"

"Sam? Yeah, we all knew him. Anything else?"

It was late and the kid was impossible. Why bother?

But still, she heard herself asking, "Do you realize how much trouble you're in, what you're facing?"

He nodded and then began picking at a small hole in his T-shirt.

"I'm cool with it."

"You're cool with spending the rest of your life in prison?"

"Sure."

"Jeremy, you're not even seventeen yet. Do you have any idea what it'll be like in prison? I can't help you if you won't let me."

"So don't."

All right then, she wouldn't. She slid her business card into her pocket, stood up and grabbed her briefcase.

"Well, if I don't see you again, good luck."

"Thanks."

She walked to the door, and was about to knock, when she turned around to face him.

"In your statement to the police, you said that Sam was 'just a faggot who deserved to die.' Did you really mean that?" She'd already made up her mind. She was just curious. Her best—really only—friends were two gay men, and Paul had been actively bisexual before he met and married her.

"Yeah, I did." He was leaning down, adjusting the back of his sneakers.

For the hell of it, she said, "I'm not sure I believe you."

"So what?"

He was right. She turned her back to him and began knocking. Within a minute, the guard unlocked the door and she left without another word.

Lee walked quickly north on Ninth and then turned left on Maxwell. A few minutes later, she arrived at her house, a sweet two-story Victorian she and Paul had renovated during their first year of living together. Before meeting her husband, Lee had never successfully cohabited with anyone, unless you counted Charlie, whom she found as a kitten hiding under a parked car during a snowstorm. When she reached for him, he scratched her face before settling down against her wool sweater. Love at first sight. Likewise with Paul, except it was the other way around.

They never planned to marry, but one day they just did. Why? It was hard to remember. Was Paul heading off to Pakistan to climb K2? Yes, that was it. And he'd wanted to make sure, if he didn't return, she'd inherit everything: a trunk full of climbing gear, four or five cameras, a thousand books, his photographs, and not much else.

As Lee searched for her house key, she figured she'd phone Peggy first and tell her to save her money, that Phil was more than competent enough to defend her nephew. And then she'd call her father, who lived alone in a condo in Braintree, Massachusetts. Most weeks, she called him every evening, usually around ten, midnight on the east coast. After playing his usual four hours of cutthroat duplicate bridge, her father always napped in the late afternoon and was wide-awake at night, happy for the company.

She dropped her briefcase in the foyer and then walked into the kitchen. Charlie hopped down from his hiding place on top of the cabinet and began crying for some wet cat food. After forking some Fancy Feast into Charlie's bowl, she stopped and considered what she was about to do: turn down a perfectly good murder case.

So that was that. She was done. No more class-one felonies where the potential sentence, if she screwed up, would be life in prison. The Lennys and Jeremys of the world would have to find some other lawyer to represent them.

So be it. Maybe she would finally slow down a little, stop fighting nature, and actually enjoy her golden years. Maybe, like Paul, she'd learn to meditate. Get up to the high country more often. Go trekking with her friends Mark and Bobby; they were always trying to convince her to leave town. Why not? After a while, she wandered back into the foyer, opened her briefcase and fished out Peggy's business card.

Peggy picked up on the first ring.

"Hello?"

"Hi, it's Lee Isaacs."

"Oh, Lee, I'm so glad you called. I've been waiting. Did you get to see Jeremy?"

"Yes, I just got back."

"Will you represent him?"

Lee glanced out the window at the cedar fence she and Paul had built the summer before his death. The fence was almost ten feet high, affording Paul the privacy to wander around naked without offending the neighbors. Declining the case would be the end of an era, the end of a good long run. Was she ready for a kinder, gentler life where she took only easy cases, the type almost any mediocre lawyer could handle? She made a face. Not really. At least not yet.

"Yes," she heard herself saying, "I'll represent him."

"Oh, that's wonderful. So it was a fit?"

Lee smiled, remembering one of her father's favorite jokes about an old woman in a nursing home who goes into the day room and announces to a group of elderly men, "If anyone can guess what I'm holding in my fist, he can have sex with me."

After a long silence, one of the men finally says, "An elephant?"

The woman thinks for a moment and then nods.

"Close enough," she replies.

No matter how many times her father told it, Lee always thought it was funny. Today, galloping toward sixty, it didn't seem quite as amusing, but the punch line fit.

"Close enough," she told Peggy.

CHAPTER TWO

There was a tall, dark man in Lee's life who regularly attempted to harm her. Today would be no exception. First, however, the rules required a deep respectful bow. In return, Lee grinned through her mouth guard and bowed back. While bowing, neither took their eyes off the other. In Tae Kwon Do, often translated as Hand Foot Way, only novices dropped their eyes when bowing to an opponent before sparring. Dropping your gaze revealed weakness and inexperience before the fight even started.

Michael Anderson, Lee's favorite sparring partner, had been practicing the martial arts almost as long as Lee. They'd been training at the same dojo in Boulder for two decades. Both were fifth-degree black belts and each taught one or two classes a week. They knew little about each other outside the dojo, but everything about what mattered inside it. For instance, Lee knew that Michael backed up a step whenever she threw an ax kick, and he knew that Lee was often vulnerable to his jump-turning back kicks. Those kinds of things.

For the past couple of years, they'd managed to arrange their schedules to accommodate an intensive workout every Saturday morning. It was one of the two social highlights of Lee's week. The other was dinner every Saturday night at Mark and Bobby's.

The workout always started with at least forty minutes of stretching followed by forms, combinations and, unless one of them was too injured, sparring. Michael was a few years younger than Lee. Both had had their share of broken bones, torn ligaments, and pulled muscles, although lately it seemed as if Lee's ribs were getting more and more brittle, breaking like sticks of wood with relatively little force. It was maddening because cracked or broken ribs took about two months to heal. Michael kept suggesting she wear a padded rib protector, but thus far she'd refused. They already wore hand, feet, and shin protection when they sparred, as well as mouth guards. Enough was enough. Besides, rib protectors were for sissies.

But the truth was, even worse than making her look like a sissy, the added protection would make her feel old. And vulnerable. Not a good way to feel when you were facing off against someone as skilled as Michael. Ask any aging martial artist: Youth was not overrated.

Today, they started circling each other slowly because Michael's hamstring was acting up again. They had thirty minutes left for what both considered the real point of the workout, the reason for the other hour and a half—the chance to pummel another human being, albeit in an elegant, socially acceptable way. For Lee, sparring required exactly the same qualities that made her an excellent trial attorney: speed, timing, technique and, above all, the ability to think on her feet. Sparring full out, like defending a murder case, demanded complete confidence and the heart of a warrior. Which meant not only courage and compassion, but a willingness to dive off a cliff and not worry about the landing.

Janis Joplin, Lee once told Michael, had the heart of a warrior but landed way too hard. Michael disagreed. Warriors aren't always admirable, she argued. Sometimes they're wild and intemperate. Okay, he conceded, Janis had been a warrior.

Every now and then, when Lee and Michael fought, when they were both at their best and the universe was aligned just right, it felt as if they were creating a gorgeous one-of-a kind work of art, like a Tibetan Buddhist sand painting, which, according to Paul, was always destroyed after its completion as a metaphor for impermanence.

But they were moving faster now and she needed to concentrate. After blocking a punch to her solar plexus, she threw a double spin kick followed by a turning back kick that slipped past Michael's guard, tagging him. In retaliation, he started throwing more jabs and hooks, forcing her to be more defensive. Inevitably, his hamstring loosened up and his jump-turning back kicks started working. Now, Lee had to scramble to avoid them.

"Nice kick," she told him when a fast one finally broke through and shoved her backward. Mouth guards made you sound as if you had a bad lisp, so it sounded like, "Nith gick."

"Thanks."

They were loose now and dancing, exchanging kicks and punches smoothly and efficiently. A few of the lower belts who had been practicing in the other room wandered in to watch. Lee was pleased to see that half of them were women. When she'd started in 1977, she'd been the only female. And it stayed that way for the next two years. Now, on the first Friday of the month, she taught an advanced women's class in which three of the students would be good enough to kick her ass someday. But not, she hoped, before she was seventy.

Lee jabbed twice to Michael's head, stepped back and threw a turning heel kick, which struck him in the chest.

"Beautiful," he said.

Lee nodded, grinning. They were fighting full out now, pulling their techniques a little, but mostly counting on each other to block or get out of the way. Michael's step-up spin kicks were barely missing her temples. Lee kept him back with a combination of side kicks and occasional reverse punches to his solar plexus. Although the room was cool, they were both sweating.

"Ouch," Michael said, after blocking one of Lee's kicks with his forearm. "Why did I bother? I'm going to have a knot the size of a golf ball tomorrow."

"You see this?" She pointed to her left elbow. "It's still purple from blocking your damn turning back kick last week." As she spoke, she faked high with a back fist to his face, then stepped up and nailed him with another side kick. Michael countered with a turning heel kick that missed her nose by an inch.

"Yikes," Lee said, backing up to catch her breath. They were both breathing heavily. Lee's gi, a traditional karate uniform made from heavy cotton canvas, was soaking wet and her hair, like Michael's, was plastered to her head.

"Should we call it?" Michael asked. His face was flushed.

"Sure. Two more minutes and we'll—"

Michael stepped up fast and hit her with a deceptively simple flip kick to the groin.

"No fair," she laughed, throwing an ax kick that caught him on the shoulder.

"I never even saw that coming."

A few seconds later, Michael threw a hard snap kick toward her chin, which she blocked with her left hand. It had come so fast, she hadn't had time to close her fist. The pain was immediate and sickening.

"Ugh," she said.

"Was that your thumb?"

Lee nodded, tried to shake it out, but knew it was a real injury. Shit. At the very least, it was sprained. Maybe a torn ligament.

"How bad?" Michael asked, spitting his mouth guard onto the floor. "Let me see."

"It's fine, Michael. Really." Thank God it was her left hand. She could still write and maneuver without anyone noticing. And she could still sleep on her thirty-year old waterbed, which she couldn't do with a cracked or broken rib. Each broken rib always required a month on the floor while Charlie got the whole wobbly bed to himself. "I'll put some ice on it as soon as I get to my office."

They bowed and then clapped each other on the back. As they walked to their respective dressing rooms on opposite sides of the dojo, Michael called out to her.

"Great dance as usual. Sorry about your thumb."

"Goes with the territory. See you next week."

She kept her head up, her back straight until she closed the door to the dressing room. No one else was in there. Good. She stripped off her gi and underwear, and then sat down naked on one of the long wooden benches that lined the room. She'd take a hot shower in a few minutes but wanted to catch her breath first. After a moment, she closed her eyes and let her head lean back against the wall. The room smelled reassuringly of sweat, deodorant, and Chinese herbal liniment.

With her eyes still closed, she began massaging the pad between her thumb and index finger, just a little and then she'd let it be. Most injuries, unless they were life threatening or needed to be cast, wanted to be left alone. She had no intention of going to her doctor, who would only shake his head, advise Lee to find a gentler sport like yoga, and tell her to ice it.

Ice is nice, she thought, but liquor is quicker. Where had that come from? Which was what her father always said when something odd or ridiculous popped out of his mouth. The aging brain. But for the record, Lee had never resorted to drugs or alcohol to alleviate pain; unlike many of the wild intemperate singers she'd admired as a youth, she wasn't that kind of warrior. Tonight, though, she'd allow Mark to make her one of his famous margaritas using his best Don Julio Tequila.

Finally, she opened her eyes and stared at a large bloodstain on the wall, a leftover from last week's grueling brown belt test. One of the students had broken her nose fending off three opponents. None of the judges, including Lee, had interfered. The rule was clear: If you were injured during a belt test, you kept on going. If you stopped, you flunked. Period. No exceptions.

Running on the last fumes of adrenaline, the student kept going and passed. She bled a lot, cried a little, but kept going. Lee was proud of her. During the awards ceremony, while the students replaced their faded blue belts with stiff new brown ones, Lee slipped out of the room and filled a plastic bag with ice. Afterward, she'd accompanied the student to the dressing room and helped clean her up.

"My first broken nose," the student told her.

"It won't be your last."

The student nodded gravely.

"You did really well, though," Lee added.

"Thank you. That means a lot. What'll I look like tomorrow?"

Lee gently removed the bag and studied the student's face.

"It's a pretty straightforward break. You'll wake up with two black eyes but, in a few weeks, only your best friends will know it's broken."

"That would be nice. And I'll still have my brown belt. They can't take that away from me."

"No," Lee agreed, "whoever they are, they can't."

They'd both laughed.

After a few minutes, Lee roused herself to take a shower. She'd procrastinated long enough. There was a ton of work to do on her new murder case. Yesterday, after a pre-trial motions hearing on a burglary that wouldn't settle, she'd stopped by the public defender's office to pick up Jeremy's file, which included dozens of crime scene photos depicting the victim's body curled in a fetal position, covered with blood, the ground around him littered with empty bottles of Southern Comfort and cigarette butts.

Phil handed the thick file over, singing, "It's my party and I'll cry if I want to."

Objectively, the pictures were shocking but, as was often the case, Lee's reaction was sadness. Whoever coined the term "homo sapiens" had run in very different circles than Lee.

Blood, blood, everywhere, she thought, stepping into the shower stall.

***

After a quick stop for sushi and an ice pack, Lee settled into her office with Jeremy's file spread out in front of her. It was quiet and peaceful. Last night, while Charlie dozed on her lap, she'd skimmed through almost a thousand pages, which would no doubt quadruple as more acid reflux-inducing information came to light. She'd also phoned the juvenile detention center and asked them to tell Jeremy she was taking his case and would see him Monday.

Yes, the facts looked bad, but a murder was always bad. A human being, often blameless, had died in an ugly, unnatural way. Initially, the details were appalling, the photographs repulsive. It took a great deal of skill and persistence to defend an accused killer, to personalize someone whom everyone else in the system referred to as "the defendant." Understandably, people wanted to do the same thing to an accused that he or she had done to a victim: dehumanize him. It was Lee's job to keep that from happening; to do that, she had to find something sympathetic, or at least pitiable, about her client and then, no other way to say it, exploit it.

Today, she planned to take extensive notes and then draft an investigation request for Carla Romano, the private investigator she used on her biggest cases. She'd phoned Carla the same night she accepted the case. Carla, who'd obviously been drinking, told Lee she wasn't sure she had the time and to call back in a couple of days.

In the nine years they'd worked together, Carla always played hard to get before accepting a job. It was annoying, but everyone had their quirks. Lee figured it had something to do with Carla's three failed marriages.

Still, despite her personal issues, Carla was an excellent PI who, once committed, worked tirelessly on behalf of her clients. On serious cases, she was always Lee's first choice.

Actually, it was probably time to call Carla and pin her down. Lee dialed Carla's cell phone number and waited. Although they'd worked together on at least a dozen murder cases, Lee realized that except for Carla's status as a triple divorcee, she knew very little about her. Whenever Carla wasn't working, she always seemed to be trawling for the next Mr. Right.

Carla's voicemail switched on, inviting the caller to leave a message. Lee simply hung up. Every three or four months, Carla would ask Lee to go bar hopping with her, but of course Lee always declined. "You need a girl's night out," Carla would say. "I'd rather have a root canal," Lee would answer. And then Carla would shake her head and laugh, no offense taken.

People never believed Carla was a PI until she showed them her card. If you had to guess, you'd peg her for John Travolta's mother in *Saturday Night Fever*. Besides her obsession with finding future ex-husbands, Carla was extremely inquisitive about other people's lives. It made her a natural investigator. When she interviewed witnesses, they could tell she was genuinely interested in what they had to say. And so they talked to her for hours, long after Lee had skipped out to sit in the car.

When Lee's office phone rang, she picked up the receiver and said, "Hi, Carla."

"Well, you're lucky. I just finished a big case for Bradley Moore."

"That rape on the CU campus? How did it go?"

"Morning of the trial, the client pled out. Judge Massey gave him sixteen to life. The guy was nice enough but deep down a real sicko. He kept telling us the girl liked it rough. Bradley told him no sane juror would believe that a girl liked having a bottle shoved up her vagina. The guy kept insisting she did. Finally, I said to him, 'Joe, I'm probably the most gullible person on the planet, and even I think you're guilty.' A few weeks later, he took the deal. Bradley was so relieved."

"I'll bet he was," Lee said, glad for the thousandth time that, as a private attorney, she could pick and choose her cases. If someone showed up in her office accused of a violent rape, she'd ask for a million dollar retainer. It was easier than explaining how she felt about the crime, and a lot more fun. One of the many perks of being self-employed.

"So, your murder case. I've been following it in the Camera. Your client's the juvenile, right?"

"Right," Lee said and then gave her a quick overview.

"Sounds terrible."

"Are you in?"

Carla took her time before answering.

"Yes, I'm in." The courtship was over.

"Great."

They agreed to meet Monday morning at ten and then go visit Jeremy together.

Lee was about to hang up when Carla said, "Oh, before I forget. I told that lawyer about you and he wants to meet you."

"What lawyer?"

"You know, the one I told you about. He does personal injury and divorces. He saw you in court last week and he's definitely interested."

Lee took a deep breath. This was a relatively new variation on Carla's hopeless quest for romance, which needed to be nipped in the bud.

"Carla, I know you mean well, but don't try to fix me up. I like my life the way it is."

It was impossible to hurt Carla's feelings.

"So you're really not interested? I think you'd be perfect for each other. He's a fitness nut, just like you."

Lee's left hand was throbbing. Over the past hour, it had turned the color of an eggplant.

"Carla, no," Lee said, as if she were addressing a big clumsy dog.

"But what'll I tell him?"

Lee resisted the urge to hang up the phone. She rarely lost her temper and even if she did, she never let it show.

"Tell him I eloped over the weekend."

"What? Oh, you're kidding."

"Carla, we have a serious murder case that needs our complete attention. I'll see you Monday."

"I still think you'd be perfect—"

"Right. Monday at ten."

"Oh fine," Carla said, hanging up.

"Food's almost ready," Bobby called from the kitchen. "Do you need another drink?"

Lee was tempted. The new ache in her neck—it still cracked when she pressed it—had settled in as promised, and her left hand throbbed. How pathetic.

"I'm good," she answered. She was curled up on an oversized leather couch in Mark and Bobby's living room.

Her friends lived in a lovely, renovated log cabin four miles up Old Stage Road in the foothills west of Boulder. Mark had inherited the house from an uncle when he was nineteen. When he first moved in, the cabin consisted of two dark rooms with hordes of mice and a family of foxes under the front porch. A few years later, when he fell in love with Bobby, the couple began fixing it up. After more than two decades, their home was stunning: airy and modern, yet somehow still cozy. And the view, the reason Mark originally stayed, was breathtaking. From where she sat, Lee could look out the picture window at a number of valleys descending to Boulder and the eastern plains beyond.

"What's for dinner?" she called.

There was a sudden clatter of pans striking each other, various cabinet doors opening and closing.

"Lasagna," Mark yelled.

A few minutes later, Bobby appeared carrying a tray of bruschetta, which he put down on the coffee table in front of her. Suddenly, she was ravenous. After wolfing down two bruschette, she stopped herself from grabbing a third.

"Great supper," she said.

"Don't be silly," Bobby replied, sitting next to her. "These are just the appetizers."

"I know." She leaned against Bobby's shoulder, the closest she came to a hug. "So, how was your week?"

"It was good. National Geographic bought six of our Pakistan pictures, the ones we took in the Karakoram Range approaching K2." Like their friend Paul, both Mark and Bobby were freelance photographers.

"That's wonderful."

"So what happened to your hand?"

"I was hoping you wouldn't notice," Lee said, tucking it carefully between her knees.

"I always notice."

"Yes, you do."

"Someone has to."

Before she could respond, Mark yelled from the kitchen.

"Bobby, I need your help!"

"To be continued," Bobby said. "The Maharaja has summoned me, but I want to hear all about it."

"There's nothing to tell."

He shook his head at her and then hurried from the room. Lee eyed the tray of food but decided to wait for the main course. Well, maybe just one more. Paul had been a great cook, but his two best friends, now hers, were brilliant. Chez Mark and Bobby was the best food in the county, bar none.

The two men met Paul in 1984 on a bus tour of Denali National Park and the three of them became instant friends. Back then, Paul lived in Seattle, spending most days rock climbing and taking photographs, and most nights dating men and women with what he called "equal abandon." Lee hadn't asked him to elaborate.

Over the next few years, at Paul's urging, the trio took up high altitude mountaineering. By 1990, their goal was to climb all fourteen of the world's eight-thousand-meter peaks. Eventually, Paul moved to Boulder, where he met Lee. By 2006, at the time of Paul's death in an avalanche on Nanga Parbat, the men had climbed ten of the eight-thousanders, including K2 and Annapurna, which Paul thought was the hardest.

After their friend's death, Mark and Bobby stopped climbing.

"We're happy just to trek," they told Lee, and maybe it was true. It would never have been true for Paul.

Since her husband's death, the two men insisted she come and have dinner with them every Saturday night. For the first couple of months, she resisted, but they'd just show up at her house instead, carrying pots of food, bottles of wine, dishes, cutlery for three, and even a tablecloth. She made up excuses, stayed late at the office, but then they'd wait for her on her doorstep. Eventually, she gave up.

"We're your best friends," they told her. "You're stuck with us."

She knew (because Paul told her everything) that a few weeks after their successful ascent of Makalu, they'd promised him they would stick by her if anything ever happened to him. She should have been furious at Paul but somehow, as usual, she wasn't. She'd understood. Her husband wouldn't have continued climbing without Mark and Bobby's promise. She also knew that loving her was Mark and Bobby's way of loving Paul even after he was gone. Surprisingly, it worked like that for her as well.

The lasagna was well worth waiting for—moist but not gooey, like Lee's would've been, and delicately seasoned with fresh basil, parsley, and fennel seeds. Lee, who ate simple salads for dinner at least three nights a week, would have never gone to this kind of trouble, but was grateful that her friends would. As Mark spooned out second helpings for everyone, Bobby asked if she was coming to the vigil the following night at the Justice Center.

"What vigil?"

"To raise awareness about hate crimes. Tomorrow's the thirteenth anniversary of Matthew Shepard's death. You know, the gay man who was murdered in Laramie."

"Ah," Lee said, guessing where this was headed. "Yes, I remember. The two perpetrators beat him, tied him to a fence in the middle of nowhere, and left him. About a week later, he died of head injuries. During the trial, his parents intervened and kept the state from seeking the death penalty. They were beyond admirable."

"Wow," Mark said. "For a straight woman, you really know your gay history. I'm impressed."

"Well, first of all, I'm a criminal defense attorney. It's my business to know. Second, I was with Paul for ten years. He was half gay. Remember?"

"Vaguely. Until you ruined him."

Lee grinned like a Cheshire cat.

"And third," she continued, "Matthew Shepard's murder was national news and anyone who was a decent human being was shocked by his death."

Bobby uncorked a bottle of Merlot and looked questioningly at Mark, who nodded yes to another glass. Lee had already reached her limit—a margarita and a small glass of Chianti.

"What's really shocking," Bobby said as he poured the wine, "is that it

happened again, thirteen years later, in a progressive town like Boulder."
He was clearly referring to her murder case.

"Supposedly progressive," Mark said.

"Well, if it's any consolation," Lee told them, "everyone, including
the victim, was from Denver."

"How do you know?" Bobby asked.

Mark set down his glass and sighed.

"Because she represents one of the killers. We should have guessed."

"You do?" Bobby asked.

He was fifty-two years old, but there was something about his soft
handsome face that made him look perpetually young and innocent, a
Boy Scout ready to escort an older woman, like Lee in the not too distant
future, across a busy intersection. She shuddered at the thought.

"I'm afraid so."

"It's what you do," Mark said. "He's lucky to have you."

"Definitely," Bobby agreed. "The newspapers said there were four of
them. Which one do you represent?"

She rubbed her eyes. Suddenly, she was tired. She'd spent six hours
that afternoon reading and highlighting police reports.

"The juvenile. Is there any dessert?"

"What's he like?" Bobby asked, ignoring her feeble attempt to change
the subject.

Lee never liked to talk about her ongoing cases. It wasn't just a
confidentiality thing. When she agreed to represent someone, especially
if the crime was heinous, she agreed to be loyal, to take his part, because
usually no one else would, including his family. Ninety percent of the
time, it was just Lee and her client versus the world.

"He's just a kid," she finally said.

"Huh," Bobby uttered, and for the millionth time she remembered
why she loved him. Lee's dream jury consisted of twelve Bobby clones,
each one saying "huh," each one inherently kind, open to surprise, ready
to listen. Mark was another story, more pragmatic than liberal. Trickier. In
the right case, he might even be better than Bobby. If he had a reasonable
doubt but thought the defendant was dangerous, he'd convict him. On
the other hand, if he believed the guy was guilty but felt bad and would
never do it again, he might just let him go. She smiled to herself, then
looked up and realized both men had started clearing the table.

"Hey, wait for me," she said, jumping up.

After clearing the table, they took their usual places at the kitchen sink. While Lee washed the wine glasses and the pots and pans by hand, Bobby rinsed everything else and then handed them to Mark, who stacked the dishwasher. They worked quietly and efficiently. When they were done, Mark announced there was homemade pecan pie in the living room.

"You guys are killing me."

"No," Bobby said, taking her good hand to escort her to the living room, "we are indulging you because—"

"You're a puritan," Mark said. "And we—"

"Are the devil," Lee muttered, eyeing the pie from the doorway.

Luckily, she could afford to pig out occasionally. Thanks to great genes—her father weighed the same now as he did at thirty—she had what most martial artists considered the perfect karateka's body: tall, lean, and muscular, not an ounce of extra fat to slow her down or put unnecessary strain on her joints.

Like actors in a well-rehearsed play, all three headed for their respective seats in the living room, Lee and Bobby dropping side by side onto the leather couch, Mark settling into the sturdy mission-style rocking chair facing them. Seconds later, they were divvying up the dessert, acting as if they hadn't eaten for days. It was delicious.

Lee had never baked a pie in her life and never would. You could only excel in so many things and in fact, as time went by, in fewer and fewer. Lately, as Lee approached the big 6-0, she felt like Alice in Wonderland, running hard just to maintain what she had. To get somewhere else, like Alice, she would have to run at least twice as fast. Alice, though, was a lot younger.

Lee ate most of her slice before managing to put her plate down. In the meantime, her friends polished off the rest. They were big guys.

"Well, I think we've outdone ourselves," Mark said, licking his fingers.

"No question," Lee agreed. "Plus, I won't have to eat until Wednesday." She placed her hands together and bowed to him. "Thank you."

Mark bowed back. He was six feet four, broad-shouldered, with steel gray eyes. Even when he was sitting down, he was imposing. They both then turned to Bobby, who seemed uncharacteristically quiet, his face blank, his thoughts obviously elsewhere.

"You okay?" Lee asked.

"What?" Bobby looked at her. "Oh, I'm fine. I was just thinking about your new murder case, all the publicity and everything. It's more complicated now that I know you represent one of the defendants. Before, I was just really horrified by what they did to the victim, but now it's not as easy to hate them, especially a kid."

"Hey," Lee said, gently punching his arm, "I'm not necessarily vouching for his character. I'm just representing him."

"Oh, I know. But gosh, there's been so much publicity. Every day, at least two or three articles. And there's the vigil tomorrow night. People might not understand why you'd be willing to represent someone like him."

"The story of my life."

Mark sat forward in his rocking chair, looking serious.

"Bobby's right, though. You'll probably get your share of hate mail on this one."

"Oh well. Death threats, hate mail—all in a day's work."

"That's not funny," Bobby said.

Lee stared at him and then glanced over at Mark. Neither of them was amused. Rats, she thought. I shouldn't have told them. But of course she had to. Inevitably, her name would appear in the papers.

"Come on, guys. You aren't actually worrying about me, are you? Because you can't. It's not allowed."

"Why not?" Bobby asked.

"Well, because there's no point. Throughout our relationship, Paul never worried about me and I never worried about him. He always said, 'You gotta do what you gotta do.' And then the three of you would head off on another adventure. I never even told him to be careful. Everyone was happy. Nobody felt guilty."

"Right, but then he died."

"True, but worrying wouldn't have prevented it."

The men looked unconvinced.

"Okay, so here's the scoop," she said, taking Bobby's hand. "The victim in my case, Sam Donnelly, isn't nearly as sympathetic as Matthew Shepard. He was a skinhead with an extensive criminal history, including at least one felony. These things shouldn't matter, but they do. The crazies won't care about him."

"Huh. So then it's better for you. And your client."

"Well, the facts are still atrocious, but you're right. It's helpful." She waited a few seconds before changing the subject. "So, are either of you going to show me the pictures you sold to National Geographic?"

"I thought you'd never ask," Mark said. "They're right here." He pointed to a leather briefcase leaning against his rocking chair.

They cleared the living room table and then Mark laid out six black and white photographs. They were exquisite. Paul had taken similar ones, but his were different. Mark and Bobby's images were more personal, moodier. Paul's were always calm, vast, and silent—no hint of the artist who disappeared before the shot was taken.

"Congratulations," Lee said. "They're so beautiful they take my breath away." After a moment, she pointed to a distant peak almost completely obscured by clouds. "Do you miss it?" She meant climbing above 24,000 feet. In the death zone.

"No," Bobby said quickly.

"Not anymore," Mark amended.

Lee stayed bent over the pictures, admiring the angles and the light in each of them. She always thought, but never said out loud, that Mark and Bobby made the wrong decision, that they should have kept on climbing. Persevered until they reached their goal. They'd climbed for twenty years, pushing their limits, enduring inconceivable physical hardships. They'd ascended ten of the fourteen highest mountains in the world. Only four peaks left. But now, for the first time, she considered the possibility that they'd exited at exactly the right moment, that they'd interpreted Paul's death as a true warning: leave while you still can.

She thought about her new murder case, the misgivings she'd had before taking it on. Had she made a mistake? Had she misread her last huge loss a year ago as an aberration instead of a true warning? Taking on a serious, high-profile murder case was a lot like climbing in the death zone. You needed skill, strength, perseverance, great instincts, and a burning desire to reach the top—to win.

When Mark and Bobby quit, they left with their heads held high, their reputations still intact. Lee was almost sixty, her body ached, and her new client was "cool" with spending the rest of his life in prison. What if she couldn't settle the case, and actually had to try it? Her last murder client was flawed, but at least he'd wanted to fight. The new kid just wanted to sleep. Which meant she'd be dragging him along behind her like a tired, cranky two-year old. She blew out a worried breath. How did you know when the party was almost over, the optimum time to thank your host, grab your coat and leave?

"Hey, Lee," Mark called. "Are you falling asleep over there?"

God, she hoped not.

CHAPTER THREE

"So, am I going to be Mutt or Jeff?" Carla asked.

"Mutt," Lee said.

Carla patted her hair, a vivid shade of red this month, and smiled.

"Oh goody. I almost never get to be the bad guy."

Lee glanced at her watch. They were standing in the parking lot behind the Justice Center. It was Monday afternoon, later than Lee anticipated. Close to one-thirty. It had taken them more than three hours to discuss Jeremy's case and then review the massive investigation request Lee had prepared. In a minute, they would press the buzzer to be let in to the juvenile detention facility.

Lee started up the stairs, taking them two at a time.

"I'm starving," Carla called from the ground. Neither of them had eaten.

"I'll buy lunch afterward," Lee offered.

"And not just salad!"

They had worked together for nine years, sometimes for days on end. During their last murder trial, Carla complained that she spent way more time with Lee than her husband, who left her a few months later for his personal trainer. Although Carla's relationships with men were abysmal, on the job she was another person, a smart savvy woman with great instincts and a huge—sometimes too huge—ability to empathize with the person she was interviewing.

Lee pressed the buzzer and waited. Carla's high heels clanked as she plodded up the metal stairs. The smell of her perfume and hairspray preceded her.

"So what's our objective?" Carla asked, slightly breathless from the climb.

Lee stared straight ahead, her heavy briefcase hanging from her right hand. Her left was still out of commission.

"To get him to talk. I'd like to know how he feels about the murder, whether he was an enthusiastic or reluctant participant. Did he know it was going to happen beforehand? That kind of thing."

"And how come we're doing Mutt and Jeff?"

The door clicked open and they headed down the hallway.

"Because our client is almost pathologically detached. I'm hoping he'll start to bond with me a little, if only to get away from you."

"Sounds like a plan," Carla said, stopping to check her face in a stainless steel security mirror mounted on the wall.

While they waited for the next door to open, Lee remained silent. A few seconds later, she watched Carla pull a Kleenex out of her sleeve and begin dabbing at the corners of her mouth.

"You're staring at me," Carla murmured. "Is my lipstick too dark?"

Too dark for what? Lee wondered. They were about to spend the next few hours in a small windowless room with a monosyllabic teenager accused of murder.

"It's fine."

"It never hurts, you know."

"What?" Lee asked, feigning ignorance.

"To put your best foot forward. You never know who you'll run into."

"In a juvenile detention facility?"

"There are guards."

"Ah."

"You're mocking me," Carla said.

The door opened, sparing Lee a response. A few minutes later, they were led into the room with the sad purple couch, the dying plant, and the two metal chairs.

"Oh well, it could be worse," Carla said, looking around and then settling into one of the chairs. "It's been a while since we represented a juvie."

And there's a reason, Lee thought. Juveniles were much more susceptible to pressure than adults and almost always confessed. As Phil said, it was simply no fun; the DA had all the cards.

Carla had pulled out her compact and was reapplying her purple eyeliner.

"You know, when I hadn't heard from you in a while, I thought maybe you were done. I would have really missed working with you." She snapped the compact shut. "Do you ever think about Lenny Hall?"

"Not anymore," Lee said, wishing it were true.

In Spanish, the word for "outdoors" was *aire libre*. Free air. The kind of air Lenny would never breathe again.

"I'm not sure I believe you."

"Then why did you ask?"

"I think about him too," Carla said, bending down to straighten her skirt. "He writes me, you know."

Lee hadn't known but wasn't surprised. Lenny was charming but needy. A bit of a con man as well. A sudden thought occurred to her.

"You haven't sent him any money, have you?"

Carla kept her head down.

"Of course not."

"Goddamn it, Carla! He's been conning you."

Carla sat up again, her face as red as her hair.

"But he needs it for his appeal. His family's all tapped out. His wife has given up on him."

"I wish you'd asked me. He has a free public defender for his appeal, which is meritless by the way. He's never getting out."

"That little rat," Carla said, frowning. It took her all of five seconds to brighten up. "Oh well, live and learn."

Live and learn? The people who usually said that didn't. Suddenly, Lee felt grumpy. Her chair was incredibly uncomfortable. Her left hand throbbed and she wondered if it needed to be X-rayed. Where the hell was her client? How many hours in thirty-four years had she spent waiting in dingy rooms like this one? Hundreds, she thought, maybe thousands. She rubbed her eyes, which ached much more than they used to. Maybe she needed glasses? Another cheery thought. Finally, she heard footsteps in the hallway.

When the guard brought Jeremy into the room, the kid looked

dazed, as if he'd been sleeping since she'd last seen him. If he'd had any hair, it would have been sticking up in all directions. He was wearing the same faded T-shirt, which was rumpled and stained with something yellow, possibly mustard. Like most teen-age males, his jeans were at least two sizes too big for him.

"Good morning," Lee said. "Have a seat." She pointed to the couch.

Jeremy froze when he saw Carla, who'd replaced her usual warm smile with a brisk, efficient one.

"Who's she?"

Carla signaled Lee not to answer.

"Jeremy Matthews? My name's Carla Romano." She leaned forward and extended a hand for him to shake. He remained motionless, shoulders hunched, his fingers curled into fists.

"Kind of rude not to shake someone's hand," Carla said, then sat back and pretended to study him. "But maybe you have some kind of phobia."

"I-I don't have a phobia. I just don't know you." After a couple of seconds, he moved to the far end of the couch, perching on the edge, his knees almost touching his chest.

"Carla is a private investigator," Lee told him. "The best in the business. I've hired her to work on your case."

"I don't need a private investigator." He glanced warily around the room, finally settling on the door. His way back to bed.

"Of course you do," Carla said. "There's close to a thousand pages of discovery, but there'll be more. This is a high-profile case. The cops are going to talk to everyone and their grandmother. So far, the DA has listed more than sixty witnesses. I have a lot of people to interview."

"You're wasting your time. This is stupid." His knees were beginning to bounce up and down. "Rab says we just have to wait. Eventually, they'll start offering us deals. When they get good enough, we'll take them."

Carla turned to Lee and asked, "Who's Rab?"

"It's a nickname. Remember the pictures of the co-defendants I showed you? He's the one with the leopard tattooed on his neck."

"It's-it's actually a jaguar," Jeremy said.

"Rab's your leader, right?" Lee asked.

Jeremy nodded and yawned.

"Excuse me," Carla said, waving her hands in front of him, "but why does Rab, who is stupid enough to get a tattoo on his neck, think they'll eventually offer you a plea bargain?"

"Because trials cost time and money."

The way he said it, a little sing-songy, reminded Lee of a nursery rhyme, the kind that ended badly. Jeremy and Jill went up the hill because trials cost time and money. Jeremy fell down and broke his crown, then later became everyone's honey.

"That's your leverage?" Carla asked derisively. "Your big bargaining chip? That it'll take the DA a couple of weeks and a few thousand dollars to send you all to prison for the rest of your lives? Lee, is he for real?"

Lee moved her chair a few inches closer toward Jeremy.

"Carla, he's never been in trouble before. He doesn't know anything about the system." She smiled at Jeremy. "Listen, I'm sure Rab means well, but we really need to work this case, even if we end up settling it."

"Okay, fine. Whatever. But I'm not testifying against my brothers." He looked resolute. "I won't."

"I don't want you to."

"You're lying. Rab said you'd try and make me."

"Well, I wouldn't. The case against your co-defendants is pretty solid. Your testimony isn't worth that much. Maybe twenty-five years in exchange for testifying. It isn't worth it. You'd have a serious snitch jacket. You'd spend a few years in protective custody and then they'd push you out. You'd be dead within a year." She leaned down and began doodling on her pad of paper.

After a while, he said, "Okay, fine."

Time for Mutt again.

"So," Carla said, "why do you hate gay people so much?" She stood up and began to pace in front of him.

"What difference does it make?"

"What the hell kind of answer is that?"

"Hey, take it easy," Lee admonished, and then turned to Jeremy. "Is that what your father taught you?"

"My father?" He looked confused. "My father's a complete asshole who hates everyone, but he's got nothing to do with this. He has no power over me. Not anymore."

"It must have been pretty scary when he threw you out."

"Not really. I found my way." He smiled bitterly. "And now I'm here." He shrugged. "At least I don't have to go to church anymore."

He was finally talking, but Lee needed to move fast.

"Tell me about the night of the murder."

"I-I was wasted. I don't remember anything."

"Bullshit," Carla said, still pacing.

He glared up at her, his knees bouncing double time.

"You know what a blackout is?" he asked.

"Yeah," she said. "Do you?"

"It's like when you're so drunk, you don't remember what happened."

"But you do remember," Lee said. "You told the police you were the lookout. You said you kicked Sam a few times."

"Right, but the rest is a blur." He began picking at a scab on his elbow. "Can I go now?"

Lee glanced at Carla again. Do something.

"So what's with the swastika on your arm?" Carla asked, standing directly in front of him. He refused to look up at her.

"I didn't put it there. Rab did. I got drunk and woke up with it. He said it was for my protection."

"Against what? Jews?"

"Of course not. Against…everyone." He was staring at the door again, ready to spring for it.

They had less than a minute.

"Jeremy, please," Lee said. "I need to know more about the murder. Did you plan it beforehand?"

"Um, I don't know."

"So you obviously weren't in on the planning," Carla said.

"I'm not sure it was planned. I kind of don't think it was. We were drunk. Someone just started kicking him. I have to go now. I'm tired."

"Okay," Lee said quickly, "one more question and then you can leave."

"And that's it?"

"Yes, and it's a simple one. If you'd known ahead of time what they were planning to do, would you have gone?" She acted as if it were the most casual question in the world. Are you good at math? Have you ever seen the ocean? What kind of music do you like? Come on, Jeremy, she thought, give me something to work with.

But he wouldn't.

"What-what difference does it make?" he asked, slamming his fist into the cushions. "It's bullshit. It doesn't matter. I *did* go." He shook his head at her, as if she'd disappointed him. "Rab said you'd try to befriend me, try to make me feel like I was different than the others. But I'm not. We're all brothers." He stood up. "I'm leaving now. By the way, in case you were thinking of contacting my parents, they won't talk to you. The public defender already tried." He pounded on the door. "Guard!" he yelled, and then turned back to Lee and Carla. "Good luck finding witnesses. No one's going to help."

Within seconds, he was gone.

"Wow," Carla said, sinking back into her chair. "So I assume you want us to go see his parents?"

"How about Friday night? We'll show up around dinner time."

"Sounds like a plan." Carla shouldered her purse and sighed. "I know he did something terrible, but I feel kind of sorry for him."

"You feel sorry for everyone. How much money did you end up sending Lenny?"

"That's none of your business," she said primly. "God, I'm starving! You know what sounds good to me?"

"I don't even want to guess."

"Some chili cheese fries at Mustard's Last Stand. What do you say?" She smiled happily. "We're partners again. Feels good, doesn't it?"

Lee nodded, trying to look enthusiastic.

Carla's directions to the Matthews home were typically vague and frustrating. Take I-25 south to exit 150A or B, whichever seems like it's going in the right direction, but you're looking for Jamboree Drive off Academy Boulevard. If you're too far north, Academy turns into South Gate Road, in which case turn around and go south. Jamboree Drive dead-ends at Outreach Park. The house is the last structure before the park. If it's dark, you won't be able to see it.

Lee had three sentencing hearings set for Friday afternoon, which should have taken a couple of hours. She'd planned to leave Boulder around three-thirty and arrive in Colorado Springs by six at the latest.

But two victims, a woman and her teenage daughter, showed up for the last sentencing, an armed robbery at a 7-11, and each wished to describe how traumatic it was to have a gun pointed in their direction, if only for a second; Lee's client had chickened out and started running when he realized there were customers in the store. He'd been busted a few blocks away with a six-pack of Mountain Dew under his coat—not even the brand he wanted.

The judge had listened patiently to the victims before sentencing Lee's client to the eight-year stipulated sentence the parties had already agreed on.

So Lee was an hour late and by the time she found Jamboree Drive and was heading toward the park, it was dark. Luckily, she recognized Carla's white Civic hatchback parked under a huge cottonwood tree. Lee pulled her old Toyota 4Runner in behind her. Both women got out of their cars.

It was another lovely October evening in the low fifties, perfect weather for a weekend in Glenwood Springs. Lee closed her eyes for a moment and thought about Paul, the way he looked after swimming laps in the hot springs pool, his wet black hair that was always a little too long, his blue eyes, those funny, tight fitting, plaid shorts he wore as a bathing suit. "I'm a sexy devil, aren't I?" he used to say when he caught her looking at him that way. You were indeed, she thought, then waved good-bye in her mind and focused on the present.

"Where's the house?" she asked. The street seemed deserted.

Carla pointed across the road toward a large metal gate.

"Behind that gate. There's a long driveway, maybe two hundred yards. It isn't as fancy as you'd think. Strictly middle-class but with its own little forest. They obviously like their privacy."

"Anyone home?"

Carla pulled her gray wool cape tight around her shoulders.

"I think so. I saw a VW van drive in about an hour ago. There were two people, a man and a woman, both about fifty. I'm assuming they're Jeremy's parents."

As Lee stared at the gate, she heard howling sounds coming from the park.

"What the hell is that?" Carla whispered.

"Coyotes," Lee said, grinning. "We hear them all the time up at Mark and Bobby's." She rubbed her eyes. It had been a long day. "I don't see any lights."

"I know, but they're on. You have to sneak in about thirty yards before you can see the house. My shoes are ruined."

"Good work."

"Thanks. I'm adding the cost of new shoes to my bill." Carla paused. "I have one of those big yellow flashlights in my car. Should I get it?"

"No. We'll look like burglars instead of professional visitors. It's not that dark. Our eyes will adjust. There's probably a buzzer on the gate and lights that come on when you get closer to the house." Lee squared her shoulders. "Come on, and don't forget your briefcase. We're professionals representing their son."

"Whom they threw out and want nothing more to do with."

"We don't know that. Maybe they'll surprise us."

The coyotes began howling again. The wind picked up slightly.

"I don't like this," Carla said, but she unlocked her car and pulled out her briefcase.

"It'll be okay. It's our only chance to speak with them without the DA there to coach them. I have to know what they told the police on the night Jeremy was arrested. They weren't present during the interrogation, which means the confession is potentially suppressible. If they said Jeremy was emancipated, it's going to make my job a lot harder."

"But that's what they're going to say, isn't it?" They were crossing the road, heading for the gate.

"Who knows? The police reports just say that they called the Matthews residence before questioning Jeremy. Maybe his parents refused to cooperate, in which case I might have a chance."

They couldn't find a buzzer on the gate, but it was unlocked, squeaking ominously as they pushed it open just enough to squeeze through. They walked ahead slowly, the road curving sharply to the right. After a minute, they could see the house in the distance. The front porch light was on, and some interior lights as well. It was very quiet.

"This gives me the creeps," Carla whispered. "It's like Waco."

Lee rolled her eyes and kept walking.

"Wait a minute," Carla said, bending down and picking up a large white sign lying in the dirt. Lee wiped it clean using the edge of her briefcase.

"Beware of Dog."

"Shit!" Carla whispered.

They looked around and listened. Nothing.

"The sign has been on the ground for some time," Lee said.

"Doesn't mean there isn't a dog."

After two or three minutes, Lee said, "Come on. Even if they do have a dog, it's obviously in the house or tied up somewhere."

"Fine. You can pay all my hospital bills too."

They walked another fifty yards before Carla grabbed Lee's arm.

"I heard something."

And then Lee heard it too: growling.

A second later, they saw it. At first, Lee thought it might be a huge coyote wandering outside the park and looking for food. The animal was standing very still about fifteen feet away from them. It was dark brown and muscular, weighing at least eighty pounds, and not on a leash. Definitely not a coyote.

"It's a Doberman Pinscher," Carla said. "See its ears? I saw a show on the Discovery Channel about attack dogs. Dobermans make great attack dogs. Whatever you do, don't run."

"I have no intention of running."

"And don't look directly at him."

"I'm not," Lee assured her. She was, instead, looking around for a huge stick or a rock, something to toss at the dog if it came any closer.

The dog growled again, baring its teeth, which looked like jagged scissors. So far, it hadn't moved.

"On the show," Carla said, "the host wrapped a blanket around his arm and shoved it into the dog's mouth."

"And then what?" Lee asked, still looking for a weapon.

"And then my phone rang. By the time I got back, the show was over."

"How about your cape?"

"My cape? It was a show, for God's sake. It probably wasn't even real. They probably used trained dogs."

"We could throw it toward him as a distraction. Then kick its head and neck if he comes at us."

"Are you crazy?" Carla asked. "I love this cape. I paid full price in

Santa Fe. I'm not going to let you throw it at a Doberman."

The Doberman growled and took a small step forward.

"Give me the cape," Lee said.

"Fine. I'll add it to the bill." Carla slipped off her cape and handed it to Lee.

Suddenly, they heard a woman's voice coming from the front porch. "Leonard! Call Henry off. I think they're women."

"They're trespassers," the man answered. "There's a sign."

"Hello," Lee called, like a seasoned hostess from Welcome Wagon. "Could you call off your dog? He's frightening us."

The Doberman took another step forward, lowering his head as if to charge. Saliva dripped from his lower jaw.

"Leonard, call Henry off, " the woman said. "I mean it! He could hurt them."

Lee and Carla waited. A number of seconds passed.

"Okay, fine," the man said. "But he wouldn't hurt them unless I told him to. Henry! Come!"

The dog hesitated, and then started trotting in the direction of the man's voice.

"Phew," Carla whispered. "Can we go get drunk now?"

"Thank you," Lee called. "My name is Lee Isaacs. I'm the lawyer who represents your son. Carla here is my investigator. She's pretty upset. Could we please come in and sit down for a few minutes? Maybe get her a glass of water. She takes medication."

"For what?" Carla whispered.

"Wing it," Lee said, starting toward the house.

"Go away," the man told them. "Our son Jeremiah is dead to us. He's in God's hands now."

No, actually he's in mine, Lee thought.

"Carla really needs some water. Please."

"I get terrible migraines that last for weeks," Carla called. "I just need to sit down for a moment and take my pills."

"Let them come in," the woman said. She stepped off the porch and headed toward them.

"My name is Mary Matthews. I'm so sorry. Leonard gets carried away sometimes. How is Jeremiah?"

"Not so good," Lee answered. "You should go and visit him."

They were almost to the house, a modest split-level built sometime in the eighties.

"I-I can't," Mary whispered. "Don't ask me again."

When Lee walked through the front door, she found herself standing in the entrance of a chapel.

"Wow," Carla said behind her. "It's a church."

"Yes," Leonard intoned, approaching them with a bible in his hand. He'd obviously been good-looking when he was younger. Now, his hair was white and his face was deeply lined, as if he'd been discontented for most of his life. "This is where we spend our days. Where everyone, if they were smart, would spend their days."

There were ten rows of pews facing a podium flanked by two giant vases filled with pink and white lilies. Because of the flowers, the room smelled vaguely like cat pee. An enormous silver cross was hanging from the ceiling above the podium. No windows, only one exit.

"Do you live here?" Lee asked.

"We live in an apartment downstairs," Mary said. "It's actually quite nice."

"No," Leonard corrected her, "we *live* up here. We sleep down there."

Mary blushed a deep red.

"That's what I meant." She was a trim pretty woman with reddish-blonde hair and freckles. Her resemblance to her sister was obvious.

"Well," Leonard said, smiling, "it's not what you said." His smile was perfect—too perfect—as if he'd practiced it a thousand times in front of a mirror.

"Could I get that glass of water?" Carla asked.

"Oh yes, of course," Mary said. "I'll be right back."

Lee looked around the room, then walked to the front and sat down in the first row facing the podium. Carla immediately followed. Leonard, still smiling, sauntered to the podium and stood behind it. The two women sat quietly looking up at their client's father. Leonard gazed benevolently down at them. No one spoke. The wait seemed excruciatingly long. Finally, Mary returned with a full glass of water and handed it to Carla, who'd managed to find two moldy white tablets in her briefcase. Lee had no idea what they were but Carla, bless her heart, immediately popped them in her mouth. Leonard motioned his wife to join him at the podium.

Lee cleared her throat. They were seconds away from being cast out of the House of the Lord.

"Listen," she said, "I want to be frank with you. We showed up unannounced and you were kind enough to let us into your home. I came here with the intention of subpoenaing both of you to Jeremiah's preliminary hearing, which is set for December 1st. Carla here has the subpoenas."

Carla stiffened for a moment, but then nodded.

"But," Lee continued, "I really just need to know about the conversation you had with the police on the night Jeremiah was arrested. If you would answer just a couple of questions about that, I'll have Carla tear up the subpoenas and we'll never bother you again."

"We have no intention of discussing Jeremiah or the reasons he is no longer living under our roof," Leonard said. Mary was silent.

"Understood. I just need to know about the night of the arrest. The conversation you had with the police. That's all."

"And we wouldn't have to come to court?" He wrapped his arm protectively around his wife's shoulders, pulling her close to him.

"Right."

Leonard began rocking back and forth, forcing his wife to rock with him.

"Okay," he finally said. "I'll answer your questions if you'll answer a few of mine."

"Of course." Lee smiled politely.

"Do you believe in God?" he asked.

"*I* do," Carla volunteered.

"Not you! *Her.*" His smile was beginning to fade, as if he'd held it as long as he could.

Lee considered her answer. She needed the interview. Although she'd been lying through her teeth all evening, she had a feeling it was time to stop, that he'd know if she was bullshitting him.

"I don't disbelieve in God," she said.

Leonard smirked. It looked much more genuine than his smile.

"So you're an agnostic?"

"I wouldn't say that I wasn't."

Leonard took a couple of steps toward her, dragging his wife along with him.

"Are you intentionally trying to piss me off?" He sounded angry, but in fact he looked pleased, excited even. He liked her answers, liked being opposed—a little resistance, a little foreplay before crushing her.

"No, sir. I'm just not a big fan of labels."

"Are you Jewish?"

"Leonard!" Mary was blushing. "It's none of our business."

"Shut up, Mary," he said without looking at her.

"Yes, I'm Jewish," Lee told him. "Is that a problem?"

"Oh, no." He shook his head and laughed. "It's perfect. You're exactly what my son deserves."

Mary pulled away from her husband's arm.

"Please forgive him. He's actually quite upset about Jeremiah. We both are."

"Actually, I'm not," Leonard said.

Lee smiled at Mary and said, "There's nothing to forgive. Since I'm one of the best attorneys in Colorado, I couldn't agree more." She turned back to Leonard. "So, Mr. Matthews."

"Oh, call me Leonard."

"Leonard. What did the police tell you on the night they arrested your son? Carla, would you please take notes."

Carla instantly pulled out a yellow pad and a pen.

"Hmm, let me see." Leonard clasped the bible to his chest. "They called and told us that they'd picked up Jeremiah and wished to question him as a suspect in a recent murder. They said they knew he was sixteen."

Lee nodded for him to continue.

"So, they asked if Jeremiah was emancipated. They—"

"Wait," Lee interrupted, "did they specifically use that word?"

"Oh yes. I told them how offensive it sounded. As if Jeremiah had been a slave and now he was free. The detectives laughed and said no, that the word was a legal term of art that had nothing to do with slavery, that it simply meant Jeremiah was no longer dependent upon us for his care, custody, or earnings. I said fine, in that case he was emancipated, that we'd had nothing to do with him since the night he left."

"You mean the night you threw him out." The interview was almost over. Lee didn't have to be quite so careful anymore.

"Correct. Jeremiah chose a different path than ours. He didn't adhere to our rules. He flouted them. And because of that, he was no longer welcome."

Mary was conspicuously silent. Her face was flushed and a little angry looking. What might she say, Lee wondered, if her husband wasn't there? But of course he was.

Lee then asked what she considered to be the most important question of all.

"Did the police invite you to come up to Boulder and be present during your son's interrogation?"

"No. They said we didn't have to. If Jeremiah was emancipated, we didn't need to come."

Lee eyed the huge silver cross hanging above them and hoped the relatively thin metal chain holding it was stronger than it looked.

"Did you speak about anything else?" she finally asked. Technically, this was beyond the scope of their agreement, but why not try?

"Nope. I didn't even ask who the victim was. We don't care."

"I do," Mary said, looking mildly defiant.

Lee searched her pockets for a business card, found one, and held it up to show Mary.

"I'll leave this here for you. If you'd like to know anything about the case, please call me. I'd be happy to answer any of your questions."

"Mary," Leonard warned. "We've agreed."

"No," Mary said. "I just wanted to say that I care about the person who was murdered. That's all."

"You can get out now," Leonard said, pointing toward the door. "And take the card with you."

Lee and Carla stood up and began walking toward the entrance of the house.

"Hey, what about the subpoenas?" Leonard called.

Carla reached into her briefcase, held up a couple of pieces of paper, tore them in half and then stuffed them into her bag.

"No longer valid."

"We can find our way out from here," Lee added.

They hurried past the pews and finally out the front door onto the porch, where they could breathe again. *Aire libre.* After they'd walked less than twenty yards, all the lights were turned off.

"Asshole," Carla muttered.

They waited until their eyes adjusted to the darkness. It was cooler now.

"What if Henry shows up again?" Carla asked, looking nervously around her.

"Don't worry. If he comes at us, I'll kill him."

"Good."

They started walking slowly. When they reached the gate, they pushed it open and then marched across the road. They stopped in front of the 4Runner.

"Well, that was fun," Carla said.

"Yup."

"Like eating ground glass."

"But funner." As she unlocked her car, Lee asked, "How many more days will you be working down here?"

"Maybe one or two. I've interviewed most of Jeremy's teachers, friends, and neighbors. I doubt anyone in their church will talk to me, but I'll try anyway."

"Anything interesting?"

"Nada. It's really weird. Everyone says Jeremy was just a nice, average kid. They're all shocked. His best friend, a kid named Ethan Mitchell, said Jeremy had been acting more aloof than usual. But that's about it. Most people blame his father."

Lee climbed into the 4Runner but left the door open.

"Well, if I were going to blame anyone, I'd blame his mother."

"His mother? Why? I felt really sorry for her."

"She chose Leonard over her son. That must have really broken his heart."

"Yeah, I see what you mean."

"But," Lee smiled brightly, "millions of people have broken hearts and most of them don't go around kicking gay people to death." She drummed her fingers on the steering wheel. "I need to speak with Mary."

"No way. Leonard will never let her."

Lee was anxious to get going. Carla was staying in a nearby hotel, but Lee had a hundred mile drive ahead of her. Charlie would be hungry. And she wanted to call her dad.

"Listen, even if you have to stick around for another day or two, I want you to follow Mary, and when she's alone, give her my card. Tell her that it's critical I speak with her about Jeremy, that he really needs her help. Tell her I'll keep anything she says confidential."

Carla looked doubtful but nodded.

"I'll do my best." She started walking toward her car but then stopped and turned around. She looked tired and deflated. "Lee, just out of curiosity, does anything scare you?"

Lee shook her head. If she were the kind of person who admitted things out loud, she might have said *losing this case, what it would mean.* But she wasn't and never had been. Paul was the same way; if climbing ever scared him, he never let on. Which was just as well, she thought. In some realms, the truth might set you free, but in others it just made the people around you uncomfortable.

"Are you heading back to the hotel?" she asked Carla.

"As fast as I can. There's a nice dark bar on the roof with lots of single men. I'll probably have a couple of drinks, see what develops."

Lee tried to think of something encouraging.

"Well, don't pick up the wrong guy."

Carla started walking again.

"Don't worry, I always pick up the wrong guy."

Lee dialed her father's number and waited. It always took him a while to hear the phone over the television. Sometimes she had to call two or three times. She'd pulled off her boots and was lying on the couch in her living room. Charlie was curled up next to her, his head resting on her thigh. For background music, she'd chosen *Highway 61 Revisited,* an old Bob Dylan album released in 1965 when Lee was thirteen. It was still great.

The room was dark and peaceful: introvert heaven. When she thought about her clients doing life in prison, it wasn't the confinement per se that horrified her. It was the inability to control her environment, to be alone when she wanted, to make the room dark or light, to decide whether it should be quiet or filled with sound. Introvert hell: a world where strangers made all those decisions for you.

She hung up and dialed again. This time, he picked up the phone immediately.

"Hey, kiddo," he said.

"Hi, Dad. Were you watching television?"

"No, actually I was on the internet watching music videos. Did you know you could watch performances by dead singers?"

"And live ones too. Who were you watching?"

"Amy Winehouse."

"Amy Winehouse?" Lee was flabbergasted. "How come? How did you even know about her?" Sometimes her father was a mystery. Actually, most of the time.

"Well, I read this article about her in the Boston Globe. She died last summer from too much alcohol. She was only twenty-seven. Can you imagine?"

Unfortunately, Lee could. More than half her clients were alcoholics or drug addicts.

"Did you like her music?" her father asked.

Lee frowned, idly running her fingers through Charlie's thick black fur.

"Well, I liked a few of her songs and I think she had talent. But she seemed so sad and lost. I guess she reminded me too much of my female clients."

"Exactly. I can't get over it. Here was this pretty, very talented girl who turns herself into a skinny, tattooed addict and then publicly self-destructs before she's thirty. At eighty-four, I find it offensive. And yet, I can't stop watching her sing."

Lee pictured him sitting in his overly bright kitchen holding an ancient white wall phone, the long rubber cord almost reaching the floor. He'd be wearing what he always wore at night, a thin blue flannel bathrobe she'd bought him years ago. It was probably time to buy him a new one. She'd long since given up asking whether he needed anything because he'd always say no. Periodically, she went shopping in Boulder and sent him pants, shirts, and underwear. When she visited, usually twice a year, she made him go shopping with her at the Braintree Mall.

"You know what, Dad? There are thousands of great singers featured on YouTube. Maybe it's time to branch out a little."

"I think you're right. Tonight, I was watching her sing 'Back to Black'—there's one really good version—and felt tears running down my cheek. In a funny way, she reminds me of a dark, skinny Marilyn Monroe."

Lee frowned again. Her father's occasional bouts of melancholy were occurring more frequently as he aged. Something else, she guessed, to look forward to.

"Hey," she said, "remember how you're always telling me to lighten up?"

"And you should. You're only sixty."

"Not quite."

"Okay, not quite. But one of the joys of being eight-four: You don't even have to try to lighten up."

She shook her head, decided to change the subject.

"So, how was bridge today?"

"Good. Freddie and I came in second."

"That's wonderful. Don't you usually play with Hal on Fridays?"

"Hal had to go back into the hospital. His diabetes is eating him alive. I think they're going to have to cut more of his toes off."

"Yikes," she said.

"Yikes is right. So, how's your new murder case?"

"Challenging."

"Not so good, huh? Well, you'll find a way. You always do."

Not always, she thought. Suddenly, she heard the unmistakable sound of a match being lit.

"Dad, you're not smoking again, are you?"

"Kiddo, I'm eighty-four. I have to die of something. If the mosquitoes don't get you, then the gators will."

"Only if you live in the Everglades."

"The Everglades." He started to chuckle. "Do you remember when we took you there? I think you were twelve. It was hotter than hell. Your mother almost fell out of the canoe."

"I was eighteen. I remember some guy wrestling with an alligator that had obviously been drugged." They were both laughing now.

"Oh, that's right! It was awful. We wanted to rescue him, but your mother convinced us it would be futile. That the alligator wouldn't last more than a day on his own if he were free." He paused. "She was very practical, your mother."

"Yes, she was."

They were silent for a while. Her mother had died of breast cancer when Lee was twenty-eight. For more than thirty years, it had just been Lee and Aaron holding down the fort, as if her mother, whom they'd both loved, had taken a trip to Paris and simply hadn't returned; she was happy there, which was all that mattered. Their grief, which must have been enormous, had gradually subsided. Lee wasn't sure if she remembered her mother's face, or if the images that came to mind of an intelligent, handsome woman with a mischievous smile were all based on photographs. No matter.

"Dad, I wish you wouldn't smoke."

"I gotta be me," he sang.

"You've already had one stroke."

"No lasting damage."

Lee glanced at the clock on her wall. It was close to eleven, one o'clock on the east coast. Time to go to sleep. She'd promised to work out with Michael in the morning. Her left thumb still hurt but it probably would for months. No sense coddling it.

"Okay," she announced, "I give up. You can smoke."

"Thanks, kiddo. You're a real sport."

"But would you at least quit watching the Amy Winehouse videos?"

"Yes, I'll move on."

"Good." She yawned. "I need to go to bed now. Don't die before I call you again." It was the way she ended every phone call since Paul had abruptly disappeared from her life.

"Okay, but call soon." What he always said back to her.

"Good night, Dad."

"Good night, kiddo."

CHAPTER FOUR

In Colorado, a preliminary hearing is the first major step in a
prosecution for murder. The DA's burden is ridiculously low: to
convince the judge there's probable cause to believe that a murder
was committed and that the defendant helped to commit it. In rare
instances, the DA can't prove probable cause and the case is dismissed.

In Lee's new murder case, the DA could have wheeled in his senile
grandfather to argue probable cause and the judge would have been
convinced. At this point, the evidence against Jeremy was overwhelming.
But it was still early in the game. Things change, she reminded herself.
There were always surprises, especially with numerous co-defendants.
Soldiers defected from the ranks. In most of her cases, the surprises felt
as if she were being slammed in the back of her head with a two-by-four,
but every now and then the surprise would be sweet and unexpected, like
manna from heaven. In this case, though, if waiting for manna was even a
small part of her strategy, her client was in serious trouble.

Lee was sitting by herself at the defendant's table in a courtroom
on the second floor of the Boulder County Justice Center. It was a few
minutes past noon. Jeremy's preliminary hearing was set for one o'clock.
In forty-five minutes, the room, which wasn't large, would be jammed
with onlookers, some of them from various newspapers and television
stations. Their first chance to see the boy, whom local reporters had
dubbed "the little savage."

Lee felt like growling. Although she wasn't happy about the level
of cooperation from Jeremy, she'd already stepped into the role of
guard dog. She, Carla, and Peggy were all that stood between him and

the hordes that wanted to lynch him. And they would make it as hard as possible. Her other longtime legal hero besides Perry Mason was Atticus Finch—both lawyers, now that she thought about it, figments of someone's imagination.

For the past few years, Lee had started showing up for major hearings at least an hour beforehand. She wanted a chunk of quiet time to arrange the table exactly the way she wanted and then to simply think. And no, she didn't have to do that when she was younger. At forty, her brain worked better. Faster. Information zipped through it without any interference, heading without hesitation to the right processing center. Nowadays, there were stops along the way, missed turns, bathroom breaks, moments of indecision. What most irked her, however, was that her perfectionism seemed to be inversely proportional to her declining powers, although it made complete sense.

She glanced at the neat stacks of manila folders on her left and her two legal bibles arranged on either side of her: the Colorado Rules of Evidence, and a book containing various sections of the Colorado Revised Statutes pertaining to criminal law. Satisfied, she set a fresh blank writing pad and three new pens directly in front of her. Lee owned a laptop but, unlike most of the younger lawyers, never took it to court. She preferred to take notes in longhand. Lately, she felt like one of the last dinosaurs roaming the earth before they'd all gone extinct. At trial, if she saw that the DA would be relying extensively on his computer, she'd intentionally pick older jurors who might identify with her and the old-fashioned legal pad she made a big show of using.

Finally, she closed her eyes and imagined the hearing—how it would go and how it would end, with the case getting bound over for arraignment on the charge of first-degree murder. The DA was calling only two witnesses, a salesclerk who worked at a north Boulder liquor store, and the lead detective in the case. The first witness had identified Rab, the skinhead with the distinctive animal tattoo on his neck, as the person who bought four bottles of Southern Comfort and five six-packs of beer from his store on the night of the murder. The clerk had helped carry the booze out to a white Chevy Nova containing four more skinheads, including a juvenile. The following morning, two CU students taking an early morning hike on Flagstaff Mountain found a body. That evening, after reading a description of the victim in The Camera, the witness contacted the sheriff's department. A few days later, after everyone had been arrested, the witness identified both Rab and the car. In the legal world, these were known as bad facts.

The DA's lead detective would fill in the rest. How an intoxicated skinhead named Johnny was bragging at the Sapphire Lounge about a boot party where they'd all kicked a "faggot" and left him in the mountains, how someone overhearing the conversation called the police, how Johnny, Rab, and Casey were arrested at the bar, how a warrant was immediately obtained to search their house, which was only a few blocks away, and how Jeremy was found sleeping in his attic bedroom during the execution of the search warrant.

The lead detective would also no doubt mention the bottles of Southern Comfort and beer they'd found at the crime scene, the bloody boots recovered from Casey's room at the house, and the sweatshirt with some blood on the sleeve that was found among Jeremy's clothes. All items had been sent to the Colorado Bureau of Investigation for DNA testing, which in this case seemed like overkill but had to be done.

And finally, the *coup de grace*: Jeremy's confession. Even without it, the judge would have bound the case over. To set up her later motion to suppress, Lee had subpoenaed the detective who'd actually interrogated Jeremy. She wouldn't get too far with her questioning because the DA would correctly argue that it wasn't relevant to a preliminary hearing. Lee would argue that it was. She would lose, but maybe she'd learn a few more facts. And then, each side would make their closing arguments. During hers, Lee would ask the court to find probable cause for second-degree murder, not first, because there was no evidence of premeditation—a specious argument at best. The judge would ignore her, and her client would once again return to his horizontal position in his cell at the juvenile detention facility.

Lee checked her watch. There was still plenty of time. Carla and Peggy would be arriving soon. Peggy had come by her office yesterday morning with a note from Jeremy. Every week since his arrest, his aunt had tried to visit him. Each time she showed up, Jeremy refused to see her and she was turned away. A few days ago, she tried again and this time Jeremy sent her a note written on a scrap of paper. Lee pulled out the note, unfolded it, and read it for the fifth or sixth time.

Dear Aunt Peggy,

I wish you'd stop trying to visit me. I don't want to see anyone. It's for the best. Thank you for trying to help but don't come again. We live in different worlds now.

Your nephew,

Jeremy

Different worlds? Lee shook her head, sliding the note back into her briefcase. As if Jeremy were in the underworld now and, unlike Persephone, had eaten way more than just a few pomegranate seeds and wasn't coming back. Ever. Still, it was Lee's job to try and drag him out of there. The problem was how. Jeremy was still a mystery to her.

Last night, she'd gone to see him and asked what had happened to him in Denver, hoping to find out how he'd metamorphosed from a nice, average kid in Colorado Springs to "the little savage" in Boulder.

"It's not relevant," he told her.

"It might be."

He shook his head, which was now covered with an inch of soft brown hair, like that of a little duckling.

"No, the only thing that matters is what we did. And I'm cool with that."

He didn't look cool—he looked sad and miserable, a duckling paddling around in circles, completely lost—but she didn't want to argue.

"Just tell me how you ended up living with Rab and the others. I'm curious, that's all."

"You're hoping I'll tell you some horrible story about being kidnapped by the bad guys, how they made me do what I did. But it simply isn't true. Rab actually saved my life."

"No kidding," she said and waited. She could be cool too.

"Yeah."

She waited some more.

"Okay, so I was like surrounded by these three guys who wanted to rob me. I was in an alley where I'd been dumpster diving. At that point, I was staying in a hostel, but my money was running out. The guys had knives and looked like they wanted to hurt me. I was cool but figured I was done for, which was fine with me. I-I was kind of depressed and lonely. Suddenly, this big skinhead shows up and kicks the shit out of the three guys. 'Go pick on someone your own size,' he yelled. He hurt them pretty bad. And then he said if I wanted, I could stay with him and a couple of his buddies. I said, 'sure.' And that's how I ended up with my brothers." He shrugged. "Satisfied?"

It was the most information he'd ever divulged.

"Thanks," she said.

"For what?"

"For trusting me enough to tell me that."

"But I don't trust you. I don't trust anyone but my brothers. I just thought you should know."

"Well, I appreciate it." She stood up to leave. "See you in court tomorrow. One o'clock." And then she'd left. Cool as a cucumber.

Lee heard the courtroom door open behind her. It was probably Carla and Peggy or maybe an ambitious reporter wanting a front row seat. Before she could turn around, she heard Phil Hartman calling her name.

"That would be me," she called back and waited until he came and sat down beside her. "Hi, Phil. Aren't you in trial down the hall on that sex assault case?"

"Turns out there's a God after all. I've been saved."

"Mistrial?"

"You guessed it. We were going down big time and then, all of a sudden, this one cop who should have known better, mentions my client's silence after giving him his Miranda warnings. Instant mistrial." He shook his head in wonder. "I thought miracles like that only happened to other people, never to me. I told my client it was a sign from God that he should plead out before the next trial. He's actually going to think about it." He grinned at her. "So now I have the afternoon free and instead of working on another sex assault or drinking myself into a happy stupor, I thought I'd drop by and watch the master do her thing. The Matthews prelim starts at one, right?"

"Don't waste your time. I'm not going to get anywhere today."

"Hey, I had the case before you. I know. It's a piece of shit. I thought maybe you'd like a little moral support."

"Well, that would be nice. I guess." She made a face. "If you still had it, what would you take?"

Phil thought for a moment. He was cute in a blonde willowy kind of way, the victim in a holdup, not the gunman. Lee had always preferred dark, dangerous-looking men. The first time she saw Paul, he'd reminded her of Jean Paul Belmondo in *Breathless*.

"I'd take twenty-five in a heartbeat," he said.

"Would they offer that?"

"Not unless he agreed to sing at his co-defendants' funerals."

"He won't," she said, "and I wouldn't let him even if he was tempted."

"You're right. He's already too pretty. So then maybe thirty."

"Would they actually offer that?" She picked up one of her pens and rolled it between her fingers.

"Not to me."

She tilted her head a little. Heard a slight crack.

"What about to me?"

"No, not to you either, sweet pea. As cute as you are."

"Christ, you never give up. I'm twenty years older than you. Stop flirting." She then busied herself with making her neat piles of folders even neater.

"You aren't." Meaning she wasn't really twenty years older than him. Actually, it was probably closer to twenty-five.

She stopped arranging the table and looked directly at him.

"All right, how old are you?"

"Forty-five," he said quickly.

"Bullshit."

"Okay, so I'm thirty-seven and you're fifty. Big deal. What's thirteen years?"

"Would you have tried to suppress his confession?"

"Of course, but it's a loser. He was obviously emancipated."

Lee disagreed. She'd been thinking about this for weeks.

"That's a determination made by a judge, not the cops. His parents threw him out. The only way he survived was by living with a group of skinheads who'd rescued him from the streets. That's not emancipated. That's not someone mature enough to decide whether to waive his constitutional right not to incriminate himself."

"I like it," he said, nodding. "It's good. It's a loser, but it's good."

"Gee, thanks for the moral support."

"Anytime."

The door opened again and this time it was Carla and Peggy. Peggy stopped in the doorway, looking hesitant, but Carla marched right in.

"Hey, Phil."

"Hey, Carla," he answered. "How're they hanging?"

She reached up and cupped her heavy breasts.

"Ripe for the picking."

"Oh for God's sake," Lee muttered.

Suddenly, Phil stood up, patted his pockets, and then pulled out a still-vibrating cell phone.

"I'd better go. I've got thirty innocent rapists all demanding justice. Good luck, Lee."

"Thanks, sweet pea."

Phil blushed a little and then hurried out.

"He's got a crush on you," Carla told her. "I think he's adorable. Not my type, but maybe yours."

"Hardly, plus he's way too young and he's married." She waved to Peggy. "Hey, I'm glad you could come."

"Uh-uh," Carla was saying. "His wife left about a year ago. Said she felt like he was married to the job."

Lee didn't bother to ask how she knew this. Everyone confided in Carla.

"That was the public defender who represented Jeremy," Peggy said, sitting down on the bench behind the defendant's table. She looked around, and then placed her green leather handbag on the floor between her feet. "I'm so glad I hired you and Carla."

"I'm not sure it'll make any difference," Lee admitted. "So far, the DA has all the cards. Your nephew, as you know, hasn't been very helpful. We need more information. Something to explain why he would have done this. Have you been able to speak with your sister? Carla managed to give her my card, but she hasn't contacted us."

"Not yet. Whenever I call, Leonard picks up the phone and then stands beside her while we talk. I can hear his breathing. What a creep. I don't want to make things any worse for her."

"Do you think he hits her?" Carla asked, sliding in beside her.

"Well, I'd like to think Mary wouldn't put up with physical abuse. But

I could be wrong."

Lee moved her yellow pad a few inches closer.

"My female clients say that sometimes the emotional abuse is worse, that they can heal from a broken bone, but that the words cause lasting damage." She adjusted her silver bolo tie, a gift from her mother when she'd passed the bar. "I could tell she wanted to speak with me, but not in front of Leonard. Keep trying."

"Oh, I will."

The room was filling up now. Lee recognized a number of reporters from the Daily Camera, the Longmont Times Call, and the Rocky Mountain News. The judge, at Lee's urging, had refused to allow any television cameras but would permit one or two at the arraignment. Finally, she saw two uniformed guards escorting Jeremy into the courtroom. They'd entered from a private door behind the judge's bench. Jeremy was handcuffed and shackled, shuffling as fast as he could to keep up with the guards. When they got to the defendant's table, she asked them to at least remove the shackles. Sheepishly, one of the guards leaned down and did so.

Peggy leaned forward and patted Jeremy on the arm.

"Hi, sweetie."

"Did you get my note?" he asked.

"I did, but I'm going to keep on coming."

He looked down at the floor and said, "No offense, but I don't want you to be here."

"I know you don't, but Lee and Carla have told me about the case. I've even seen the pictures."

"What pictures?"

"The DA will be introducing a number of autopsy photos as well as pictures that were taken at the scene," Lee explained. "Do you want to see them?"

"No, I was there."

Unfortunately, the hearing went exactly as Lee predicted. At four-thirty, the judge returned from a ten-minute recess and announced his ruling.

"I'm specifically finding probable cause to bind the case over on the charge of first-degree murder," he said. "Ms. Isaacs has argued that there's no evidence the murder was planned beforehand, which is true, but I believe the crime itself—kicking the victim to death over a period of time—is more than enough to support a finding that the murder was committed intentionally and after deliberation. So I reject her argument that there's probable cause to support only a charge of second-degree murder. Ms. Isaacs has also pointed out that there's ample evidence of intoxication, which could negate the culpable mental state of intentionally. At this stage, however, there is no way to know how drunk anyone was when the beating began. In any event, that is not an issue for this hearing. And so, as I've said, I'm binding the case over on the original charge of first-degree murder."

He glanced at the calendar on his desk.

"I'm setting this for arraignment on the first Monday after the New Year. That should be enough time for the parties to finish their investigations and to communicate about any possible plea bargains. Ms. Isaacs, will that work with your calendar?"

Lee flipped through her appointment book to January and said, "Yes, Your Honor."

The judge then turned to Dan Andrews, the lead prosecutor.

"Mr. Andrews, will it work for you as well?"

"Absolutely, Judge. It gives us plenty of time to talk. If we can settle this, we'll let you know before the next hearing."

"I'd appreciate that." The judge removed his glasses and pinched the bridge of his nose. He was the same age as Lee but looked considerably older, or at least she hoped he did. He was peering at her client now. "Mr. Matthews, I'm remanding you back to the juvenile detention facility. Your next appearance date is set for January 2nd at nine in the morning. This is a very serious case. If convicted, you'd be facing life in prison. Listen to your lawyer. Trust her." He replaced his glasses. "Mr. Andrews, I'm assuming the co-defendants' cases were severed from the beginning because of the statement made by the juvenile?"

"Yes, Judge," Dan said. "We think the Crawford case prohibits the introduction of the statement against the co-defendants. We made the judgment call to sever the cases from the beginning."

Plus, Lee thought, it'll make it easier for Jeremy to testify against the others, except he's not going to.

"Thank you, Mr. Andrews. That's what I thought." The judge banged his gavel and stood up. "Court is adjourned."

Everyone immediately began leaving. Dan was striding confidently toward the defendant's table. Jeremy turned to Lee, his handcuffs clinking as the deputies helped him to his feet.

"Does that mean I won't be tried with the others?" he asked.

"I'm afraid so," Lee said. "I'll come see you after I've spoken with the district attorney." She stared at her client's body, which seemed to be getting thinner and thinner. "You have to start eating, Jeremy. If you end up going to prison, you'll need to be big. Eat as much as you can." Finally, she looked up at Dan, who was standing next to her. "Hi, Dan."

"Long time no see," Dan said.

The guards had finished shackling Jeremy and were escorting him toward the door. Peggy and Carla had already left to have drinks at the Boulderado. Lee had declined to join them. She had a class to teach at the dojo, she told them. Which was true, although the class didn't start until seven. She just didn't feel sociable, didn't feel like commiserating with the two women about how bad the case looked. She didn't feel like talking to Dan either, but there he was. Dan only took the biggest cases. The last time they'd crossed swords was over Lenny Hall and Lee had come out the loser.

"Hey, sorry about the Remmington case," she said. It was the only case Dan hadn't won in the past year.

"I didn't really lose it. The jury just found him guilty of a lesser charge. He's still in prison where he belongs."

"Well, that's a good way to look at it."

He smiled evenly and said, "So, you want to talk about the case?"

"It can't hurt. The usual spot?" Over the years, when she and Dan needed to discuss a serious case, neither wanted to meet on the other's turf. A few years ago, they'd settled on Spruce Confections on Pearl Street as a neutral meeting place.

"Sure. How about tomorrow at ten?"

Lee pulled out her appointment book and peeked at her week. She was free all day tomorrow.

"I'm busy. How about Friday at ten instead?"

"That's okay too. My whole week is pretty light. You've got a tough case, Lee. I don't envy you." He was actually a nice guy, very ethical, and almost always kind. Lee had to work hard during a trial not to like him.

"Oh please, I've had much tougher cases than this one. See you on

Friday."

Dissemble or find another profession.

On Friday, Lee arrived at Spruce Confections at a quarter to ten and staked out a table in the corner. It was cold and blustery outside. A major snowstorm was being forecast for late that afternoon and continuing all day Saturday. Lee had her fingers crossed. Last night, while talking to her father, she'd weatherproofed her old cross-country ski boots, hoping there'd be enough snow to go skiing on Sunday.

This was the time of year when she and Paul always got their winter gear ready, waterproofing their boots, scraping last year's crud off the bottom of their skis, adding new wax, and checking the condition of their gloves, hats, and ski masks. They both loved spending at least one day a week cross-country skiing, often returning in the dark wearing their headlamps. They'd ski for miles and miles, mostly not talking except when they stopped to eat. It was one of their favorite ways of being together and not being together, the key, as far as they were concerned, to a happy, healthy marriage.

They actually met each other skiing. It was dumb luck. They were each skiing alone and had stopped at the Guinn Mountain warming hut to have lunch in front of the wood stove inside. It was Christmas, a holiday that meant little to Lee except that after weeks of frantic buying and endless songs piped into every place you went, including bathrooms, the world finally quieted down again. Neither of them spotted any other skiers the entire day. The hut, built by the Colorado Mountain Club at the top of a long steep trail in the Roosevelt National Forest, was dark and full of mouse droppings, but the fire made it seem warm and intimate.

"Lee?" someone whispered.

She looked up and saw her old adversary standing less than a foot away from her. The coffee shop was packed. Dan was wearing a black wool coat and a maroon scarf. His gray hair was mussed from the wind.

"You were lost in a daydream," he said. "Seemed like a good one. I didn't want to interrupt. I almost left."

She hated when someone crept up on her unannounced. It unnerved her, made her feel naked and defenseless.

"I wasn't lost in a daydream," she snapped. "I was just thinking."

"Is this a bad time?"

"Oh stop being so fucking sensitive. You're trying to disarm me." She pointed to the chair across from her. "Sit down."

He sat down, sighing.

"It's so unfair. I *was* being sensitive."

"But you were also trying to disarm me."

He took off his coat and laid it carefully over his lap.

"Okay, that too." He smiled at her. "People like us, do we ever just say or do anything without an ulterior motive?"

"I don't think so. We've been doing this for too many years. It's automatic. We can't help it."

He leaned forward as if to confide in her.

"One day about ten years ago," he began, "I was talking with this defense lawyer. We had a tough case together and I was working him hard to take my latest offer. Out of the blue, he said his wife had just been diagnosed with breast cancer. I knew he was telling me this because he trusted me, but he was also working me. I told him how sorry I was, that I'd agree to a continuance if he needed one. 'Hell,' I said, 'I'll even make the deal a little sweeter.' And I'm thinking to myself, who's working whom?" He shrugged. "You're right, it's automatic. But still, it's kind of creepy."

"You're doing it again. But it's okay."

"Thanks. I think I've missed you. Maybe." He had a Spencer Tracy face, not handsome but hugely appealing. Like the late actor, he came off as strong, confident, emotional, and fatherly. Juries loved him. But they also loved Lee's grace, wit, and fierce intelligence. When both shticks were equally good, they cancelled each other out. Then, all that mattered were the facts and the burden of proof, the way it was meant to be. "Who's buying the cappuccinos?"

She pushed her chair back and stood up.

"I am. You bought the last time."

"It's been a while. Are you sure?"

"Positive. I'll be back in a few minutes."

At the counter, she ordered two cappuccinos—half decaf, two percent milk, dry with lots of foam. They both happened to like it the same way.

When she returned, they took a moment to enjoy their drinks.

"Best coffee in town," Dan said, cradling the cup in his hands.

"I agree. So, do you want to talk?"

"Sure, although I think you know what I'll say."

"I do. You're going to make me what you believe is a pretty good offer if my client will agree to testify against his co-defendants. Right now, you won't even negotiate with them—your boss thinks they all deserve life—but eventually, when the press coverage dies down, you might want to offer them second-degree murder with a stip to forty-eight years. The victim, after all, is another skinhead. If so, you want my client's agreement to testify as leverage to make them take it." She paused. "How'd I do?"

"Good. I'll offer your client thirty years if he agrees to testify."

"You'd offer him twenty-five, but he still won't take it. He gets a snitch jacket whether he testifies or not."

"Lee, I'm not sure you get how bad your case is."

"The night is young. It might get better." She took another swallow and waited.

He studied her face, which gave nothing away.

"You think you're going to suppress his confession," he said.

"Well, I'm certainly going to try."

"I figured that and did all the research. You're not going to win it, but even if you do, it won't make any difference." He finished his drink and set it down.

"Because the judge will still find the statement to be voluntary?"

"Exactly. Your client will have to take the stand. There's too much circumstantial evidence. When you put him on, we'll still be able to impeach him with the statement. As good as you are, you can't pull it out, Lee."

"What if I convinced the judge that the statement was involuntary?"

"It'll never happen."

"Well, I guess we'll see. Just out of curiosity, when you finally get around to offering the co-defendants forty-eight years, what will you offer my client?"

"I never said I'd be offering them forty-eight years." He leaned back and surveyed the room, which was jammed with casually dressed Millennials staring at their phones.

"Theoretically," Lee said. Nothing, of course, would be settled today. They'd be talking for months. Today, they were merely sniffing around, establishing the perimeters.

"Theoretically, I'd offer your client forty." He started to put his coat on.

"Which means thirty-six, which is still too much. He's just a kid." She shook her head. If her client took it, he'd either die in prison or wish he had.

Dan shrugged sympathetically, then stood up and wrapped his scarf around his throat.

"Just out of curiosity, Lee, what would you take after the judge finds the statement admissible?"

"Well, no matter what the judge rules at the motions hearing, I can't see taking more than fifteen." She'd picked the lowest number she could say with a straight face. She actually had no idea what she'd settle for.

"Which means you'd take twenty, and even if he agreed to testify, which I understand he won't, I'd never go that low."

Lee stood up to face him.

"Well, it's always good to talk."

"Absolutely." Dan stuck his hand out. "This'll be interesting, Lee. I love it when I have a worthy opponent."

"No, you don't," she said, shaking his hand. "You hate it. So do I. We have to work too hard."

"Oh, you're good, Lee. You're really good. But this time, I have all the cards. It hardly seems like a fair fight. I actually feel kind of bad."

"You couldn't be happier."

"Walk me to my car," he said, smiling.

She pulled on her own black wool coat and fell in behind him. Outside, she recognized his classic dark green Jaguar. It was a beautiful car.

"Frankly," he said, "beating you twice in a row will be a huge boost for my morale. Especially after the Remmington case, which should have been a slam-dunk. I don't know what happened."

"Do you ever think about retiring?"

He was searching through his pockets for his car keys.

"Sometimes, but my wife says she'll divorce me if I quit before I'm seventy. She thinks I'd be lost without the job. Which is true."

A few snowflakes were just beginning to fall, dissolving before they hit the ground.

"How old are you?" she asked, shivering a little. She was getting nosy in her old age.

"Fifty-three."

"So you're probably fifty-eight."

"What about you?" he asked.

"I'm a year older than you. Which makes me fifty-four."

"Right."

Lee sat in her 4Runner, the heater running. It was later that day and, in the past hour, the snowstorm had begun in earnest. The temperature, meanwhile, had been steadily plummeting since noon. A strong wind was blowing the snow sideways and the world outside her car was disappearing under a layer of heavy white mush. From only twenty feet away, the metal stairs leading up to the detention facility were barely visible.

Why was she here? Why not go home, change her clothes, and go for a walk in the foothills? During a snowstorm, the landscape she knew so well looked totally different. Magical. The usual intrusive sounds got lost in the hush of falling snow. The few people, like Lee, wandering around on foot always grinned and waved. Fellow travelers. Lee could never stay unhappy when it snowed. Go home and play, she told herself.

Ethically, she was supposed to convey every offer a DA made to her client, but in this case, Jeremy had already told her he wouldn't take any deal that required him to testify against his co-defendants. So why bother? Did she think he'd be impressed that she'd come during a blizzard to see him? That he'd suddenly open up and tell her all his secrets? Fat chance. So why was she sitting here freezing her ass off in this parking lot?

Because she couldn't bear to lose. And pleading the kid out to forty years, or even thirty-six, was the same thing as losing. It's what a competent, unexceptional lawyer would do. Not Lee. No matter how bad the facts were, she was an alchemist. Or at least she used to be. Pleading him out to so many years would be a public acknowledgement that she'd devolved into mediocrity, that she was now just an old entertainer who'd run out of rabbits and could barely pull a few yards of cheap, brightly colored cloth out of her sleeve. No, she thought. Not yet.

Plus, although she'd never admit it to Carla or anyone else, she felt bad for the kid. He kept insisting he was fine, but he wasn't. Each time she visited him, he was thinner and sadder than before. It was almost as if he were on an undeclared hunger strike. Privately, she was beginning to think her client wanted to die, so of course she had to save him. No one died on her watch. She wouldn't allow it.

Finally, she turned off the engine and climbed out of her car, leaving her briefcase behind. There was at least five inches of snow on the ground. Her short black boots were completely inadequate and would be soaked before she made it inside.

On her way up the stairs, Lee grabbed a handful of snow, packed it into a tight ball, and stuck it in her coat pocket. She had no idea what she would say to her client. Begging was useless; she'd already tried. Maybe she'd just hand him the snowball and go.

As soon as she sat down in the room, a huge bald guard with an earring in his left ear, like Mr. Clean, brought Jeremy in to see her.

"There's no rush," the guard told her. "He's yours for as long as you like. Looks pretty gnarly out there."

"It's not for the faint-hearted."

"My shift doesn't end till midnight. I live in Longmont. Maybe I'll find a spare bed, hole up until the morning."

"Do you have four-wheel drive?" she asked.

"I don't even have front wheel drive."

"Then you should spend the night."

"Yeah, I think I will. Just knock when you're ready." He paused and then placed a hand on Jeremy's shoulder. "I don't think he's doing so well. Lots of nightmares."

"I-I told you," Jeremy said. "They're just dreams. I'm fine." As usual, he looked anything but. There was something about his affect, his complete lack of concern, that reminded Lee of another client, a Vietnam veteran suffering from post-traumatic stress syndrome who'd strangled a man trying to steal his backpack. When Lee suggested a mental health defense, he fired her, went *pro se*, and took a deal for forty-two years.

"Whatever," the guard said, and left.

Jeremy took his usual seat on the edge of the couch, as if he might need to spring up at any moment and dash for the door.

Lee reached into her pocket and handed him the snowball.

"What's this?"

"A present," she answered and was rewarded with a rare smile from her client.

He tossed the ball back and forth in his hands, looking pleased.

"Thanks."

They sat quietly for a while. Eventually, Jeremy tossed the ball into a wastebasket.

"It-it was starting to melt."

She nodded amiably but didn't say anything. The room, after so many visits, was beginning to feel like a second office.

Finally, Jeremy asked, "So did the DA make us an offer?"

"Not one you'd accept. Thirty years if you agree to testify. I told him no."

"Well, Rab said to be patient, that they won't make any real offers until it gets closer to trial."

"You know Rab and the others might not end up in the same facility as you. In which case they wouldn't be able to protect you. Even if you were in the same prison, they can't watch your back 24/7."

"I know." He was staring at the floor.

Go home, she told herself. Soon, the roads would be clogged with abandoned cars, hysterical drivers, and snowplows trying desperately to maneuver around them.

"Jeremy, is there anything else you can tell me that I could use as leverage to get you a better deal?"

"Not that I can think of."

"You're holding out on me," she said quietly. "I don't know what it is or whether it's important, but it's something. Everyone has secrets. Normally I wouldn't pry, but I'm your lawyer. I was hired to protect you. I need more ammunition."

Finally, he looked up at her. His eyes seemed vacant, as if he were standing on the window ledge of a tall building and had already decided to jump.

"You just wish I was innocent, but I'm not," he said, turning to face the door. He obviously meant to leave.

Lee put her hand out to stop him.

"Just tell me why."

"Why what?"

"Why you went along with it."

"I don't know." He shrugged. "I guess it was just easier. You should probably get going. The snowstorm sounds pretty bad."

"Okay, I give up. Would you at least make an effort to start eating? Right now, you wouldn't last a day in the penitentiary. There's an invisible bulls-eye on the back of your head."

He actually reached up to touch the back of his head.

"What-what do you mean?"

"You're a ninety-eight pound weakling, a walking target."

He looked indignant, which was what she'd hoped for.

"I'm stronger than you think."

"Great, let's arm wrestle."

His mouth dropped open.

"Are you right-handed?" she asked.

He nodded, looking uncertain. Lee stood up, walked over to the side of the couch, and squatted down beside it. She put her left arm, her weaker one, on the armrest.

"Come on," she said.

"This is stupid."

"Are you chicken?"

"No!" He scooted back a little, his feet planted firmly on the floor.

Lee waited a few seconds and then smiled at him.

"I'll bet you a thousand dollars I can pin your arm in a second."

"I don't have a thousand dollars." He was trying not to smile back.

"You can owe me. Put up your arm."

After a moment, he did. In a split second, she'd pulled it all the way toward her.

"All right," she said, "that was practice. This time, try as hard as you can."

In another split second, she'd pinned his arm on the top of her knee. His face was red, mostly from embarrassment.

"You're like really strong,"

"I am," she said, standing up, "but seventy-five per cent of the inmates in your pod will be stronger. Everyone will be able to push you around."

"What should I do?" He actually looked concerned.

"Eat everything they give you and then beg for more. You also need to start exercising."

"How? There's nothing here. Just a yard outside."

"You can exercise in your cell. Start with fifteen pushups and a hundred sit-ups four times a day. As soon as that's easy, double it."

"Wow," he said. "Can you do that?"

She walked over to the door and knocked.

"It doesn't matter what I can do, Jeremy. I'm not the one going to prison." She knocked again. "I'll see you in a couple of weeks. We can arm wrestle again if you like. I'll still win, but maybe it won't be as easy."

"Maybe I'll beat you."

"It'll never happen," she said. Goading him to try harder. To live.

Outside, it was a full-blown blizzard. She scraped her car windows, and then climbed into the driver's seat, waiting for the heat to come on. She shivered stoically. The case was going nowhere, but maybe her client would at least get fit enough to survive his first few days in prison. Christ, was that all she could hope for? Eventually, she pulled out of the parking lot into a line of cars that were barely moving. She'd be lucky to get home before dark. She thought of Jeremy's sad grateful face as he tossed the snowball back and forth in his hands. At last, there was plenty of snow. Time to pray for manna.

CHAPTER FIVE

Lee had been asleep for almost two hours when the phone rang. According to the alarm clock on her bedside table, it was 2:08 in the morning. Lee cursed, turned on the light, and fumbled for the phone. She knew it was her investigator. She'd talked to her dad earlier, and Mark and Bobby weren't in the habit of making inappropriate late night phone calls.

But Carla was, especially on the weekend.

For the past few days, Carla had been canvassing the neighborhood in Denver where Jeremy lived at the time of his arrest. She was determined to find one more character witness, someone who could say that Jeremy had been a peaceful cooperative neighbor. Lee was skeptical of her efforts. All the character witnesses in the world wouldn't help, she told Carla, unless their client suddenly remembered he was innocent and was willing to explain to a jury why he'd told the police otherwise. World peace seemed likelier.

"This better be good," Lee said, struggling to sit up.

"Hey, Lee. I didn't wake you, did I? It's Carla."

"I know. And yes, for some inexplicable reason, I was sleeping. What's up?"

"Man oh man, in your wildest dreams, you wouldn't believe it."

"How much have you had to drink?" Lee asked.

"What makes you think I've been drinking?"

"Just a guess. Are you driving?"

"How else am I going to get home?"

"You could take a cab. If you get busted for DUI, I'm not going to represent you." The room was freezing. With one hand on Charlie, who was curled up next to her, she pulled the comforter up to her chin. Much better.

"Oh stop being such an old fart. I've had three and a half Manhattans. I'm fine."

"That's a lot."

"They were watered down with too much cherry juice and were a complete rip-off. Anyway, what was I . . . Oh, so I called to tell you that I just found the most amazing character witness. The kind you dream about but almost never find. Her name is Mrs. Weissmann and she's ninety-one."

"You found her in a bar?"

"No, silly. I found her this afternoon. Then I went to the bar, a new one at the Westin that my friend Sheila told me about. I only meant to have one drink, but I met this cute guy who told me he'd recently separated from his wife. We talked for hours, and not just about him, which is the usual give-away. I was really starting to like him. And so then, guess what?"

Lee shook her head, assuming some kind of betrayal.

"What?"

"His wife calls and he tells her, right in front of me, that he had a flat tire and was waiting by the side of the road for someone to come and fix it. And he's smiling at me as if the whole thing is just a big joke! So I toss the rest of my watered-down, ridiculously expensive drink in his face and leave."

Lee politely counted to three.

"The witness?"

"Oh right. Mrs. Weissmann. Did I tell you she was ninety-one?"

"You did." Lee was wide-awake now and curious. "So, why was she so amazing?"

"Well, for one thing, she's a concentration camp survivor. She spent a year at Auschwitz."

"No kidding?"

"No kidding. Anyway, she said that she and Jeremy were friends. It started with Jeremy shoveling her walk a few times when it snowed. He lived across the street from her. He always came over when his roommates were gone. In the spring, he helped her with other things, like carrying her groceries inside and putting them away. Sometimes he rang her doorbell and asked if she needed anything. He clearly wanted to help, so she asked him to move the dresser in her spare bedroom, change some light bulbs in a chandelier she couldn't reach, that kind of thing. Afterward, she always served him lemonade and chocolate chip cookies. 'He was even lonelier than me,' she said."

Lee was silent. The new information didn't surprise her as much as it should have.

"Lee?"

"Yes, go on. I'm listening."

"Okay, so mostly they talked about Jeremy's future. He was studying to take the high school equivalency exam. Wanted to go to college. He never discussed his parents or why he wasn't living with them. Mrs. Weissmann didn't pry. Occasionally, she tried to warn him about his roommates, but he'd smile and say they weren't as bad as they looked. Twice, she offered him money, but he wouldn't take it.

"One day in August, when it was very hot, he removed his sweatshirt and she saw the swastika. She could hardly breathe. When he asked what was wrong, she pointed at his forearm. He immediately put his sweatshirt back on and apologized. 'I'm sorry,' he told her. 'I didn't mean to scare you. I don't hate anyone.' For some reason, she decided to trust him. 'After all those years,' she said, 'it was time to trust someone.' So she told him about her year in Auschwitz and Jeremy was horrified. He'd read about the Nazis in high school but it hadn't sounded quite so bad. Mrs. Weissmann was his first Jewish friend. When he left that day, she wondered if he was ever coming back. But he did, two or three times a week until the police arrested him."

Lee stared at one of Paul's dramatic photographs on the opposite wall. He'd taken it from the top of K2 after almost turning back twice because of storms. A few days after his return, three South Korean climbers were blown off the mountain and killed. Paul was philosophic, but for once, Lee wasn't. Her husband was tempting fate, risking their happiness. But asking him to quit would have been like asking him to stop taking deep breaths. And then, she thought, there was Jeremy, living a dangerous surreal life and longing for the safe predictable one he no longer had.

"Is there anything else?" she asked Carla.

"Isn't that enough?"

Her investigator was right. Mrs. Weissmann was the kind of witness every lawyer dreams about and almost never finds.

"So, what do you think?" Carla asked excitedly. "She's everyone's dream grandmother. Ten minutes into the interview, I wanted her to be mine. And she's willing to help. Can we use her? She thinks Jeremy acted under duress. Why can't we argue that?"

"Two reasons. First, our client has never indicated that he acted under duress. And second, duress is not a defense to a charge of first-degree murder."

"Oh."

"But you found us a great witness, and if there's any way to use her, we will."

"Shit," Carla muttered.

"Are you almost home?"

"Yeah, I'm two blocks away."

"Go home and go to sleep. We'll talk some more on Monday."

"I can't believe this. I just found the best character witness in the world and we're not going to be able to use her."

"We don't know that yet, Carla. Let's discuss it on Monday."

"Are we screwed?"

"No, we're just stalled. There's a big difference."

"If you say so."

"Good night, Carla."

Lee hung up the phone, turned out the light, and slipped back under her down comforter. After circling around, Charlie dropped onto the pillow beside her—Paul's pillow, but for the past five years, Charlie's. "Just stalled," Lee repeated, settling into one of her two favorite sleeping positions. A few seconds later, she tried the other. Okay, so they were stalled. Which simply meant that nothing was happening at the moment. Things always changed, not necessarily for the better, but they changed; and when they did, she'd act. In the meantime, she would keep the faith, work the case, and wait.

When the alarm beeped at seven, Lee ignored it. At eight-fifteen, she scrambled out of bed, splashed some water on her face, fed Charlie, and made a fruit smoothie to go. There was no time to shower. She was supposed to meet Michael at nine.

A few minutes later, she was speeding down Broadway heading for the dojo, which had relocated a few years earlier to a building in the back of the Table Mesa shopping center. Although it wasn't quite nine and most of the stores didn't open until ten, Lee noticed a large number of shoppers already wandering along the Pearl Street Mall. It was the Saturday before Christmas. Five more days to go.

As she passed the shoppers, Lee thought about Mrs. Weissmann, wondering if the old woman had any other friends or relatives who would visit her during the holiday season. Lee hoped so.

The first three weeks of December could be a bit strange for a Jew. In every American city, it was hard not to feel like an alien from outer space wandering through an unfamiliar landscape where huge red and white candy canes affixed to lamp posts lined the major roadways, where thousands of box-shaped houses lit up spectacularly when the sun went down, and trees that were ordinarily leafless in winter were strung with dozens of tiny colored light bulbs. Where eight hundred variations of a song about jingle bells played continuously wherever you went. And all day long, determined-looking earthlings hurried in and out of stores searching for scarves, toys, sweaters, ties, and jigsaw puzzles to exchange for similar presents on December 25th, the day it all suddenly ended.

Once, when Lee was nine or ten, her father brought home a Christmas tree, which he set down a few feet away from the beautiful bronze menorah in their living room window. Lee's mother was livid when she saw it.

"No," she told him, "it's too confusing. Our daughter needs to know who she is."

"What's the big deal?" her father asked. "We're not religious."

Her mother pointed toward the door through which she expected the tree to exit.

"The Nazis didn't care that my Uncle Joseph and his family weren't religious."

Her father conceded the point and the tree was donated to a neighbor down the street. It was the Isaacs family's one and only attempt to assimilate.

Like most of the Jews they knew, Lee and her parents spent Christmas day eating lunch at one of the many Chinese restaurants in Boston (thank God for the Chinese), and then off to a four-star movie where there were plenty of empty seats to choose from. Lee hadn't minded any of it. She'd never wanted a tree, never cared about fitting in, which seemed boring. Aliens from outer space were different; she liked being different. Separate from the herd. Of course she was aware of the Holocaust, where the last thing you wanted was to stand out, but growing up Jewish in cosmopolitan America didn't feel dangerous. So as far as Lee was concerned, December 25th was an odd pleasant day when the earthlings did one thing and she did another.

Lately, though, after having weathered fifty-nine holiday seasons, Lee felt more like a tourist than an alien—the way Mark and Bobby felt standing off to the side in Allahabad, India, during a religious festival when millions of Hindu devotees plunged into the Ganges River to wash away their sins and break the endless chain of reincarnation. They'd planned to take pictures, but hadn't. "It would have been intrusive," Bobby explained.

Lee felt equally respectful, but still for the month of December, a tourist.

Mrs. Weissmann, on the other hand, was a true alien as well as a Jew. Did she ever feel at home? Hard to imagine, but at least the skinheads on her street were gone. That must have helped, although her faithful young friend had been swept away with them.

Lee finished the last of her smoothie as she pulled into a parking space in front of the dojo. She was ten minutes late. After grabbing her workout bag, she hurried to a side door she knew would be open. Michael had brought a friend's son to work out with them. The son, who'd studied Muay Thai since high school, was in the military now, had done two tours in Iraq, and was due to leave for Afghanistan on Tuesday. He'd wanted to spar with a couple of black belts before returning to his usual job teaching basic kickboxing to new recruits.

"Hey, Lee," Michael called as she entered the dojo.

"Hi, Michael. Sorry I'm late."

A young man in his twenties was stretching on the floor beside Michael. The man, who was obviously strong and fit, wore a black muscle T-shirt and gray sweatpants. His hair was very short. Michael nodded at him.

"Lee, this is Cary."

"Hi, Cary," Lee said. "Welcome to the dojo."

"Thanks," Cary grunted as he widened his legs to more than a hundred and twenty degree angle and then slowly bent forward until his chest was touching the floor.

"Christ, were we ever able to do that?" Michael asked.

"Sure," Lee said. "About a hundred years ago."

Cary straightened up and smiled.

"It's been a while since I worked out with civilians. This is nice."

"He says he's going to go easy on us," Michael assured her.

"I certainly hope so," Lee said. "I'll be back as soon as I've changed."

When she returned, Michael and Cary were doing Japanese pushups, a variation of a regular pushup but much more strenuous. Cary was faster than Michael, but each of them moved smoothly and effortlessly.

"Come on, Lee," Cary said, "it'll warm you right up."

"I'll say," Lee muttered, but she dropped to the floor and kept up with them. Finally, after about forty of them, Cary ground to a halt. Lee and Michael gratefully stopped when he did, and when he wasn't looking, exchanged mock looks of horror.

"Youth," Michael mouthed.

"We're in the army now," Lee mouthed back.

A few minutes later, Cary started doing jumping jacks.

"Come on, guys. We do five hundred of these every morning."

"Do we have to?" Michael asked.

Cary laughed but didn't stop.

"I leave for Kabul on Tuesday. I've got to be in tiptop shape. Keep me company."

"Let's go, soldier," Lee said to Michael. They both started jumping. After five straight minutes, Lee and Michael stopped and began to stretch. Eventually, Cary joined them.

They were quiet until Cary asked, "So, when do we get to spar?"

"Let's throw a few kicks first," Michael suggested. "I need to warm up my hamstrings. We usually fight at the end."

Lee walked over to a cardboard box in the corner of the room and pulled out a kicking shield, a large pad made of thick foam with handles on the sides and back.

"Let's use this. I'd like to work on my turning kicks. My timing's been off for weeks."

For the next twenty minutes, they each took turns holding the pad while the other two practiced their kicks. When Lee held the pad, she took as strong a stance as possible, but was still shoved backward, especially by Michael's jump-turning back kicks. Cary was fast and powerful, but his kicks weren't nearly as polished as Lee's and Michael's. Occasionally, he missed the pad or lost his balance. Which meant he didn't have as much control as they did. Lee would have to be vigilant when she fought him. She knew Michael was thinking the same thing. The most dangerous people to spar with were always strong, fast, limber, and sloppy.

Although she could have made numerous suggestions that would have improved Cary's kicks, Lee decided to remain silent. Some guys reacted badly to feedback, especially from a woman. They'd bide their time and then take it out on her later. She didn't know Cary. Better to be safe than in an ambulance heading for the hospital.

Finally, at Cary's urging, they stopped and got ready to spar. Lee searched through the box until she found extra hand, feet, and shin protection for the young man. Everything she touched smelled slightly rancid—an old familiar scent of blood, sweat, and tears. The whole place reeked of it, but no one seemed to mind. It smelled like effort, triumph, courage, and defeat: the universal dojo smell.

Michael volunteered to fight Cary first. They decided on three 15-minute rounds, which seem short if you're watching and long if you're fighting. Lee stood to the side, acting as the referee/time keeper. When they were ready, she had them bow to each other. Then she checked the clock and said, "Go."

Michael fought Cary the way Lee planned to: thoughtfully and conservatively, dancing just slightly out of the younger man's range, and moving in with a flurry of well-placed kicks and punches. Toward the end of the fight, Cary got lucky with a knee to Michael's stomach and an ax kick to his shoulder, but mostly Michael eluded him. When Lee called time, she could see that Cary was winded and frustrated. He needed a break.

"I want to fight Michael while he's tired," Lee told them. "Then it'll be Cary and me." She turned to the younger man. "You don't mind, do you?"

After the briefest hesitation, Cary said, "Of course not. I can use the rest." He took a couple of steps back, perfectly polite.

Michael might have been more tired than Lee, but he was looser and, after a few minutes, their fighting settled into a fast and elegant duet, each of them throwing full power kicks and punches, sidestepping when they could, blocking and counterpunching if they couldn't. It was one of their magical days when everything worked and they flowed around each other like water. When the round was up, they were grinning. At least something in her life wasn't stalled, Lee thought.

"That was beautiful," Cary said. "It looked almost as if it had been choreographed."

"Well," Michael replied, "we've been sparring together for ages. I guess we sort of know what to expect from each other."

"Not always," Lee said. "You surprised me with that side kick to my face. I thought you were done after you faked high and stepped up with a kick to my solar plexus. Then, suddenly, there was this heel heading straight for the bridge of my nose."

"Yeah," Michael laughed. "That kind of surprised me too. And your crescent kick came out of nowhere. You almost never throw them. I was completely caught off guard."

"See," Lee said, "we don't always know what to expect."

Cary nodded but was obviously impatient to fight.

"Do you need a few minutes to rest?" he asked Lee.

"Nope," she said, slipping her mouth guard back in. "I feel great. Let's go."

Cary walked up until he was about two and a half feet away from her.

"Bow to each other," Michael said.

As they bowed, Cary murmured, "I don't think I've ever fought a woman as good as you. This should be fun."

Lee said nothing. She bowed deeply, keeping her eyes on the younger man. A split second later, she leapt backward so that his very first kick, a come-around spin, missed her by a foot.

"You're very fast," Cary said.

"When I have to be."

Eventually they settled into it, Lee playing it safe the way Michael had. She bobbed and weaved, staying just out of range, skipping in occasionally to tag him. Nothing too hard because she had no desire to antagonize him. Halfway through the fight, Cary threw a powerful spin kick to her front leg, catching her right below the knee. She froze for a moment, wondering if her knee was injured. Cary immediately stepped up and hit her in the side with an uppercut.

"Break!" Michael shouted.

Cary looked surprised and upset.

"Why?"

Lee put up a hand to keep Michael from talking.

"That was a little too close to my knee."

"But very effective," Cary argued. "In fact, it's the first technique that worked on you."

"You're right. It's an excellent street technique, but it's too dangerous. We don't kick to the knee in our dojo. If we did, we'd all end up crippled." She bent down and palpated her knee. The joint felt slightly tweaked but okay. Later, she'd take a few Advil as a precaution. Finally, she straightened up.

"How is it?" Michael asked.

"I think it's all right," she said, nodding.

"Great," Cary said, smacking his fists together.

Michael shook his head and frowned.

"You were lucky. Should we call it?"

"Are you kidding?" Cary asked. "Come on, man. She's fine. There's more than seven minutes left."

There was a part of Lee that knew she ought to stop, that it was the prudent thing to do. If Cary had something to prove, let him take it to Afghanistan and prove it on the enemy. Calling it now would be wise; it would be mature; it would be boring. Lee was tired of waiting, tired of playing it smart. It's what she did all day long as a lawyer. Gravity be gone. Today she wanted to fly.

"I'm happy to finish the fight," she told them.

"It isn't worth it," Michael said.

"Probably not, but what the hell."

"As you wish. Bow to me. Bow to each other."

"Wait a minute," Lee told Cary. "Neither of us can afford to get hurt. You're heading off to Afghanistan, and I want to last forever. Let's just take it easy and have fun."

"Sounds good to me," Cary replied.

"Just stay away from my knees, okay?"

"Or what?" Cary asked.

"Don't be an ass," Michael said.

"I was just kidding, man. I'm not going to hurt her."

"It's not her I'm worried about."

"What? You're worried about me?" The young man looked incredulous.

"Let it go, Michael," Lee said. "We'll be fine."

After bowing in again, Cary smiled at her. A big open smile that was meant to disarm her. Lee smiled back, wondering if she'd made a mistake. Maybe yes, maybe no. They started slow but things picked up quickly. Cary was mixing it up, using his elbows and knees as often as possible. Lee had to block and kick almost continuously just to keep him away. About five minutes into it, they were both sweating profusely. Lee was beginning to relax. Finally, she saw an opening and threw a perfect turning heel kick that she pulled at the very last moment. If she hadn't, she'd have broken his nose.

"Nice control," Michael called.

"How many more minutes?" Cary asked, sounding tired and frustrated.

"Two," Michael answered. "Might as well take it easy now. Cool down a little."

"You're right," Cary said, but Lee had been a lawyer too long. She looked in her opponent's eyes, at the wild blue yonder behind them, and saw the words "fuck it." He'd been good for as long as he could. A lot of her clients were like that; they just couldn't help themselves. It almost wasn't their fault. Although she was ready, he skipped in so fast she could barely react. When his foot was an inch from her knee, she raised her leg high and side kicked him hard in the stomach. She pulled it, but not as much as she could have.

The kick shoved Cary backward until he lost his balance and fell down. He immediately rolled to his feet, his hands clutching his solar plexus.

"What the fuck?" He was panting a little in order to control the pain.

Michael looked at him and shrugged.

"Hey, she warned you."

Cary's face contorted with rage.

"She's just a girl," he cried, lunging toward her.

Ah, the real Cary—Lee wished she felt more surprised. Good thing she'd practiced her timing. Instead of turning too quickly, she waited until he was close enough to punch her, and then in one smooth motion executed a turning high knee side kick that caught him squarely in the chest. She didn't pull it this time. Fuck it.

Cary flew back about twelve feet into a wall and then slid to the floor. At first, he made no sound, which was worrisome, but finally he began to groan. Lee and Michael walked over to him.

Michael spoke first and said, "You're an idiot, Cary."

"She broke my rib, man." His voice was hoarse, his breathing shallow.

"Not just one. I'm guessing more like four. Maybe even five. What do you think, Lee?"

She didn't answer. Cary was rocking back and forth, his arms crossed in front of him.

"I'm supposed to report for duty on Tuesday. My gig's all fucked up."

"Maybe she saved your life." When Cary didn't respond, Michael turned back to Lee. "It's possible, you know."

Lee wiped the sweat out of her eyes and said, "I feel kind of bad now. I should have stopped when you told me."

"I guess you're not perfect."

"I guess not."

"Well, for what it's worth, I wouldn't have stopped either."

"Yes, but you're a few years younger than me. You've always been less mature."

"True," he said, smiling. "You might as well go change. I'll deal with Cary. I'll get him dressed and then take him to the emergency room. Make sure there are no other injuries besides the ribs." He made a scooting motion with his hand. "Go on."

"Okay." She began limping toward the women's dressing room. "You'll call if he's hurt worse than we think?"

"Absolutely," Michael said. "Did you break your baby toe on that last kick?"

"Feels like it."

"Was it worth it?"

"Hell yes."

"Why are you limping?" Bobby asked as the three of them retired to the living room for an after-dinner drink of Grand Marnier and homemade pound cake. Lee's baby toe was firmly taped to its neighbor and hadn't been bothering her until now. It was late, almost ten o'clock, and she was tired.

Her first inclination was to feign ignorance, but her toe hurt too much. She needed more Advil.

"I kicked someone," she said, limping to her usual spot on the couch. "He's hurt a lot worse than I am."

Bobby immediately sat down beside her while Mark lowered himself into his beloved rocking chair. After a moment, Mark picked up the bottle of Grand Marnier and began pouring a few inches of the liqueur into three small glasses. Lee hadn't been intending to partake, but changed her mind and sipped greedily at the soothing liquid.

"Ah, that's nice."

"Who'd you kick?" Mark asked. "Michael?"

"No," she said, putting the drink down before she finished it in one go. "A friend of Michael's. Actually, a son of a friend of Michael's, a soldier."

"A soldier?" Bobby asked. "Sounds like an interesting story."

"It's not. And it wasn't my finest hour."

"Now you've really piqued our interest," Mark said. "You kicked some soldier's ass and you regret it."

"Regret is probably too strong a word. I'm disappointed that I wasn't able to restrain myself." She picked up her glass and drained it. "More," she said, setting it down in front of Mark.

Mark looked surprised, but picked up the bottle and poured her another few inches. Lee was a lightweight. If she drank much more than that, she'd have trouble driving down the mountain. He capped the bottle and slid it away from her.

"Enough of the prefatory remarks. Tell us what happened."

When she finished the story, both men shrugged, much as Michael had.

"Sounds like he deserved it," Bobby said, putting his arm around

Lee's shoulder.

"He did, but I sort of knew it would happen. I was just tired of being a grown-up. I've been feeling frustrated. My murder case is stalled, and I think I took it out on him."

Both men were silent. She finished her drink, reached over, and poured herself another inch.

"What?" she finally asked. "Am I drinking too much?" After a couple of seconds, she kicked off her left shoe. Her toe was killing her. So was her hip where Cary had punched her. She'd have a fist-sized bruise for at least a week.

"You need a reality check," Mark told her.

"Reality is overrated," she said, feeling old and weary.

"But it's the truth," Bobby said. His sweet handsome face had that look of concern that signaled a reluctant but necessary reproach—the Boy Scout pulling her back onto the sidewalk. "We've been thinking about this for weeks."

Then it'll keep, Lee thought. She'd reproached herself enough. She was tired and wanted to leave. What she needed was eight hundred milligrams of Advil and an uninterrupted night of sleep.

"No advice," she said, standing up.

Mark looked exasperated.

"Lee, we've been reading the papers, attending vigils, and talking to people. You're out of step with reality. You actually think we care that your case is stalled. But we don't. We're glad."

"Fine," she said, limping toward their bathroom to find some Advil. "I never expected you to be sympathetic. Why should you be?"

Bobby stood up and followed her.

"But you still don't get it, Lee. Everyone, including us, wants you to fail. We don't want you to save your client."

"I know."

"Would you please sit down," Mark said. "I doubt it'll change your mind, but I want to tell you what it was like when I was your client's age." He pointed to the couch. "Please."

She sighed, limping back to the couch.

"Mark, I can just imagine what it was like back then to be gay."

"No, you can't. I was sixteen years old and knew that I was different than everyone around me. I was in the closet but hated it. One day, a group of my friends started picking on this effeminate kid who was obviously homosexual. I didn't even like him. I was a quarterback on the football team, a jock. This kid was everything I wasn't and didn't want to be. But somehow I knew I had to protect him. I waded into the middle of the fight and told everyone I was gay, that if they wanted to pick on someone different, to pick on me instead." He ran a hand through his thick blonde hair. "The fight broke up and the kid scuttled away. He never even thanked me. I lost my friends and spent the last two years of high school on my own. It really sucked."

"Yes," she said. "Paul told me a number of similar stories. "Just because I want to help my client, that I'm ethically required to help my client, doesn't mean I don't understand homophobia."

"But the point is," Mark continued, "I was sixteen and made a choice. Your client could have made a choice. He was old enough. He could have decided not to go along with it. It would have been tough, but he could have walked away. I think he's despicable."

"Duly noted." She turned to Bobby. "What about you? Come on. Say everything you think. Let's get it all out." The liqueur had already given her a headache. Actually, her entire body ached, even her chest muscles. Those Japanese push ups—why did she have to do so many?

Bobby looked conflicted.

"I wasn't as brave as Mark was. I never came out to anyone until I was twenty-two. I listened uncomfortably to all the faggot jokes, kept my mouth shut, and never stood up for anyone." He paused. "But I would never have participated in a 'boot party.' At the very least, I would have run away and tried to call for help."

"Okay," Lee said, "I've heard you both and I'm not surprised. But here's the thing: I represent a sixteen-year old boy accused of a heinous murder. Everyone hates him, including my two best friends. I'm all he has. I can't be swayed by the victim's agony, or by anyone else's. I can hear your truths, but I have to set them aside. If I succumb to 'reality,' if I take anyone else besides him into account, then I'll have violated my oath, which requires me to diligently represent my client no matter what he's allegedly done."

"Allegedly?" Mark's eyes flashed angrily. "He confessed!"

"It doesn't matter," she said, standing up again. "He's still presumed to be innocent. So whether you like it or not, I'm going to do everything in my power to get my client acquitted."

"Even if he's guilty?" Bobby asked.

"Oh come on, guys! It's what I do. Where the hell have you been for the past fifteen years? And, now that I think about it, where was your horror when the victims were women and children?"

Suddenly, the room was quiet. The only sound was wood crackling in the fireplace. It was their first real argument since Paul died. Lee searched for her down jacket, which she'd either hung up or thrown over the back of a chair. There was nothing more to say. When she found her jacket, she pulled it on.

"You can't go out like that," Bobby told her.

"Why? Because we've had a disagreement? Friends occasionally fight. We'll get over it."

"No. You're missing a shoe."

She looked down at her feet.

"Oh. I must have kicked it off. It has to be around here somewhere. Probably under the couch."

The two men got down on their hands and knees, peering under the massive leather couch. Lee remained standing. If she got down on the floor, she'd want to spend the night there.

"Here it is," Bobby said, reaching up and handing it to Lee.

"Thanks." She bent down and tried to pull it on. After a couple of seconds, she gave up. "My foot's too swollen. I'll just hop to my car."

"You're so fucking macho," Bobby muttered. "I'll find you a slipper." He headed for the bedroom.

After a while, Mark said, "I'm sorry, Lee. I don't know what got into me. Your case just struck a nerve, I guess."

"I think I drank too much of your Grand Marnier. Did I sound as priggish as I think I did?"

"Yes, but we deserved it. Despite everything we said, we really do understand what you do and why. If I ever commit a dreadful, disgusting crime, I'd want you to be my lawyer."

"Thanks."

Suddenly, Mark grabbed her shoulders and pulled her to him. The hug was tighter than she liked, but she decided not to struggle. She'd been kicked and punched till she was black and blue. How bad could a five-second hug be?

"You're impossible," Mark whispered in her ear. "But as gay as I am, I know why Paul fell for you."

It was the highest compliment he'd ever paid her.

CHAPTER SIX

December 25th was a perfect ski day: cold but not windy, with tons of new snow in the past week. While most people in Boulder were sitting around in their L.L. Bean pajamas opening their presents (oh, another waffle iron—how thoughtful), Lee headed for the warming hut in the Roosevelt National Forest. Today was the fifteenth anniversary of the day she'd first met Paul. For the past five years, she'd skied to the hut every Christmas and toasted him with a cup of hot chocolate. The first year was the hardest—she almost turned back—but then it got easier. In time, it became a lovely way to mark the occasion and a great excuse to spend the holiday alone.

When Lee got home, she checked for messages on her cell phone, which she'd intentionally left behind. There was only one voicemail, from Dan Andrews, who sounded as if he was hiding in a closet in the middle of a raucous party.

"Hey Lee, I'm not sure you'll be able to hear this, but I've got some brand new evidence to disclose in the Matthews case. You know how ethical I am, so I'm making the call today. I won't be coy. The evidence is great for me, not so good for you. If you feel like it, call me this afternoon. I'm at a family reunion and wouldn't mind an excuse to skip out for a while on business. I've got my cell phone in my pocket. Merry Christmas."

Lee fed Charlie, went upstairs to shower, and then returned to the kitchen, where her phone still lay on the counter. Forget it, she thought. I'm not going to make your day. Enjoy your family reunion. She slipped the phone into her pocket and wandered into the living room, turning in a circle as she often did to admire a collection of photographs Paul took on his trek to the Annapurna Base Camp. Finally, she sat down on the couch. She had loads of work to do but no desire to do it.

What kind of new evidence could Dan have? If there were any eyewitnesses, they would have surfaced long ago. Had Jeremy made any other statements besides the one to the police? Possibly, which would be disastrous, but Dan hadn't sounded quite that happy. So probably it was a jail snitch, who had come crawling out of the woodwork looking to make a deal. What kind of information could he have?

After a moment, she fished the phone out of her pocket and dialed Dan's number. He picked up on the first ring.

"Lee?" He was clearly at a party.

"It's Christmas, for Christ's sake."

"Oh please, I know you're Jewish. Wait a minute. I need to go outside. Thank God you called." Thirty seconds later, he said, "Okay, I'm back again."

"How's the reunion?"

"Awful. I feel guilty saying this, but I have the most boring relatives on the planet. I almost fell asleep during dinner. Now it's time for fruitcake. Everyone brought her own. Whose is the best? Who cares? I hate fruitcake."

"You're trying to disarm me and you're succeeding. I hate fruitcake too."

"Thanks for calling, Lee. I know I could have waited till tomorrow, but I needed some immediate gratification. I knew I'd hear from you."

"Well, you were right." She settled deeper into the couch and waited for Charlie to hop up and snuggle next to her. "So how bad is the new evidence? I'm standing in my bathroom in front of the medicine cabinet. Can I get by with regular Alka-Seltzer or do I need the extra strength?"

"For most attorneys, I'd say the extra strength, but since it's you, maybe just the regular."

So it wasn't as bad as it could be. She relaxed a notch.

"Shall I guess?" she asked.

"Sure, go ahead."

"A jail snitch just contacted your office."

"I hate you," he told her. "Go on."

"The snitch has information that hurts the co-defendants more than me, but now you feel confident that they'll take a deal and testify against my client if I refuse to cooperate."

"Why did I even bother calling you?"

"Because you're trying to wear me down."

"Am I succeeding?"

Lee looked out the window and saw a group of people ringing her next-door neighbor's doorbell. As soon as the door opened, they immediately linked arms and began singing. She stifled a groan. If they continued on to her house, she'd pretend she wasn't home.

"What's the information and is it credible?" she asked.

"Very. The snitch was the victim's roommate. He said there was a party at his house about a week before the murder. Someone found paperwork indicating the victim was facing charges for soliciting in Cheesman Park. The solicitee was a male undercover police officer."

"Was the victim at the party?"

"Nope. But all the co-defendants were. And, according to the snitch, they were talking about a possible boot party for the 'cocksucker.'"

Lee thought for a bit, then smiled.

"The snitch can't say whether my client was there or not."

"Unfortunately, that's true. This isn't as much fun as I thought it would be."

"This is actually great news for me. It proves that everyone but Jeremy knew what was about to happen. It explains his shock and paralysis during the attack. I'll call the witness even if you don't."

"Nice try, Lee. You're a real pro. But it doesn't actually prove that at all. In fact, arguably it's proof he knew exactly what was going to happen. These guys all lived together. The co-defendants were pretty agitated when they left the party. Stands to reason they shared the news with your client. At least that's what I'll be arguing." He paused. "And you're ignoring the real import of this bad news: that I have the co-defendants exactly where I want them. If you go to trial, three eyewitnesses—not one, not two, but three—will testify against your client. You can impeach the hell out of them, but three eyewitnesses are simply too many. He's going down, Lee."

She counted to five while scratching Charlie's head.

"What's your real best offer?"

"Now you're talking."

"Would you have called me today if I weren't Jewish?"

"Absolutely," he said.

"So what's your bottom line?" There was never a bottom line.

"I am authorized to offer your client thirty-five years. The offer will be withdrawn after the arraignment."

She stared at one of Paul's pictures, a frozen bone-colored landscape where nothing could survive for long.

"I need more time."

"Why should I give it to you?"

"Because you owe me. I called you back when you were about to sample a dozen fruitcakes."

"True. And my mood has definitely improved. How long do you need?"

"Until the motions hearing." The doorbell rang but she ignored it.

"Uh-uh," he said. "That's too long. I'll give you to February 15th. If you don't take it, I'll never offer it again."

"Which means you'll offer me thirty-eight any time before the trial."

"Don't be so sure."

"Enjoy the rest of your day, Dan."

"Merry Christmas, Lee."

"Shit," she muttered after hanging up the phone. If this were a chess game, she would soon lose her queen, and in another few moves, the game would be over. Had she missed anything? Was there something she couldn't see? There had to be. Today was her client's birthday. He was seventeen. Lee Isaacs did not plead seventeen-year old children out to thirty-five years. Period.

Without waiting to think it over, she dialed the Matthews residence.

Hi, she would say, *today is Jeremiah's birthday. His life is essentially over.* Mary would care; Leonard wouldn't. But she'd say it anyway.

"Hello?" It was Mary's voice. She either had a cold or she'd been crying.

"Mary? It's Lee Isaacs, your son's attorney."

"I know who you are."

"Is Leonard there?" Lee asked quickly.

"Not at the moment." She sniffed loudly. "It's Jeremiah's birthday."

"I know. When is your husband coming back?"

"I'm not sure. I wouldn't go with him. Sometime around eight, maybe earlier."

Lee checked her watch. It was a quarter past four. She stood up and began to pace.

"I need to ask you some questions about your son."

"I can't help you. I promised."

"Leonard doesn't have to know."

"Not Leonard," Mary said, beginning to cry. "Jeremiah."

"Jeremiah?" Lee was confused. "What did you promise Jeremiah?"

"It's all my fault. What kind of mother lets her son leave home at sixteen? I'm a monster." Mary was crying so hard now, it was difficult to understand her. "If I could drive up there tomorrow and take his place in prison, I would."

Lee was losing patience.

"Well you can't, Mary. But you could help him by answering my questions. I need to know what your son was like when he lived with you. He seems pretty passive to me. Depressed. Not the kind of person who could have done what he's charged with. Did Leonard preach excessively against homosexuality?" Lee hesitated. "Did he abuse him?"

"No!" Mary cried. "No one abused him. I'd have known and prevented it."

"I'm glad to hear that. So what led up to his being thrown out of your house?"

"I-I can't tell you. I promised."

"Please, Mary, you have to. Your son's not going to make it in prison. He'll die there. Please help him by talking to me."

"I need to hang up," she said, sounding desperate. "Leonard could come home early. He always says one thing and then does another. Testing me. Always testing me."

Lee squeezed the phone in her hand, but her voice remained calm and reasonable.

"Mary, you're my last hope. I've run out of ideas. What did you promise not to say?"

"It doesn't matter anymore. It won't help. I think I heard something. I have to go. I'm sorry." And then she hung up.

"Goddamn it!" Lee shouted, and then made her third phone call. To Carla.

"Hello?"

"Where are you?" Lee asked. She'd stopped pacing and was staring out the window. The carolers had obviously moved on.

"Lee, in case you hadn't noticed, it's Christmas. I'm celebrating."

"Can you meet me in fifteen minutes?"

"For what?"

"We need to drive down to Colorado Springs. Mary is by herself. I just got off the phone with her. We need to go down there and persuade her to talk to us."

"Are you crazy? Unlike you, I'm a Christian. Christians don't work on Christmas. I've got people to see, parties to go to . . ."

"Okay, listen, remember when you asked if we were screwed?"

"Yeah?"

"Well, we are. The case keeps getting worse. I don't know if Mary can help or not, but she's all we have left."

"You sound pretty desperate."

"I am." Lee rarely groveled, but it always worked with Carla.

"I'll go on one condition."

"What?" As if she had a choice.

"When we get back to Boulder, you have to go to the Boulderado and have a drink with me. It's only fair."

Lee thought fast.

"I think it's closed on Christmas."

"It's not. I checked. If you won't have a drink with me later, then I'm not going to spoil the most wonderful day of the year running off to the Springs with you. Find a Jewish investigator. And if Henry attacks us, I'm going to charge you an extra ten thousand dollars. So, do we have a deal?"

"Yes, we have a deal." Lee checked her watch. "I'll meet you at the Basemar shopping center in fifteen minutes."

"That's not enough time."

"Twenty," Lee said and hung up.

Twenty-two minutes later, her trusty investigator drove up beside Lee's old 4Runner. Lee rolled down her window and motioned for Carla to do the same.

"You're the best," Lee said, and meant it.

Carla actually blushed.

"I'll drive," Lee told her. "It's the least I can do. I don't think there'll be much traffic."

Carla exited her Honda carrying two small flashlights. She was wearing sensible boots, thick leather gloves, and her wool cape.

"You came prepared."

"You bet," Carla said, hopping into the passenger seat. "If I owned a stun gun, I'd have brought that too. Hey, maybe we should buy one for the future."

"There is only now," Lee intoned, parroting what Paul used to say in all seriousness.

"Well, that's true."

Lee turned right on Baseline road, heading for the freeway. The forecast was for snow later in the evening.

"Listen," Lee said, "this could be a huge waste of time. If Leonard's back, she'll never talk to us."

"Which is why we're going to have a drink afterwards."

Lee forced herself to smile. She hated bars, hated the inevitable come-ons when two women were drinking alone together. Tethered goats waiting for the lions and jackals to sniff them out, gauge their defenselessness, and then swoop in for the kill. In Lee's experience, they came in droves and weren't easily dissuaded. It took extreme rudeness or just walking out, which was what she usually ended up doing. But if Mary was alone, Lee needed her investigator to witness her statements. So she was stuck. And on Christmas of all days.

The traffic on I-25 south was almost non-existent. Fruitcakes took a long time to eat, Lee figured. And, because they were so dense, you couldn't just get up and leave right away. Coffee helped. And time. Hence the empty highway.

It was barely six-thirty when Lee's Toyota approached Jamboree Drive.

"We should park a few streets away," Carla said, shifting into investigator mode.

"Good idea."

They circled the neighborhood until they found an inconspicuous spot on a busy street, and then jumped out with their flashlights. It was dark and just beginning to snow.

"Merry Christmas, ho, ho, ho," Carla muttered as they squeezed through the metal gate on Jamboree Drive and headed down the long driveway to the house. There were no outside lights on. Until they got much closer, they wouldn't know if Leonard, or Henry, was there.

"I don't think I ever told you this," Carla whispered, "but after my first divorce, I considered becoming a dental hygienist. My heart was broken and I wasn't thinking clearly. At the last moment, I decided it would be too boring. Somehow, I convinced the public defender to interview me as a rookie investigator. I didn't look at all like the other applicants, which I guess they liked. In any event, I talked and talked until they gave me the job. I thought it would be more exciting than cleaning people's teeth. But I didn't expect it to be like this." She tripped over a branch and cursed.

"You picked the right profession. We're almost there."

"It's really snowing out. I wish I'd brought a hat."

"Take mine," Lee said, handing her a black wool beret.

"Thanks. I think it looks better on you. Because you're taller."

There were no cars in front of the house, no porch lights, but there was at least one light on downstairs. Lee marched up to the front door and knocked loudly. After a couple of minutes, they heard footsteps approaching the door.

"Who's there?" Mary called. "Leonard, did you forget your keys?"

"It's me, Lee Isaacs, and my investigator, Carla Romano. Can we please come in?"

"No. Go away."

"I need to speak with you. I drove all the way down from Boulder because I'm desperate. I'm going to lose Jeremiah's case without your help. Would you please open the door?"

"There's no way I can help you."

"We're freezing out here. It's snowing pretty hard. Could you at least let us in to get warm? Carla's feet are numb."

"Why is it always my feet?" Carla whispered.

"My feet are numb too," Lee added.

"Well, you certainly don't give up easily," Mary said and finally unlocked the door. There was a lovely waft of warm air coming from the downstairs apartment as well as the mouthwatering smell of freshly baked cookies. "You can't stay here long. Leonard could come home at any moment."

"Where's Henry?" Carla asked. She was trying to peer inside.

"Henry? He's with Leonard."

"Were you making chocolate chip cookies?" Lee asked, shutting the door behind them.

"Yes, I make them every Christmas." A couple of tears slid down her face. "They're-they're Jeremiah's favorite." A few seconds later, the tears began in earnest.

"You obviously love your son," Carla said, putting her arm around Mary's shoulder. After a moment, they were hugging. "Please talk to us, Mary. I know you want to help him."

"He'll never forgive me," Mary cried. "And I certainly wouldn't blame him." Suddenly, she straightened up and stared at them. "But I do want to help. I don't care if Leonard approves or not."

"Good for you," Lee said. "How about if we—"

Carla shook her head and Lee immediately shut up.

"Are you afraid of him?" Carla asked gently.

"Not physically. But I'm tired of his bullying. I've been thinking of leaving him for a while, but I-I guess I'm just not ready."

"It takes a lot to leave somebody," Carla said. "I know."

Mary was starting to look worried again.

"You'd better go. I don't want him to see you here."

"When can we talk?" Carla asked.

"After his arraignment. I'll talk to you then."

"Great," Lee said. "The arraignment is—"

"I know when it is," Mary interrupted her. "I was at the preliminary hearing."

"You were?" Carla asked. "We didn't see you."

"I know. I sat in back and, well, I was wearing a disguise. My friend Brenda has breast cancer. I told Leonard I was going to spend the day with her. Instead, I borrowed her wig and drove up to Boulder. I left as soon as the judge announced the next court date. Leonard would kill me if he knew."

Both Lee and Carla were stunned.

"Oh yes," Mary said, smiling at their expressions. "And one of these days, I'm going to walk out for good. One of these days."

Then they all heard a car drive up to the house. Less than a minute later, they heard the sound of the van door opening and a dog barking happily as he jumped to the ground.

"Oh my God, that's Leonard," Mary whispered. She looked terrified.

"Oh well," Lee said. "It's too late now."

"No, wait! There's another way out downstairs. When you get outside, there's an overgrown path that leads to the park."

"How overgrown?" Carla asked.

"Come on," Lee said, grabbing Carla's arm. "Let's go." She turned to Mary. "I hope you won't change your mind."

"I won't."

They found the back door and opened it. Outside, it was pitch dark and snowing even harder. Lee gently closed the door behind them. In seconds, they were covered with snow. They turned on their flashlights, searching for something resembling a path. Lee stood very still for a moment, getting her bearings. Finally, she pointed to the right.

"I think that's the direction we want to go."

"You *think?* I should have become a dental hygienist. They never work on weekends or major holidays."

"Too late. Follow me. The park is only a quarter of a mile away. Maybe a little longer."

"Oh great."

"Hey, we should be celebrating. Our client's mother is going to talk to us. This could be a turning point."

"Maybe, but I can't wait until we're sitting in a warm bar."

"Soon."

"Oomph," Carla uttered, falling sideways.

Lee turned in a circle.

"Where are you?"

"In a snow bank," Carla cried.

"Shhh."

"Shhh? I'm suffocating!"

"You couldn't talk if you were suffocating. Stick out your arm and I'll pull you out."

After a moment, she saw Carla's cape and then her arm. She'd obviously fallen off the path into a hole filled with snow. Lee stuck the flashlight into her mouth, wrapped her left arm around a small tree, and then grabbed Carla's hand. In a second, she'd pulled her out. Carla was covered with snow and sputtering. It took everything Lee had not to laugh. This was one of the best Christmases she'd had in years. In the distance, two coyotes had begun to yip.

"I won't even ask what that sound is," Carla said, wiping her face.

"Come on." Lee took her arm. "In two hours, we'll be sitting in a dry cozy bar surrounded by droves of good-looking single men. We'll be laughing about all of this, when one of them will sit down beside you and ask why it's taken him so long to find you."

"Ah," Carla sighed happily. "And then what?"

About fifteen minutes later, they climbed into Lee's Toyota. It was snowing heavily and the temperature had plummeted. On the way back to Boulder, the highway was busier and the driving chaotic. The earthlings, having digested their fruitcakes but still high on eggnog, were now heading home.

They were halfway there when Carla cleared her throat.

"I have a confession to make."

"I hate confessions," Lee said, trying not to become mesmerized by the snow darts hitting her windshield.

"Well, too bad. I lied to you. When you called earlier, I was sitting at home in my pajamas. I had no plans whatsoever for the evening."

"Why? You have plenty of friends. And doesn't your mother live in Boulder? I think you told me that."

Carla slumped forward, her face in her hands.

"Ever since I was little, I've spent every Christmas with my mother, even when I was married. About three years ago, she was diagnosed with dementia. Last month, she stopped remembering who I was. I didn't want to spend the holiday with someone who didn't know I was her daughter. It's just too depressing."

"I'm so sorry, Carla. I had no idea. That must be awful."

"So you did me a favor by calling. You don't owe me a drink. If you want to go home, it's okay."

Lee considered the idea but of course rejected it.

"One drink won't kill me."

"Really?" She sat up straight again. "Great. Thanks, Lee. It was kind of fun today, wasn't it?"

"Yes," Lee said, "it was."

Although it was almost ten-thirty when Lee returned from the Boulderado, she decided to call her father anyway. She and Carla had spent a pleasant hour drinking wine and imagining various unlikely miracles occurring in Jeremy's case: that another juvenile skinhead would suddenly confess, that all three co-defendants would refuse to testify against their teenage brother, and so on.

When a couple of grinning jackals approached them, Carla looked at Lee, who shook her head.

"We're nuns, brides of Christ," Carla told them, "toasting the birth of our Savior."

The men looked skeptical but eventually left. Better to be safe than sorry.

Her father picked up on the first ring, which meant he hadn't been watching television.

"Hey, Dad," Lee said, settling against the pillows on her couch. She'd slipped into an old plaid bathrobe that used to belong to Paul. It was pretty ratty and one of these days, she'd drop it off at the Salvation Army. Maybe after the holidays. Or not.

"Hey, kiddo."

"Merry Christmas."

"Thank God it's over," her father grumbled.

Only another Jew would say that, she thought happily.

"Not so merry?" she asked.

"They don't play bridge on Christmas."

"Bummer." Charlie had finished eating and was waiting to be invited onto her lap. She patted her legs and he immediately hopped up. "So what did you do instead?"

"What we always did when you were little: Chinese food and a movie."

"What movie?" she asked, figuring a war story, or maybe an intelligent comedy. Which was pointless because she never guessed right.

"A new one called *Shame*, about a male sex addict in New York City. It was kind of heavy. Sad but good."

Lee shook her head. Her father's tastes in movies, art, and literature were always edgier and heavier than hers. Then again he didn't spend his days staring at pictures of dead bodies. Lee liked thoughtful movies but stayed away from the more disturbing ones. She had enough wretched images in her head to last a lifetime.

"What made you go see something like that?"

"Sweetheart, I'm eighty-four. I've lived a pretty sheltered life. But before I go, I want to see as much as I can."

"Okay, so what did you think?"

He was silent for a moment while he lit a cigarette.

"Well, it's funny. Part of me was envious and part of me felt really sorry for the guy."

"Huh," she said, like Bobby. Although she'd asked him before, she decided to try again. "Did you ever want another serious relationship after Mama died?"

"Nope. Once was enough."

She glanced at one of Paul's beautiful frozen landscapes.

"Am I going to end up just like you?"

"Would that be so bad?" He chuckled a little.

"Well, I don't particularly like card games."

"Neither did I when I was your age. Later, when your arthritis gets worse, you'll change your tune."

"Now there's a gloomy thought." Charlie was beginning to stir, which meant he wanted her to scratch his head again. "How come you rarely focus on happy, positive things?"

"I'm old. Why should I?"

Because it would make me feel better, she thought. Which hardly qualified as a reason.

"So listen, Dad," she said, changing the subject, "I won't be getting out there in January unless I end up settling this murder case. Are you okay with waiting until the summer?" This time, she knew the answer. Her father was even more independent than she was. Whoever said no man was an island had never met Aaron Isaacs.

"Of course. Which doesn't mean I don't enjoy your visits."

She adjusted the pillow behind her neck. It had been a long emotional day. Time to get horizontal and travel to the land of Nod, a wild, lawless place where she often ran into her husband, and sometimes if she was really lucky, her mother.

"How's the case going, anyway?" he asked, puffing at his cigarette.

Lee suddenly thought of Mary sneaking into her son's preliminary hearing wearing her friend's wig. The image was both sad and amusing.

"We might have had a breakthrough today. I'm not sure."

"Well, you're an Isaacs, so you won't give up until you find a way to help your client. It's in your DNA. An Isaacs never gives up."

She wanted to ask if he'd ever considered just the possibility of giving up—not for long, maybe a day or two—especially after the death of his beloved wife. But of course she didn't. An Isaacs never even thinks of giving up; it was her legacy.

"Hey," her father said, "today's your anniversary. The day you first met Paul."

"You're right." She was surprised. "You have an excellent memory."

"An elephant never forgets."

"Where did that come from?" she asked, laughing.

"Hell if I know. It just popped into my head."

She heard a tiny hiss, the sound of his cigarette being dropped into a tumbler of water. For as long as she could remember, he'd never used an ashtray.

"Listen," he said, " if it really bothers you, I'll try to focus on happier, more positive things."

She stood up, dislodging Charlie from his perch.

"No, you're perfect just the way you are."

"Am I your funny valentine?" He hummed a few bars of the song.

"You are indeed. So don't die before I call you again."

"Okay, but call soon."

"Good night, Dad."

"Good night, kiddo."

CHAPTER SEVEN

On the first floor of the Justice Center, there was a small cafeteria with a sitting area for about thirty people. Lee sat at one of the tables, eating a sesame bagel with cream cheese. All the other tables were occupied by lawyers studying their files or reading the newspaper. Because she'd been practicing forever, Lee knew everyone in the room and, for the most part, liked and respected them; and if she didn't, she pretended otherwise. Politics 101: You never knew when or from whom you might need a favor.

It was eight-thirty on the first Monday of the New Year. Jeremy's arraignment was at nine. Carla and Peggy were supposed to meet her there in fifteen minutes. As usual, she'd staked out the table beforehand. It was silly, but she couldn't help it. All good lawyers were control freaks.

It had snowed all weekend and she'd skied for miles on Sunday. Her toe had finally stopped hurting and she was feeling strong and well. Ready to disappoint Dan and set her client's case for trial. She still had no idea what her defense would be, but sometimes you had to remain calm and respectful, waiting until it revealed itself. The Gods did not reward fearful, panic-stricken defense attorneys.

One of the first things her then-boss, a recovering alcoholic, told her as a public defender—"Fake it till you make it"—had stayed with her all these years. It worked unless she was up against someone like Dan, who'd obviously received the same advice when he'd started.

As she ate, Lee had her fingers crossed that Mary would show up at the hearing and then follow through with her promise to help. She also hoped they wouldn't have to spend too much time comforting the woman and reassuring her that her son's life wasn't ruined, because it probably was. But who knew? Maybe Mary would reveal something crucial, something that would prevent Dan from moving confidently ahead toward checkmate.

She finished her bagel and sighed. Dreaming was allowed up to a point, after which it would be a sign of premature trial psychosis, a state of mind where the lawyer ignores everything negative and focuses only on the possibility of a miraculous intervention from above.

Lee looked across the room and saw the judge in Jeremy's case standing in front of the pastry counter. Judge Samuels was a portly, bespectacled man with pink skin and thinning white hair. As she watched, the judge picked up a fresh croissant, held it to his face almost as if he were sniffing it, and then put it back. After rejecting a donut and an apple turnover, he grabbed a bag of peanuts, stood in the checkout line, and waited to pay for it. A minute later, as he was heading for the door, he noticed Lee and changed course, limping toward her.

"Hi, Judge," she said, motioning to the empty chair across from her. "Why are you limping?"

"Gout." He lowered himself into the chair. "Can you believe it?"

Lee could but shook her head.

The judge ripped open the bag of peanuts and poured some into his hand.

"This is what my doctor considers an acceptable snack." He popped them into his mouth and shuddered, as if they were pills he was required to take.

"I like peanuts," Lee said with a straight face.

"You would." He was staring at her. "You look great. As always."

"Thanks, Judge."

He ate another handful, then closed the bag and dropped it on the table.

"Ugh. You know what I really love?"

"Wine and lobster?"

"How did you know?" He looked genuinely surprised.

"Just a guess."

He glanced around the room, and then leaned in closer.

"There are only three things I really love: good wine, good food, and good sex. And these days, the occasional third isn't enough to compensate for the lack of the other two."

"That's too much information, Judge."

"Sorry. I guess I've always just thought of you as one of the guys."

"I'm assuming that's a compliment?"

"Oh, yeah. And not only that, you're one of the best attorneys who's ever practiced in my courtroom. Which doesn't mean I'm going to cut you any slack on the Matthews case."

"I wouldn't expect you to, Judge." She peeked at the clock on the wall. It was a quarter to nine. Carla and Peggy would be here any moment.

"Here," he said, handing her the rest of the peanuts. "I'd rather starve." He hesitated. "Speaking of the Matthews case, any progress toward a settlement?"

"Not yet." She tucked the bag into her briefcase. "Thanks for the nuts. I'll probably eat them for lunch."

"To each their own." He stood up to leave. "I know you know what you're doing, Lee, but objectively speaking, it doesn't look so good for your kid."

"Not to worry. I've pulled out worst cases than this."

"I know you have. I've watched you. Well, see you in court."

She thought for a moment. It would be hokey, but what the hell.

"Have you brought home any flowers recently?"

He seemed to know what she was getting at.

"No, not for a while."

"Hmm. I'd suggest tulips." Surely a new low in terms of trial advocacy.

"Tulips?" he whispered. "Women like tulips?"

Lee was now the spokeswoman for half the human race.

"Yes, Judge. We love tulips." Actually, she really did, so it wasn't totally ridiculous. And if it helped, it might make a difference somewhere down the line.

"Thanks," he said, smiling. "I'll get some on my way home."

"Don't tell me how it went."

"Right, I won't. See you in court." He limped toward the door and then disappeared into the crowd of people rushing toward the courtrooms on the first and second floors.

The arraignment was quick. Lee pleaded not guilty on behalf of her client and Judge Samuels set the trial for May 23rd.

"I'm guessing two weeks," the judge told them.

"More than enough time," Dan agreed.

So of course Lee disagreed.

"Only if the prosecution puts its whole case on in the first week. If not, it might take longer." She was bluffing and everyone knew it. She could hear Dan chuckling in the background.

"Judge," he said, "I'll bet a hundred dollars we can do the case in less than two weeks."

"Any response to that, Ms. Isaacs?"

"I don't bet for chump change, Judge."

"Well, it probably wouldn't be appropriate anyway." The judge flipped through the calendar on his desk. "I'll set a one-day motions hearing for April 17th. Is that okay?"

Both parties checked their appointment books and then nodded.

"Ms. Isaacs, I'm assuming you'll be filing a motion to suppress your client's confession. Anything else significant?"

Lee pretended to think about it.

"Well, Judge, there were numerous searches and seizures. There may be discovery issues, and of course there are the usual matters that should be ruled on *in limine*. So, the truth is, I don't know." Actually, she did. None of the other issues would take more than an hour to litigate.

"That's fine, Ms. Isaacs. If we have to find another day to finish the motions, we will."

"Thanks, Judge."

When the arraignment was over, Lee looked behind her and saw Mary sitting in the back row without her wig. She was wearing a pretty blue dress that complimented her figure. Her face, in repose, was almost identical to her sister's.

The guards were about to escort Jeremy back to bed. Here came the shackles, as if he had anywhere else to go. Vegas. Buenos Aires. Casablanca. Jeremy Matthews: master escapologist.

"Jeremy," Lee whispered. "Your mother is here. She was at the preliminary hearing as well."

Jeremy kept his eyes on his feet and didn't respond. Lee could hardly blame him.

"She feels really bad, Jeremy. She's not asking you to forgive her, but she wants to help."

"Well, it's kind of too late, but you know what? Tell her it's all good."

"But it's not good. She abandoned you."

"It doesn't matter." He patted Lee's arm with his handcuffs. "Really. What's done is done. I'm cool with it."

"We have to take him now," one of the guards said.

"All right," Lee told them, then turned back to her client. "I'll see you next week. Keep eating and exercising."

"Yeah, sure. Whatever."

Mr. Cool was turning into Mr. Frozen.

<hr>

"I'll start with a little sympathy," Carla whispered, "and then you can take over from there. Go easy."

They were walking down the hall toward a small conference room on the second floor of the Justice Center. Mary and Peggy were following close behind, Peggy's arm around her younger sister's shoulders. Lee felt vaguely irritated by Carla's remark. Of course she would go easy. Anyone with half a brain would go easy. It wouldn't take much to send Mary fleeing from the interview.

Carla must have sensed Lee's reaction because she whispered, "Sorry. I'm just nervous. I can't believe she actually showed up. I've interviewed over a hundred people in this case and Mary's our last hope for any new information."

"I know." Carla was right; there was no one left but Mary. It took great discipline not to keep peeking over her shoulder to make sure the two sisters were still following them.

Finally, they reached the room. Lee opened the door and motioned for Mary to enter.

"May I come in too?" Peggy asked. "I promise I won't say anything. I think it would make Mary feel more comfortable."

"It would," Mary agreed.

"Sorry," Lee said, reaching in and turning on the light. "Whatever your sister tells us will be confidential, but not if there's a third party present. We don't want to turn you into an involuntary witness in the case."

"Oh. Well then of course not." Peggy kissed her sister on the cheek.

"I'll be right outside, waiting. And then we're going to lunch. You promised."

"I did, but we can't dawdle. Leonard will get suspicious if I return too late."

"I'm proud of you, little carrot."

Carla grinned at the two women.

"Is that a nickname?"

"Yes," Mary answered, "it's what she always called me when we were kids."

"Oh that's so funny," Carla said, nudging Lee in the ribs. "I wish I had a sister."

Both women smiled gratefully at Carla. Lee merely nodded. Personally, she'd never wanted a sister. She'd loved the attention of two doting parents. Why would she want to share it? In the meantime, all three women were hugging again. Lee tried to hide her impatience.

Inside the conference room, there was a round wooden table and four chairs. Carla sat down next to Mary while Lee took a seat across from her. Carla started by assuring Mary that everything she said was confidential and that no one was going to judge her. They just needed to know the truth. Mary nodded, tears running down her face. They let her cry for a while until Lee couldn't stand it anymore.

"Okay," Lee told her, glancing at Carla, who immediately pulled out a pad of paper and a pen. "We can't undo the past, so let's see what we can do to help Jeremy now. I mean Jeremiah."

"No, you were right the first time." Mary dabbed her eyes with the handkerchief Carla had loaned her. "I only called him Jeremiah in front of Leonard. Jeremy hates the name."

"You love him very much."

"Oh yes. No matter what he's done." She dropped the handkerchief onto her lap and straightened her posture. "And I won't waste any more of this interview berating myself. I did what I did. At the time, I wasn't strong enough to stand up to my husband. There's simply no excuse. Ask me whatever you want."

Suddenly, Mary looked strong and determined, like her sister. Lee couldn't help staring. *What happened to you?* she wanted to ask. But of course she already knew. Since the first caveman clubbed his future wife and dragged her to his grotto, Leonard and other men just like him happened to millions of Marys. If Lee had her way, the martial arts would be mandatory for all girls beginning in the first grade. And little boys would be discouraged from fighting.

They started by talking about Jeremy's unremarkable childhood and his father's increasingly overbearing behavior as his son entered adolescence.

"Leonard was afraid of something," Mary said, shaking her head. "But I didn't know what it could be. As far as I was concerned, Jeremy was the perfect son. He was kind and polite and funny. He even went to church, although it was clearly beginning to bore him. I tried to shield him as best I could from Leonard's rage, especially because I couldn't understand the reason why. Leonard knew, but I didn't. I really didn't."

"Knew what?" Lee asked, although she'd already guessed.

Mary bowed her head in shame.

"That our son was gay."

"What?" Carla asked, clearly surprised.

"Yes," Lee said, "that's what I thought." She waited for Mary to compose herself, then asked her to describe the day she watched her son leave home with nothing but his backpack and a couple of dollars. The day her son changed from a polite middle-class boy from the suburbs to a desperate street kid picking through dumpsters in the back alleys of Denver.

"I have relived this a thousand times," Mary whispered, and then slowly, almost involuntarily, shut her eyes. For the next few minutes, she recited the facts as if she were watching them on a screen inside her head, a movie where bad things happened to other people. People who never saw things coming and were floored by life's surprises. Her face was calm and expressionless, like a doll's.

"Every Friday afternoon, Leonard preached at a small church in Manitou Springs, and I always went with him. I enjoyed it, actually. It was a chance for us to get out. Jeremy never expected us to return before dinner. One afternoon in February, when we got to the church, only one old man was present. Everyone else had the flu. After less than an hour, the old man started coughing, so we decided to call it a day.

"When we got home, the first thing we saw was this dark blue station wagon parked in front of the house. And there they were, Jeremy and another boy, sitting in the front seat making out. Like teenagers at a drive-in, except both of them were male. At first, I tried to pretend it was platonic—just two good friends saying good-bye—but it obviously wasn't. And they weren't really saying good-bye. More like hello.

"I looked over at Leonard and his face was purple with rage. I've never seen him look angrier. When he started to get out of the car, I tried to grab his arm, but he pushed me away and ran toward the boys. I got out too and began shouting. I wanted to warn them, but it was freezing out and their windows were closed. Leonard pounded on the passenger door, screaming at the top of his lungs. For a moment, Jeremy stared at us, his face bright red with embarrassment. Then, after zipping up his jacket and saying something to the driver, he got out of the car. He looked sad and resigned." She hesitated. "But-but he also looked relieved, as if a heavy burden had been lifted from his shoulders.

"After the station wagon took off, Jeremy wouldn't look at me. Leonard was still screaming, but neither of us paid any attention to him. It was just a lot of noise in the background. I reached up and smoothed Jeremy's hair, which was mussed, and asked why he hadn't told me. 'I couldn't,' he said. 'I just couldn't.'

"Leonard was now ordering Jeremy to leave. 'You are an abomination,' he screamed, 'to your parents, church, and community!' Jeremy just nodded and began to walk away. I was too stunned to think. 'Wait!' I finally shouted. 'What about counseling?' Jeremy stopped and turned. The look on his face told me everything I needed to know. There would be no miracle. A hand would not reach down and save us. 'Mom,' he said, 'if years of prayer couldn't help me, counseling won't make any difference. I am what I am. This is all for the best. Promise you won't tell anyone, okay?' Of course I promised. By then, Leonard had grabbed my arm and was pulling me toward the house. I might have tried to break free, but then what? No, I simply lacked the will. In less than a minute, my tall, funny, beautiful boy was gone."

Finally, she opened her eyes.

"So that's it. I never heard from him again. I knew he went to Peggy's and that she gave him money, but after that, until the police called, I had absolutely no idea where he was or what he was doing. How can you both not judge me?"

"That took a lot of courage," Carla said. "We're proud of you."

"But it doesn't help him, does it?" Mary asked, looking first at Carla and then at Lee.

No one said a word. Probably not, Lee thought. If anything, it was the missing motive. The reason her client behaved the way they said he did. Internalized homophobia. Self-loathing.

Carla was thinking hard but reaching the same conclusion.

"We don't have to tell the DA. They'll never find it out on their own."

"True," Lee said. "But I need to talk to Jeremy. Make sure it all went down the way he said it did. Maybe they threatened him and he's been too ashamed to tell us."

Suddenly, both Carla and Mary looked hopeful. Lee didn't bother to remind them that duress was not a defense to murder. At best, it was a mitigating factor, something she could use to get a better deal. Not that Jeremy had ever intimated he'd been threatened. Why would he change course now? He'd been living with men who openly hated gay people. He obviously detested himself. From the very beginning, he'd wanted to go to prison. Welcomed it. Was it because he was gay or because he was guilty? If she asked, he'd probably say both. Great. So Mary's disclosure was irrelevant—just another sad fact about a sad boy whose life would soon be over.

No, she thought, Dan can't win again. And Jeremy couldn't lose; he was simply too young. And Lee? Lee was simply too old. There had to be something else. Something more. Lee would just have to jumpstart her aging mojo and find the missing information. Their futures were totally intertwined, hers and Mr. Frozen's.

Forty-eight hours later, Lee was standing on the stairs leading up to the juvenile detention facility. Yesterday, in an all-day trial before a judge, she'd successfully represented a client who'd answered the door with his penis hanging out of his boxer shorts. The victim, a female FedEx employee, said it was intentional; her client, an investment broker, claimed it wasn't, that he'd just woken up (it was two in the afternoon). Lee argued reasonable doubt, and after she won, privately advised her client to seek counseling.

She'd been on the stairs for at least ten minutes. It was a cheerless winter day. A pale weak sun was vainly trying to keep things from freezing.

If Paul were alive, she might have driven home later and suggested they spend the weekend in Puerto Vallarta, holed up in a cheap hotel on the beach. They'd had fun there, even fantasized about buying a condo in the Old Town when they were eighty. "We'll eat and drink whatever we want and let ourselves go," Paul joked. Two fat, old, alcoholic expats sitting on a bench overlooking the sea. It might not have been so bad.

But it wasn't her own future that worried Lee. It was Jeremy's. The kid was starting to get to her. Like most lawyers, Lee tried not to get emotionally involved with her clients, but sometimes she couldn't help it. It wasn't fatal; it just made the job harder. The more she cared, the more she had to make sure it didn't affect her judgment or advice. Mary's revelation had struck her as incredibly sad, and for the past two days she'd wavered about whether to confront Jeremy with his sexuality or to ignore it. He'd kept it a secret for a reason, but secrets between a client and his lawyer were never good; they often backfired or, at the very least, prevented the two from bonding. Jeremy and Lee clearly hadn't bonded yet. Ergo, she ought to confront him no matter how ashamed he felt. Except the secret in this case was either irrelevant or harmful, so why put her client through it? Because—she repeated the mantra—secrets between a client and his lawyer were never good.

Fine, she'd go inside and wing it.

As she entered the room with the couch and the two metal chairs, she noticed that the large dead plant had finally been carted off. There was a new poster on the wall depicting a teenager turning down a bag of drugs. It was hard to tell what race he was, something that was no doubt intentional. The words above his head were simple: "Today is the first day of the rest of your life." Lee approved. It was much more sophisticated than the usual depiction of a teenager in handcuffs who'd already made the wrong decision.

When Jeremy was finally brought into the room, she asked what he thought of the poster.

"I don't know. It's kind of irrelevant, I guess. But it's also sort of depressing, like they're rubbing it in."

"Hmm. Well, have a seat. There are all kinds of things for us to talk about." As he headed for his usual seat at the far end of the couch, she said, "No, not there. A little closer."

He hesitated, and then sat down in the middle. The act spoke volumes about their relationship, which hadn't progressed much in the three months she'd been courting him. He no longer glared at her, which was nice. Sometimes he even smiled. They'd arm wrestled and joked, but he'd never let her into his world. He'd revealed a couple of things but never what truly mattered. That he was gay, for instance, and obviously wished he wasn't, that he'd surrounded himself with men who would have killed him if they'd known his secret. What had that felt like? Maybe she'd ask him, maybe she wouldn't.

"There's a new jail snitch in the case," she began.

Jeremy was studying the boy in the poster, the boy whose future was still in his hands. The boy who still had a future.

"Sam's roommate," she continued. "He's willing to testify that your three co-defendants found out Sam was gay about a week before the boot party. He'll say they were outraged and were planning to kill him."

"Yeah, Sam's roommate was a real creep. Sam was going to move out as soon as he had the money."

"Well it's too bad he didn't move out sooner," Lee said.

"How did they find out anyway?" He turned to face her. "Did-did his roommate know?"

"Why do you care?" Come on Jeremy, she thought, tell me what's in that head of yours. I'm tired of pulling teeth.

"I don't really," he said. "I'm just, you know, kind of curious."

"They found some paperwork in Sam's bedroom—a summons to appear in court for soliciting an undercover male police officer."

"Okay, I was just wondering."

"So you obviously didn't know beforehand that they planned to kill him?" She moved her chair a little closer, hoping to create more intimacy.

"No, but they never told me anything. I-I was just a kid. No one but Rab paid any attention to me." He was studying the poster again.

Lee stared at it too. Her client was right. It *was* kind of depressing. But it didn't have to be.

"Today is the first day of the rest of your life, Jeremy. Do something to affect it."

He smiled at her, sad as always.

"How? By changing my story? You never give up, do you? Okay, fine, I didn't know it was going to happen beforehand, but once they started kicking him, I just kind of went along with it."

They were circling the drain. What did she have to lose?

"Because you were afraid you might be next?"

"Why? Because I'm a faggot just like Sam was?" He jumped to his feet, more angry than embarrassed. "I knew my mother would tell you. She probably thought she was helping, but it doesn't, does it? They'll think it's why I did it." He flicked his hand in the air. "Fuck it. Who cares?"

Lee stood up as well. They were face to face, just a couple of inches between them.

"I do."

For a moment, she thought she had him, but then he took a few steps backward. Waved his hand again as if to dismiss her.

"Stop trying to save me, Ms. Isaacs. I'm not worth it. Whatever the DA offers is fine. I'll take it."

Suddenly, she felt exhausted. She'd spent thirty-four years engaging with thousands of lost and unhappy clients. Freeing them if she could, plea-bargaining if she couldn't. But either way, she'd always tried to steer them in a better direction, away from the oncoming cars.

"I would never use the term 'faggot,' Jeremy. It's demeaning. Like calling someone a nigger or a kike."

"What's a kike?"

"A derogatory term for a Jew." She paused. "Like your friend, Mrs. Weissmann." Like me.

Suddenly, his eyes lit up.

"Mrs. Weissmann?" He looked genuinely concerned. "Have you seen her? Is-is she okay?"

Use this, she thought. Use anything.

"She's fine, but she misses you."

"I miss her too. Yeah. She was a very nice lady."

"She doesn't think you're guilty, Jeremy." And then Lee surprised herself. "And frankly, neither do I."

"Well, you're both wrong." The light in his eyes was gone. Extinguished. He turned his back on her and headed for the door. He was leaving her the same way he left his parents: for good. There would be no miracle. Nothing would make him change his mind. Lee imagined how his mother must have felt. Desperate and then resigned.

"Jeremy," she said.

He was knocking for someone to come.

"What?"

For once in her long career, the great Lee Isaacs was speechless. Nothing, she thought. Her shoulders sagged. No more trying to manipulate him. She'd hold out for thirty years, plead him out, and wish him well. Maybe she'd take another murder case, or maybe it was time to stop. The universe had sent this sad little boy as a messenger: You've used up the last of your mojo. Stop trying to save every dying thing around you; there are just too many of them.

A couple of seconds later, a young Hispanic guard showed up to escort Jeremy back to his cell. She could hear their footsteps echoing down the empty hallway.

Going, going, gone.

It was snowing again. Hard. Which meant the skiing would be great for weeks. A good reason to cheer up, Lee thought. She was staring out the picture window in Mark and Bobby's living room. Thick white snow blanketed the landscape, making parts of it, including the long steep driveway down to Old Stage Road, completely invisible. There was at least a foot of new snow since she'd arrived at six. It was almost ten-thirty now. She yawned surreptitiously and gave up any hope of leaving that evening. Even a large 4Runner wouldn't make it down the driveway without getting stuck. She knew because she'd tried three or four times before under similar conditions. With this much snow, her truck always slid to the left and ended up in a ditch that ran along the driveway.

So she might as well accept the fact she'd be spending the night in Mark and Bobby's well-appointed guest room. Charlie had plenty of dry cat food and could survive for weeks on the extra fat he'd gained from the Fancy Feast he'd convinced Lee to add to his diet.

Earlier, they'd gorged on turkey, mashed potatoes, and green beans, one of Lee's favorite winter meals. Now, they were seated in the living room drinking peppermint tea in a fruitless effort to digest Mark's decadent mashed potatoes. Bobby had disappeared a few minutes earlier and was just returning.

"Your suite has been made ready for you," he announced, bowing slightly in Lee's direction. "The covers have been turned down, a blue bathrobe is hanging on a hook behind the bathroom door, and the pink fluffy slippers you hate so much have been set on the floor beside your bed. Will there be anything else, Wooster?"

"I don't believe so. Thank you, Jeeves."

Bobby bowed again and then dropped down beside her on the couch. Mark, as usual, was sitting in his rocking chair. They were like an old married couple, except there were three of them: two gay men and a widow (but not, at least tonight, a very merry one).

"How about if we go snowshoeing in the morning?" Mark asked. "The plow won't arrive before noon."

"Sure," Lee said, glancing at her watch. "Is breakfast included?"

Mark pretended to look offended.

"Of course. On Sunday, we always have pancakes and bacon."

"Pancakes and bacon? Yikes. How come you guys aren't fat?"

"We're gay. It's not allowed." But Lee knew they both worked out daily at an expensive gym on 30th Street.

Lee smiled but felt tired and sad. She couldn't stop thinking about Jeremy, how she'd lost him. All through dinner, she kept picturing the boy in the poster, the one who still had a choice: What'll it be, heaven or hell? Her client had already decided, but she wondered when. On the night of the murder, the day his parents threw him out, or even earlier, the moment he finally stopped praying and acknowledged who he was?

There was silence for two or three minutes before Lee suddenly realized both men were staring at her.

"What?" she asked.

"You seem a bit down," Bobby said, "that's all."

"I'm just tired."

"No, it's more than that. Something's going on." He moved even closer to her and tried to take her hand. She rubbed her eyes instead, wondering for the hundredth time whether she needed glasses. She'd spent the afternoon reading back issues of the Colorado Lawyer. She hadn't learned much, but it filled the time. And kept her from thinking.

"And when we asked you to consider trekking with us in April," Mark continued, "you actually said you'd consider it."

"So?"

"So it's not like you. And your murder trial is set for the end of May. You'd never leave before a major trial."

Lee picked up her cup of tea, cradling it in her hands. It was still warm.

"Well, I've recently decided to settle it. My client doesn't want to go to trial, and it's probably just as well since the evidence is overwhelming." She stared into her cup. "So you'll be happy to know that 'the little savage' will soon be where everyone thinks he belongs. And, as an added bonus, he probably won't survive there for long."

Both men were silent.

"So, that's that," she said, sipping her tea.

Mark stopped rocking and leaned forward.

"Wait a minute. Last week, you mentioned that his mother was going to cooperate. That you were finally going to learn why his parents had thrown him out. What happened?"

"It wasn't helpful."

Bobby nodded, but Mark shook his head.

"What did she say?"

"It isn't relevant and it'll probably make you mad. I'm too tired to fight tonight. In fact, I think I'll go to bed now. What time should I be ready in the morning?"

"Not so fast," Bobby said, managing this time to grab her hand. His handsome face was creased with concern. "Most cases don't get to you, but for some reason this one has. Why? What did she say?"

"It'll just make you angry, Bobby."

"No it won't. I swear." He raised his right hand, like a witness promising to tell the truth, the whole truth, and nothing but.

Mark was looking skeptical.

"All right," she said. "His parents threw him out because he's gay."

"Goddamn it!" Mark exploded. "We should have guessed. Of course he's gay. Most homophobic bullies are. Oh, that makes him so much more despicable. J. Edgar Hoover as a teenager."

Bobby looked from Lee to his partner.

"It's also kind of sad, though."

"Don't feel sorry for him," Mark warned. "He's a little traitor."

"Well, I think I'll go to bed," Lee told them.

123

"Hold on," Bobby said. "Did you ask him about it? What did he say?"

Lee's neck had begun to ache. She was sick of being a lawyer, sick of advocating on behalf of mute, downtrodden clients, of explaining their motives and begging for mercy. Tonight, at least, she was done.

"He acknowledged it. Said he'd take whatever deal the DA offered." Then, what the hell, she decided to tell them the rest of it. "Not that it makes any difference, but I actually don't think he's guilty."

"What?" Bobby blurted.

"He confessed!" Mark said. His expression was three parts furious, one part confused.

"I know."

"What evidence do you have to suggest he's innocent?"

"None. Just my gut." Which, until recently, had never misled her. But it wasn't infallible. A year ago, it had dragged her off a cliff.

"Could you be wrong?" Bobby asked.

"Possibly, but I don't think so. I've spent a lot of time with him. He's not a killer. He doesn't have it in him. I'm guessing he just hates himself for being gay and wants to be punished."

"Well then, what are you going to do?"

"Nothing. He's determined to go to prison, where he'll be dead within a year, or wish he was."

"Christ," Mark said. "That's awful. I mean if you're right."

"It *is* awful. And there's nothing I can do." She started to rise.

"Wait a minute," Mark said. "You sound so calm, so resigned, but you can't be. You're a great lawyer, which means you're a great faker." He thought for a moment. "Fuck the peppermint tea. This calls for strong whiskey."

She turned back to face them: her two best friends who believed her in spite of everything they knew and, when it really mattered, would always take her side. Her brothers who merely wished to comfort her. Suddenly, she decided to let them.

"You're right. Fuck the peppermint tea. Bring on the whiskey."

CHAPTER EIGHT

At first, she thought the ringing had to do with the start of the first round in a world championship-boxing match being televised to millions of viewers. Lee, so far unscathed and remarkably calm, was perched on a metal stool in a corner of the ring. Her eyebrows were slathered with Vaseline and she was wearing heavy black boxing gloves that felt like anvils. Considering the weight, skill, and experience of her opponent, Lee figured she'd be face down on the mat in less than twenty seconds. Maybe thirty if she bobbed and weaved like a pro, which she wasn't. How did she get here anyway?

She tried to remember, but there was no time to figure it out. She'd just have to do her best, that's all. In any event, it would be an embarrassingly short fight, at the end of which Lee would be unconscious and seriously injured—at the very least, some broken bones in her face. Maybe she'd get lucky and there would be no permanent damage. The ringing continued. She was just getting ready to rise when it occurred to her that it sounded more like a telephone than a bell.

She reached out a hand and grabbed for the receiver.

"Ms. Isaacs?" It was a male voice she didn't recognize.

Lee glanced at her bedside alarm. It was a quarter past two.

"Who is this?" She was trying to wake up as fast as possible.

"Tim Reynolds. The guard that looks like Mr. Clean."

"Oh, right." How funny. Then she stopped smiling. "Has something happened? Is Jeremy okay?" It had been a week since she'd seen him. In the interim, she and Dan had met and hammered out a deal for thirty years.

"He's not," the guard was saying. "He tried to kill himself. One of the newer kids smuggled a knife into the facility and Jeremy asked to borrow it. He cut his wrists."

She fumbled for the lamp, almost knocking it over.

"When?"

"I found him a few hours ago. It really freaked me out. There was blood everywhere. I don't know if he's going to make it."

Lee was sitting up in bed, fully conscious now.

"Thanks for calling, Tim. Where is he now?"

"They took him to the psych ward at Boulder Community Hospital. It's the closest place."

"Is that on Broadway and Balsam?"

"Yeah, I think so. We called his parents, but I doubt they'll come. Are you going over there?"

"Yes," she said, climbing out of bed.

"Would you mind calling me back when you find out how he is?"

"Not at all."

"I'll be here until eight in the morning. Just ask for Mr. Clean. It's what everyone here calls me."

"I'll get back to you, Tim. I won't forget." She was already pulling on a pair of jeans and a black turtleneck sweater.

Five minutes after hanging up, Lee was in her 4Runner heading for the hospital. As she drove, she dialed Carla's cell phone and waited. After a few moments, she hung up and dialed again. On the third try, Carla picked up and Lee filled her in.

"I'll call Peggy," Carla said.

"Okay, good." They were speaking in the hushed tones people use when death is closer than usual.

"I'll be there in about thirty minutes," Carla added.

Lee signaled for a right turn onto Broadway, although there were no other cars in sight.

"You don't have to."

"Of course I do." Carla sounded indignant. "He's my client too."

"Well then, I'll see you soon. The psych ward is on the third floor."

A few minutes later, she turned right onto Balsam, then left into the hospital parking lot, which was almost empty. She switched off the engine and sat for a minute. The world outside was sleeping, unaware that yet another sentient being had made a run for it. Headed for what he hoped was sweet oblivion. And, given her client's bleak prognosis, Lee could hardly blame him. Perhaps it was even for the best. But as she hurried from her car toward the revolving doors at the hospital entrance, she hoped Jeremy's desperate bid for freedom hadn't worked, and that he was still alive and miserable. But why? Because no one died on her watch?

No, it was more than that. As long as her client was alive, there was hope. Every case had dozens of unseen, unimagined variables. Until the last appellate court ruled against you, or your client killed himself, there was always a possibility that one of those variables would unexpectedly morph in your favor. This wasn't optimism, just a simple recognition, after thirty-four years of lawyering, that the universe was a squirrelly place where anything could happen.

As she stepped out of the elevator onto the third floor, Lee saw a double set of thick glass doors. There was a telephone on the wall with instructions for reaching the on-duty nurse. Lee picked it up and dialed.

"Can I help you?" a woman asked.

"Yes. My name is Lee Isaacs and I'm here to see my client, Jeremy Matthews. He's an inmate at the juvenile detention facility."

"We generally allow only relatives to see patients after hours."

Lee thought quickly and said, "I'm here in lieu of his parents. They can't make it."

The line was silent.

"Listen," Lee added, "I can call Judge Samuels, but he really hates to be woken up unless there's a true emergency."

"Can you prove you're the attorney of record?"

"Absolutely. I have my bar card and some motions that I've filed in district court identifying me as the attorney on the case." Good thing she'd thought to bring them.

Suddenly, Lee heard a buzzer and the door clicked open. As soon as the first door closed behind her, the next one opened. A heavyset blonde wearing bright pink scrubs waved to her from behind a desk. Lee hurried toward her.

"Thank you," Lee said, handing her a sheaf of papers. "How's my client doing? Will he be all right?"

Up close, Lee could see that the woman's hair was dyed and guessed she was in her late forties. The nurse studied the papers and was apparently satisfied.

"We think so, but only because they found him so quickly." The woman hesitated. "This wasn't just a cry for help, you know. The gashes were deep. He clearly intended to die." She gave Lee back her papers. "He looks so young. What's he in jail for anyway?"

"Felony self-hatred."

"Is that really a crime?"

"No." Lee smiled at her. "I was being facetious. He just happened to be in the wrong place at the wrong time. Can I see him?"

"He's sleeping."

"That's okay," Lee said, stuffing the papers back into her briefcase. "I won't wake him. I'll just sit there. Oh, and my investigator will be arriving in about twenty minutes with my client's aunt."

"Anyone else?" She was trying to look stern but was obviously sympathetic.

"Nope, that's it."

"I'll bring a couple more chairs into the room. But you have to be quiet. I mean it."

"Scout's honor. Which room is he in?"

"Third door on your right." The nurse pointed down the hall. "I'm glad you cared enough to come. I'm not sure most lawyers would do that."

The room was very plain—just a hospital bed and a single chair in the corner. No windows, no plants, no pictures, nothing. A grim, no frills way-station whose inhabitants, as soon as they were stable, were headed somewhere else. After shutting the door, Lee picked up the chair, moved it near the bed, and sat down. A small overhead light shed a calm white glow on her client's sleeping face. In repose, he looked like an innocent twelve-year old, someone who lived at home with two loving parents who'd managed to shield him from any true understanding of evil. His wrists and forearms, wrapped in thick gauze bandages, however, suggested a different, darker story.

She continued to study him, the mystery boy who'd been entrusted to her care.

"What am I missing?" she whispered, but as usual he didn't answer.

The room was very quiet. There was nothing to do but watch her client sleep. In his dreams, he was on the lam, weightless and gloriously free. Lee hoped he was enjoying every second. After a while, her eyes felt heavy and her body leaned forward. Sometime later, she heard the door opening and sat back up again. Carla and Peggy had entered the room and were coming toward her.

"I guess I fell asleep," Lee said. "What time is it?"

"Three-thirty," Carla whispered. "The nurse is looking for more chairs."

The two women tiptoed over to the bed and stared at Jeremy, who hadn't moved.

"Oh dear God," Peggy moaned.

"He's heavily sedated," Lee told them. "Blissfully unaware."

"I want to be here when he wakes up," Peggy said. Her voice was shaking, but her face looked resolute.

"He won't be blissful then," Carla sighed, putting an arm around Peggy's shoulder.

The nurse walked in, carrying two more chairs.

"There's a cafeteria in the basement," Lee announced. "I'm going to look for some coffee and call the detention center. The guard who found him saved his life."

When Lee returned, both Peggy and Carla were fast asleep. Off to the land of Nod, as far away from this sad bare room as possible. Lee shut the door behind her, removed her shoes, and then tiptoed inside. She didn't feel like sitting. Time was of the essence.

There was a clue somewhere that Lee had missed, something her client told her that she somehow hadn't heard. There had to be. Pacing back and forth, she painstakingly replayed every conversation she'd had with him. When she was finished, she started again.

Finally, she stopped. Maybe there wasn't a clue. Maybe anyone in Jeremy's situation would have opted for the quick exit. Except in the thirty-four years she'd been practicing, no one ever did. Even the ones facing a lifetime of tedium and violence never wavered. So what else could it be? If Lee was right, that her client wasn't guilty, what was it about the murder he couldn't bear? Was it the victim's suffering? For Lee, the hardest thing would be the feeling of helplessness. Not being able to save him. Even so, would it make Jeremy slash his wrists? Not likely, unless he'd truly cared for Sam, which he hadn't.

Or had he? When she'd informed him that Sam's roommate was the jailhouse snitch, he'd said, "Sam's roommate was a creep. Sam was going to move out as soon as he had the money." How did he know that? Sam must have confided in him. Had they actually been friends? Sam was twenty-two, six years older than Jeremy. Had either of them guessed about the other? Mark and Bobby swore that most gay men had "gaydar"—the ability to sense another man's homosexuality. Had Jeremy cared for Sam? Standing there helpless, while his "brothers" kicked his friend to death would have been a truly horrifying experience.

Lee walked back to Jeremy's bed.

"You knew him," she whispered. "He was your friend and you couldn't save him. That would be awful." She shook her head. "But still not a reason to die."

"What's not a reason to die?" Carla asked, stretching her arms and yawning. "It's so quiet, I think I fell asleep."

"Nothing. I'm just making up stories."

They were both looking down at their client, the boy whose secrets continued to elude them.

"He looks so peaceful," Carla said. "I'm having a hard time picturing him in prison."

"Me too," Lee agreed, glancing at her watch. It was a quarter to six.

"He's going to die in there, isn't he?"

"Probably."

"Well then we just can't plead him out. I don't care what we have to do, but it would be—"

"Shh, you'll wake up Peggy."

"Okay, fine," Carla whispered. "But we have to do something."

"What do you suggest?"

"Me?" Carla's voice was starting to rise again. "I'm not the lawyer. You are."

"My supernatural powers seem to have deserted me."

"You'll figure something out, Lee. You always do."

"Not always. What about Lenny Hall?"

"Oh for God's sake. Lenny was an asshole and you had bronchitis during the trial. That doesn't count."

Of course it did, but there was no point arguing.

"How much did you send him anyway?"

"I told you. It's none of your business." Carla was searching through her purse. Finally, she pulled out a comb and her compact.

"Listen," Lee told her, "I'm going home to shower. I've got two arraignments at nine and a sentencing at eleven. Tell Peggy I'll be back as soon as I can."

"All right." Carla was staring at herself in the mirror. "Ugh, my makeup is ruined. Why didn't you tell me?"

"Because it's fixable."

"But not our client?"

"I'm not sure, Carla. Maybe not."

She grabbed her briefcase and shoes before leaving. As she shut the door behind her, a young man carrying a bouquet of yellow roses slipped quietly into one of the other rooms. Lee pulled on her shoes and hurried down the hallway. As she approached the thick glass doors, she suddenly stopped. *Eureka!* A faint new path in the case had just been revealed. It was either a way out of the maze or the last dead end.

When she returned to the hospital, Carla and Peggy were standing near the nurse's station, buttoning their coats and pulling on their gloves. It was twelve-thirty.

"Perfect timing," Carla told her. "Peggy and I are headed to the Hungry Toad. Do you want to come?"

"No," Lee said. "I have a sandwich in my briefcase. Is he awake?"

"Since ten," Peggy replied. "When he opened his eyes and saw us, he groaned and then rolled over to face the wall."

"Has he said anything?"

"Oh yeah." Carla snorted. "A regular chatterbox. Two words in two and a half hours: 'Go away.'"

"I love him," Peggy said as she shouldered her leather handbag, "but he's a royal pain in the ass."

"I'll say," Carla agreed. She patted Lee on the shoulder. "Good luck. If anyone can get him to talk, you can."

I have to, Lee thought. If not, it's game over.

A few minutes later, she was sitting on a chair less than a foot from Jeremy's bed. He was still facing the wall.

"Hi, Jeremy," Lee said. "We have a lot to talk about."

"Go away."

"I can't. I'm your lawyer. So I think I'll just cut to the chase: Sam was your boyfriend. You watched him die. You couldn't save him."

Jeremy flinched as if he'd been shot.

"What? How did you find out?" He rolled over to face her.

"I wasn't sure, but you just confirmed it."

"But-but how did you guess? Nobody knew."

"Some comments you made about Sam's roommate being a creep and that Sam was going to move as soon as he had the money. I wondered how you knew that."

"Well, it doesn't really matter."

"Of course it does," Lee said calmly. "You loved him and you couldn't save him."

"I didn't even try." His voice sounded strangled.

Lee took a couple of breaths. She had to be careful here.

"I can't imagine what it must have been like to watch him die. But you know, of course, you couldn't possibly have saved him."

"I loved him so much. I would have done anything for him."

"But you couldn't have saved him."

His dark brown eyes flashed angrily.

"I didn't even try. I just—"

"You just what?" He was shutting down again. Any second, he would turn away from her. "You just stood there?"

He was shaking his head, seeing things that nobody in a better world should ever have to see. The senseless violent death of someone they loved.

"Hey," she said. "Remember when we arm-wrestled? Remember how strong I was?"

"So?"

"So if I'd been there instead of you, I could have taken one of them, but certainly not all three." This wasn't strictly true. With a little help from Sam, she would have disabled all of them, but of course it didn't matter. Nothing mattered except to keep him talking. "They each outweighed you by forty pounds, and they each knew how to fight. How many times have you been in a serious fight? Once, twice, never?"

"Never, but it doesn't matter. A real man would have tried."

But you're just a kid, she wanted to say, but of course didn't.

"How did the two of you meet anyway?" she asked instead, hoping now that someone finally knew, he'd want to talk about it.

"I-I was at the Sapphire Lounge with my brothers," he began, clearly willing, even eager to tell her. "Sam showed up with his roommate and some other skins. At first, he didn't notice me. He was really handsome, kind of like George Clooney but younger." He tried to raise his arms and winced. "With a shaved head. A little while later, I was standing near the jukebox and suddenly he was like standing next to me. My heart was pounding. I'd never been so attracted to anyone in my life. I guessed he was a homo just like me. I don't know how I knew, but I did. He asked what I was into and I tried to think of something cool, you know, like hunting or wrestling, but I couldn't think of anything except what I was really into, which was music and looking at guys in magazines. So I said, 'I'm into the same things you are.' He looked surprised, then asked if I wanted to go to another, quieter bar with him. I was so nervous, but I said, 'yeah sure,' like I was totally cool with it." He paused to catch his breath. Lee had never heard him talk so much.

"So you went to this other bar?" she prompted.

"Yeah, it was just a dark quiet bar that no one hardly went to. By the end of the night, I knew he was the one." He blushed. "I know it sounds stupid, but it's true."

"It doesn't sound stupid to me. It sounds like you fell in love."

"Yeah, I did. After that, I was just so happy. He was everything I'd been dreaming of. He looked tough, but he really wasn't. He was just protecting himself, you know, like I was."

"I understand," Lee said. She'd seen two photographs of Sam taken by the police when he'd been arrested for soliciting. In the pictures, his neck and arms were completely covered in tattoos. Lee tried to imagine him with hair and flawless skin. No George Clooney, but handsome enough. "Can I ask you a nosy question?"

"I think I know what it is. But sure, go ahead."

"Was Sam your first real boyfriend? Did the two of you make love?"

Jeremy nodded, managing not to blush again.

"Yeah. We had to go to parks because of our roommates. It was okay once it got warmer outside. I didn't mind. My favorite was Cheesman Park because there were lots of other guys there." He hesitated. "That's where Sam made all his money. He was going to quit as soon as we had enough. He told me about this section of San Francisco called The Castro where thousands of homos lived and where we could, you know, be out in the open. I couldn't wait to go." He licked his lips, which were badly chapped. "Except I was worried about Mrs. Weissmann. Her family rarely came to see her."

Lee made a show of scratching her head.

"Jeremy, I'm confused. Your roommates killed your boyfriend. Why do you still call them your brothers? Why don't you hate them?"

Jeremy tried to sit up, but he couldn't use his arms.

"Hold on," Lee said. "There's a button." She pushed it until Jeremy signaled her to stop. He'd used the time to compose an answer.

"I know it's weird, but I don't really hold them responsible. They were just being themselves, like . . . like a pack of coyotes killing a rabbit. I was the one who was different, the one who should have stopped them. But I just, I don't know, stood there like you said. And then when Sam was gone, my-my brothers were all I had left."

"Okay, it's weird, but I think I understand." She made a face. "Sort of."

Jeremy almost smiled. For the first time ever, her client was actually talking to her. Revealing his deepest secrets. Would he stop if she asked about the night of the murder? He was obviously innocent; he'd loved the victim. But in order to craft a viable defense, she had to know how it all went down.

"Jeremy, tell me about the night Sam died."

His face immediately darkened.

"Why? I don't want to fight this. I'll take whatever deal my brothers take."

Lee sat very still. If they were climbing a mountain, this was the crux move, the one that would make all the difference. They would both either fall to their death or move even higher toward the summit.

"Jeremy, remember the kid in the poster? The one who had to choose?"

"Yeah, I remember."

"Well, today you're the kid in the poster and you have a huge decision to make. It's time to break your allegiance to your roommates. You're not like them. When they go to prison, they'll do okay because they'll be with other coyotes. You, on the other hand, will die there. You didn't kill your boyfriend. Your housemates did." She thought for a moment. "You said they were all you had left."

"So?"

"So it isn't true. Not anymore. You have me and Carla and your Aunt Peggy. You have Mrs. Weissmann. You even have your mother if you can ever forgive her. We all know who you are and fully accept you. We want to help, but you have to say what happened. You have to say it out loud."

"I can't."

"Yes, you can." Then she waited patiently, as if she had all the time in the world. Which, in a way, she did.

A couple of minutes passed. And then for the second time in twenty-four hours, the God of Lost Boys intervened and her client spoke.

"Okay, I'll say it."

After four long months of waiting, they were finally at the starting line. The words came out haltingly at first and then quickly gathered steam.

"So-so first we went to this liquor store, but then we didn't know where to go. So we kind of drove around and then Rab remembered this place on Flagstaff Mountain that had a really nice view. We all said, 'great.' By the time we got there, it was getting dark, but the moon was almost full. Rab said, 'Come on,' and we followed him up a path to an open area. It was really pretty, like he said. So we sat on the rocks and passed around bottles of Southern Comfort. Sam was sitting next to me, but-but not too close. We were having a good time.

"Suddenly, out of the blue, Casey jumps up and screams, 'You're a fucking cocksucker,' and runs at Sam. So then, while Sam is facing Casey, Johnny gets up and kicks Sam in the back. Like a lot of skins, Johnny wears Doc Marten boots, which have steel toes and are really heavy. Sam almost falls, but then grabs hold of Casey. He's obviously in a lot of pain. I'm not sure what to do. I'm just, you know, so shocked.

"Before I can think of anything, Rab punches Sam in the face and I'm pretty sure breaks his nose. Sam cries out and falls. As he's falling, Johnny kicks him in the ribs. They're saying he's a faggot who deserves to die. They're in a circle now, taking turns kicking him. Everyone's wearing boots. There's blood coming out of Sam's nose and mouth. I'm screaming but no one notices. They're all just laughing and yelling, 'Boot party! Boot party!' Finally, I reach down and grab his arm. One of his eyes is swollen shut. I try to pull him up, but he can barely move. 'Come on, you have to get up,' I tell him. He shakes his head and whispers, 'leave me.' I'm crying and then someone grabs the back of my sweatshirt and pulls me away from him.

"And then, I don't know, I think I just start to run. I have no idea where the path is. I'm crying and I can't see and at some point I trip and fall. And then I'm throwing up. Pretty soon, Rab finds me and tells me to quit crying and be a man. Then he drags me up the hill and I can hear Casey and Johnny yelling. They sound really drunk. Rab orders me to stay put and then goes back to them. Casey's saying I'm a yellow belly deserter, but Rab says, 'No, he's cool. He's acting as the lookout.' I'm totally numb by now. I'm guessing Sam is dead and I wonder how I'll go on living without him.

"So I start like thinking of ways to kill myself. Finally, Rab shows up and leads me to where Sam is lying on the ground. His face is so swollen I can hardly tell it's him. There's blood leaking out of his ears. All his teeth are broken. 'Kick him,' Rab orders, 'so they'll know you're down with it.' I shake my head no, but Sam is dead and my brothers are all I have. So I kick him twice and when I do, I feel nothing. I might as well be on the ground beside him. When they finally leave, I follow them to the car. There's nowhere else to go, so I get in and close the door. We drive to Denver and a few days later we get arrested."

He stopped and stared at her.

"So that's it. He's gone and I'll never see him again." A single tear rolled down his face.

For a moment, Lee considered telling him everything she knew about grief—how it comes and stays and threatens to last forever, but then one morning you wake up and realize you no longer feel invaded, that somehow over time it's been incorporated into your deepest self, bridging the gap between who you were before the loss and who you've now become. And so then the last thing you want is to get rid of it, because along with your photographs and memories, your precious grief is all you have left of your beloved.

But she knew it would sound like gibberish. Long-term grief was a private experience, not a communal one.

Time passed.

"So now what?" Jeremy finally asked.

"It depends," she said. "What would Sam want you to do?"

"He'd-he'd want me to go to trial."

Suddenly, the room felt bigger. There was a huge influx of oxygen. Lee felt almost giddy with relief.

"Well, then that's what we're going to do."

"I could end up with a life sentence."

"You could."

"Will my brothers testify against me?"

"If they get the chance." She smiled ruefully. "It's what coyotes do."

CHAPTER NINE

Sunday afternoon. Lee was lying on the couch with Charlie on her stomach. *Ballads*, one of her favorite old jazz records, was playing in the background. John Coltrane on the saxophone, McCoy Tyner on piano. Her father bought the album in 1963 when Lee was eleven. She loved it from the very beginning and her father finally gave it to her as a present when she headed off to law school in Boulder. It was a major sacrifice because Aaron loved the record as much as his daughter. When her mother died, Lee flew back to Boston with the album wrapped carefully in her suitcase. But the music reminded Aaron too much of his wife and he couldn't bring himself to play it. And so, after a year or two, Aaron gave it back.

Lee listened with her eyes closed, remembering the five-room shotgun style apartment in Mattapan where they lived until Lee went to college. There was a box-shaped hi-fi in the living room, and a large murky tank that her father kept filling with exotic fish, though none of them lasted long. "I know you mean well, Aaron," her mother used to say, "but fish aren't meant to swim in circles. You're basically torturing them. Get rid of it." Her father refused until one evening when her mother demanded a vote. It was a democratic household where all votes counted equally. Her father voted to keep the tank and her mother voted to give it away. So it was up to Lee, who sat down cross-legged in front of the tank, studying its inhabitants. Finally, she sided with her mother. "They never smile," she explained. Her mother burst out laughing. Lee was nine. Her father groused but eventually got rid of the tank.

On Sunday mornings, her family listened to music. Mostly jazz, but occasionally opera (which put both Lee and Aaron to sleep). When the music started, her father dropped into his leather chair, her mother reclined on the couch, and Lee lay down in the middle of the carpet. "Now close your eyes," her mother always said. "So you can really hear it." Afterward, they would watch movies on television. They all loved *Twelve Angry Men, The Bridge over the River Kwai, Ben Hur,* and anything directed by Hitchcock. When the movies ended, they drove to the nearest Howard Johnson's for an early supper. Later, when she described these days to Paul, he was astounded. Hadn't she gotten bored, the same things over and over? But no, she never did.

When Lee was six or seven, she asked her parents if they wished they had more children. Both shook their heads. "We scored big with you," her father said. It wasn't until Lee was in college that her mother admitted she'd had a hysterectomy when Lee was three. "Early stage endometrial cancer. Nothing to worry about." And so of course Lee didn't. But a few years later, when her mother was fifty-five, she was diagnosed with an aggressive form of breast cancer and was dead within six months. After that, it was just Lee and Aaron, two instead of three. And for years, although they never acknowledged it, Sunday was the hardest day. It wasn't until Lee met Paul that the very last traces of Sunday sadness were vanquished. But then Paul died too.

These days, Lee hiked, skied, or snow-shoed on Sundays and then she worked. Early this morning, she'd driven up Flagstaff, past the lookout where Sam died, and skied the seven-mile Walker Ranch loop twice. After a shower and lunch, she'd sifted through her stack of records and decided on this album. But now it was time to call Dan and tell him their deal for thirty years was off. She doubted he'd be surprised. In the decades they'd worked together, had she ever truly surprised him? Maybe not, she thought, reaching for her cell phone.

"I was wondering when you'd call," Dan answered.

"I was waiting until everything stabilized." It had only been three days since Jeremy tried to kill himself. Despite Lee's request to keep him for another week, he would be transferred back to the detention center on Tuesday.

"Well, it sounds like he's going to be fine."

"At least physically," she admitted.

"So you're going to renege on our deal."

"How did you guess?"

"Because you've always been a sucker for the underdog. The moment I heard he'd cut himself, I knew you wouldn't plead him."

"Well, as usual, you were right."

"You sound annoyed."

"Maybe a tad. I didn't think I was so predictable."

"Well, you are," he said. "And you're making a terrible mistake. If you really cared about the kid, you'd plead him out. Instead, he's going to end up with a life sentence. Is that Coltrane in the background? Sounds like *Ballads*."

"I didn't know you liked jazz."

"I love jazz. Listen, just because he tried to kill himself doesn't mean he's innocent. It just means he has a conscience." He was fishing.

"That's one possibility," she agreed. "Who do you like besides Coltrane?"

"I love Miles Davis. *Kind of Blue* is my all time favorite jazz album."

"I actually like *A Tribute to Jack Johnson* better."

"Well, it's a close call."

Lee stood up and walked into the kitchen. Charlie, ever hopeful, raced to his empty food bowl and then looked up at her. She shook her head no, but as usual relented.

As she was opening the refrigerator, she asked, "Have you already started talking to the co-defendants?"

"Why would I?"

"Because you guessed I was going to renege. What did you offer them?"

"Second-degree murder, stip to forty-eight, and of course testify against your client."

"Will they take it?" Of course they'd take it.

"They're not ecstatic about testifying."

"Oh, that's nice. They have scruples." She was searching in the kitchen drawer for a fork and then stopped. "You're actually miffed about this, aren't you?"

"Well, maybe a tad. I'd much rather deal with you and convict the grown-ups of first-degree murder."

"Then don't deal with them," she said, closing the drawer. "Convict them instead. You'll be a hero."

Dan laughed appreciatively.

"And what about your case?"

"You can beat me without their testimony. Make it a fairer fight."

"I don't like fair fights," he told her.

"So you're going to deal with the grown-ups just to make sure you don't get defeated by a suicidal, seventeen-year old boy."

"Exactly. Do you like Chet Baker?"

"I love Chet Baker." She bent down and put a few dollops of food into Charlie's dish.

"Me too. Sometimes, when he plays 'Almost Blue,' I get tears in my eyes. I'll tell you what: I'll go down to twenty-eight years if you take it before the co-defendants plead."

"Wow, that's very generous." She stood up. "When are they pleading?"

"Tomorrow at one."

"I guess you didn't think I'd take it." Christ, he always seemed to be one step ahead of her.

"You know, I actually do feel sorry for your client."

"Then offer him probation and convict the bad guys."

"You've got a great sense of humor, Lee. I hope it's still intact after I've beaten you twice in a row."

God forbid, she thought.

"Well, tally-ho," he said brightly and then severed the connection.

"Ouch! What's that?" Carla asked.

Lee reached down into the grass and found a lime green plastic disk.

"A Frisbee. Chill out."

"Chill out? I almost broke my ankle."

They were walking across a vast expanse of grass in Denver's Cheesman Park headed for the white marble pavilion. Both women carried small yellow flashlights. It was the last Friday night in February. It hadn't snowed for a week, but the grass was cold, wet, and spongy. They wore hiking boots, hats, gloves, scarves, and their heaviest coats.

"I'm freezing and I'm hungry," Carla said.

Lee was too, but of course she wouldn't admit it.

"We can get something to eat after we leave."

"I vote pizza!"

It was like dealing with a four-year old.

"How about something healthier with vegetables?" Lee asked.

"Oh, don't be such a killjoy."

A four-year old who just happened to be the finest investigator Lee had ever worked with.

"Okay, I give up. Next week, I'll bring a sandwich."

"Good." Carla checked her watch under the flashlight. "It's almost eleven-thirty. How much longer?"

They'd arrived at ten—the time when, according to Jeremy, he and Sam used to visit the park—and had questioned over twenty men. No one recognized either Sam or Jeremy's picture. Each time they approached someone, Lee explained that she and Carla represented a boy who'd been falsely accused of murder. "Would you be willing to look at some photographs?" The men were initially reluctant, but out of curiosity they all agreed to look.

"It could save our client," Carla told them, "if you've ever seen the two of them together. You know, like romantically."

Everyone looked incredulous. Two gay skinheads? Lee merely shrugged. "Hey, love can be mysterious." Most of the men laughed knowingly.

Still, the night was a bust.

When they reached the pavilion, it was empty. Then, something low and fast, a cat or a fox, rushed past their feet, disappearing into the darkness. Carla yelped and then turned to Lee, who was smiling.

"Oh, fuck off," Carla muttered.

They wandered past the pavilion trying to decide which path to follow.

"There's a bench over there," Lee said, pointing west in the direction of the State Capitol Building. "Do you want to sit down for a while?"

"Actually," Carla replied, "I'd like to keep going until I drop dead from exhaustion."

Lee nodded guiltily. During the week, Carla spent most nights combing the bars along Colfax Avenue, but she'd refused to come to the park alone. Lee could hardly blame her.

"Do want to call it quits?" Lee asked. "It's okay if you do."

"No, I was just being a sourpuss. We can stay till midnight. And if we don't find a witness tonight, we'll just keep coming back till we do."

"You're the best, Carla."

"I know. So are you. Are we really going to pull this case out?"

"We have to. There's no Plan B."

They reached the bench, which was lit by a nearby street lamp. A piece of newspaper cartwheeled by in the breeze.

"Listen," Carla said, wiping the seat with the edge of her coat, "if we don't win the case, it doesn't say anything about you."

Lee snorted. Somewhere in the Milky Way, it might be true, but not on Lee's planet.

"Have you always been this competitive?"

Lee sat down and nodded.

In the distance, they could hear the sound of traffic. Suddenly, a lone owl hooted, a low-pitched *hoo-hoo-hoo-hoo*. Probably a Great Horned Owl, Lee thought. She smiled and stretched her legs out. A number of stars were visible now, including the seven that made up Orion, one of the few constellations Lee could reliably identify. When he was lost in Alaska, Paul had used the Big Dipper and Cassiopeia to locate the North Star and find his way back to camp.

"So tell me about your childhood," Carla said, wrapping her red wool scarf tight around her throat.

"Why?" She hated small talk.

"Jesus Christ, Lee. It's called conversation. What two people do when they're sitting on a bench in the middle of nowhere freezing their asses off."

"Why not just enjoy the silence?"

"Oh, I don't know. Maybe because we've worked together for years and I hardly know anything about you?"

"So what? We're a great team and we work really well together. That's all that matters. Why gum it up with nonessential details?"

"Well, if that's how you think, fine. By all means, let's just enjoy the silence."

Lee began counting: one Mississippi, two Mississippi, three . . .

"Okay, so maybe you don't need to talk, but I do. I visited my mother last night and I'm still having feelings."

"Uh-oh. Has she gotten worse?"

"Are you sure it won't gum things up to tell you?"

"You can always talk about your mother, Carla."

"Well, all right then. So for the last few months, she's been living in a home that specializes in 'memory care.' I visit every other day, which is a lot, but I'm only there for an hour. Anyway, last night I walk into her room and she's cowering near the doorway. So I ask what's wrong and she points toward the window on the opposite side of the room. 'I'm afraid,' she says. 'Of what?' I ask, wondering what in the hell she's talking about. She points toward the window again. 'I'm afraid I'll fall out.' So I walk to the window and check to see that it's locked. Her bedroom is on the third floor. 'The window is locked,' I tell her. 'You can't fall out of it.' She shakes her head. 'It could break,' she says. I thump the windowpane to show her how sturdy it is. 'No, it can't.' So then she begins to wail. 'Anything can break,' she says.

"And for a moment, my heart stops because it seems as if she's actually talking about herself, about her mind. I have to control myself because I don't want to cry in front of her. She finds it very distressing. So I thump the window again and decide to be honest. 'Okay, you're right. Anything can break. In the extremely unlikely event the window breaks and you somehow fall out of it, the worst thing that could happen is you'd die.' She immediately stops wailing and stares at me. 'I'd die?' she asks. And I nod. 'Yeah, that would be the very worst thing.' So then she smiles and says, 'Oh, I can live with that.' And then, there's this familiar twinkle in her eyes and I know she's back for a moment. We both start laughing and we laugh so hard, I almost pee in my pants. After a while, she drifts away again and I leave. On the way home, I sob, but I'm also grateful that for ten or fifteen minutes, I had her." Carla stopped. "I miss her every day."

"I'm very sorry, Carla."

"Yeah, me too. It's called 'The Long Good-bye.' It's excruciating. I wouldn't wish it on Hitler. Well, maybe on Hitler." She leaned forward to adjust her knee-high boots. "I don't suppose you'd like to talk about your mother? I know she died a while ago, but other than—"

"You're right, I wouldn't."

"Hey, just thought I'd ask." Suddenly, Carla pointed down the path. "Oh look, two guys just emerged from the bushes. Should we approach them?"

"Might as well. It'll be our last interview for the night. Then we'll go get some pizza."

Neither of the men recognized Jeremy, but finally the taller one—who reminded Lee of Michael Perlman, one of her closest friends in high school and in retrospect, a closet gay—admitted hooking up with Sam the previous summer. The other, shorter man looked aghast.

"A skinhead! Are you crazy?"

The taller man waved his arms as if to ward off the memory.

"I know. I know. I know. But it was dark and I was somewhat inebriated."

The shorter man was shaking his head.

"What were you thinking?"

"I don't know. Urban guerrilla chic?"

Both men started to laugh.

"So what happened?" Lee asked, smiling in spite of herself.

"Well, as you might have guessed, it was a disaster. When we finished, he stuck out his hand and demanded a hundred dollars. I told him I didn't pay for sex and he said, 'Well, you are now.' I looked around and it was pretty deserted. Suddenly, my head cleared and I realized the situation, how dangerous it was. I pulled out my wallet and gave him everything I had: sixty-seven dollars. He took it and left. My hands were shaking so hard, I dropped my wallet twice before putting it away."

"Christ," Carla told him, "I thought I took chances. Maybe you should find somewhere else to meet people."

"Yep. Looking for love in all the wrong places."

Lee pulled out Jeremy's picture again and showed it to him.

"Are you sure you didn't see this boy as well?"

"No. He's very cute. I'd remember."

"Thanks anyway," Lee said, holding one of her business cards out to him. "Here's my card. Maybe you could ask your friends if they've ever seen two skinheads in the park together."

Both men agreed they would ask around and then started to walk away.

"And be more careful!" Carla called.

"Yes, Mom."

"It's not fair," Carla said. "All the nicest, best-looking men are gay."

Lee smiled to herself. Not always, she thought. Sometimes, if you were lucky, they were bisexual instead.

The wind picked up and snowflakes began swirling around them.

"Too cold for love," Carla announced. "Time to go."

Lee agreed. They switched on their flashlights and headed for Lee's Toyota, which they'd left on the other side of the park. It was cold and dark. They were halfway across the grass when Lee heard a sound. She quickly twirled around. Two strange men wearing gray hoodies were following them. Lee shined her light into their faces and assessed them: white, mid to late thirties, not gay, probably drunk. Both men lifted their hands to shield their eyes, which were bloodshot.

"We're not looking for trouble," she told them.

"But we are," one of them said. His words were slightly slurred.

"Just kidding," the other one said. "We're looking for some company, that's all."

"Not interested," Lee told them, removing her gloves and tucking them into her pocket.

"Definitely not interested," Carla added redundantly.

The first one tried to grab Lee's arm.

"Oh come on. Don't be a frigid bitch."

Lee easily evaded him. She could have knocked him out with her flashlight, but decided to hold off.

"If you reach for me again, I'll hurt you."

"Dude," the other man said. "I don't think they're interested."

"Course they are. They're just playing hard to get."

"Let's go," Lee whispered, moving closer to Carla. "Walk quickly but don't run."

As they started walking away, the first man staggered toward them, pawing the back of Lee's wool coat. It didn't hurt, but she'd warned him. So she spun around and punched him in the face. Bright red blood immediately spurted from his nose. He clutched his face and screamed.

"Fuck me! I'm bleeding!"

"Oh for God's sake." Lee was feeling tired and crabby now. "It's just a broken nose. Come on, Carla."

"Hey, man, do something," the injured one cried. He was rocking back and forth, smearing blood on his sweatshirt. Making it look worse than it was.

"Like what, dude?"

"Get her. She fucking broke my nose."

"Leave it, dude." He turned to the two women. "Sorry for bothering you."

"He needs some ice," Lee replied. "Let's go, Carla."

"Fucking dykes!" the first one called. "They're fucking dykes, man!"

"Sure, dude. Whatever you say."

Carla giggled as they crossed the grass.

"Well, that was exciting."

"I should have pulled it more," Lee confessed, "but he was very irritating."

"The other one was actually kind of cute."

Lee glanced at her investigator and said, "Please tell me you're kidding."

"Dude, you'll never know."

It took them half an hour to find a pizza place that was still open. Lee and Carla were the only customers. The woman behind the counter was painfully thin and had sores on her face. Lee guessed she was a meth addict. Hard to look at, but it was none of her business.

At Carla's insistence, they ordered a whole pizza and then sat down at a booth to wait. The light from a plastic, low-hanging fixture made their skin look green. The woman turned up the volume on the radio and asked if they minded. Neither of them did.

A few minutes later, they heard Chaka Khan singing "Ain't Nobody Loves Me Better," which became an instant hit in 1983. At the annual public defender conference that year, Lee and her colleagues danced to the song, all of them singing along at the top of their lungs. By then, Lee was a seven-year veteran handling the most serious cases and had recently represented a mentally ill client whose husband had tortured and killed their baby while the client lay awake a few feet away from them.

It was the first time Lee had received death threats. At the conference, Lee got drunk and spent the night with a lawyer from the Denver office who was representing a serial killer. After making love, they stayed up till dawn telling each other the worst facts of their cases. They'd alternated between hysterical laughter and sudden fits of crying. Lee had never felt more alive.

When their pizza was set down in front of them, Carla announced she was famished. Suddenly, Lee was too. Without a word, they tore into the pie like lions ripping at the carcass of a freshly killed zebra. Whatever else it was, defending a murder case was still hard work, requiring copious amounts of fat and protein. When they were finished, Carla checked her watch.

"Four minutes, fifty-three seconds," she said.

"Is that a personal best?" Lee asked, licking some cheese off her fingers.

"Not even close."

CHAPTER TEN

It was April Fools' Day when Phil Hartman called and asked to see Lee in her office. For the first time in months, her caseload was under control and she'd been thinking about leaving early and wandering the Pearl Street Mall. Perhaps ending up at the Boulder Bookstore, where she could spend hours reading indiscriminately before rousing herself to stumble back out into the daylight. But maybe not today.

"I'm free after three o'clock," she told him. "What's this about?"

"A friend of mine who doesn't qualify for the Public Defender needs your services."

"Great. Just tell him to call me."

"Well, he wants me to come see you first, explain the case, and make sure you'll take it."

"This isn't an April Fools' joke, is it?" she asked.

"Definitely not. I'll see you at three."

A few minutes past three o'clock, Phil was sitting in her office, eyeing the art on the walls and studying her fake silk tree.

"I've never been here before," he said. "The tree's not real, is it?"

"No, but most people think it is. How did you guess?"

"Elementary, my dear Watson. The tree is too perfect—not even one yellow leaf. You're a workaholic like I am, which means you wouldn't purchase anything requiring maintenance, and to be honest, you don't strike me as at all domestic."

"I have a cat," she reminded him.

"Except for the cat."

They were both smiling. Phil wore loose faded jeans, a black T-shirt, and old, scuffed cowboy boots. Lee had never seen him in anything but court clothes.

"Tell me about your friend," she said.

"What can I say? He really fucked up."

"All our clients have fucked up. That's why they're our clients."

Phil looked around the office again, pointing at her faceless purple horse.

"Who painted that?"

"An artist named Fritz Scholder. Do you like it?"

"I do, but I can't say why."

"I know. Like most art, it either sings to you or it doesn't." She waited a couple of seconds. "So, how did your friend fuck up?"

"I brought the police report, but I'll summarize it first."

"Great." Lee put her own boots up on her desk, leaned back, and closed her eyes. It would take a while; she could tell. "Just start from the beginning."

Phil cleared his throat and said, "It's a rather predictable story."

"They almost always are, but only in retrospect. When they're happening, each one seems unique and mysteriously unavoidable."

"Yes, I suppose that's true. No wonder your clients like you."

Lee waited. Stories came when the teller was good and ready. After clearing his throat again and commenting on the details in one of Paul's rare urban photographs, a street scene in Katmandu, he finally began.

"Let's see, my friend and his wife have been separated for more than a year. They own a large two-story home in Longmont, anticipating children they never got around to having. At the present time, only the wife lives there, but each pays half the mortgage."

"Excuse me," Lee interrupted, "but does your friend have a key?" A relevant fact if things went the way she guessed.

"I knew you'd ask that, and yes, he still has a key. Occasionally, he drives over to feed their St. Bernard, whose name is Eleanor."

"After Eleanor Roosevelt?"

"No, Eleanor Rigby. My friend and his wife both love The Beatles."

"Okay," Lee said, her eyes still closed. "Go on." She'd laced her hands behind her neck and made herself comfortable.

"So in the past few months, my friend and his wife have considered reconciling. They've made love on a number of occasions, twice in a bathroom at the public library where his wife works, but mostly in their home. As far as my friend was concerned, things were looking up. Then, about a week ago, his wife calls with bad news. She's changed her mind and is finally clear about wanting to get a divorce. She's sorry for any confusion, but sometimes you have to go back to go forward, blah, blah, blah. Understandably, my friend is distraught. He stops eating and sleeping. All he can think about is how he'll end up alone and miserable in someone's dreary basement apartment while everyone else lives happily ever after."

"So then what?"

"So then a couple of days ago, after finishing work, my friend drives to the house in Longmont and sits in his car just staring at it."

"Does he bring alcohol?"

"Of course, but he doesn't start drinking until he's parked the car and put the keys in his pocket."

"Better than leaving them in the ignition." She nodded approvingly. "So what happens next? I assume this is worse than a defensible DUI?"

"How did you know?"

Lee smiled with her eyes closed.

"A lawyer's intuition. So then what?"

"So then a man named Bob Wheeler shows up in a brand new Land Rover, parks it directly in front of the house, walks up to the door, presses the buzzer, and is let in as if he's expected."

"And this upsets your friend?"

"Inordinately. Bob Wheeler had once been their couples counselor, albeit a few years ago. Whether it's unethical or not, it's certainly—"

"Cheesy?"

"Yeah, that's just what my friend thought. So, after flinging his wedding band into some bushes, he decides to confront his wife and her visitor."

"Your friend is somewhat drunk by this time?"

"Oh, he's FUBAR." As a criminal defense attorney, the acronym for "fucked up beyond all recognition" was very familiar to Lee.

"Unfortunate but not surprising. Go on."

"So my friend staggers up the stairs, pounds on the door, and waits. When his wife opens the door, she looks surprised and uncomfortable. My friend begins shouting, so she slams the door shut, but of course he still has a key. When he gets the door open, he pushes his wife aside, and immediately lunges for Bob, who flees to the bedroom. Which is just what you'd expect from a therapist who throws up his hands and advises his clients to quit. Frustrated and heartsick, my friend threatens to kill Bob and then kicks a few holes in the door."

Lee opened her eyes and sat up.

"Okay, so we have burglary, harassment, criminal mischief, menacing, and trespass. Does it get any worse?"

"Legally, not much. Since Bob is in hiding, my friend joins his wife in the kitchen, where he notices that the table is set for dinner. There's a loaf of bread on the cutting board, two glasses of Chianti, and a pot full of hot bubbling water. Pasta, bread, and wine: his favorite. He feels like crying, but his wife has just found her cell phone and is about to call the police. So he grabs for the phone, which accidentally falls into the pot."

Lee picked a yellow pad off the credenza and began writing.

"Accidentally falls into the pot," she murmured, scratching the words onto a page already full of notes. When she was finished, she looked up. "So another count of criminal mischief, and tampering. Anything else?"

"Well, it sounds a bit weird, but since his wife won't stop yelling, he gets the brilliant idea they should dance. In his head, he's thinking 'Hey Jude' because his wife's name is Judith."

Lee wrote the name on her yellow pad.

"And how does that go?"

"Not like he'd hoped. As he reaches for her waist, he slips on some water and falls, hitting his face on the edge of the table."

"Which accounts for the shiner," Lee said, referring to his huge black eye. "I was going to ask you about that eventually."

Phil patted his face and sighed.

"Well, it was kind of you to wait."

"Not at all. Speaking of injuries, though, can I ask about your arm?" She pointed to his left arm, which was encased in a bright purple cast. "Nice color, by the way."

"I almost chose red, but I'm glad I didn't."

"So how did you break it?"

"Well, let's see, after hitting my head, Bob came out and then he and Judith escorted me to the front door and then pushed me through it. On my way down the stairs, I pulled the railing loose and then stumbled. I think that's when I broke it. But it might have been while I was jumping up and down on the Land Rover."

"Ah. Well I'm guessing the Rover damage is a felony."

Phil barely nodded. He was staring out her window at the foothills, which looked brown and parched. In a month, if it snowed again, everything would be green and lush. Maybe it would rain in May, as it used to, and they'd have a proper spring. But probably it wouldn't and the spring would last barely a month before the hot weather came.

"So, will you represent me?" Phil asked, still looking out her window.

"Of course."

"Do you think I'll get disbarred?" For most lawyers charged with a crime, it was the crucial question.

"Not if I can help it. But you might get suspended for a couple of months."

"That's what I figured," he said, turning back to face her. "As soon as I got out of jail yesterday, I went to my boss and told him what happened. We agreed that I would take a leave of absence. I can probably keep my job if I return by the beginning of August."

"That was very smart. I'll try to make any bar suspension run concurrent with your self-imposed leave of absence. What will you do in the meantime?"

"It depends." He was studying her face. "I have a proposition."

"I'm not condoning this, you know."

"Why would you?"

"You scared your wife."

"I know." He rubbed his eye and winced. "I wish I hadn't, but I think I wanted to make sure she never changed her mind again. Or something like that."

"The DA will want you in therapy."

"I'm already on it. I have an appointment tomorrow afternoon."

"Great. I love representing criminal defense attorneys." She glanced at her notes, reread the part about the cell phone, and said, "Accidentally falls into the pot."

At that moment, someone knocked on the door.

"Are you expecting anyone?" Phil asked.

"Carla?" Lee called.

"Are you busy?" Carla answered.

Phil walked over to the door and opened it. When she saw him, Carla put a hand to her mouth.

"Oh my God, Phil! Does the other guy look worse?"

"Fortunately not," Lee said.

"You poor boy." Carla reached out and touched Phil's cheek. "Does it hurt?"

Phil made a show of looking brave.

"Only my heart."

"I heard about it this morning," Carla admitted. "It's all over the courthouse." She turned to Lee. "Are you going to represent him?"

"I am."

"Good. I'm glad." She patted Phil's cast.

"Oh, I just remembered," Phil said, looking embarrassed. "How much will you need as a retainer? I've been a public defender too long."

Lee considered the question.

"Well, you won't be working and the restitution will be considerable. Repairing just the Land Rover will cost thousands. How about I do it *pro bono?*"

"Okay," he said, sitting down again. "So I was hoping you might say that. Here's my proposition: How about I work for you until I get my job back? For free, of course. You'd be doing me a huge favor. If I have to sit around with nothing to do, I'll become a true alcoholic and kill myself. Or Bob." He leaned forward, cradling his cast with his good arm. He was obviously still in pain. "When's the pre-trial motions hearing on the Matthews case?"

Lee flipped through the calendar on her desk and said, "April 17th."

"I'll do all your legal research. I'll do anything you want." He gave her his best, most winsome smile. "What do you say, babe?"

"Babe?"

"Yeah, no, that was a mistake."

"You can start next Monday. Go home and take some Advil."

"Thanks, boss." He stood up to go.

Lee was staring at her calendar, which looked impossibly busy. There were hearings set almost every day until the end of the month.

"Wait a minute," she said, raising her hand. "Are you free on Friday night?"

"Um, sure. You're not asking me out on a date, are you?"

Lee glanced at Carla, who nodded. After five weeks, they still hadn't found a witness who'd seen Jeremy and Sam together. But they were determined.

"Not with me," Lee told him. "With Carla. Ten o'clock at the pavilion in Cheesman Park."

"Be there or be square," Carla added.

It was almost eight o'clock when Lee finally left the office. Phil and Carla ended up staying till seven discussing the Matthews case. Before leaving, Carla promised to copy her entire file and get it to Phil by Sunday. He had a lot of catching up to do.

Outside, it was dark and cool, no hints of spring, but in Colorado there almost never were. The seasons changed overnight. When Lee reached the corner of Ninth and Canyon, she was aware that someone was following her. A figure in a raincoat wearing sunglasses and a red kerchief was darting in and out of the shadows, staying about a hundred yards behind her. When the traffic light changed, Lee remained where she was, trying not to laugh. A couple of minutes went by. Finally, the figure approached her. It was Peggy.

"You look like a courier in a World War Two spy movie," Lee told her.

"Busted. Please don't call the Nazis." She surveyed the intersection. "Can we move to a darker place?"

"What's going on?"

Peggy retied the knot on her kerchief and said, "A strange, seedy-looking policeman came to my house a few hours ago. He might have waited till I left and then followed me. I'm guessing it has to do with Jeremy's case."

"Are you sure he was a policeman?"

"Well, he acted like one." She reached into her pocket, pulled out a card, and handed it to Lee. "He left this under my door. It says I have to call him immediately, but I didn't."

Lee examined the card, which was from the Boulder District Attorney's Office.

"Okay, so it was Jason Tyler, a retired cop who now works for the DA. Did he have any paper in his hand?"

"I think so. I saw him coming up the stairs and pretended I wasn't home. He shouted my name and even jiggled the doorknob. I'm guessing he would have come inside if the door hadn't been locked. I was really scared. Finally, he slid the card under my door and yelled he was leaving, as if he knew I was there. I could use some advice."

"Right." Lee ran a hand through her hair. "Walk with me while I think. I'm heading up Ninth."

"Fine with me."

They crossed Canyon and began walking up Ninth toward Mapleton. Lee glanced over at Peggy.

"It's pretty dark out. Can you see well enough with those sunglasses?"

"Not really." She took them off. "I tripped and almost fell near your office."

"I saw that."

They walked for a couple of blocks while Lee considered her options. Finally, she was ready.

"So here's what I can say: In a criminal prosecution, a witness is not legally obligated to submit to an interview with anyone. Ethically, neither side can encourage or advise any witness not to cooperate with their opponent." Lee shrugged and waited.

"Okay," Peggy said carefully. "I think I understand."

"Good."

"So all I want is some information. Is that all right?"

"I don't see why not. What do you want to know?"

Peggy put a hand on Lee's arm.

"First of all, could we walk a little slower?" She was panting a little.

"Sorry," Lee said, slowing down. "I usually walk by myself."

"Okay, so I think the main issue at the next hearing is whether my nephew was emancipated. If he was, then the judge won't suppress his confession."

"Correct."

"So is there anything I could say that would affect the issue one way or the other?"

"Well," Lee said, looking straight ahead, "you could testify that your nephew came to see you after his parents threw him out, and that you offered him money and a place to live. You could testify that Jeremy turned down your offer, choosing to live on his own. That would be some evidence, I suppose, that he was in fact emancipated."

"But he was too ashamed to stay with me! He wasn't thinking straight. He was a mess."

"Well, that's what I would argue."

Peggy was silent for a while, thinking.

"Okay, thanks for answering my question. Do you think Mr. Tyler was going to subpoena me for the hearing?"

"Probably. At the very least, he wants to talk to you."

Peggy took off her kerchief and stuffed it in her pocket.

"Could they subpoena me if I were in, let's say, Bismarck, North Dakota? My best friend from college lives there."

They'd reached the corner of Ninth and Maxwell. Lee's house was just down the street.

"They could," Lee said, "but it wouldn't be easy." She made herself look serious. "I'm in no way suggesting, however, that you skip town to avoid a subpoena."

"I understand. It's just that I've been planning to see my friend, and there never seems to be a good time. I'm thinking I might just go . . . tomorrow."

"I see. Well, nobody can make you stick around if you don't want to."

"Right. Besides, Bismarck in April, how fabulous is that?" She grimaced a little.

"You're a good aunt," Lee said, smiling.

"Well, he was a great kid until his parents threw him out. I want to do whatever I can to help."

"Including paying for his therapy," Lee reminded her. "Which is probably quite expensive." After Jeremy's suicide attempt, she'd asked if Peggy would be willing to hire a therapist who could visit him at the detention center. A week later, Peggy had arranged it.

Peggy checked her watch.

"Oops, it's getting late. I have a lot to do if I'm leaving. Where *is* Bismarck anyway? Actually, where the hell is North Dakota?"

"Right above South Dakota?"

Peggy nodded and began heading back the way they'd come.

"Good luck on the 17th," she called.

"Thank you."

Lee turned west in the direction of the foothills. When she reached her house, she stopped in front to admire it. Paul had wanted to paint it yellow, but she'd insisted on blue and white, which he thought would be boring. A good lawyer knows the limits of rational persuasion. "I just can't see myself living in a yellow house," she told him. "That's your irrefutable argument?" he asked, incredulous. She said it was. A month later, her beloved home was painted blue and white.

CHAPTER ELEVEN

When Lee was twenty-five and had been a public defender for all of twelve months, she was assigned her first felony, not because she was ready, but because no one in the office would take it. Everyone was drowning under the weight of too many cases.

Ellen Lang, one of the office's most experienced attorneys, had just been ordered to spend the rest of her pregnancy in bed or risk losing her child. Suddenly, a caseload of ninety active felonies had to be divided among six lawyers who could barely handle what they already had. So Lee, the virgin newbie, was being tossed into the fire. If she emerged unscathed, it meant they had been right to hire her.

When she'd shown up for work, Lee's supervisor had ordered her to accompany Ellen, who was leaving for court in five minutes. This would be Ellen's last hearing and her last interaction with the client. From what Lee could gather, the hearing was to suppress a critical search. If Ellen lost the motion, which was likely, then Lee would take over the case and try it.

"Why won't any of the others take it?" Lee asked, grabbing her briefcase and buttoning her coat. It was snowing hard outside.

Her supervisor tossed his paper cup into a wastebasket across the room.

"The case is a piece of shit and the client won't deal. You're going to lose the trial and then he's going to grieve you."

"My first felony," Lee groaned. "And my first grievance."

"Welcome to the practice of law." Her supervisor patted her on the shoulder and then escorted her to the door. "The guy's name is Felix

Garcia. He thinks all white lawyers are prejudiced. Good luck."

On the way to the courthouse, Lee hurried behind Ellen, who was carrying a huge heavy box overflowing with paper. As they approached the courthouse, Ellen grunted a few times and held her stomach. Lee watched in silence, terrified she might have to take over even sooner than expected.

"I'm okay," Ellen reassured her, chuckling. "When we get inside, just follow my lead. You'll be fine." Ellen pushed back a lock of curly brown hair that fell across her face. She was maybe four years older than Lee but was clearly an adult, whereas Lee was still in the wings, practicing.

After passing through security, they took the elevator to the second floor. Until then, Lee had never been in district court. The room was almost twice as large as the county courtrooms downstairs and much quieter. The stakes were obviously higher here. In county court, which heard the misdemeanors and petty offenses, first-time offenders were looking at a fine and a lecture or maybe probation; only persistent offenders, usually those with drug and alcohol problems or the mentally ill, actually got sent to the local jail. In District Court, where the felonies were handled, defendants had already been warned and slapped, and clearly that hadn't worked. Now, they were looking at years in the penitentiary, maybe for the rest of their lives. Rehabilitation was still a possibility, but punishment was the overriding objective. In county court, it was nice to have a competent attorney, but in district court it was crucial.

When Lee and Ellen first entered the courtroom, it was empty. Lee's heart was racing as she followed Ellen to one of the two large wooden tables facing the judge's dais. Lee set the box down and waited while Ellen pulled out various stacks of paper and arranged them in the order she expected to use them. The amount of legal research was impressive. Lee had no idea how much time the defendant was facing, but guessed it was a lot.

"What exactly is our client charged with?" Lee asked.

Ellen surveyed the table, moving two piles of paper forward and one pile back.

"I think that's good," she murmured, and then turned to Lee. "Okay, let's see." She thumbed through a thick folder. "Right. At this point, it's down to three counts first-degree burglary, three counts second-degree burglary, three counts first-degree criminal trespass, two counts theft by receiving, two counts possession of a weapon by a previous offender, one count false information to a pawn broker, one count criminal impersonation, plus two counts of being an habitual offender. Yeah, so that's it."

Lee nodded, trying to stay calm.

"What's an habitual offender?"

"You're kidding, right?"

Lee felt her face grow hot.

"Is it some kind of sentence enhancer?"

"Um, yeah." Ellen shook her head. "I can't believe they gave you the case." She was about to say more but then stopped. "Okay, so we'll just have to make the best of it. I have a ton of research in my office, which should be helpful, although it's complicated. But you can call me."

"Thanks," Lee said, wishing she could disappear through a hole in the floor.

Just then, two guards escorting a middle-aged, handcuffed Hispanic man entered through a side door. The defendant was short and husky with muscular arms covered in black and green tattoos. He looked around, spotted Ellen, and nodded. As he approached the table, Lee could see that his face was pitted with acne scars.

Ellen smiled at her client as the guards removed his handcuffs.

"Felix, this is Lee Isaacs. She'll be taking over your case after the hearing. I'm sorry but I have to take a sabbatical. Doctor's orders." She patted her protruding stomach.

Felix stared at Lee and then snorted.

"Are you shitting me? She looks fifteen."

Ellen put her hand on Felix's arm and said, "She's older than she looks and very well qualified. Give her a chance."

"But I want you to be my lawyer."

"Sorry, Felix. I would if I could. Give her a chance. I think you'll like her." Suddenly, she grunted and clutched her stomach. Sweat broke out on her forehead.

Both Lee and Felix watched anxiously until she started to relax.

"Okay, false alarm. I think I'll hit the ladies' room before the hearing starts. Give you a chance to get acquainted."

After Ellen left, Felix looked glum.

"When does her sabbatical start?"

"At the end of today," Lee said, attempting to sound casual.

"Fuck me," he muttered. "And you're really going to be my lawyer?"

"I am, yes."

"Man oh man, am I fucked." Suddenly, a thought occurred to him. "How many bitch cases have you handled?"

Lee guessed he was talking about the habitual offender counts, but wasn't sure. In any event, she knew better than to admit the truth.

"Look, I just got the case today. Give me a week to get up to speed and then we can discuss your options."

He looked at her in disbelief.

"Which means none. Oh man, I am so fucked." He crossed his arms and turned away from her.

Lee wondered what she could possibly do if she quit being a lawyer.

Finally, Ellen returned and the hearing began. For the next ninety minutes, Lee sat woodenly beside Felix, staring straight ahead. A number of witnesses took the stand and were examined by both sides. Lee followed along as best she could, straining to understand the constitutional issues at stake. Although she knew it was irrational—she was just a baby lawyer—it was hard not to feel stupid and inadequate. Eventually, she gave up listening and watched the judge's face for any sign that he might miraculously grant the defendant's motion; she didn't see any. Finally, the prosecutor made his closing argument and it was Ellen's turn.

Ellen stood up slowly and walked to the podium. She was obviously tired. Turning sideways, she pointed at the various piles of paper on the table.

"Lee, could you hand me the cases as I mention them?"

Lee nodded, grateful for something to do. She moved the first pile closer and read the name of the case, *Mapp v. Ohio, 367 U.S. 643 (1961).* As Ellen began her argument, Lee decided to pour her a glass of water. Careful not to make any noise, she reached for the stainless steel pitcher and a few of the unused cups. Maybe she'd pour a glass for Felix as well. When she turned the pitcher upside down, the cover, which should have been screwed in tight, dropped with a clunk onto the table. A flood of water followed, immediately swamping the paper and dripping over the sides of the table.

Ellen looked down from where she stood and gasped. Lee used the arm of her blazer to sweep some of the water away. The two uniformed guards sitting behind Felix reached into their pockets and pulled out identical white handkerchiefs. Lee grabbed them and began blotting as many pieces of paper as possible. The judge cleared his throat and then ordered Ellen to continue.

When Lee glimpsed her future client's expression, a mixture of horror and despair, she wanted to die but kept on blotting. Each time Ellen mentioned a new case, Lee stopped and found it, shook it out, handed the limp wet pages to her colleague, then continued blotting. Somehow the time passed and the hearing finally ended. As expected, the judge denied their motion. Ellen sighed and then gathered up her things.

"Sorry, guys, I have to run. I have loads to do before I leave the office." She wiped her forehead with the edge of her sleeve. "Look, Felix, we knew it was a long shot, but I'm sorry. I really am. You and Lee will just have to make the best of it. Good luck." She reached out her hand and Felix, after a moment's hesitation, took it.

"Thanks anyway," he said.

"You're welcome. Take care of yourself, okay?" Then she hurried out.

Once again, Lee and Felix were alone. The guards behind them waited at a respectful distance. Felix seemed lost in thought, which was fine with Lee. Finally, she stood up.

"I'll see you next Friday."

"Wait," Felix said, grabbing her arm. "This isn't some kind of joke? You're really my new lawyer?"

It was yet another insult, but Lee was way beyond caring.

"Yes, I'm really your new lawyer."

"Okay then." He was nodding to himself. "So as soon as you see Ellen, ask her to call the DA and see what he'll offer."

"You want her to plea bargain the case?"

"Well, it has to be reasonable, but yeah."

When Lee returned to the office, she told Ellen what Felix had said. Ellen was delighted. Within minutes, everyone in the office knew about it. Suddenly, Lee was a hero. They clapped her on the back and congratulated her. Half the lawyers wanted to give her their most recalcitrant clients.

"No way," her supervisor said, laughing, "but it *was* a great result."

At the end of the day, as Lee was ready to leave, she knocked on her supervisor's door and then strode into his office. He was sitting at his desk, surrounded by stacks of manila folders. His gray hair was mussed and his eyes looked bloodshot.

"Would you have really allowed me to try it?" Lee asked.

He knew she meant the Garcia case.

"Of course. You've tried more than a dozen misdemeanors and won most of them." He studied her face. "What? You think we set you up?"

"It crossed my mind."

"Well, we didn't."

"Good, because I would have quit."

"See you tomorrow, Lee. Close the door on your way out."

Lee drove straight to a dojo on Pearl Street, where she'd just started taking karate. Learning the movements was hard, but she'd already glimpsed the possibility of elegance. Halfway through class, she fell and sprained her ankle. Limping back to her car, Lee swore she would pay her dues to become a great lawyer and an equally great karateka. But after that, she would never be a beginner again.

Thirty-five years later, she was sitting in the same district courtroom on the second floor of the Boulder county courthouse. That day with Felix was just the beginning of countless humiliating experiences that quickly thickened her skin and forged her into the lawyer she would finally become. Tales from the trenches, she thought, and smiled. Felix had probably been released and imprisoned two or three more times in the intervening years, Ellen had eventually become a judge, and Lee? No longer a beginner. She smiled again and checked the clock on the wall. The Matthews hearing would begin in twenty minutes. She'd been sitting there since eight, enjoying the peace and quiet, the lull before battle.

The courtroom door opened and a woman in a blonde wig entered. It was Mary Matthews, except she wasn't supposed to be there. Lee had instructed Carla to dissuade her from coming because the DA would request the sequestration of all witnesses that might later be called at trial. Sequestration meant she would have to sit in the hall outside the courtroom. She might as well have stayed home.

"Hello, Mary," Lee said, swiveling around to make sure there were no other people in the courtroom. "I wasn't expecting to see you today."

"I know, but here I am." She was refusing to make eye contact.

"Why don't we go to that conference room down the hall? If the DA sees you, it could be awkward." An uneasy thought occurred to her. "He hasn't subpoenaed you for this hearing, has he?"

"Not that I know of."

When Lee and Dan last spoke, they'd agreed on four witnesses between them: Detective Bruno, the lead detective on the case, Detective Roberts, who'd telephoned Jeremy's parents and later interrogated their son, Detective Armstrong, who'd escorted Jeremy to the juvenile detention center, and Ethan Mitchell, the kid who'd been Jeremy's best friend in Colorado Springs. Lee had specifically decided not to call Mary because she wanted to keep Jeremy's sexuality a secret for as long as possible.

"Someone called a few weeks ago," Mary was saying, "but Leonard told him to leave us alone, that we didn't want to participate, and that if he tried to subpoena us, we wouldn't be cooperative." She stared at the floor. "Anyway, I guess it worked."

"Well, good." Something was up and, whatever it was, Lee needed to nip it in the bud. She rose to her feet. "Come on, let's go to that conference room. We can talk in private there."

"There's nothing to talk about." But she let Lee take her arm and lead her out of the courtroom.

When they reached the conference room, Lee escorted her inside. The light was on and the blinds already closed. There was a briefcase and a box of Kleenex on the table. Lee pushed them to one side.

"Have a seat, Mary." As soon as they were both sitting down, Lee said, "So what's up?"

"Nothing," Mary said. "Really."

Lee glanced at her watch. She had thirteen minutes before the most important hearing in her client's case.

"Come on, Mary. I don't have a lot of time."

"Well, then how important is it that I testify at Jeremy's trial?"

Lee's stomach lurched, but she wasn't especially surprised. Witnesses routinely balked at testifying. As hearing and trial dates drew closer, Lee spent much of her time rounding people up, quelling their fears, reminding them of their promises or obligations, and then urging them to do the right thing.

"Mary, if you don't testify, your son will be convicted. He'll go to prison and very likely die there. You are a critical witness."

"But he could still lose even if I testify."

"That's true, but you're the only witness that can corroborate his sexual orientation. Without your testimony, the jury will almost assuredly convict him. You have to testify."

Mary was shaking her head.

"And-and if he loses, then both our lives will be over."

Lee wanted to strangle her, but nodded sympathetically instead. Dissemble or find another profession.

"Have you talked to Leonard about testifying?"

"Of course not. He would order me not to." Mary took a deep breath and then leaned in closer as if to confess something important. "Things have been going better at home."

"Good. I'm glad."

"Leonard has been making a real effort to control his temper. He's been taking me out regularly and acting like, I don't know, like a real gentleman. He's even asked my opinion about things."

"That's wonderful," Lee said. "Can I ask you one more question?"

"Of course." Mary reached up to adjust the wig, which had slipped a little. Her pale blue eyes blinked nervously.

"If you choose your husband over your son again, will you be able to live with yourself?"

Mary burst into tears. Lee sat still for a moment and then handed her a Kleenex. Someone knocked on the door and started to come in. Lee jumped up, blocking the doorway.

"Hey," the intruder said. He was a young, good-looking lawyer in a sleek Italian suit. A heavily made-up woman stood meekly behind him.

"Sorry," Lee said. "This room is being used."

The young lawyer tried to push his way in.

"We were here earlier. We need the room again."

Lee reached back and grabbed the briefcase off the table.

"I'm sorry," she repeated, handing him the briefcase. "You'll have to find another one."

"Why don't *you* find another one?"

"I'm in the middle of an emergency," she whispered. "Don't embarrass your client by getting into a pushing match with me."

The lawyer hesitated, and then turned to leave.

"Come on," he told the woman, "there's a room down the hall."

"Thank you," Lee whispered.

"Crazy bitch."

Lee shut the door and then checked her watch. Four minutes until show time.

"Mary, I have to run. We can talk next week. In the meantime, think about how you'll feel if you betray your son again." If kindness didn't work, there was always brutal honesty.

Mary stood up, clutching her Kleenex.

"That isn't fair, Lee."

"Actually, I think it is." She reached for the doorknob.

"Wait a minute," Mary pleaded. "Leonard says it's in God's hands, that if Jeremy is guilty, he should be punished, and if he isn't, God will intervene."

"Cut the crap, Mary."

Mary's shoulders sagged and she began to weep. Not cry, but weep.

Lee checked her watch again.

"Mary, please, we can talk about this later. You don't have to decide now. Talk to your sister. Pray, if that helps. But not to Leonard's God. To yours."

A few seconds later, Mary wiped her eyes and nodded.

"Okay, I will. Thank you." She reached out for a hug.

No, no, no, Lee thought, but then relented.

A good lawyer will do almost anything for her client. A great lawyer, everything.

As Lee expected, Dan started with the lead detective to give an overview of the facts and show how the defendant's confession fit with the evidence. Because Phil was still a lawyer in good standing, Lee allowed him to sit at the defense table on the other side of Jeremy. Carla, who'd accidentally dyed her hair black, sat directly behind them with Mr. Clean, who had brought Jeremy over from the detention facility. It was a nice little cheering squad.

As Detective Bruno described how the victim's body looked when it was first discovered by the college students, Jeremy seemed more agitated than usual. He kept kicking the table leg and squirming.

"You've heard all this before," Lee whispered.

"I know, but he makes it sound like Sam wasn't real, that he was just a thing on the ground."

"That's true, but they didn't know him and they didn't see him die. So they're just describing what he looked like after you'd driven away."

Jeremy's knees began bouncing up and down.

"I shouldn't have left him."

"Help," Lee mouthed to Phil, who'd promised to babysit their client if necessary.

"I'm on it," Phil mouthed back and then put his hand on Jeremy's arm. "Hey, buddy," he whispered. "Check out the detective's hair."

"What about it?"

"Well, it looks like . . . an animal pelt."

Jeremy's knees stopped bouncing.

"What-what kind of animal?"

"I'm not sure." Phil was squinting at the detective. "I once had a cat who looked just like that. Two Halloweens ago, he disappeared."

"I don't think—"

Phil interrupted him with a gasp.

"Oh my God, it's moving! Juju, is that you?"

Jeremy had begun to giggle, which reminded Lee how young he was. And vulnerable. How his entire future depended on this hearing. There was a famous song that David Bowie and Queen sang in the '80s, called "Under Pressure." One of Lee's colleagues used to sing it constantly until everyone in the office made him stop. Lee hummed a few bars before going back to note-taking.

When Dan finished his direct, Lee stood up and walked to the podium. She had a couple of goals on cross: to nail down testimony for later use at trial, and to highlight any details suggesting Jeremy's statements were involuntary, and that he was not in fact emancipated.

"Detective Bruno," she began, "you saw Sam Donnelly's body at the scene before it was moved?" For Jeremy's sake, she would try to personalize the victim.

"Yes," the detective answered, running a hand through his glossy black hair, careful not to muss it. Although he was short, about 5'7, his voice was loud, confident, and authoritative. In numerous cases over the years, his obvious and unshakeable confidence had persuaded jurors to dismiss their own doubts as inconsequential and to vote for the prosecution.

"And from studying Sam's body and the surrounding area, you and your team could determine that he had been kicked by multiple assailants?"

"Yes," he said. When the answer was a simple yes, Lee knew from past experience that the detective would not equivocate.

"But you can't say for sure how many."

"We know there were at least three assailants."

"But no conclusive proof beyond that?"

"You are correct." As if Lee were a student managing to answer the question right.

"You collected various items at the scene for possible DNA analysis?" she asked.

"Correct."

"My client's DNA was not on any of the items."

"Correct." Someone else might have tried to explain what that did or didn't prove, but the detective was a pro.

And so was Lee, who knew when to move on.

"The jailhouse snitch in the case told you there was a party at Sam's house a week before the murder?"

"Correct."

"The three adult co-defendants were at the party, but not my client."

"The snitch, Mr. Heller, wasn't sure."

Lee continued, undeterred.

"You can't prove my client was at the party."

"No." He paused. "Not yet."

"The snitch also told you that the co-defendants discovered paperwork suggesting Sam was gay."

"Yes."

"And that there was talk about having a 'boot party' in Sam's honor?"

"Yes, that's correct."

"There's no proof my client knew about these plans."

"No, not yet."

In a neutral voice, she said, "Detective, you either have proof or you don't. Which is it?"

"We don't." But he couldn't help himself. "Not yet."

Lee deliberately closed her notepad, signaling her intention to improvise.

"When you say 'not yet,' you mean not until the co-defendants testify at my client's trial?"

"Exactly."

"And you're hoping they'll implicate my client?"

The detective crossed his arms and said, "I'm sure they will."

"And if they don't?" She made it sound like a challenge, hoping he would take the bait.

"They'll lose their deal."

"Ah," she said, nodding as if he'd cleared things up for her.

Dan immediately jumped to his feet.

"Objection! The deal requires them to be truthful, not—"

"This is outrageous," Lee interrupted. "The prosecutor is coaching the witness."

Judge Samuels put up a hand.

"I agree. Sit down, Mr. Andrews. You can ask the witness to explain his answer on redirect."

"Thank you, Your Honor." Dan sat down, smiling. He'd accomplished what he needed to do.

"Right." The detective was nodding in agreement. "They just have to be truthful."

Lee shook her head and opened her pad again. For the next thirty minutes, she questioned the detective about the facts leading to the arrest of the co-defendants and the seizure of their car outside the bar.

"And so once you'd arrested the co-defendants, you obtained a search warrant for the house where they lived?"

The detective stifled a yawn.

"Sorry. I've been on night shift for the past two weeks. The answer is yes."

"We appreciate you being here," Lee said. "And so during the execution of that search, you climbed a ladder and found my client sleeping in the attic?"

"Yes, he was fast asleep."

"The attic was not intended for human occupancy?"

"Well, he was living there."

She ignored his answer.

"There were no walls, just exposed rafters?"

"True."

"The attic had no windows, no fan, no obvious ventilation?"

The detective carefully scratched his head and said, "I think you're right."

"The space where my client was sleeping had none of the usual things you'd find in a bedroom."

"True."

"No bed, no table, no lamps, no bureau, no mirror, no closet, no rug, no computer, no television, no desk, no pictures."

"Correct. I think there was a sleeping bag and some personal items."

"Yes," Lee said, pulling out a copy of the detective's report. "In addition to the bag, there were three piles of clothing, two pairs of sneakers, a baseball bat, a leather jacket with a broken zipper, a gray sweatshirt, six paperback novels, a plastic bag containing a toothbrush, toothpaste, and deodorant, and a wallet. Does that sound correct?"

"If that's what my report says."

"The rest of the house was a mess?" She took a sip of water and glanced at Jeremy, who was clearly paying attention.

"Yeah, pretty much."

"Piles of unwashed dishes, beer bottles everywhere, garbage in the kitchen, sheets tacked up over windows, overflowing ashtrays, unmade beds, cigarette burns on the furniture, broken lamps, et cetera."

"It definitely needed a woman's touch," the detective joked.

Both the judge and the DA were smiling, so Lee smiled too. *No wonder your marriage failed*, she wanted to say, but of course didn't. A smart lawyer always takes the high road; it's no fun, but it's safer.

"Detective, you seized my client's sweatshirt because there was a drop of blood on the sleeve?"

"Yes. Later on, we tested it and the blood matched the victim's."

Lee closed her eyes for a moment and then opened them. She needed to word the next few questions carefully.

"You found blood on two pairs of boots worn by the co-defendants?"

"Correct. They were wearing them on the night we arrested them."

"And the blood matched Sam's?"

"Correct."

"And you found blood in the front and in the backseat of the co-defendants' car?"

"Yes," the detective said. "And the samples matched Sam's as well."

"Okay. So the blood on my client's sweatshirt could have come directly from contact with Sam?"

"Yes."

"But it also could have come indirectly from riding in a car that had Sam's blood in it."

The witness took his time before answering.

"I guess so."

"Thank you," Lee said. She was in the home stretch now. "My client's wallet contained seven dollars and thirty-two cents?"

"Yes."

"You found no evidence that he had a bank account?"

"True."

"You found no evidence that my client was employed?"

"True."

"You found no evidence that my client was married?"

"True."

"No evidence he was in the military?"

The witness was beginning to fidget.

"No, there was no such evidence."

"Just a few more questions, Detective. If he wasn't working, was my client enrolled in school?"

"Not to my knowledge."

"Before handing him over to your colleague, you determined that my client was only sixteen years old?"

"True."

"And that his parents had thrown him out?"

"That's what he said."

"One final question: Did my client also tell you *why* his parents had thrown him out?" She knew the answer but wanted the judge to hear it.

"I'm not sure. Can I refer to my notes?"

"Please," she said.

The detective thumbed through a sheaf of papers he'd brought with him to the witness stand.

"Let's see. Oh yeah, now I remember. 'For being a disappointment.'" He shook his head and chuckled.

"What's so funny?" Normally, she'd never ask a question when she didn't know the answer but decided to risk it.

"Well, if that's all it takes, I'd have tossed my kid out years ago." He turned to the judge and the DA, expecting them to laugh, but they didn't. "Christ," he muttered. "I was just kidding."

"Well, thanks for your candor," Lee said. "No further questions."

As soon as she sat down, Phil leaned over to congratulate her.

"You got more than you should have. Well done." He squeezed their client's shoulder. "Oh, and both Jeremy and I think the detective's an asshole."

"I'd have to agree." Outwardly, she was calm, almost nonchalant, but inwardly she was taut, focused, and ready, a state of mind she could easily sustain for weeks. If she were younger. She could still do it now, but after a couple of days, it would become exhausting—one of the many reasons she charged as much as she did.

Then Dan stood up and said, "The State calls Detective Roberts to the stand." A moment later, the witness came sauntering up the aisle.

In a contest for the best Marlboro Man lookalike, Detective Roberts would be considered a shoo-in. He had the requisite physique: tall, lean, and muscular. And the requisite wardrobe: boots, jeans, cowboy hat, a blue western style shirt, and a belt with a huge silver buckle. Jurors couldn't get enough of him. After taking the stand, the witness removed his hat and placed it on his lap, then grinned ruggedly at the judge.

"I know he's the enemy," Carla whispered behind them, "but he's so good-looking."

"Gag me with a spoon," Phil said.

"You're just jealous." Carla tapped Jeremy on the shoulder. "What do you think?"

Jeremy swiveled from Carla to Phil and back again.

"Um, I'm not sure."

"Good man," Phil laughed.

"Shh," Lee told them. "I have to pay attention now."

Dan's direct examination was quick and effective. In less than thirty minutes, the detective explained where the interrogation had taken place, the time of night, the suspect's demeanor, the phone call to the suspect's parents, what the parents said, and finally, after waiving his Miranda rights, what the suspect eventually admitted. No muss, no fuss. The implication was clear: The defense, as usual, was making a mountain out of a molehill.

"No further questions," Dan said, looking pleased. "He's all yours, Ms. Isaacs."

"Thank you, Mr. Andrews."

God is in the details, she thought, as she walked to the podium and began spreading out her notes.

"Good morning, Detective," she said.

"Morning, ma'am." Short for: I'm just a simple cowboy who tells it like it is.

That'll be the day. Lee held up a sheaf of papers in each hand.

"Detective, I have two reports detailing your contact with my client, an official-looking typed report and your handwritten notes."

"Yes, ma'am."

"The typed report is an accurate summary of your handwritten notes?"

"Yep. That's the way I do it."

"Do you have both reports in front of you?"

"No," he said. "I've only got the typed report."

Lee turned to the judge and asked if she could approach the witness. After getting permission, she walked up to the detective and handed him the handwritten notes.

"My questions will mostly refer to these."

"Not a problem."

Back at the podium, Lee waited a beat.

"So, to begin with, you knew my client was only sixteen?"

"Yes, ma'am." Then he winked at her.

She guessed it was a facial tic and ignored it.

"You knew he had no criminal history?"

"Yes, ma'am."

"No experience being questioned by the police?"

"Not as far as I know."

"He'd been thrown out of his home in Colorado Springs and had come to live with some older skinheads in Denver?"

"That's what he said, ma'am."

"You offered my client a sandwich and he wolfed it down and asked for more?"

"Yep, he was pretty hungry."

"He gave you the name and phone number of his parents and you called them?"

"I sure did, ma'am."

"And after speaking with them, you determined that my client was legally emancipated?"

"Yes, ma'am."

"At first, they didn't know what the term meant?"

"Correct, so I read them the statute and they agreed their son was emancipated."

Lee kept the pace fast and friendly.

"And then you told them they didn't have to come to Boulder?"

"Yep, that was about it." And then he winked again.

Was he actually flirting with her? She smiled tentatively.

"Did you tell them they could come if they wanted to?" According to Leonard, he hadn't.

"Nope, it wasn't necessary. Their son was emancipated."

Excellent, Lee thought.

"And so you never read them their son's Miranda rights?"

"No, ma'am. It wasn't necessary."

"Because you'd determined that their son was emancipated?"

"Exactly." He made it sound like two words.

"You'd agree that the question of emancipation is ultimately the judge's call, not yours?"

"That's right, ma'am. I make the preliminary determination and then talk to the suspect. Later, after the charges have been filed, the suspect's attorney files a motion to suppress claiming the suspect wasn't emancipated, and then the judge either grants the motion or more often than not, he doesn't."

"Fair enough," Lee said. "And because you'd made that preliminary determination, you never told my client he was entitled to have his parents or some other adult be there?"

"No, ma'am."

"You never even asked if he wanted his parents or some other adult to be there?"

"No, ma'am." The detective glanced at his watch.

Lee pretended to be solicitous.

"Do you have somewhere else you need to be?"

The detective stroked the stubble on his chin and said, "I do, but it'll have to wait. This is important." Another wink.

It had to be intentional. What the hell. This time she smiled back warmly.

"When you asked if he wanted to speak with you, my client simply shrugged?"

"I think that's right."

"And then you read him his rights?"

"Yep, and he said he understood them."

Lee held up the detective's report.

"According to your handwritten notes, when you asked if he was willing to waive his rights, my client said he didn't care."

"Yes, ma'am. So I asked him to sign his name, indicating his willingness to speak with us, and he did."

"And then you gave him two more sandwiches."

"Yep, the kid was pretty hungry." He chuckled at the memory.

"I'll bet. And then you asked if he knew Sam Donnelly?"

"Yes, ma'am."

"And according to your handwritten notes, my client said, 'It doesn't matter anymore.'"

"That's right, but when I pressed him on it, he said the victim was 'just a faggot who deserved to die.'"

"How bitter that sounds." She hadn't meant to say it out loud.

"Yeah," the detective agreed. "Pretty hateful. Although it's not in my notes, I remember saying something like nobody deserves to die for being different and the kid said he didn't believe me."

Lee looked toward Phil, who was busy scribbling down the detective's last answer. She decided to move on.

"You asked my client what part he played in the murder, and he looked down at the floor and said, 'I didn't help him.'"

"Yeah, he was pretty evasive but eventually admitted kicking the victim."

Lee found the page she was looking for.

"Actually, it went like this: You asked if he'd kicked the victim and my client said, 'A couple of times, but he was already dead.' So then you asked if he was a hundred percent positive the victim was dead, and he said, 'Well, I'm pretty sure.' And then you said, 'but not a hundred percent,' and he said, 'I guess not.'"

The detective smiled innocently and said, "Right. He wasn't sure."

A lousy lawyer would have argued with the detective and gotten nowhere. Lee moved on.

"Let's talk about the last 'admission' by my client, that he was the lookout."

"Not a problem."

Lee held up the two reports.

"In your official-looking, typed summary, you said my client admitted being the lookout."

"Yes, ma'am."

"In your handwritten notes, it went like this: You asked what my client was doing while the others kicked the victim, and he said, 'I don't remember exactly.' So then you confronted him by saying, 'Come on, Jeremy. You had to be doing something.' And that's when he said, 'Okay fine, I was the lookout.'"

"Yes, ma'am. Then he put his head down on the table and said he needed to sleep. I asked Detective Armstrong to take him to the juvenile detention center."

As she gathered her notes to leave, Lee asked, "Did my client mention how he ended up living with the skinheads?" It wasn't in either report, but Jeremy thought he'd told the detective how Rab had saved his life.

"Hmm," the detective said, as if he was trying to remember.

Lee straightened up and met his gaze. *Come on,* she telegraphed. *Throw me a bone.*

The detective's eyes narrowed. *Why should I?*

Because it's the right thing to do. She hesitated. *And I'm cute.*

The detective put on his big white hat and grinned.

"Yeah, he said something about a fight and how the skinheads rescued him and gave him a place to stay."

"Thank you very much, Detective. No further questions."

Dan immediately stood up and said, "No redirect, Your Honor." He was frowning a little, which meant he hadn't liked the answer.

As she was sitting down, Phil leaned over and said, "You were flirting with him!"

"So?"

"So it was incredibly effective."

"It helped," she admitted, "but it's still a long way to the finish line."

Detective Armstrong's direct examination lasted till noon. According to this detective, the suspect wasn't under the influence of either drugs or alcohol, he was coherent, mostly calm, and seemed to understand everything that was going on. He was handcuffed without incident and placed in the back of the detective's car. On the way to the juvenile detention facility, the suspect became upset when he realized his "brothers" were being housed elsewhere. The detective told him he'd be safer at the juvenile facility, but the suspect said he didn't care. He demanded to be taken to the jail and began pounding his fists on the plexiglass partition. The detective ordered him to stop, but the banging continued. Finally, the detective braked to a halt and said, "Look kid, it's not up to me, okay? You're going to juvie and that's the end of it. Pound all you want, but if you break the glass, I'm going to be pissed." Then he started driving again. After a while, the suspect lay down in the backseat and a few minutes later, began to snore.

Lee's cross was very short.

"Did my client say anything else during the drive to the detention center?"

"No, I don't think so," the detective answered.

Like all good attorneys, Lee stopped when she had what she needed.

"Thank you. No further questions."

CHAPTER TWELVE

After the lunch break, Lee called her only witness, Ethan Mitchell, who had been Jeremy's best friend in Colorado Springs. Ethan's family belonged to the same congregation as Jeremy's, The Word of God, and considered Pastor Matthews to be their spiritual leader. According to Ethan, who blushed almost constantly, both boys were the same age and had been friends since they were ten. In the past few years, they'd begun to rebel against their strict upbringing. For example, they'd refused to go to church more than four times a week and sometimes snuck out to "normal" movies, which their parents had forbidden them to see. They'd tried cigarettes a couple of times and had once shared a bottle of Boone's Farm apple wine and gotten very sick.

In high school, both boys were straight A students and were often mocked by the normal kids. As soon as they graduated, both planned to move as far away as possible—maybe to Florida or California, somewhere warm—and never go to church again. In the meantime, they fantasized about being free to hang around with people who weren't religious zealots.

Pastor Matthews often preached against homosexuality, calling it an abomination, but neither boy felt strongly about condemning people who were different. After all, *they* were different and knew firsthand what it felt like to be shunned by the normal kids. As far as Ethan was concerned, both he and Jeremy were "live and let live" kind of guys who didn't hate anyone. Jeremy, especially, was kind and courteous to everyone.

Ethan had been shocked when Lee first showed him his friend's arrest photo. For one thing, it looked like Jeremy had lost about thirty pounds and for another, the tattoos on his arms were totally out of character; Ethan couldn't imagine what had happened to his friend, but it must have been bad. When he lived at home, Jeremy had never been in trouble. Ethan couldn't imagine Jeremy surviving on the street for more than a couple of days.

Toward the end of her examination, Lee asked Ethan to describe his last interaction with Jeremy in Colorado Springs.

"It was right after his parents threw him out," Ethan said. "He called and asked if I would meet him at the Denny's on Academy Boulevard. He sounded upset. I got there an hour later and tried to calm him down. He couldn't stop crying."

"Did he tell you why he'd been thrown out?" She knew her client hadn't told him the real reason.

"For just, you know, not honoring his parents' wishes."

"Regarding?" Lee prompted.

"Regarding almost everything, I guess." Ethan blew out a breath. "His father was incredibly strict. Nothing Jeremy did was ever good enough. His mom was actually okay, but his father was always mad at him for something."

"Did Jeremy have a plan for the future?"

"Well, he wanted to stay with me, but my parents wouldn't have allowed it. They'd never go against their pastor."

"So then what?"

"We were both pretty hungry, so we ordered grilled cheese sandwiches and apple pie. I kept begging him to apologize and ask for forgiveness, but Jeremy said no, his father would never take him back. So I gave him all the money I'd brought, about a hundred dollars that I'd been saving since I was twelve, and made him take it. I also gave him my leather jacket." He wiped a few tears away. "It was really hard because he was my best friend and I wasn't sure when I'd see him again."

Lee gave him a few seconds to compose himself.

"Do you know where Jeremy went that night?"

"Well, at nine o'clock, he took a bus to Denver. I waited till he got on. He was going to look for a place to stay, you know, like a youth hostel. And, well, that's all I know."

"Did you ever hear from him again?"

"Just once," Ethan said. "He called on May 5th, which is my birthday.

He said things were finally looking up and that someday we were going to laugh about all this. I wanted to come and see him, but he said it was impossible, that we lived in different worlds now. And then he hung up. I never heard from him again."

"Thank you, Ethan."

After Lee took her seat, Dan asked a couple questions and then sat down. At trial, he probably wouldn't ask any. He would make it clear to the jury that the witness, a nice, sympathetic kid, was irrelevant to the only issue that mattered: whether the defendant aided and abetted a murder.

At that point, Judge Samuels announced a thirty-minute recess and started to rise.

"I'm guessing you've both prepared written briefs. If so, could you hand them in now? You don't have to exchange them until after you've argued, but I'd like to read them during the recess."

Dan and Lee both pulled out their briefs, approached the bench, and handed them over. While they were still in front of the judge, Dan asked Lee if she wanted to exchange them now; he would if she would.

Fat chance, Lee thought, but smiled sweetly and said, "What would be really gallant is if you'd give me yours and wait for mine at the end of the hearing."

Dan smiled just as sweetly.

"If only I could be gallant but, alas, I must be cowardly. You're just too good a lawyer."

"You're both full of shit," the judge said, laughing. "I'll see you in thirty minutes."

Lee walked back to the defense table. As Mr. Clean was preparing to take Jeremy back to the holding cell, Ethan approached them. He wore a short-sleeved white shirt and a clip-on bow tie. With his reddish hair and wide-open face, he reminded Lee of Andy Griffith's fictional son, Opie. In this episode, Opie's long lost friend from Mayberry resurfaces as a skinhead arrested for murder.

"Hi, Ethan," Lee said. "Thanks for testifying."

"You're welcome." He was staring hard at Jeremy.

"Hey, man," Jeremy said. "I'd shake your hand, but I can't." He showed Ethan his handcuffs. "Do your parents know you're here?"

"Uh-uh. I'm hoping they won't find out." He hesitated. "Look, I just want to apologize."

"For-for what?"

"Oh, you know, for not helping you more." His face was pink with embarrassment.

"Hey, man, you gave me your money and the jacket off your back. What more could you have done?"

"I should have gone with you. I'm really sorry."

"That's ridiculous. You wouldn't have survived. I barely did."

"Still."

"Hey, man, it's all good. Take care of yourself, okay?" Jeremy turned toward Mr. Clean. "I'm ready to go now."

"Yeah," Ethan said, checking his watch. "I'd better go too. My bus leaves in half an hour." He was trying hard to smile.

"Well, thanks for coming."

"I've really missed you," Ethan blurted and then quickly walked away.

"He's just a kid," Jeremy murmured.

After the recess, Dan slipped quietly to the podium and spread out an impressive number of pages. Since he usually argued without notes, it was his way of signaling to the judge that the motion really mattered and that he needed to prevail.

His argument was vintage Dan: smart, organized, and cogent. As Lee expected, he spent almost half his time on the issue of voluntariness, arguing that even if the defendant wasn't emancipated, his statements to the police weren't coerced and were therefore voluntary.

"Ultimately," he said, "it's a question of fairness. Allowing the defendant to take the stand and deny any participation in the murder without also allowing the state to impeach him with his voluntary statements would be grossly unfair and seriously hamper our ability to prove the defendant's guilt beyond a reasonable doubt. We only want what is fair. Thank you, Judge."

Lee closed her eyes for a moment. Dan's argument made perfect sense; it would be a hard sell to convince the judge otherwise. But she had to.

As she walked to the podium, she made a number of decisions. First, no passion—it would only make her seem desperate. Second, she would address the issue of police coercion head-on. And third, she would hijack Dan's fairness argument and make it her own.

"Your Honor," she began, "we, too, only want what is fair. And what's fair for my client is to grant his motion to suppress and to prohibit the prosecution from using any unlawfully obtained statements against him." She took a drink of water. "It's been over thirty years since the Colorado legislature enacted section 19-2-511, recognizing that juvenile defendants needed special protection when dealing with the police and the criminal justice system. Recently, the American Psychological Association, the American Psychiatric Association, and the National Association of Social Workers filed amicus briefs in two landmark cases before the United States Supreme Court, *Graham v. Florida* and *Miller v. Alabama*, arguing that research in developmental psychology and neuroscience documents juveniles' greater immaturity, vulnerability, and changeability.

"These organizations urged the Court to treat juvenile defendants differently than similarly situated adults because juveniles are less capable of mature judgment than adults, are more vulnerable to external influences, and their psychosocial immaturity is consistent with recent research regarding adolescent brain development. These amicus briefs have been included in my written material along with some of the newer research on adolescent brain development."

Lee waited until the judge nodded, then began again.

"According to section 19-2-511 (1) of the Colorado Revised Statutes, a statement given by a juvenile during custodial interrogation is not admissible unless a parent, guardian, or legal custodian is also present during the interrogation. Under section (2), however, the statement may be admissible, notwithstanding the absence of an adult, if the court finds that, under the totality of the circumstances, the juvenile made a knowing, intelligent, and voluntary waiver of rights *and* was emancipated. An emancipated juvenile, as defined in section 19-1-103 (45), means a juvenile over fifteen years of age and under eighteen who has, with the real or apparent assent of his parents, demonstrated independence from his parents in matters of care, custody, and earnings. The term may include, but shall not be limited to, any such juvenile who has the sole responsibility for the juvenile's own support, who is married, or who is in the military.

"According to Ethan Mitchell, who was my client's best friend in Colorado Springs, my client grew up in a strict, religious home. His life, as the son of a strong-willed pastor, was extremely sheltered and narrowly circumscribed. He rebelled by drawing the line at four church services a week and by occasionally sneaking off to see a 'normal' movie. He'd never been in trouble with the police and had never been questioned by them. Just after his sixteenth birthday, his parents threw him out and he was forced to live on the streets. At some point, a group of skinheads saved his life and adopted him. They allowed him to live in their attic and taught him how to survive. To fit in, he shaved his head and got the same tattoos that they had.

"At the time of his arrest, he wasn't in school or in the military. He wasn't married. He had no job, no bank account, and no visible means of income. He lived in an attic, had almost no possessions, and was very, very hungry. If, at that time, he'd petitioned a civil court for emancipation, the judge would have laughed at him."

She stopped again, checking to make sure Judge Samuels was still with her.

"Judge, there's no question my client was alone when he was interrogated by Detective Roberts. If he was emancipated and the court finds he made a knowing, intelligent, and voluntary waiver of his rights, then his statements are admissible. But, given the definition of emancipation and the facts surrounding my client's exodus from his home and his subsequent living arrangement with a group of older skinheads in Denver, there's no way this court can find he was truly emancipated.

"And, because Detective Roberts was aware of these same facts, there's no way he could have made even a good faith determination of emancipation. Calling my client's parents and asking them if their son was emancipated just isn't enough. If it were, then any child who gets thrown out of his house would automatically be emancipated and wouldn't be entitled to any of the special protections that the courts and legislatures have determined to be necessary."

Now for the hard part, she thought, although her face gave nothing away.

"Because my client wasn't emancipated and his rights were intentionally violated, section 19-2-511 requires this court to suppress his statements and to prohibit the DA from using them. The statute also states that if the juvenile wasn't emancipated, it doesn't matter that he voluntarily waived his rights. The statements are still inadmissible. Implicit in this is the determination that, under such circumstances, any statements made by the juvenile are to be considered involuntary. Which means that the DA should be prohibited from using these unlawfully obtained statements in any way, either in its case-in-chief or to impeach my client should he decide to testify. That is what's fair."

Both the judge and the DA looked surprised. Lee immediately put up a hand.

"Judge," she said, "I'm fully aware of the DA's argument: that there should be a separate voluntariness inquiry apart from the statute, that even if the court rules that my client's statements should be suppressed, unless he was subject to undue influence or police coercion, his statements should be considered voluntary under the due process clauses of the Fifth and Fourteenth Amendments and therefore available as impeachment material."

She looked at Dan and said, "That's your argument in a nutshell, correct?"

Dan hesitated but eventually nodded his head. To nitpick her language would appear peevish and obsessive.

"Okay then," she told the judge. "So, for all of the reasons stated, it is still our contention that the statute precludes using the statements for any purpose. If, however, Your Honor agrees with the DA that there is in fact a separate voluntariness inquiry, I will address it." She took a deep discreet breath. What she said next would very likely determine where her client would spend the next forty years of his life.

"According to the Court in *People v. Lucas*, a case concerning an obviously emancipated juvenile who ran away from home and was arrested for murder, statements are inadmissible for any purpose unless they are made voluntarily. Whether statements obtained during a custodial interrogation are voluntary depends upon the totality of the circumstances surrounding the interrogation. Primary factors to be considered are: (1) the juvenile's age, experience, background, and intelligence; and (2) his capacity to understand his Fifth Amendment rights and the consequences of waiving those rights.

"In that case, the Court found that the statements were voluntarily given, and not the result of undue influence or coercion on the part of the officers. But unlike the defendant in *Lucas*, my client had no experience dealing with the police, and because he wasn't emancipated, had every right to have an adult assist him to understand his rights and the consequences of waiving them. This much-needed assistance, however, was deliberately withheld by an officer who wished to take advantage of his youth and immaturity. An officer who knew exactly how to get a scared, hungry, sleepy kid to talk.

"So how much coercion is necessary? Do the police have to slam my client around to obtain his confession? Why bother, when all you need to do is feed him, withhold any information that might help him, and ignore any answers you don't like. It's easy. But just because it's easy doesn't mean you haven't used undue influence to get him to talk. In this case, Detective Roberts knew or should have known that my client was not in fact emancipated. He should have ordered my client's parents to either come to Boulder or arranged for another relative to stand in for them. He should have told my client that he didn't have to decide whether to waive his rights without the advice of an adult. My client obviously thought he was alone. His so-called brothers were elsewhere. There was no one to help him except the nice friendly detective who gave him sandwiches and acted kind. Undue influence? You bet.

"Judge, for all of the above reasons, I'd ask you to suppress my client's statements and to prohibit the DA from using those statements for any purpose. Thank you."

After everyone was seated, Judge Samuels told the parties to return at five o'clock for his ruling. Then he banged his gavel.

"The Court is in recess."

Both the judge and the DA immediately left the courtroom. Phil and Carla crowded close to Lee.

"Whew," Phil said. "I think we actually have a chance. I couldn't imagine how you'd argue against the *Connelly* case, but you did. I'm very impressed."

"What's the *Connelly* case?" Carla asked, her hand on Jeremy's shoulder.

"It's our biggest hurdle," Phil explained. "The case where the U.S. Supreme Court held that a confession is voluntary unless the defense can prove it was the product of police misconduct."

"But we argued that, right?" Carla asked.

"As best we could," Lee answered. She was tired and didn't feel like discussing anything with anybody. She stared at her watch. "I have to be somewhere at 3:30." *Somewhere* was the Boulder Teahouse on 13th Street, where she often hid during trials and major hearings. Even if it was busy, she never ran into anyone there who knew her.

"How are you holding up?" she asked Jeremy.

"Just, you know, kind of scared." His chin and fingers were covered with blue ink. The pen she'd given him to take notes or draw pictures must have leaked.

"But basically okay?"

"Basically? Um, I guess so. Yeah, sure."

She studied his face, but it was unreadable.

"Great," she said. "I'll see you at five."

At exactly five o'clock, Judge Samuels entered the courtroom, sat down and cleared his throat.

"First of all, I want to congratulate both parties for their professionalism throughout the day. I know how much you both want to win. And I realize my rulings will very likely affect Mr. Matthews' chances at trial." He then picked up his notes and began reading them into the record.

"After reviewing the written material, the witnesses' testimony, and the arguments of counsel, I find the following: Concerning whether the defendant was emancipated at the time he made statements to Detective Roberts, I am not convinced that he was. Although Mr. Matthews had been on his own for almost eight months with his parents' consent, there wasn't nearly enough evidence to show he could actually take care of himself. It seemed from the limited amount of evidence presented, that in lieu of his parents, he was simply living off another set of adults.

"I also found it highly persuasive that unlike the defendant in *Lucas*, Mr. Matthews hadn't chosen to live on his own, that he'd been thrown out of his home and was distressed by his parents' action. Because the defendant wasn't emancipated, section 19-2-511 of the Colorado Revised Statutes requires that I suppress his statements. The DA is hereby prohibited from referring to or using any of these statements in its case-in-chief.

"Now, as far as the issue of voluntariness goes, I disagree with Ms. Isaacs' contention that a violation of the statute requires me to find that her client's statements were involuntary. Instead, I agree with Mr. Andrews that a separate voluntariness inquiry is required and that according to *Colorado v. Connelly,* a statement will not be considered involuntary unless it was the product of coercive police activity. Which means more than the usual amount of coercion required to get someone to talk.

"Ms. Isaacs argues that because Detective Roberts knew or should have known that her client wasn't emancipated, his interrogation amounted to coercive police activity and that he used undue influence to extract those statements from him. Mr. Andrews argues that the *Connelly* case requires much more coercion than that. I agree with Mr. Andrews. Although I disagreed with the detective's preliminary determination of emancipation, there's no evidence, beyond Ms. Isaacs' allegation, that it was made in bad faith. Furthermore, I am unconvinced that the detective used undue influence to get Mr. Matthews to talk. In fact, I find the opposite: that Mr. Matthews was inclined to talk and was easily persuaded to do so.

"And so, for all of the above reasons, I find that the defendant's statements were voluntary and that the DA may use those statements to impeach the defendant if, and only if, he chooses to take the stand. Thank you everyone. This court now stands in recess." Without looking at either party, the judge gathered his notes and left. A few seconds later, the lights in the room were dimmed.

Lee sat very still, her face impassive.

"So we lost, right?" Jeremy asked her.

"Well, they can't bring up your statements in their case-in-chief, which is helpful, but they can bring them up if you take the stand."

"Do I have to take the stand?" But he already knew the answer.

"If you want to win," she confirmed.

"So the jury will hear what I told the detective?"

"Unfortunately."

"And my-my brothers are going to say I'm guilty?"

"It's what coyotes do."

"I can't believe it," Phil muttered. "It'll be a great appellate issue if we lose."

"We won't," Carla said behind them. "We've pulled out cases worse than this. What do we do now, boss?"

Good old Carla, Lee thought, finally managing to smile.

"Well, first of all, we find a witness who saw Jeremy and Sam together, then we make sure that Jeremy's mother will testify, and then we prepare for trial. With a little luck and a huge amount of work, we'll win." Because there was no Plan B.

Or was there? Out of the corner of her eye, Lee saw Dan approaching. She told everyone to be quiet and waited until he was a few feet away from them.

"Hi, Dan. Congratulations."

"Thanks. Listen, at the risk of sounding like I never mean anything I say, I'm hereby re-offering your client thirty years. You have twenty-four hours to accept. After that, I'm done."

"Except Judge Samuels doesn't take deals after motions have been litigated."

"That's generally true," Dan said. "But he'll make an exception for your client. I just asked him."

"Okay, then we'll think about it." They wouldn't take it, of course, but it never hurt to keep the prosecutor guessing.

Tomorrow, she had back-to-back hearings from eight till noon. Tonight, she was supposed to teach an advanced weapons class at the dojo. Maybe she could get Michael to stand in for her while she spent the evening deconstructing the hearing with her client.

"Um, I'll take it," Jeremy said, scraping his chair back from the table. "I'll take the thirty years."

Everyone stared at him, including Dan.

Mr. Clean, who was standing a couple of feet away, walked up to Jeremy and put a hand on his shoulder.

"Hey, why not discuss it with your lawyer first?"

"It won't help. I'm-I'm just not strong enough. So I'd better take the deal."

"Which would be totally fine," Lee assured him. "If you decide to plead, everyone including me will respect that. But let's at least talk for a moment. I want to understand your reasoning, that's all. I'm sure the DA can wait a few more minutes, right?" She glanced at Dan, who reluctantly nodded. "Okay, so let's just sit here and go over it. Can everyone give us some space?"

Carla, Phil, and Mr. Clean immediately jumped up and hurried toward the judge's dais while Dan headed in the opposite direction. Once they were alone, Lee moved her chair closer. Ideally, she would have a conversation as important as this one in an intimate setting with no time constraints. But when her clients couldn't make bail, her options were limited to strange, impersonal, and always depressing places. A shadowy courtroom at the end of the day was better than most of them.

"So, first of all," she whispered, "it's perfectly okay if you're scared. Anyone in your place would be. It's only natural."

"*You* wouldn't be." He was gazing down at his ink stained fingers.

"Jeremy, look at me. Of course I would." When he looked up, she smiled reassuringly, but he was shaking his head.

"No, you're just saying that to try and make me feel better. But I'm not like you. I'm a ninety-eight pound weakling, just like you said. I won't hold up when Mr. Andrews starts questioning me. So I'd better take the deal."

"And if that's your ultimate decision, I'll honor it. But to be clear, you're not a ninety-eight pound weakling. I only said that to get you to start eating. I think you're the bravest person I've ever represented."

"You don't know me then. I'm the opposite of brave, and I would just end up disappointing you."

"That's impossible. As long as you did your best, I'd be completely satisfied. Everyone gets scared. It doesn't mean you should necessarily take the deal."

"Okay, so like what are you scared of?"

"What difference would that make? Besides, this isn't about other people. It's about you and whether you want to fight the case or take a deal for thirty years. The decision is yours, but it's a life-changing one that shouldn't be made without lots of discussion. Why don't we postpone this until tomorrow? We can spend tonight going over all the pros and cons."

"No." He rubbed his eyes, smearing more ink on his face. "It won't help. I don't have what it takes to fight. I-I barely have what it takes to live. Inside my head, I just keep thinking about Sam and how I'll never be happy again."

"You're grieving, but those feelings won't last forever. Trust me."

"I-I want to, Ms. Isaacs, but I just don't feel like I can. I'm not even sure I know how." He was looking right at her now. "So I think I'll take the deal." Whatever uncertainty he might have felt earlier was gone.

"I see. Well, it sounds like you've made up your mind. Are you sure?"

"I think so. Yeah."

"Then I'll tell Mr. Andrews." She glanced around the courtroom. Dan was sitting in the back row, reading the newspaper. "Dan," she called. "My client will take the deal. When can we set it?"

"Next Monday at four. That's when the judge has time." He stood up and made his way to the aisle. "I'll go tell him now. I didn't expect him to take it on the spot."

Carla and Phil looked shocked but of course didn't comment.

After the case was set for a change of plea, everyone left except Carla, who for once seemed at a loss for words. She kept straightening her skirt and brushing invisible lint off her sweater.

"So that's it?" she finally asked Lee.

"That's it."

"Well, maybe it's for the best." She was trying to look hopeful.

"Right. I'll see you next Monday."

After her investigator left, Lee packed up her rolling briefcase, looked around the empty courtroom, then sat down to think. Her client had decided to plead. Although she'd promised to respect his decision, should she try one more time to dissuade him?

Like all baby lawyers, Lee had memorized the most important sections of the American Bar Association's Standards for Criminal Justice and could recite them almost verbatim. According to one of the standards, certain decisions relating to the conduct of the case were ultimately for the accused, and others were ultimately for the defense counsel.

After consulting with his lawyer, an accused had the right to decide what pleas to enter, whether to accept a plea agreement, whether to waive a jury trial, whether to testify in his own behalf, and whether to appeal. Counsel was free, of course, to engage in fair persuasion and to urge the client to follow her advice. Ultimately, however, because of the fundamental nature of these decisions, the accused had to make the determination himself.

Jeremy was no longer suicidal. He was immature, but he wasn't incompetent. His confession had just been ruled admissible. Objectively, the evidence against him was more than sufficient to convict him. To chip away at what little confidence he had in the rightness of his decision would be selfish, inappropriate, and possibly unethical. She would not do it.

It was over.

CHAPTER THIRTEEN

D
inner on Saturday night was superb. Her friends made roast chicken, steamed artichokes, and salad followed by a platter of cheeses that looked moldy but were of course delicious.

Lee hadn't realized how hungry she was until she started eating. As she dug in, she thought of Jeremy wolfing down sandwiches at the police station and then asking if there were any more. Since the motions hearing three days ago, he'd been almost constantly on her mind: the way he shrugged, the way he giggled, the way his knees bounced when he was nervous, the gentle but unmistakable way he'd said good-bye to Ethan and their shared childhood. How he'd metamorphosed into what her father would term a *mensch*, a decent, upright, honorable person. No longer a kid, but not quite yet an adult. *Kid interruptus.*

As she sipped some of Bobby's excellent Merlot, she realized she felt proud of her client—he'd had to make a tough decision—as well as terribly sad. But that was the price of caring. In time, she'd get over it; she always did. The tough cases broke her heart and, what? Made her stronger? More compassionate? So far, yes, but they also took a toll that Lee had always gladly, carelessly accepted. Was there a limit? Possibly, but she hadn't reached it yet. Or had she?

"Lee?" Bobby asked.

He was holding the bottle of Merlot and pointing at her glass, which was almost empty. He was wearing one of his lovely cashmere sweaters and a pair of pleated khaki pants, which fit him perfectly. Mark, as usual, wore loose jeans and a faded denim shirt. Both men were still what Paul called lookers.

"I'd better not," she answered. She'd already had two glasses and felt moderately buzzed.

"You could spend the night here," Bobby said.

"Thanks. Hey, have I told you both lately how much I appreciate your friendship?"

"Uh-oh," Mark said. "It's worse than we thought. She really is in the dumps."

"That's not why I said it," she replied, draining the last of her wine. "Look, I'm sad and disappointed but I'll be fine. I'm thinking about taking a sabbatical."

"Really?" Bobby asked.

"Don't look so surprised. I haven't taken any real time off in years. I'm thinking about heading east, visiting my father, and then traveling around New England. I haven't been to Maine since I was twenty." She set her glass on the table. "Who knows? Maybe after that, I'll join your next trek in the Himalayas. If you'll have me."

"Sounds like you're thinking about retiring," Mark said.

Was she? The idea of never being responsible for another person's fate sounded superficially pleasant, but then her mind went blank. Who would she be if she weren't a lawyer?

"I can't think that far," she admitted.

"You don't have to," Bobby said, standing up. "Come on. There's brandy in the living room."

After they'd settled into their respective places—Mark in his rocking chair, Lee on the couch with Bobby sitting too close to her—Mark poured some caramel-colored liquor into three identical snifters and passed them around.

Lifting her glass, Lee said, "Here's to the end of something and the beginning of something else." Hell, in less than two months, she'd be sixty. According to the prevailing culture, she was a crone now, in the final chapters of her life. Time to make a few changes.

"Are you sure you're all right?" Bobby asked her.

"Absolutely."

Both men looked skeptical.

Outside the picture window, she could see the dark outlines of Spruce trees surrounding the house. Up here, at seven thousand feet, it still felt like winter, but down in Boulder, which was seventeen hundred feet lower, everything was beginning to bloom. In another week, the lilacs in front of her house would be out and then, after that, it would be summer. Jeremy would have already gone to prison and the people who'd cared for him, including his lawyer, would still be grieving but becoming more and more resigned to his absence. The big Oh Well.

She sighed, then stood up and walked toward the kitchen, her gait a little unsteady from too much alcohol.

"You're not leaving, are you?" Bobby asked. "It's only eight-thirty."

"Just getting a drink of water."

"Oh, okay."

Lee rolled her eyes. His concern was beginning to chafe. When she reached the kitchen sink, she poured herself a large glass of water and drank it in one gulp. A few seconds later, she drank another. Better. In a couple of hours, she'd be able to drive home safely without worrying about being stopped. Cops just loved arresting lawyers.

She ran her hand along the black granite counters, admiring their cool sophistication, and then glanced around the room. Everything, from the gleaming stainless steel refrigerator to the automatic espresso maker, matched perfectly. A bit too sterile for her taste, but it was beautiful. Hey, if she stopped lawyering and got tired of traveling, she could always remodel her kitchen: the time-honored middle class response to existential angst. For a nanosecond, she actually considered it.

"Do you want to watch a movie?" Bobby called.

"Sure."

"Happy or sad?"

Whatever she said would be telling. She walked back into the living room. Both men were standing in front of a black metal cabinet, scanning through a large collection of DVDs.

"Sad," she said decisively.

"Good," Mark replied.

"Why is that good?" Bobby asked.

"She needs to wallow."

"I'm standing right here," Lee told them. "I can hear you." But she couldn't help smiling.

"Hey," Mark said, picking out one of the DVDs, "how about *Philadelphia*? We haven't seen Tom Hanks die of AIDS in a while."

"Sounds good," Lee said, dropping onto the couch. A moment later, Bobby sat down next to her. After the movie started, Mark squeezed in on the other side of her.

"I can't breathe," she complained, but as usual they ignored her.

At a quarter to eleven, both men walked her to the door. As she headed out, she promised to call them Monday night after Jeremy's plea hearing. On the drive home, she thought about the movie, which had been one of the first mainstream Hollywood films to acknowledge the AIDS crisis and homophobia. It had come out in 1993, the year before Jeremy was born. He would never see the film, never hear the haunting aria sung by Maria Callas that so famously comforted the main character. The list of all he'd miss was staggering. The best-case scenario: He'd survive the way he had in Denver. Find someone not too awful to protect him and eventually learn to fit in. She turned onto Broadway, passed a barefoot man wearing a blanket, and stopped to give him some money.

On Monday, her client would be sentenced to thirty years and that would be that, a small-time miscarriage of justice in a system that worked moderately well but wasn't perfect. On Tuesday, she had a preliminary hearing on a kidnapping case, a probation revocation hearing, and two run-of-the-mill sentencings. No haunting arias, just business as usual.

"The Court calls People v. Matthews, 11CR1059."

Lee walked to the podium and waited for Jeremy to join her.

"Good afternoon, Judge. For the record, Lee Isaacs appearing on behalf of Jeremy Matthews, who is present and standing next to me at the podium."

Dan, smiling broadly, stood up and said, "Your Honor, Dan Andrews for the prosecution. As the Court knows from last week, we've reached an agreement in the case. In exchange for a dismissal of count one, the defendant will be entering a guilty plea to an added count two, second-degree murder."

"Is that your understanding, Ms. Isaacs?" the judge asked.

"Yes, Your Honor. In addition, both parties will be stipulating to a sentence of thirty years in the Department of Corrections."

"Very well."

Jeremy was bouncing from foot to foot. Lee put a hand on his shoulder to settle him.

"Everything's all right," she whispered. Hardly, but it seemed to calm him down. He wore jeans, sneakers, and a white button-down shirt Mr. Clean had bought him. He'd combed his thick brown hair with water and smelled like Listerine, a boy on his first (and last) date.

Judge Samuels flipped through a sheaf of stapled papers. When he was finished, he selected a single grape from a bowl in front of him, rolled it between his fingers, and finally ate it.

"Mr. Matthews, do you understand the terms of your plea bargain?"

"Yes sir," Jeremy mumbled.

"You need to speak loud enough so that the court reporter can hear your answers and record them."

"Yes," Jeremy said, louder.

"Good." The judge smiled and then slipped on a pair of glasses. "So, first, we'll go over all your rights to make sure you understand them. These are the rights you'll be giving up by pleading guilty. Then, we'll go over the elements of second-degree murder. You need to understand everything I tell you. If you have any questions, ask your lawyer."

"Okay," Jeremy said and then glanced at Lee. He looked scared but determined.

Ten minutes later, the colloquy was almost finished. The advisement had been careful and thorough, what everyone in the biz would call bombproof. If her client changed his mind later, any post-conviction motion to withdraw his plea would fail.

"So," the judge said, "any questions before I take your plea?"

Jeremy shook his head.

"Again, you have to say yes or no, so the court reporter can record your answer."

"Sorry, no," Jeremy said, sounding a little out of breath.

Lee stood quietly next to her client. Soon it would be over. Mr. Clean, with his kind face and huge arms, would escort Jeremy back to his cell. Later, tonight or tomorrow, he'd be taken to the Denver Reception and Diagnostic Center for processing before being placed at one of the permanent facilities in the system. He would be terrified. Lee moved closer to her client, willing him to breathe.

The judge cleared his throat and said, "All right then, Mr. Matthews, to the added count two of second-degree murder, how do you plead, guilty or not guilty?"

"Guilty."

The judge removed his glasses and closed his file.

"We're almost done, Mr. Matthews. But before I accept your plea, I'd like some acknowledgement of your guilt. If a jury had already found you guilty, I wouldn't be asking you."

"Like, what do you mean?"

"Well, at the motions hearing, your lawyer argued that your statements weren't trustworthy, that they might not be true."

"I-I said everything they said I did." He was starting to bounce again.

"Judge," Dan interrupted. "I'm sure Ms. Isaacs would stipulate that the facts presented by the prosecution at the motions hearing last Wednesday provide a sufficient basis for the plea." He motioned Lee to back him up.

Before she could, the judge said, "Thank you, Mr. Andrews, but I'm looking for a bit more reassurance here. The defendant is very young. He could later claim he was confused. That would be difficult if he acknowledged some culpability."

Lee simply nodded now. She had no obligation to make the court's advisement any more airtight than it was.

"Mr. Matthews," the judge began again, "did you act as the lookout while the others kicked the victim?"

Jeremy looked up at the ceiling and then down again. Twice, he opened his mouth to speak but then closed it.

Finally, he said, "Not really."

"Not really? Mr. Matthews, would you like a moment to speak with your lawyer?"

"Please Judge," Lee said. Then she and Jeremy stepped back a few feet.

"Jeremy," she whispered, "you have to make up something to satisfy the judge or he won't accept your plea."

"I'm supposed to lie?"

"Well, yes. If you want the deal."

"That's fucked up."

"Only if you're innocent."

Dan jumped in again, sounding desperate.

"Your Honor, would the court accept an Alford plea?" Like a *nolo contendere* plea, an Alford plea allowed a defendant to enter a guilty plea without admitting guilt. Essentially, a defendant did not admit committing a criminal act but acknowledged that the prosecution would likely prove the charge at trial. It was entirely up to a court's discretion whether or not to accept the plea.

Lee waited silently, a tiny hope having sprung deep inside her.

The judge was shaking his head.

"Mr. Andrews, I have never accepted an Alford plea unless there was an ongoing civil case. I will not accept it here."

"What do you want, Jeremy?" Lee whispered.

"What do I want?" He shrugged helplessly. "I don't know. I want this all to be a dream. I-I want to be somewhere else. I want Sam to be alive again."

"Well, this isn't a dream. It's your life. What do you want to do here?"

He leaned in close, his face only a few inches away from hers. There were tears in his eyes, but he looked more angry than sad.

"How should I know? I'm only seventeen!"

"Which is why you're so scared. But you know what," she heard herself saying, "I'm fifty-nine and I'm almost as scared as you are."

"You're fifty-nine?" He looked astonished.

"Yes, but the point is, I'm scared too. If you take the deal, you'll do thirty years for a crime you didn't commit. If you go to trial, you could end up doing life and I'd feel terrible for not being able to save you."

"Except it wouldn't be your fault."

"It wouldn't matter. You'd be sentenced to life on my watch. I'm not sure I could go on lawyering after that."

"Well, so then what would you do?"

Their noses were almost touching. He had a small dimple above his right cheekbone that she'd never noticed, and flecks of green in his eyes.

"You mean if I quit being a lawyer?"

"Yeah."

Judge Samuels and Dan were waiting, but for once she didn't care. This—whatever the hell it was—was more important.

"Good question. I've spent my entire adult life being a lawyer. I always meant to travel but never found the time. Maybe I'd spend five or six months hiking in the Himalayas."

"But-but wouldn't your husband get upset if you went away that long?"

"I don't have a husband. I mean, I had one, but he died five years ago."

"Sorry, I didn't know. Did he, like, get cancer?"

"No. He was a mountain climber. He died in an avalanche."

"Oh wow. But then you never got another one?"

"Hey, five years isn't that long."

"Were you afraid if you got a new husband, he'd die too? Because, you know, that's what I'm afraid of. That if I ever get a new boyfriend, he'll die just like Sam did."

Lee made herself stop and think. A knee-jerk reaction to any of his questions could sink them. Although this was new and unfamiliar territory, it felt surprisingly right. As if they'd always been headed here, even if they hadn't known it.

"Honestly," she told him, "I don't think so. Unless of course I married another mountain climber. Which I wouldn't."

"Yeah, I wouldn't either."

They both smiled.

"But here's an opposite thing," he whispered. "I'm also afraid that I'll never meet anyone that I'll love as much as Sam."

"Well, I might be afraid of that."

"Yeah."

"Ms. Isaacs," the judge said, "I don't mean to pressure you, but we don't have all day."

"I'm sorry it's taking so long, Judge. This is a difficult and important decision."

"Can we resolve this in the next five minutes, or should we continue the hearing?"

"For the record," Dan stated, "the People object to any continuance. The defendant has been adequately advised and pled guilty. The facts presented by the People at the motions hearing in this case provide a sufficient basis for the plea."

"Ms. Isaacs?" the judge prompted.

Lee turned to Jeremy and whispered, "Any chance you're ready to decide?"

"I'm still pretty scared, Lee." It was the first time he had called her Lee. "What-what do you think I should do?"

All right then. Some very good lawyers might differ, but Lee agreed with Harry S. Truman that the buck stopped here. When a client asked what she thought he should do, he had the right to an unequivocal answer. Other lawyers might list the various options but leave it up to the client. Lee thought that was bullshit, that lawyers and other professionals, if asked, should be forced to make the ultimate decision. It's what they were paid for.

"Go to trial," she said. "It's your only chance to be free."

"But what if I lose?"

"You'll be sentenced to life in prison and I'll end up trekking in the Himalayas."

"Would you come back sometimes and visit me?"

"Regularly."

He thought for a moment and then said, "Okay."

"I'll tell the judge."

"Will he be mad?"

"He'll get over it." They both stepped up to the podium. "Your Honor, after thinking it over, my client continues to maintain his innocence."

"Why am I not surprised?" The judge sighed as he reached for his glasses. "In which case, I won't accept his guilty plea. The trial is once again set for two weeks beginning May 23rd. I'll rule on all miscellaneous motions by the end of the week. Good luck, Mr. Matthews." He banged his gavel. "Court is adjourned."

As soon as the judge left the courtroom, Phil and Carla rushed up to her, grinning like lunatics.

"Thank you, Lord Jesus!" Phil shouted.

Carla looked as if she'd been crying.

"I knew you'd do something, Lee. I just knew it."

"But I didn't," Lee protested. "Not really."

"Yeah, right."

Out of the corner of her eye, Lee saw Peggy hugging her nephew while Mr. Clean hovered over them, beaming.

"Let's meet tomorrow in my office at ten," Lee told them. "And then we should all visit Jeremy. He's going to need constant reassurance."

"I'll have to call Mrs. Weissmann," Carla said. "I told her last Friday that Jeremy was going to plead. She'll be so relieved."

"Drinks anyone?" Phil asked. He was pretending to swing a tennis racket.

Lee shook her head and said, "You can't drink, Phil. It's a condition of your bond."

"Is she always such a Grinch?" he asked Carla.

"Often but not always. Come on, I'll buy you a nice, cold cranberry juice."

"Cranberry juice without vodka tastes disgusting."

"I'll see you both in the morning," Lee said. She would pick up a sandwich at Alfalfas and then head to the office, where she'd probably work till midnight. Life was good again.

As she exited the courtroom, she saw Dan standing near the window pretending to read the Boulder Weekly, which he held upside down—a major clue.

"Hey, Dan," she said.

"Oh hi, Lee. Do you have a minute?" He looked calm and cheerful, as if the hearing had gone exactly the way he'd expected.

"Of course." She walked over to him and glanced out the window. "The days are getting longer."

"Thank God. Do you suffer from SAD?" He meant seasonal affective disorder.

"No, do you?"

"Nope, but I'm pretty sure my wife does. We get along so much better after the spring equinox. No more arguments till October. Today's our twenty-fifth anniversary."

"No kidding? Congratulations. Did I ruin your day?"

"Of course not. Well, kind of."

"I didn't plan it, you know."

"Oh, I know. That's why I'm not angry."

Suddenly, a distraught woman holding an infant in her arms burst out of another courtroom shouting, "How am I gonna feed my baby if they lock him up?" One of her eyes was swollen shut and there were various green and yellow bruises around her face. A number of people were standing close by, but no one responded. A moment later, a teenage girl ran up and took the baby from her.

"Come on, mama," she said. "Let's go."

Everyone watched in silence as the girl led her mother down the stairs.

"It's an imperfect system," Lee observed sadly.

"I agree," Dan said, "but it's the only one we have." He folded the newspaper under his arm. "Oh, before I forget, do you know of a good Italian restaurant? I'm taking my wife out tonight."

"I've always liked Carelli's." It had been her and Paul's favorite restaurant, the place where he'd asked her to marry him.

"Carelli's? I'll make a note of it." Then, affecting a look of nonchalance, he asked, "So, what's going to be your theory of defense?"

"I don't know exactly. I'm still working on it."

"Oh sure."

"Jesus Christ, Dan. You have three eyewitnesses and my client's statements. Can't I have anything?"

"Ideally, no." He unbuttoned his suit jacket and loosened his tie. "All right, fine. Do you have a favorite dish at Carelli's?"

"I always order the eggplant Parmesan. It's very good." She set her briefcase on the floor. "So was twenty-eight your real bottom line? I'm just curious."

"When your client was wavering, I almost came over and offered you twenty-five."

"Yikes, I'm glad you didn't. It would have been very hard to turn down."

"Should I be kicking myself for not offering it?"

"No. We would have turned down anything over fifteen."

"Yeah, well that's what I thought." He checked his watch, which looked expensive. Lee had never spent more than thirty dollars on a watch and never would. Her court clothes, on the other hand, had cost a fortune, but that was different. By definition, anything that helped you win was essential.

"So, would you like the chance to interview the three co-defendants?" he asked.

"Of course."

"Well, if you'll tell me your theory of defense, I'll ask their attorneys."

"Great. I'll think about it."

"No, you won't." Suddenly, he looked genuinely thoughtful. "Setting aside all the strutting bullshit, you know what I really feel?"

"That it's too bad we both can't win?"

"Yeah," he said, nodding.

"But we can't, can we?"

"I don't see how."

"So it's back to the strutting bullshit?"

"I'm afraid so."

After a moment, she picked up her briefcase and headed for the stairs.

"Happy anniversary," she called over her shoulder.

"Thanks, Lee."

It was eleven-fifteen and she was still at the office. She'd stopped working because the words on the page had gotten blurry. Maybe she needed glasses? Of course she did, but she'd managed so far without them. If she closed her eyes for a while, they might perk up again and let her work for another hour. In the meantime, while she rested, she'd call her father.

"Hey, Dad," she said when he picked up.

"Hi, kiddo. How'd it go today?"

She closed her eyes, put her feet up on the desk.

"Jeremy couldn't go through with it."

"That's good, isn't it?" He was lighting a cigarette and not even trying to disguise the sound.

"Yes, it's very good." Then she told him what happened. "Everyone thinks I did something to make him change his mind, but all I did was talk to him. Somebody besides me is looking out for him."

"The God of Lost Boys again?" he asked, inhaling deeply.

"Yup, showed up at the last possible moment. I wasn't sure she'd make it."

"Well, I'm glad she did. Is there a God of Lost Old Men?"

"If there was, what would you pray for?"

"May I be purely selfish?"

"You may."

He took another puff and then extinguished his cigarette.

"I would pray for Miriam Adler's bridge partner to move away from Boston."

"So no world peace?"

"I'd rather be Miriam's partner." Suddenly, he started coughing. When he could finally speak again, he said, "That's what I get for being selfish."

"No, that's what you get for smoking."

"Honey, I've decided to die by having a massive cerebral hemorrhage. It won't matter if I smoke."

"You could get lung cancer first. The chemo could interfere with your ability to play bridge."

"Hmm," he said, pretending to take her seriously. "I never thought about that."

She smiled, laced her fingers behind her head, and let her mind drift for a moment. It had been a long surprising day. Lots of hard work ahead and maybe, in the end, not the outcome she hoped for. But she couldn't think that far and more importantly, she wouldn't. For once, she would take Paul's advice and be here now.

"Speaking of chemo," her father was saying, "Ed, my Tuesday bridge partner, just got diagnosed with stage four liver cancer. He drank too much for years but finally went to AA and got sober. Reconciled with his wife. Six months later, he gets the big C."

"That's terrible."

"Yeah, he's a goner. We had a party for him this afternoon and he basically said good-bye. Nice guy, decent player. Not even eighty yet. It's going to be hard to replace him."

"I'm so sorry, Dad." She tried to think of something wise and comforting to say, but nothing came to mind. Although she was well acquainted with violence and tragedy, there was something about her father's stories that often left her speechless. "What about Hal and Freddie?" His two longest-standing bridge partners. "Are they still okay?"

"Freddie's fine."

"Oh good."

"But his son wants him to move to Florida. He thinks his father would be better off in one of those soulless, one-size-fits-all retirement communities."

"Does Freddie want to go?" She hoped, for her father's sake, he didn't.

"Not really. He hates the weather, his son's never available, and his daughter-in-law is a biggie in the Florida Right to Life movement."

"Now that's depressing."

"Tell me about it." Her father sighed. "Eventually, of course he'll go, but hopefully not for a year or two."

"And Hal?" Her father hadn't mentioned him in a while. What was his problem again? Diverticulitis? Prostate cancer? Diabetes? That was it: diabetes.

"Hal's turned out to be a real survivor. He's only got one toe on his right foot and two on his left, but he still shows up to play. It's really something."

"Yikes. Can he walk?"

"He totters."

"Jesus," she muttered.

Her father began to chuckle and then they both started laughing. For a while, they gave themselves up to it. Eventually, she sat up and wiped her eyes.

"On that note, I think I'll say good-night. Promise you won't die before I call you again?"

"Okay, but call soon."

"Ciao, Dad."

"Ciao, kiddo."

CHAPTER FOURTEEN

On the first Saturday in May, Lee and Carla were sitting in The Cave, a dark, nondescript joint that Carla had found on a side street about four blocks from Colfax Avenue. The bar was filling up fast with locals who waved to one another and were obviously regular customers. At ten p.m., Lee and Carla were supposed to meet a guy named Barry Simmons, a former bar employee who might or might not recognize Jeremy and Sam from their pictures. Lee sipped lukewarm coffee while Carla nursed a watered-down whiskey sour.

"Come on, Barry," Carla muttered. "Don't stand me up."

A few hours earlier, Carla had wandered in, her sixth time in three months, and asked the bartender, whom she didn't recognize, if he'd worked there the previous summer. No, but his friend Barry had. Carla then asked for Barry's number and called him. Barry had been asleep but was happy to speak to an unknown female trying hard to sound playful and mysterious.

It took an interminable amount of foreplay, but ultimately she was rewarded for her efforts. Barry had occasionally filled in for the regular bartender, his cousin, when he was too hung over to work. After a bit more prodding, Barry remembered serving two young skinheads but couldn't remember much about them. To him, he admitted, they all looked alike. So Carla offered to buy him a beer if he'd drive over and look at some pictures—she would be "extremely grateful"—and he'd finally agreed to meet her at ten.

Carla then called Lee, who was at Mark and Bobby's house watching a new documentary about American climbers that included interviews with both her friends. Halfway through the movie, the filmmaker asked them about Paul's death on Nanga Parbat and their subsequent decision to quit climbing. It was a natural question, which they'd obviously anticipated, and if you didn't know them well, you would have thought they'd completely recovered from the trauma. Lee, however, *did* know them well and was grateful when her phone rang.

"Excuse me," she told them as she answered it.

"This could be nothing," Carla began, "or it might be the break we've been waiting for." After she'd finished explaining, Lee decided to join her in Denver.

"Sorry, guys," Lee announced, looking for her jacket. "I'll watch the rest of it later."

"You don't have to," Bobby offered.

"Of course she does," Mark said.

"I want to," she told them, "and I will." But she'd watch it by herself.

After surveying both rooms of the bar, they picked a booth facing the bar's entrance. The lighting was dim and cave-like. In the past few minutes, a noisy group of bikers had entered and were greeted by the bartender. One of the bikers, a big swarthy man wearing a black leather vest and chaps, was heading straight for their booth.

"Oh great," Lee muttered.

"It's okay," Carla said wearily. "I know him."

"Carla baby," the biker said. "Give me some sugar." His arms were covered with brassy tattoos featuring buxom, cartoonish-looking women. Better than racist slogans, Lee decided. If you had to choose.

Carla pursed her lips and gave him an air kiss.

"Hi, Elliott. I thought you hung out at Willie's Tavern."

The biker stopped a few feet away from them and adjusted himself.

"Willie's got shut down by the IRS."

"Bummer," Lee said.

"Yeah, so now we're here. Any luck tonight?"

"We hope so," Carla replied, holding up two crossed fingers. "We're meeting someone in a few minutes."

Another biker at the bar called, "El, what do you want to drink?"

"Milk," Elliott yelled back, "if they have it." He leaned in closer and confided, "My ulcer's acting up on me."

"Ah," Lee said.

"Yeah." He grimaced. "Well, I hope your person shows."

"Thanks," they said.

When they were alone again, Carla pulled out her compact, checked her reflection in the mirror and, a few seconds later, put the compact away. She took a sip of her whiskey sour, then set the glass down hard.

"I love my job, Lee, but this Colfax bar scene is getting old. I need a break." She shook her head and sighed. "You see that cowboy near the jukebox?"

"Sure."

"Well, in another minute, he's going to play 'Crying,' by Roy Orbison. Which I used to love but now I hate. And then he's going to ask if I'd like to dance with him."

"Really?" Lee tried to keep from looking amused.

A moment later, Roy Orbison's plaintive voice filled the room and a cowboy in a huge black hat walked over and asked if Carla wanted to dance.

"Not tonight, honey."

"You sure?" He had a gravelly voice and a sweet, irresistible smile.

"We're waiting for someone."

"The mystery witness?" the cowboy asked.

"God, I hope so," Carla told him. "I really hope so."

Lee started to laugh.

"It's not funny," Carla said, but she was already beginning to smile.

Over the next thirty minutes, they spoke with six more cowboys, a couple of locals, and a group of rowdy biker chicks wearing the tightest jeans Lee had ever seen. Nobody remembered two skinheads sitting alone in a bar the previous summer.

They had just ordered another round of drinks when a sad-looking man in an orange sweatshirt and black slippers entered the bar. His thin blonde hair was tied in a ponytail.

"That's him," Carla said. "I'm sure of it."

"How do you know?" Lee asked.

"I just know." Carla stood up and waved. "Barry, we're over here."

As he approached the booth, his shoulders sagged.

"I thought you'd be alone." He looked around fifty but might have been younger.

"I thought so, too," Carla replied, "but I called the lawyer I work for and she wanted to meet you, too." She turned to Lee. "Lee, this is Barry Simmons."

Lee stood up and stuck her hand out.

"Pleased to meet you, Barry."

"Yeah," he said, offering a limp hand in return.

"Thanks so much for coming. What would you like to drink?"

"Um, I'll have a Coors Banquet." He'd turned sideways and was gazing at the bar's entrance as if he might make a run for it.

"I'll get it for you," Carla said, nudging him toward the table. "Lee can explain what we're looking for."

"Have a seat, Barry." Lee pointed to the space across from her. After he slid in, she added, "Carla says that you served a couple of skinheads last summer."

"Yeah, but I don't remember much about them." He looked tense and uncomfortable.

"Sure. Carla also said that you weren't officially working here, that you were filling in for your cousin."

"Yeah, just when he needed me. The owners didn't know."

"So your cousin paid you?"

He smiled weakly. His two front teeth were missing.

"Well, he was supposed to pay me, but he got robbed. I'm still, you know, kind of waiting."

"That's a drag. So where do you work now?"

"Um, right now I get unemployment, but that'll run out in a week."

Carla returned with a beer for Barry and a bowl of Cheez-its.

"I don't know about you," she told Barry, "but I'm starving." She slid into the booth beside him, close enough so that their shoulders were touching.

"So you served a couple of skinheads last summer," Lee continued, "but you don't remember much about them."

"Right," Barry said, taking a long swig of beer. "Hmm, that's good." He took another swig before elaborating. "The older one ordered shots of tequila and the younger one drank Coke."

"How many times did you serve them?" Lee was beginning to feel excited.

"Two or three times. They always sat at the table over there." He pointed to a small table in the corner. "I thought maybe they were cousins, like me and Clark."

"Really? How come?"

"I don't know. Just the way they sat together. Like they were close. Plus, they kind of looked alike." He took another swallow of beer.

"Did they hold hands?" Carla asked.

"Are you shitting me? They were skinheads."

"Anything else you remember?" Lee asked.

"Just that they were real quiet. Skinheads don't usually come here. Neither do bikers, until recently. Times are changing, I guess." He smiled again.

"Barry, what happened to your teeth?" Carla asked, sounding genuinely concerned.

Barry put a hand up to cover his mouth.

"It's kind of a long story, but Clark and me owed this guy some money. The guy got impatient and one night he just punched me."

"Ouch," Lee said. If he ended up being their witness, he'd need new teeth. It wasn't fair, but the middle-class jurors in Boulder would dismiss him as a loser—someone they wouldn't easily trust. If Peggy couldn't swing it, Lee would have to pay for it herself. A haircut wouldn't hurt either.

"Should I show him the pictures?" Carla asked Lee.

"In a minute. Barry, listen, we don't want you to lie. If you don't recognize them, just tell us. But if you do, you could end up saving a young boy's life."

"How?" Barry asked, grabbing a handful of Cheez-its.

"The younger one is accused of murdering the older one."

"No shit! So like, what? You guys represent the younger one?"

"That's right," Carla said, pulling out the pictures. "Here they are. Do you recognize either one of them?"

Barry nodded immediately.

"Yeah, those are the ones I served."

"Are you sure?" Lee asked. Her voice was calm and matter-of-fact.

"Yeah, it's them. Um, can you get me some more snacks? I forgot to eat dinner."

"Absolutely," Carla said, standing up. "Would you like another beer?"

"Don't mind if I do."

After Carla left, Lee asked if he'd ever been convicted of a felony.

"Nope, my record's clean. My cousin's lawyer asked me the same thing."

A warning bell went off inside Lee's head.

"Your cousin Clark's lawyer?"

"Yeah," he sighed. "This time it's serious. He's charged with vehicular homicide. His lawyer says if I don't have a felony, I could be his alibi witness. That means—"

"I know what it means, Barry. Would you be telling the truth?"

"Well, not really, but the lawyer says it's important."

"Does the lawyer know you're lying?"

"I'm not sure. I don't really want to testify, but if I don't, my cousin will go to prison. So I have to."

"Actually, you don't."

When Carla got back to the table, Lee explained what Barry intended to do. Carla nodded slowly.

"So you and Clark are close?" she asked, although she already knew the answer.

"He's my only living relative. My parents died when I was nine. Clark's parents took me in. I don't know what I would have done if they hadn't. Eventually, they died too and now it's just me and Clark." He reached back and refastened his ponytail. "I know he's a fuck-up, but he's family. You know?"

"Family's important," Carla agreed, "but this time you could get in real trouble. If you weren't with Clark that night, where were you?"

"The truth? I was here, working."

"For free," Lee added drily.

"I sound like a real chump, don't I?"

"You do," Lee said. "But worse than that, there are witnesses who can dispute where you were. Perjury is a class-four felony, carrying two to six years in the penitentiary."

"What should I do?" he asked, looking upset.

Carla put her hand on his arm.

"Honey, it's easy. On Monday morning, call the lawyer and tell him the truth."

"He's going to yell at me. I just know it." He took a huge swallow of beer, and then turned to Lee. "Could you, like, call him for me?"

"Sure, why not? Do you have his name and number?"

Barry reached into his back pocket, pulled out a crumpled business card, and handed it to her. On the front, it read "Derek Cooper, Criminal Defense and Debt Relief," and below it an address in Denver. The phone number had been crossed out and a new one penciled in. On the back was another number.

"The one on the back is his cell phone," Barry explained. "He said I could call anytime."

Lee glanced at her watch. It was a quarter past eleven. What the hell. "I'll be back in a few minutes."

Lee walked outside the bar and sniffed the air, which smelled like Chinese food. She looked around until she spotted a restaurant on the corner. A group of laughing teenagers—the boys in tuxedoes, the girls in long dresses—emerged from the restaurant and headed toward Colfax. Prom night, she thought, smiling. Lee had gone to her high school prom with her friend Michael Perlman, who moved to New York City after graduating. Had he come out in the intervening years? She hoped so. And then she started to laugh. According to Paul, women who habitually hung out with gay or bisexual men were affectionately referred to as fag hags. She'd been one all her life.

A few moments later, Lee dialed Derek Cooper's cell phone, expecting to leave a message.

"Hello?"

"Is this Derek Cooper?"

"Hey, what's up?"

"Hi. My name is Lee Isaacs. I'm an attorney in Boulder."

"I've heard of you. You did the Eisner case a few years ago. That was a great result." Barbara Eisner had been charged with suffocating her infant daughter. Lee had convinced the jury to convict her client of criminally negligent homicide, a lesser offense than murder, and then at a highly publicized sentencing hearing, had persuaded Judge Samuels to give her client probation.

"It was," Lee acknowledged. "So, I'm calling about a client named Clark Simmons."

"Mine or yours?"

"Yours," she said. "He's charged with vehicular homicide. The trial should be coming up soon. There's an alibi witness named Barry

Simmons—"

"Oh, right. What a sad sack, but he's all I've got. The DA has three eyewitnesses. I'm fucked."

"Well, now you don't even have Barry."

"Goddamn it! What's he charged with?"

"He's not charged with anything," she said. "But after consulting with me, he's decided not to testify for his cousin. He'd be committing perjury if he did."

"Oh fuck. Well, in that case, I won't call him."

"Thank you. Can I tell him to ignore his subpoena?"

"Yeah, I guess so. You know what really sucks?"

"What?"

"My client owes me five grand and I'm beginning to think he won't pay me. The trial is in two weeks."

It was none of her business, but she spoke anyway.

"Maybe you should ask for a continuance? You just lost a critical witness."

"Hey, I think I will. Thanks."

"Good luck, Derek." She ended the phone call.

Back inside the bar, Lee ordered a celebratory shot of Grand Marnier, another beer for Barry, and a whiskey sour for her investigator.

"Good news," she announced as she set the drinks on the table.

"Was he mad?" Barry asked, reaching for the beer.

"Of course not."

Carla put her arm around their witness' shoulder.

"So I've arranged for Barry to get his hair cut next week and we're going to buy him some clothes for the trial."

"Excellent," Lee said. "Find him a dentist as well."

"I wondered about that," Carla murmured.

"Um, I'm sorry," he said, "but I can't afford a dentist."

"It's okay," Carla told him. "We'll take care of it." She picked up her whiskey sour. "Here's to never hearing Roy Orbison sing 'Crying' ever again."

To settle a domestic violence case, Lee always contacted the victim to see if she, or occasionally he, would be helpful or hurtful to the defense. Half the time, the victim was ambivalent about prosecuting the defendant. Whatever Lee privately felt about the harm allegedly caused by her client, a reluctant victim was always good news. Prosecutors were understandably hesitant to spend their time and resources on cases where the victim was trying to recant or take responsibility for some or all of the harm. No matter how misguided the victim, it was Lee's ethical duty to take advantage of her lack of enthusiasm, and she did, often convincing the DA to either drop the case or offer her client a sweeter deal than he otherwise deserved. On the other hand, if the harm was great and the victim had been brutalized before, Lee almost always refused to take the case, a luxury she hadn't enjoyed as a public defender.

In Phil's case, Lee guessed his wife would be somewhat sympathetic to the defense but not a pushover. Her initial anger, Lee hoped, would be tempered now by feelings of guilt and loyalty. From Phil's description of his wife, Lee expected a strong, intelligent woman finally ready to divorce her husband, who wished, albeit unrealistically, that he would understand and accept her decision.

"She won't be vindictive," Phil had promised. "She'll be worried about my career. Ask her about Eleanor, our dog. She'll want to share custody. In a few years, she'll want us to be confidantes, best friends who tell each other everything. Ugh! But it'll probably end up that way. She's been my best friend since college."

"Can you continue to leave her alone?" Lee asked. "Can I promise her you'll comply with the restraining order?"

"Yeah. I mean I have to, right?"

"You do." She'd made herself sound firm. "You can't save your career unless you agree."

"Then I agree."

Lee was sitting on a black metal bench outside the entrance to the Boulder Public Library, where Judith Hartman worked. Judith had agreed to meet her at noon. She'd sounded kind on the phone, a good sign. A few minutes past noon, a pretty woman with long blond hair exited the library. She wore a green linen pantsuit that flattered her petite figure. When she saw Lee, she stopped and smiled, managing to look both innocent and sophisticated. Lee was inclined to like her.

"Are you Lee Isaacs?" she asked. She was carrying a fashionable canvas handbag on her arm.

"Thanks for agreeing to meet me."

"Not at all. Shall we go find a bench near the creek?"

Lee immediately agreed. They walked east until they spotted a bench facing the water. It was a glorious spring day, the temperature in the low seventies. Both women took off their jackets and turned their faces toward the sun. A flock of Canada geese waddled past, squawking loudly. Lee had brought two sandwiches from Alfalfas in case Judith was hungry.

After they settled themselves, Lee pulled a paper bag out of her briefcase.

"I've got hummus wrapped in a gluten-free tortilla, or a turkey, Swiss, and tomato sandwich. Which would you like?"

Judith started to shake her head, but then said, "I'll take the hummus if you don't mind." She paused to unwrap it. "Did Phil tell you I was gluten-free?"

"He did." Lee tore into the other sandwich. She'd missed breakfast and was starving.

Judith took a tiny bite and asked, "How come you took so long to call me?"

"I was waiting for your anger to evaporate, hoping it would be replaced with bittersweet memories of the past."

"Are you being serious?" Judith asked. "I've always had a hard time telling if Phil was joking or not. I think you're like him."

"I probably am. Most defense lawyers have a dry sense of humor. But in fact, I was being serious."

"I'm not sure I believe you, but I guess it doesn't matter because you're right. I'm no longer angry and I want to help. I'd feel terrible if Phil lost his job. It's all he has. He's a workaholic, one of the many reasons I don't want to be married to him any more. I still love him, but he's never going to change. His work makes him too melancholy, too sad. There has to be some lightness to balance it all out, something hopeful. Instead, it's just one dark drama after another." She stopped and sighed. "Is he all right?"

"He will be. But right now, let's see if we can save his career."

"How can I help?"

Lee then explained the various charges in the case and how she hoped to get most of them dropped.

"What I'm worried about is the harassment charge involving you, and the menacing and criminal mischief involving Bob. The burglary and trespass should never have been filed since Phil had a key and was always welcome." Lee paused. "That's true, isn't it?"

Judith thought for a moment. She wasn't stupid.

"Yes, I'd say so."

"Good," Lee said. "But if he was always welcome, how come you tried to lock him out?"

"That's easy. He was being a drunken asshole."

"No doubt, but is there another answer that would also be true, something about the timing?" Lee kept her face impassive.

Three or four seconds later, Judith nodded.

"Yes, I could say it was an inconvenient time and I was embarrassed."

"Good, let's run with that." Lee took another bite of her sandwich and said, "In the police report, you told the detectives that Phil pushed past you, trying to get at Bob."

"That's true."

"So he didn't push you, he simply pushed *past* you in an effort to catch up with Bob, who managed to elude him?"

"Right."

"So any physical contact with you was inadvertent and, in your opinion, not made with the intent to harass, annoy, or alarm you? He was just trying to get to Bob?"

"Exactly."

"When he kicked the wall, do you think he knew what he was doing?"

"No," Judith answered. "He was stinking drunk and really frustrated that Bob was able to elude him. Plus, the wall was in bad shape anyway. Actually, so was the bannister."

"You should have been a lawyer."

"That's what Phil always told me." Her face darkened. "I'm really going to miss him." She leaned down, picked up a rock, and threw it at the nearest bush. "Damn him," she muttered.

Lee gave her a moment and then said, "I'm assuming the cell phone falling into the pot of water was an accident?"

"Yes, it was."

"I appreciate your cooperation, Judith, and I've instructed Phil to have absolutely no contact until you're both ready, which might be a long time."

"Just until he accepts that we're done."

"That could be a while, Judith." Lee's voice was gentle but firm.

"Okay then." She reached into her pocket, pulled out a Kleenex, and blew her nose. "Oh, I almost forgot. Bob just wants Phil to pay for the damage to his car. The bill came to forty-eight hundred dollars, which seems like a lot, but if I were you, I wouldn't haggle. Though I'm not supposed to tell you, he doesn't want to testify. He's worried about the publicity, how it might affect his reputation."

"That's good to know."

"Yeah. Mostly he's embarrassed."

"Because he hid in your bedroom?" Lee asked.

"What a wuss. You can tell Phil I'm done with him."

"I can't. News like that would only make him hope again."

"Oh." She looked dejected. "You're right. This is hard."

"I'm sure it is." Lee waited a few seconds. "Would you be willing to come with me when I talk to the DA on Thursday? It could make a huge difference. I'll also need a statement that I can send to the Office of Attorney Regulation."

"Saying what?"

"The truth in the most helpful way you can phrase it. In addition, if you have absolutely no fear of your husband, it would be great if you would say that. Oh, and also that he's never behaved this way before."

Judith pushed a strand of hair off her lovely, troubled face.

"I can say both of them, but I'm concerned about his drinking. It's getting worse."

"Fine, I'll make alcohol counseling a condition of his probation."

"He won't like it." Judith stood up, brushing crumbs off her linen pants.

"Too bad. You're being a very good sport about this. If you think he needs counseling, I'll make it happen. It's the least I can do." Lee crushed the paper bag into a ball and stuffed it into her briefcase. "Will you come with me on Thursday?"

"I'd prefer not to. Would it really matter?"

"Yes. I'll get a better deal if you come with me."

Suddenly, a large wet dog appeared in front of them. He'd obviously been swimming in the creek and hadn't shaken himself off yet.

"Shoo," Lee said, sliding as far away as she could.

Judith immediately bent down to scratch his ears.

"Hello, big fella. You're a beauty, aren't you?"

After a couple of minutes, the dog took off and Judith straightened up again.

"I guess I owe him that much. What time is the meeting?"

"Thank you." Lee pulled out her appointment book to check. "Four-thirty. I can make it earlier if you want."

"Four-thirty's fine. I'll meet you in the cafeteria on the first floor. It's where I always met Phil. Could you at least tell him I wish him well?"

"Sure."

"You won't, will you?"

"No," Lee said. "If you're really done, you need to stay away. A complete news blackout is best."

"Thanks for your honesty, Lee. No wonder Phil thinks so highly of you. I'll see you on Thursday." She turned and started walking toward the library.

Lee watched until she disappeared around a corner. With her looks and intellect, it wouldn't be long before she found another man. But he wouldn't have Phil's dark, disturbing, funny sensibility. Would she miss it? Lee thought she would. But then again, she and Phil were *landsmen*, members of the same legal tribe that spent too much time in the underworld.

A week before the trial, Lee drove to the back of the Justice Center with Mark and Bobby in tow. Both men were uncharacteristically quiet while she parked her 4Runner in a space between two police cars. For months, she'd toyed with the idea of introducing Jeremy to her friends, but had only recently asked her client if he was interested in meeting two gay men who'd been in a relationship for thirty years.

Jeremy's response had been lukewarm.

"Are they like really old?" he'd asked.

So then Lee told him about their long and dangerous career as high altitude mountain climbers and, for good measure, hinted that they looked like fashion models—true but extremely superficial—which worked.

"Okay," he'd said quickly. "I mean if you think I should meet them."

As she turned off the ignition, Lee wondered if it was a mistake to mix her personal and professional lives. For thirty-five years, she'd scrupulously kept her clients in the dark about who she was when she wasn't their lawyer. At the last hearing, she told Jeremy more about herself than she'd ever divulged to a client. It made a huge difference and she was glad she did.

But taking her friends to meet him would further blur the lines between them. Was that a good thing as well? Normally, it wasn't. Most clients needed to look up to her as the calm and distant captain who would steer them through the rocks and shoals of the system, delivering them to a safer place. Undue familiarity could easily weaken the blind allegiance often necessary in a defendant-attorney relationship. Unlike most clients, however, Jeremy craved authenticity and closeness. He'd had enough secrecy to last the rest of his life.

Most of all, though, he needed confidence and self-esteem. Without it, he'd never withstand Dan's sly, skillful cross-examination, which could be surprisingly gentle, until it wasn't. To fight for his life, Jeremy needed to believe it was actually worth fighting for. Hence the decision to let him meet her friends, two gay men whose lives were rich and interesting and who thanked God every day for their sexuality.

After parking the car, Lee glanced at her friends.

"Well, we're here." She pointed to the stairs that led to the facility. At the top of the stairs was a plain door and a large metal buzzer.

Both men looked confused. They'd never been in a jail or prison, but like most people had seen movies and photographs depicting guard towers, massive steel gates, barbed wire, and ominous signs announcing a detention center.

"It doesn't look like much," Lee admitted, "but it's the real thing. Come on."

While they waited to be let in, Lee asked if they had any last-minute questions. They shook their heads. Both men were dressed casually, Mark in his usual jeans and blue denim shirt, Bobby in black pants and a green cashmere sweater. If she looked at them objectively, they were gorgeous. Hardly representative of any population, but they were all she had.

"Remember, he's only seventeen," she said. "Like most teenagers, he's self-absorbed, immature, and stubborn. In addition to that, he's depressed. And, as you might expect, he suffers from post-traumatic stress disorder." She smiled at them. "And yet, despite all that, he's quite delightful."

Her friends looked unconvinced.

"One last caveat: You can talk about anything you want, but don't lie to him or make empty promises. He's very sensitive and has a well-developed bullshit detector. I'm taking a chance bringing you to see him, but I think it'll be worth it." The door buzzed open. "Well, in you go."

She herded them down the hall and eventually into the room with the couch and the two metal chairs. The poster was still on the wall—"Today is the first day of the rest of your life"—although someone had scribbled "fuck that" in response. The guard, a barrel-shaped man with a crew-cut, agreed to bring her client. Her friends tried the couch and grimaced, but stayed where they were. Lee took one of the chairs.

After a couple of minutes, the guard brought Jeremy to the room. Her client stood shyly in the doorway and wouldn't come any further. He was wearing a black T-shirt with a picture of Bob Marley on the front, a pair of baggy jeans, and new purple high-tops without laces. His thick brown hair was almost too long now. Lee smiled encouragingly.

"Come on in," she said, "and meet my friends." She pointed to the two men, who looked almost as nervous as Jeremy.

"I'm Mark," Mark said, slowly standing up. "And this is my partner Bobby." Bobby stood up as well. Jeremy simply stared at them.

"Are we your first visitors?" Bobby asked.

"No, my Aunt Peggy comes three times a week." He blushed a little. "But she's, you know, my aunt."

"And Mrs. Weissmann is coming this weekend," Lee reminded him. Lee had called the old woman, identified herself as Jeremy's lawyer, and asked if she would come to Boulder on Saturday if Carla picked her up. She could meet with Lee and then see Jeremy if she wanted.

"Oh yes!" Mrs. Weissmann had replied. "I didn't think I'd ever see him again. What time should I be ready?"

There was a brief, awkward silence in the room, but Bobby broke it.

"Well, it's great to meet you, Jeremy. I've never been in a jail before. It must have been hard to get used to."

"Not really," Jeremy said.

"Oh. Well, how's the food in here?"

"I don't know. I guess it's okay." He shrugged. "Kind of salty. And the vegetables all come from a can."

"Yuck," Bobby said, making a face.

Jeremy finally smiled.

"It's not so bad. What-what else do you want to know?" He walked into the room and sat down. Mark and Bobby then lowered themselves onto the couch, which sank to the floor.

"So what do you do all day?" Mark asked.

"Not much. We get an hour in the yard if it's nice. I kind of walk around in circles. And there's television, but I don't like it. Mr. Clean says I sleep too much. So I'm beginning to read."

Bobby's face brightened.

"Have you read *Catch-22*? That was my favorite novel in high school."

"Um, I think I've heard of it."

Bobby turned to Lee and asked if he could send the book to her client.

"Sorry," she said, "it's not allowed."

"That's okay," Jeremy told them. "If I ever get out of here, I'll find a copy and read it."

The room was quiet again. Someone was coughing in the hallway. A toilet in an adjacent room suddenly flushed. Lee began counting all the cracks in the brown linoleum floor.

"Hey," Mark finally said, "would you like to hear how we almost lost our fingers and toes on Everest?"

"Sure. I guess so."

When Mark finished his story, Jeremy was silent. Most teenage boys would have asked a thousand questions: about their gear and clothing, how they stayed warm at night, what they ate, how they went to the bathroom, et cetera. As she studied her client's face, Lee tried to imagine a childhood where almost everything was prohibited—books, television, movies. The world divided into two warring camps, zealots versus heathens. *Us* and *them*, Jeremy once explained; *us* ending up in heaven of course but first living a life in hell, and *them* doing the opposite. To a boy fantasizing about just being "normal," mountain climbing would have seemed as remote and as unlikely as space travel. How could he possibly relate?

But Jeremy was trying.

"Lee said you don't climb anymore. So did you just, you know, get tired of it?"

"Are you kidding?" Mark asked, looking stupefied. "Climbing is one of the most exciting things you can imagine. Everyday life pales in comparison. When you're climbing, you feel totally alive. There's nothing like it."

"So then why did you stop?"

Bobby glanced at Lee before answering.

"Our best friend died in an avalanche. After that, we just didn't want to."

"Oh, right. So your best friend was Lee's husband?"

"How did you know?"

"Because she told me." Jeremy pointed at Lee, who nodded.

"Lee *told* you?"

"Well, duh," Jeremy said, smiling a little. "I mean, how else would I know?" But then something occurred to him and his smile faded. He sat forward and asked, "Were you, like, right there when he died?" His voice sounded strained.

"We were, yes," Mark said.

"Oh wow. Did-did you try and save him?"

"We couldn't. It all happened so fast, thousands of tons of snow traveling at about ninety miles an hour. When it all stopped, it set up like concrete. We searched until dark and then gave up."

"We came back every day for a week," Bobby added, "but we never found his body."

"Oh wow. So-so even though it wasn't your fault, did you kind of blame yourselves anyway?"

"Why would they blame themselves?" Lee asked. "It was an accident. There was nothing they could do."

"It doesn't matter," Jeremy explained. "It's just, you know, how people feel when they can't stop something bad from happening. My therapist says it's normal."

"You're right," Bobby told Jeremy. "We *did* blame ourselves. Mark's nightmares got so bad, he had to go to therapy, just like you."

"But that's terrible!" Lee said. "I never blamed you guys for a second. Why didn't you tell me?"

"You were kind of a mess," Mark answered. "You didn't want to talk about it. Besides, if you'd felt responsible too, you wouldn't have told us."

"Why would I have felt responsible?" She was beginning to feel uncomfortable.

"You wouldn't," Bobby said. "It would've been totally irrational." He was staring at Mark.

"Of course it was," Mark agreed, "but for all we know, you might have blamed yourself for never telling him how you felt about the risks involved, the danger we continually put ourselves in."

Bringing her friends and her client together might have been a mistake.

"But there was nothing to tell. I felt fine about it."

"No concerns at all, even after K2?" Mark asked. Bobby reached over to hold his hand. They were both looking at her, waiting.

Lee started to deny it, but then stopped. Why did it matter? But somehow it obviously did.

"Okay, fine. I was concerned after K2 but kept it to myself. There was an unspoken pact between us that I wanted to honor. And after a while, I mostly accepted it again."

"We kept it to ourselves, too," Mark said.

"How come?" Jeremy asked, clearly enjoying the conversation. At least somebody was.

"Well, we weren't at all sure we wanted to stop, but mainly, just like Lee, we hated to disappoint him."

"It was one of his few real flaws," Lee acknowledged. "He couldn't stand to be disappointed."

"He wasn't willing to compromise much either."

"That, too," Lee said.

"But other than that," Bobby added, "he was just so great."

"The best," Mark agreed. "And we'll miss him forever."

Lee looked at her friends and nodded.

"So, now that we've admitted Paul wasn't perfect, could we possibly talk about something else?"

Everyone laughed, including Jeremy, who seemed completely at ease.

"Well, I'm very curious about Sam," Bobby said. "Would it be all right to ask a few questions about him?"

"Sure," Jeremy replied. "I mean, if you guys really want to know."

"Absolutely," Mark said. "What was he like?"

"Truthfully, like everything I'd been dreaming of: tall and strong and really good-looking. And-and very protective. He wouldn't, for instance, let me shoplift or do anything illegal. Didn't want me to get into trouble like he did. His childhood was really crummy, much worse than mine. His dad died when he was five. A few years later, his mother married a creep who began, you know, to molest him. So then he started getting into trouble. One day, he kicked this kid in the face and the kid lost his eye. Sam felt really bad. They arrested him and sent him to juvie prison, where he worked out every day and got streetwise. He liked it better than being at home. And after that, he lived on the streets."

"Did he ever tell anyone about being molested?" Lee asked, guessing that he hadn't.

"No, I was the first person he told. We were saving up to leave Denver and start a new life in San Francisco." He smiled confidently. "I think we would have lasted like you guys did."

"Sounds like you would have," Mark said.

Lee glanced at her watch. She had thirty minutes to drop her friends off at their gym and then make it back to the courthouse for a sentencing on a kidnapping case with injuries.

"I'm really sorry, guys, but we're going to have to leave soon."

The men looked genuinely disappointed.

"Have you ever been to the Castro district in San Francisco?" Jeremy asked them.

"Oh, lots of times," Bobby replied. "We have a number of friends who live there."

"Is-is it like the way Sam said it was?"

"You mean full of gay men?" Mark asked. "Yes, it's great."

Jeremy smiled wistfully. The way, Lee thought, European Jews during the Second World War might have smiled at the idea of a homeland. A safe place where you finally fit in, where you were surrounded by people who looked and acted like you did. Maybe not paradise, but damned close.

Lee stood up, signaling the end of the visit. Mark and Bobby got to their feet as well. Finally, Jeremy stood up too.

"It was very nice to meet you," Mark said.

"Thanks for coming," Jeremy mumbled, looking shy again.

Bobby put out his hand and Jeremy shook it.

"Good luck at the trial," Bobby said.

"Thanks. We'll need it."

Because her friends looked so worried, Lee forced herself to smile.

"Hey, if there's any justice in the world, we'll win." She waited a moment. "So did that sound as idiotic as I think it did?"

No one bothered to respond.

CHAPTER FIFTEEN

Dan stood at the podium, readying himself to give his opening statement. He was dressed in a somber navy-blue suit he hoped would convey his sincerity and trustworthiness. Lee, guessing he'd wear something dark, had chosen a light, gray silk pantsuit as contrast, aiming for openness and transparency. Ladies and gentlemen, unlike our opponents, we've got nothing to hide. *Fanciful thinking?* Probably, but if even one juror was subliminally affected, it was worth it. And for a trial that mattered this much, you couldn't overlook anything.

It had taken three full days to pick a jury because the vast majority of prospective jurors had either read or heard that Jeremy had confessed and that his co-defendants had been busted after bragging about a boot party. Lee could have successfully filed for a change of venue, but never seriously considered moving the trial. Boulder was notoriously liberal compared to most jurisdictions in Colorado and, despite all the negative publicity, it was still her best bet. If there were twelve sympathetic people who might acquit her client of murder, they probably lived in Boulder.

When Lee and Phil had strategized about the perfect juror for the case, they'd both agreed she was a well-educated, bleeding-heart liberal, someone who worked outside the home but still had kids, and who made her living helping others: a doctor, lawyer, nurse, therapist, social worker, yoga instructor, teacher, librarian, et cetera. And besides all of the above, she had to be accepting of gay people; ideally, have a gay or lesbian friend or relative. In some of the nearby jurisdictions like Weld, Adams, Jefferson, or El Paso, such women existed, but good luck finding them. In Boulder, they were everywhere.

Of course, the prosecution would have engaged in similar thinking and come up with their own ideal juror: a middle-aged or older male, ex-military, conservative, religious but not seriously homophobic—he had to believe that killing a gay man was still murder. If Lee were Dan, she'd want engineers, accountants, financial analysts, bankers, blue-collar workers, and men who worked in cubicles for major corporations. Men whose hearts were unavailable for tugging.

The end result was the usual one, a jury neither side particularly liked or hated. After challenging each other's dream jurors, they were left with twelve ostensibly neutral people who swore they could be fair and impartial. Lee was pretty sure who the foreman would be, a self-assured manager at Wells Fargo whose wife was a "homemaker," but whose younger brother was gay. Dan, who still didn't know what Lee would later argue, looked surprised when she didn't strike him.

Lee sat as close to Jeremy as possible, partly to keep him calm, but mostly to demonstrate how fond she was of her client, which in this case happened to be true. Over the next two weeks, she would make a point of touching his arm and shoulder many times, another subliminal hint that her client had been wrongfully accused and wasn't at all dangerous. Although at some point the jury would see his tattoos—Lee hadn't been able to convince the court that they were irrelevant and prejudicial—for now he wore simple long-sleeved shirts that hid his arms and made him look like an ordinary schoolboy. What he still might be if his parents had come home just a few hours later that day in February.

While Dan methodically previewed the state's evidence against the defendant, Lee calmly took notes. As he described the crime scene and the various injuries suffered by the victim, a number of jurors began to frown. By the time he finished, most of the jurors would be shaking their heads and wondering why they had to sit through a whole trial before they could convict the kid and go home. If Lee was stupid enough to waive or even reserve her opening statement, she would never catch up, and the chances of an acquittal would be as likely as a snowstorm in Haiti.

As instructed, Jeremy sat quietly next to her, looking serious and interested but not worried.

"You're on stage whenever the jury is present," she'd warned. "Any signs of anger, defensiveness, or boredom will sink you. Don't blow it."

He promised he wouldn't.

Carla and Phil sat directly behind the defense table, both of them watching the jurors' faces for anything that might indicate a reluctance to follow the herd. Because she might be called as a witness, Carla had dyed her hair brown and exchanged her contact lenses for glasses. She'd wear smart professional suits throughout the trial, forgoing her usual glitter until after the jury's verdict. Phil's cast had been removed a few days earlier and his face no longer showed any signs of trauma. His heart was still shattered, but at least now it was a private affair.

Thanks to Lee and his wife, Phil's career was still viable. After much arguing, they had convinced the DA to offer a one-year deferred judgment and sentence to misdemeanor criminal mischief and menacing, naming Bob Wheeler as the victim. Because all charges against his wife would be dismissed, there would be no domestic violence designation. Based on the deal, the Office of Attorney Regulation agreed to a twelve-month suspension with all but two months stayed, which meant Phil would keep his job. As promised, Lee stipulated that her client would undergo six months of outpatient alcohol counseling.

Phil was relieved and grateful. When the one-year deferral was up, he would be eligible to seal his record. He'd work for Lee until August and then go back to the Public Defender. It was as good as it got. And although he couldn't imagine ever falling in love again, Lee suspected he would. In the meantime, there would be no shortage of women who would want to soothe and mother him, who would listen to his dark, disturbing stories with wonder and puzzlement and then try to lighten things up.

Dan was taking his time now, making eye contact with as many of the jurors as possible. He'd saved the best part for last: the three co-defendants who would take the stand and testify under oath that the defendant had actively taken part in the murder, that he'd urged the others on, that he'd kicked the victim several times, and had acted as the lookout. Finally, Dan stopped talking.

After a long pause, he said, "So you see, ladies and gentlemen, this won't be a difficult trial. Unlike some cases where the evidence is murky or conflicting, we have plenty of direct, compelling proof of the defendant's guilt. And although you might feel a bit queasy passing judgment on another human being, especially someone as young as the defendant here, it's your job to do just that: to look inside yourselves and, without sympathy or prejudice, ask if you have any reasonable doubt that the defendant aided and abetted the murder of Mr. Donnelly. If it's clear to you that he's guilty, then it's your sworn duty to say so and let the system deal with his punishment. That's all the prosecution will ask of you. Thank you."

Lee gathered her notes together and surveyed the crowd. As expected, there were representatives from numerous local and national media in the audience hoping to capitalize on the Matthew Shepard aspect of the case. How would they feel if it turned out that the real culprits had all made a deal and the only innocent person was the one on trial? It was a delicious thought, which made her smile. Besides the media, there were the usual rubbernecks who showed up at gruesome, high-profile murder cases for the free entertainment. Better than reality TV!

The rest of the benches were filled with various personnel who worked in the courthouse, a large contingent of local gay men and lesbians wearing Matthew Shepard pins, prosecutors and defense attorneys who wanted to see Dan and Lee in the ring together, and a group of strange-looking people dressed in cheap black suits and plain white dresses, each of them clutching a bible. Had Leonard sent them? He must have.

The air conditioning didn't seem to be working and everyone's faces looked flushed. A few of the religious women were fanning their faces with their bibles. From what Lee knew about Sam, she hadn't expected anyone from his family to show up, but still it was sad. A life had been brutally extinguished and there was no one here who cared, except his accused murderer. Shortly after Sam's body had been identified, the police had located his mother, who merely said she wasn't surprised at her son's violent end.

"I'm amazed he lived as long as he did," she admitted. "As a child, he was always getting into trouble. We couldn't control him."

Before the trial started, Judge Samuels had agreed to a single camera in the courtroom, the feed to be shared by all requesting media groups. Despite repeated requests for interviews, Lee had turned them all down. Years ago, both she and Dan had agreed that neither of them would make any statements to the press concerning a case they were trying. In any event, the Rules of Professional Conduct severely restricted what a lawyer could say to the press. For instance, neither side could ethically offer an opinion concerning the defendant's guilt or innocence.

After Dan settled into his chair, Judge Samuels waited a few moments before asking Lee if she intended to make an opening statement.

She stood up and said, "Yes, Your Honor."

Over the years, she'd experimented with dozens of opening statements, some of them managing to say almost nothing depending on the defense. In this case, after trying and rejecting a number of approaches, she'd decided on a straightforward story, which they'd ultimately buy or they wouldn't. She took a deep breath. For now, she'd simply tell it.

"Ladies and gentlemen," she began, "this is what the defense will prove: On his sixteenth birthday, Jeremy Matthews was living with his parents in a modest, middle-class home in Colorado Springs. His father was a self-proclaimed minister of a small fundamentalist congregation called The Word of God. Jeremy's life was an extremely sheltered one that revolved around going to school and attending almost daily church services with his parents. Unlike other kids his age, he was prohibited from watching television, reading fiction, listening to music, or attending movies unless they were appropriately 'Christian.'

"For years, Jeremy lived with a terrible secret that he hoped his parents would never discover—that he was gay. He wished he wasn't, but no matter how hard he prayed, there it was. God couldn't or wouldn't change his sexuality, even though, according to Jeremy's father, God condemned homosexuality as an abomination. And then one day, disaster: A few months after turning sixteen, his parents came home early and found him sitting in a car with another boy, kissing. Jeremy's father ordered him to leave the house forever. There was no reasoning with him. Jeremy called his best friend Ethan, crying. With Ethan's leather jacket and a hundred dollars, he decided to leave Colorado Springs for good. His childhood, he figured, was over."

Lee paused for a moment, nodding at each of the jurors. A few nodded back, a good sign. She glanced at her notes and continued.

"So Jeremy took a bus to Denver, where he stayed in a youth hostel until his money ran out. After that, he lived on the streets, rummaging through dumpsters for food, sleeping on park benches, and trying to avoid anyone who might harm him. Physically, he was cold and hungry, but mentally he was worse: generally depressed and scared, but sometimes filled with so much guilt and self-loathing that he wanted to die. One evening in early spring, he was cornered by a group of would-be attackers with knives. Part of him didn't particularly care. 'Bring it on,' he thought. 'Get it over with.'

"But a tall, dangerous-looking skinhead came to his rescue. The skinhead took him to a house where a group of them lived, and said Jeremy could stay if he wanted to. Like a stray dog who'd finally found a home. Yes, they were rough, older men who hated Jews, blacks, and homosexuals, but they were willing to take him in. Better than nothing. So Jeremy went back into the closet, dutifully shaved his head, and let them cover his arms with hateful tattoos. It didn't matter. He had a new family of sorts and, at least for the moment, he was safe.

"Weeks went by. Jeremy settled into the attic of the house, ate whatever food they gave him, and surreptitiously made friends with an old Jewish woman who lived across the street. With her encouragement, he daydreamed about going to college. And then one day, something really wonderful happened. He met Sam Donnelly, a twenty-two year old Denver skinhead who was also secretly gay.

"They started a clandestine love affair and, for the next few months, life was actually good. No, it was great. As far as Jeremy was concerned, he'd met the man of his dreams, someone who was strong, good-looking, and protective. They hid their love from the men around them, knowing—but not really—what a dangerous game they were playing. Eventually, they planned to leave Denver and start a new life in San Francisco, a city where they hoped they could be themselves. In the meantime, a deadly combination of inertia and delusion kept them tied to the only group of people they knew, their so-called brothers."

Lee shook her head and sighed.

"If only they'd saved their money and left, they'd both be alive and well today, and none of us would be here." She paused again. "But, they didn't. One evening, while Sam and Jeremy were elsewhere, the others found evidence suggesting that Sam was gay—a citation charging Sam with soliciting a male undercover police officer in Cheesman Park. Outraged, they made plans for a boot party in the mountains where they'd kick the traitor to death. If Jeremy had known, if the others had told him of their plans, he would have warned Sam and they would have run away together. But he didn't know, and so he accompanied his brothers to Boulder expecting a typical party where everyone would sit around, get drunk, and laugh.

"Eventually, they ended up on Flagstaff Mountain, where the view was magnificent. Bottles of beer and Southern Comfort were passed around and everyone began to drink. Jeremy was relaxed and happy. For an hour, nothing happened. But then, without any warning, the party turned ugly. One of the three co-defendants called Sam a 'fucking cocksucker' while another one kicked him in the back. As Sam was falling, a third one punched him in the face, breaking his nose. After that, it was awful. Jeremy could only watch in horror; he was simply too young, too weak, too helpless to stop the attack, which seemed to last forever.

"After killing Sam, they all drove back to Denver. Jeremy was in a state of shock. He felt suicidal. He'd watched his best friend, his lover, get kicked to death and hadn't been able to save him. Nothing mattered now. It was as if he'd been killed along with his boyfriend. Time passed and then the police woke him up and arrested him for the murder of his beloved Sam."

Lee took a deep breath, watching the jurors' faces for any signs of sympathy or disbelief. She worried, now that she'd heard it out loud from her own lips, that the story was too incredible to believe, that it might be dismissed as an elaborate tale concocted by the defense to explain the defendant's otherwise inexplicable behavior. God, she hoped not.

"So that's what the defense will prove," she said. "During the second half of the trial, I'll be calling numerous witnesses, including Jeremy's mother, his best friend from Colorado Springs, a bartender, and a guard at the juvenile detention facility. In a criminal case, the defendant is presumed to be innocent. The burden is on the prosecution to prove the defendant's guilt beyond a reasonable doubt, which means if you have any doubt about my client's guilt, you are required to find him not guilty.

"Who is Jeremy Matthews? Is he a seventeen-year old monster who intentionally aided and abetted the murder of Sam Donnelly, or is he a teenager who got in over his head and was unable to stop a group of older, homophobic men from killing the one person in the world he loved? Ultimately, it'll be up to you to decide. Please make the right decision. Thank you."

When Lee sat down, the judge called a twenty-minute recess, after which Dan would begin presenting his witnesses. Lee guessed he'd start chronologically with the two college students who'd found Sam's body on Flagstaff.

Phil and Carla both assured Lee that her opening had been effective.

"I mean I'm scared," Phil said, "but I think it was good." He closed his notepad and placed it face down on the bench beside him. "I've had a lot of trials where the truth was stranger than fiction, but this one takes the cake."

Lee simply nodded. Once a trial had started, it was her policy never to reveal how nervous she was to anyone, not even to the members of her team. And of course never to her client, who in this case was sitting quietly beside her, looking very grave.

"Hey, buddy," Phil told him, "you've got the best lawyer in Colorado defending you."

"What do you mean in Colorado?" Carla asked, pretending outrage. "In the country!"

Lee smiled at them and said, "I'm going to the bathroom and then I'm going outside to think. Jeremy, watch the table for me. Make sure no one touches anything."

"Okay," he said, brightening a little.

Inside the bathroom, Lee gazed at her reflection in the mirror. In a couple of weeks, whether she was ready or not, she'd turn sixty. Did she actually look that old? After turning her head from side to side, she decided no. Her face looked tan and healthy, with only five or six wrinkles and a sunspot or two. Not bad at all. Thanks to her favorite hair stylist, who was Dan's as well, her silver hair had been cut so that it swept almost carelessly past her ears. Her eyes, which looked almost black in the bathroom light, were the only giveaway. They were tired; they'd seen too many sad, unconscious people fucking up and doing terrible things. She shrugged. The cost of doing business.

As she headed down the hallway toward the stairs, she saw Dan waiting for her. He looked relaxed and confident, as if he were on vacation. Tennis anyone? Sure, Lee thought. Why not.

"Hey, Dan," she said, stopping in front of him. "What's up?"

"That was quite a story."

"Thanks." She smiled innocently. "Anything else?"

He started to laugh.

"You are so good, Lee."

"You're not so bad yourself. I'd better go, though. We don't have much time."

"Okay, fine. So at first I thought it was you. That in complete desperation, you'd imagined the perfect defense and then somehow convinced both yourself and your client it was true. But then I realized only your client could have concocted such a bizarre, unbelievable story. Upon further reflection, I wondered if he was really that clever and decided he wasn't. So then what?"

"Right," Lee said. "So then what?"

"So then I put myself in his shoes. He's scared, in pain, and in denial. How can he live with himself if the allegations are true? So they can't be true. Maybe they aren't. And so eventually he comes up with an alternate version of reality—wishful thinking about him and Sam and how he might have behaved if only he'd been a better, more principled person. How's that?"

Christ, it was brilliant. She pretended to think about it.

"Not bad."

"Not bad? Oh come on, it's brilliant."

"Okay, it's brilliant."

"That's why you're such a difficult opponent, Lee. Most of the time you actually tell the truth. It's only now and then, you don't."

She glanced at her wristwatch.

"So the upshot is . . ."

"That you're not going to win." He said it almost kindly. "You're not going to pull one last tired rabbit out of a hat. I've not only come up with a brilliant explication and defense to your defense, but I have the co-defendants' testimony and your client's statements."

"Well, you're right," she said. "Except for one thing."

"What thing?"

"The thing it always comes down to: reasonable doubt."

His shoulders slumped a little.

"I hate reasonable doubt."

"Well, of course you do. It's how I win cases. I don't have to prove that my defense is true. The jurors just have to worry that it might be."

"The evidence against him is overwhelming."

"Yes, but what if the defendant is telling the truth? If so, it would be a horrible miscarriage of justice to send him to prison for the rest of his life."

"Well, thank goodness he confessed, so we don't have to worry. Who do you think will be foreman?"

"The bank manager from Wells Fargo," she replied, "the one whose brother is gay."

"Yeah, I should have struck him."

"Why?"

"Because you didn't."

"Yes," she said, "that was a mistake." She thought for a moment and then groaned. "I asked if he liked his brother and he said he respected him, but I didn't follow up. What if he respects his brother, but doesn't actually like him? What if it all comes down to whether he likes his younger brother?"

"You know what?" He was massaging his right temple. "I think I'm getting a headache."

"Me too. We'd better get back to the trial."

"I'm going to kill myself if I lose," Dan said.

"Me too."

After the college students, Dan called two crime-scene investigators, who described finding Sam's body curled into a fetal position, his face contorted by "pain, exhaustion, and a dawning sense of despair." This last observation was clearly objectionable, but Lee remained seated. She wouldn't object to anything unless it challenged or contradicted her defense. The investigators carefully discussed what they'd found: footprints in the dirt surrounding the body, and cigarette butts, empty beer cans, and broken bottles of Southern Comfort littering the ground.

In her cross-examination, Lee emphasized that the evidence implicated the three co-defendants, and not her client.

"The footprints surrounding the body had all been made by heavy boots?" she asked the second investigator.

"From what we could tell."

"No footprints made by sneakers?"

"Well, many of the footprints were smeared and distorted by other prints on top of them."

"But from what you could tell, none of them were made by sneakers?"

"From what we could tell."

"Thank you," Lee said. "All the evidence you collected was tested by CBI, the Colorado Bureau of Investigation?"

"Correct."

"None of it could be linked to Mr. Matthews?"

The crime scene investigator hesitated.

"We didn't do the testing ourselves. You should ask one of the CBI techs."

"I will, thanks," Lee said, smiling. "But it's your understanding there was no physical evidence at the scene that could be linked to Mr. Matthews?"

"That's my understanding, yes."

The art of pulling teeth.

"Thanks. No further questions."

After lunch, Dan showed the crime-scene video. It was only eight minutes long, but it seemed to last forever. Lee, of course, had seen it many times, but the jurors hadn't. When it was over, their faces registered shock and disgust. During the last fifteen seconds, the videographer had slowly pulled her camera back from the scene. With each backward step, Sam's body got smaller and smaller until it eventually disappeared. The effect was extremely disconcerting, as if Sam's death meant very little in the scheme of things, which unfortunately was true. During the screening, Jeremy remained totally still. Afterward, Lee saw tears running down his face. She would have tried to comfort him, but worried it might look staged or disingenuous. Better to just let him cry and hope that some of the jurors noticed.

The Boulder County Coroner then testified about the various injuries Sam had suffered and opined that the cause of death was a combination of blood loss and suffocation due to broken bones. Lee had very few questions.

Finally, a forensic expert from CBI testified that the three co-defendants' DNA had been found on most of the items submitted by the Boulder Police Department. He also confirmed that Sam's blood had been found on two of the co-defendants' boots, in the car that had been impounded, and on Jeremy's sweatshirt. During Lee's cross-examination, the expert agreed that the blood on her client's sweatshirt could have come from sitting in the car sometime after the murder.

After Lee's opening statement, there had been no other surprises, but there undoubtedly would be—there always were—which was the fun and horror of trying cases. Court adjourned early at four-thirty.

When most of the spectators were gone, the guard from the juvenile detention center placed Jeremy in handcuffs. The guard, a heavyset man with a goatee, was someone new. Mr. Clean, like all of the defendants' proposed witnesses, had been sequestered. Lee approached the man and introduced herself. The guard grinned at her.

"Leroy Atkins," he said. "Pleased to meet you. Mr. Clean told me to take good care of your client." He looked at Jeremy. "The cuffs aren't too tight, are they?"

"They're fine," Jeremy said. His face looked pale and drawn. There was a large ink stain on the front of his shirt. Good thing Carla had bought him a dozen.

"Okay, good." The guard turned back to Lee. "This is a real interesting trial. I'm enjoying being here." He obviously meant well.

"So what do you think about the case?" Lee asked.

"Well, if what you told the jury was true, it would be a shame if the kid was convicted."

Phil had come up behind them.

"A shame? Is that all it would be? A shame?"

The guard looked confused.

"As you can tell," Lee said, smiling warmly, "we all feel strongly about Jeremy's innocence. Thanks for taking such good care of him. We really appreciate it."

"Sure, no problem," the guard replied.

When they were alone, Phil apologized.

"I understand," she said. "But it doesn't help to get angry."

"Sometimes it does." Then he looked contrite. "But not often. So what do you do to blow off steam?"

"That's easy. I go to the dojo and beat the crap out of as many people as possible."

Phil started laughing, and then stopped.

"You're kidding, right?"

"Only a little," she conceded.

On Friday, Dan called the clerk from the north Boulder liquor store, the one who'd identified Rab as the tall, menacing skinhead with the animal tattoo on his neck who came into the store on the night of the murder to buy beer and Southern Comfort. The clerk also identified the white car Rab was driving. "The passenger door was all bashed in from an accident." The clerk helped Rab carry the liquor out to the car and saw four more skinheads sitting inside the car, waiting. One of the passengers was obviously younger than the others.

"So you could see the passengers?" Dan asked him.

"Yes, but only for a couple of seconds. I can't identify them."

"That's okay. Did all of the skinheads have tattoos?"

"I think so, yes."

"Even the youngest one?"

"Him too. They were all kind of scary."

Lee nodded to herself. Dan, having guessed she might revisit the issue of whether Jeremy's tattoos were admissible, was eliciting as much testimony as possible concerning their relevance.

After a short recess, Dan called two waitresses from the Sapphire Lounge who'd overheard Rab, Casey, and Johnny bragging about how they'd kicked a gay man to death. Both women were pale, skinny blondes who'd worked at the lounge for more than a decade. The first one, Donna, had three kids under fifteen and worked two other jobs besides this one. She was nervous about testifying and was worried about taking time off from her day job as a maid at a Motel 6. During the preliminary questions, she made a point of checking her watch every few minutes.

"I'll be as quick as I can," Dan promised, but then took his time setting the scene and making sure she repeated everything the men had said.

"So why did you call the police?" Dan finally asked.

"Do I have to say?" She looked embarrassed.

Judge Samuels cleared his throat and said, "Unless it's going to get you in trouble."

"Oh no," she replied, "nothing like that."

"Then you have to answer the question," the judge said.

"Okay, so the truth is, my ex-husband was gay. He died a few years ago from AIDS. Right before he died, he called to say he was sorry and wished things had gone differently between us. I kept thinking about him while those jerks were yukking it up. Usually, I tune out what my customers are saying, but this time I couldn't. So I called."

The other waitress, Joy, had a scar running down the side of her face, a souvenir from a boyfriend now serving time in prison.

After being sworn in, she stated, "I don't really want to be here. I'm scared for my safety."

"I understand," Dan said, "but as I've already told you, the men in the bar have all pleaded guilty and been sentenced to forty-eight years. No one's going to hurt you."

"Yeah, well, I'm still scared. I mean, they have friends, right?" She fingered the scar on her cheek. "I'm thinking about moving away, but I don't want to say where."

Dan hid his annoyance well.

"That's fine, although I think you're safe where you are."

"You don't know those guys."

"Tell me about them." He knew Lee would ask if he didn't.

"Well, let's see. Casey's just plain crazy. Half the time, he comes in barefoot, even when it's snowing. And Johnny? Johnny's mean. But it's Rab who's the most dangerous. If he says he's going to hurt someone, he means it. They all do what he says."

"So Rab's the leader?"

"Uh-huh, yeah." Suddenly, she started coughing.

"Would you like some water?" the judge asked.

"No thanks. I cough all the time. It used to drive my boyfriend crazy." She coughed for another five seconds and then stopped. "I think I'm all right now."

"Are you sure?" the judge asked.

"Yeah, I should probably stop smoking. My mom died of emphysema."

Dan was pretending to study his notes. Finally, he looked up and pointed at Jeremy.

"Have you ever seen the defendant before?"

The witness squinted toward the defense table.

"I think so, although he looked really different then."

"How so?"

"Well, his head was shaved and he looked a lot thinner, like he never got enough to eat."

"Was he friends with the guys we've been talking about?"

"Definitely."

"Did he have tattoos similar to the ones they had?"

"Uh-huh, but he wasn't nearly as creepy. He was real quiet. Actually, I thought maybe he was Rab's younger brother."

"Really? How come?"

"Oh, I don't know. He just kind of stuck close to him."

At the end of his examination, Dan assured her again she was safe. The witness looked doubtful.

"Well, I sure hope you're right."

Lee waited until Dan sat down and then slowly walked to the podium.

"Sounds like you've had too many experiences with violent men," Lee said.

The witness smiled ruefully and answered, "I've definitely had my share."

"The three men we've been talking about—they're really dangerous, aren't they?"

"Uh-huh, yeah."

"They wouldn't be easy to stand up to."

"No, they wouldn't."

Lee looked back toward the defense table. Both Phil and Carla were leaning forward in their seats, their hands resting on Jeremy's shoulders. It was hard to tell if he even noticed.

"Joy, this is important. Are you sure my client wasn't at the Lounge on the night the others were bragging about the boot party?" She'd interviewed the witness, of course, and knew what she'd say.

"Yes, I'm sure."

"Did the others mention anything about my client's involvement in the murder?"

"No."

"Did they say anything about anyone helping them murder the victim?"

"No."

"Did they say that anyone acted as the lookout?"

"No."

"Did you get the sense the three men had acted alone?"

"Yes."

So far so good, but Lee wanted more.

"So the three older men seemed violent and dangerous to you?"

"Definitely."

"Which is why you're still afraid of them?"

"Exactly."

"Did Jeremy seem dangerous too, or did he seem different?"

"Different."

"Did he in fact seem kind of gentle?" She was taking a little bit of a chance here.

The witness glanced at Dan before turning back to Lee.

"Yeah, he did seem kind of gentle."

"Thanks very much," Lee said. "No further questions."

Detective Bruno was Dan's advisory witness, which meant he'd been sitting next to Dan at the prosecution table since the first day. Years ago, Dan had confessed to Lee how much he disliked the detective, but during a trial, no juror would have guessed Dan's feelings. He was unfailingly polite to his advisory witness and listened attentively to his many suggestions. As soon as Dan called Detective Bruno to the stand, Lee asked if she and Dan could approach the bench.

"You may," the judge said.

Once they were huddled together, Lee whispered, "I'd like to make further argument concerning the admissibility of my client's tattoos."

"I object, Your Honor," Dan said. "We've argued this already and the court has made its ruling."

"We have a supplemental brief," Lee told them, "and a number of new arguments. If nothing else, I need to make a record for appeal." She handed a sheaf of papers to the judge and a copy to Dan, who was frowning and pretending to be surprised.

"Judge," he said. "I thought this was already settled."

The judge skimmed through Lee's brief, which Phil had drafted the night before, and then nodded.

"I doubt that I'll change my ruling, but I'll allow further argument. Mr. Andrews, if you'd like, you can have until Monday to write a response."

"Thank you, Judge."

"Can you wait until Monday before asking the detective about the defendant's tattoos?"

"I don't want to, but I can."

The judge smiled and said, "I appreciate your flexibility, Mr. Andrews. So, this is what we'll do. First thing Monday morning, before the jury comes in, Ms. Isaacs can make her record. Mr. Andrews can submit his response and then I'll make my ruling. Are we clear?"

"Yes, Your Honor," they said.

"Excellent. It's such a pleasure when both sides act like grown-ups."

Dan spent the rest of the day questioning Detective Bruno about his role in the case. The detective's answers were certain and matter-of-fact. No jokes, no mistakes. He wanted to win as much as Dan did.

When court was adjourned for the weekend, Lee asked Leroy, who'd volunteered to be Jeremy's guard for the rest of the trial, if she could speak privately with her client.

"Sure. Take your time. I'm really enjoying this case."

"Glad to hear it," Lee said. Good thing Phil had already left the courtroom.

Leroy wandered to the side of the room and leaned against a wall. Lee turned to her client, who was sitting quietly, staring straight ahead. For the last few days, Jeremy hadn't said a word. Except for his tears during the video, he'd shown no emotion. One way that many of her clients dealt with being on trial was to dissociate: I'm not here, this isn't happening to me. Lee guessed Jeremy had chosen this way as well. For now it was fine, but when it was time to testify, he needed to be extremely, excruciatingly present.

"Hey," she said, sitting down beside him.

He didn't respond.

"Jeremy, I know how difficult this is. No, actually, I don't. But I can imagine."

His face looked so haggard, it was hard, even for Lee, not to just grab him and pull him close.

"Do you believe in God?" he asked suddenly.

Six months earlier, his father had asked her the same thing. She'd been flippant then, but she wouldn't be now.

"I don't know. I don't think so. Do you?"

"For the first time in my life, I'm not sure. God and prayer were always part of our lives. We prayed every day: at services, before meals, on holidays, at bedtime. Every other word out of my father's mouth was God. Whatever happened was God's will. If there was, like, a hurricane in Florida, praise God. If there was a massacre in the Middle East, praise God. Even when God wouldn't make me heterosexual, I-I never questioned whether he existed or not, although it was kind of hard to praise him.

"When I lived in Denver, I still prayed every night, but of course I didn't tell anyone. My brothers would have laughed their heads off. And then, you know, when I met Sam, I thanked God all the time. It-it wasn't until the night Sam died that I wondered if there really was a God, or whether he was my father's God after all. A God who punished gays and everyone else who displeased him, a mean and nasty God. So then, I just stopped praying. Every night in jail, I think I'm going to start, but then I don't. Maybe I'm still too angry but maybe, I don't know, maybe I just don't believe in him anymore."

At first, Lee was speechless. What could she possibly say that wouldn't sound like bullshit? Jeremy's agony was real. *I'm just your lawyer,* she wanted to say. *This isn't within the realm of my expertise.* But he was waiting. Finally, she thought of something.

"Do you know the story of Job?" she asked.

"Of course."

"Well, I studied it in college. Back then, I was concerned with the question it was supposed to answer: Why do bad things happen to good people? But when Job demands to know, God yells at him and says that humans can't possibly understand what he is doing. And somehow this satisfies Job and he stops questioning his fate. To me, it made no sense."

"Yes, that's how my father explained it. God is beyond our understanding, so humans have no right to question him."

"Well, that's not very satisfying. I remember thinking that if God existed, he was a jerk, especially because he'd made Job suffer on purpose."

Jeremy was beginning to smile.

"But we're not supposed to judge God because God is . . ."

"Incomprehensible," Lee finished. "To me, what's weird is how Job doesn't abandon his faith in God. He just accepts that he can't possibly understand what God is doing and stops complaining. Although, at the end, God makes his life better again." She made a face. "I don't get it."

"Yeah," he said, crossing his arms, "neither do I."

"So the question is: Would you rather have an incomprehensible God or no God at all?"

Suddenly, Jeremy looked confused.

He uncrossed his arms and asked, "Is-is that my only choice?"

Was it? Almost nothing in Lee's world was ever simply black or white. If it were, she'd have been out of a job a long time ago. She'd just have to dig deeper.

"Well, maybe not," she said. "Maybe the author of the story wanted us to stop blaming God when things go badly and to stop thinking that whatever happens is God's will." She was kind of making things up now, but what the hell. "Maybe the author wanted us to change our conception of God altogether."

Jeremy was listening hard.

"And so," she continued, "it's only when we want a personal God that we can pray to or to blame that God seems incomprehensible. But if we imagine God more like the intelligence behind creation, which has nothing to do with whether people suffer or not, then that kind of God can be appreciated by anyone who stands in awe of the universe." Wow, she thought, that's pretty good. "In which case, God isn't someone you know. It's something you're part of." She looked to Jeremy to see if he agreed. He didn't.

"But God talks to Job."

Whoops. She'd gone too far. Maybe asking your agnostic lawyer about God wasn't such a great idea after all.

"That's absolutely true," she said, nodding. "So I guess it's back to whether you want a God you can't understand or no God at all."

Jeremy was silent for almost a minute.

"You know what, Lee?"

"What?"

"I think I'm too young to decide."

"Well, of course you are." And for the first time in her long career, she willingly hugged a client.

CHAPTER SIXTEEN

In the law, nothing stays put. Anything that seems final isn't. Appellate courts issue rulings that are contrary to settled precedent; new facts pop up requiring further argument; a party to a lawsuit thinks of yet another reason why the judge should reverse an order. Motions for reconsideration are filed, argued, decided, appealed, reargued, decided again, and appealed once more. Like the ultimate scene in *Fatal Attraction*, when Michael Douglas drowns Glenn Close in the bathtub and we think she's finally dead. Forty seconds later, she rears up again, gasping, and the fight begins again.

On Monday morning, Judge Samuels heard further argument concerning the admissibility of Jeremy's tattoos. As promised, Lee offered new reasons why her client's tattoos shouldn't be revealed to the jury, including an assertion that because the evidence was being offered for its expressive content, its admission would violate the defendant's Fifth Amendment right against self-incrimination. Dan had done his homework, however, arguing that even if the evidence was testimonial, it wasn't the product of government compulsion.

After an hour, the judge put up his hand.

"Enough," he told them. "I'm ready to make my ruling."

Both sides sat down. Lee expected to lose, but she'd made her record for appeal. Although Phil's brief was well written and persuasive, Dan's was better, and the law was on his side.

"All right," the judge said, removing his glasses and pinching the bridge of his nose. "The issue, once again, is whether the prosecution can show pictures of the defendant's tattoos to the jury without violating the rules of evidence or the Constitution. First of all, the tattoos are highly relevant to prove the defendant's allegiance to the skinheads and to show that he and his co-defendants all shared the same values. The evidence is also relevant because it makes it more probable that the defendant possessed the requisite intent. Although the tattoos are certainly prejudicial, their probative value is not, in my opinion, substantially outweighed by the danger of unfair prejudice. Secondly, contrary to Ms. Isaac's contention, the tattoos are not being offered to prove the defendant's bad character; instead, they're part and parcel of the criminal episode and are admissible as *res gestae*."

The judge paused to eat a couple of blueberries, his newest healthy snack.

"All right, concerning the defendant's Fifth Amendment argument, the tattoos do seem testimonial in nature, but as Mr. Andrews pointed out, they were not compelled; nobody forced the defendant to cover his arms with incriminating words and pictures. In the absence of government compulsion, the defendant's Fifth Amendment claim fails.

"Finally, revealing the defendant's tattoos to the jury does not undermine his constitutional presumption of innocence." He paused. "Okay, I think that covers it." He nodded toward Dan and Detective Bruno. "As soon as the jury is seated, you may resume your case."

After Detective Bruno finished testifying about finding Jeremy in the attic and arresting him, Dan pulled out a number of 8 x 12 inch photographs from one of his trial notebooks and asked if he could approach the witness. When he was standing in front of the detective, Dan handed him the pictures.

"Detective Bruno, can you identify these photographs and describe them for the jury?"

"Certainly. They're photographs of the defendant on the night I arrested him. I took them myself, mostly to document the various tattoos on his arms and to memorialize the way he looked in case he later changed his appearance for trial."

Sweat dripped silently down the sides of Lee's blouse but, to judge by the expression on her face, she remained unconcerned. Dissemble or find another profession. Although Jeremy's body sat beside her, his mind had clearly slipped its bonds and fled. In an alternate universe, he was walking hand in hand with Sam through the streets of San Francisco.

"Judge," Dan said, "may I show the photographs to the jury?"

"You may."

As each of the jurors looked at the pictures, their expressions tightened. Some glanced at Jeremy and then back to the photographs, making sure there was no mistake; there wasn't. The gaunt kid with the shaved head and the odious tattoos was in fact the defendant.

When Lee finished her cross, Dan called Detective Armstrong to testify concerning Jeremy's demeanor on his way to the juvenile detention facility and his demand to be incarcerated with his "brothers." Lee's questions focused on how naïve and childish he'd seemed, and the detective tended to agree. A tiny bone, for sure, but she'd take it.

At noon when he stood up to leave, Dan looked positively merry. He was on a roll now. He'd saved the jailhouse snitch and the three co-defendants for last. On their way out of the courtroom, the jurors no longer glanced at Lee and Jeremy, which was always a bad sign.

In his direct examination of the snitch, Dan took a long time reviewing the witness' prior criminal history. It was a typical preemptive move meant to take a little of the sting out; Lee would go over it again in detail but, by then, the jury would already have heard it.

Like Jeremy, the snitch had let his hair grow out in jail, but unlike Jeremy, he didn't necessarily look better. His reddish-brown hair was combed straight back from his forehead. With his small nose and sharp features, he reminded Lee of the ferret her father had brought home to surprise her and her mother. Both of them thought the animal smelled funny. A few days later, her father agreed and they gave the ferret away.

According to the snitch, the three co-defendants were definitely at the party where Sam's "secret" was discovered. The defendant could very well have been there too, but the snitch wasn't sure.

"It's real possible, but I'm not positive."

Toward the end of his examination, Dan focused on Jeremy's connection to the skinheads.

"When you saw Casey, Rab, and Johnny, was the defendant almost always with them?"

"Um, yeah. He was a definite part of their gang."

"Did you spend a lot of time with the defendant?"

"Well, not a lot of time, but enough to know that he, um, shared the same feelings as the others." He'd been well coached.

Dan nodded approvingly.

"What do you mean by 'the same feelings'?"

"Um yeah, so like he was prejudiced against Blacks, Jews, and faggots. Homosexuals." He paused to think. "And, um, he made cracks about them, just like we all did."

Dan flipped to the next page of his notes.

"Mr. Heller, did you ever see the defendant and Sam hanging out together?"

"Now and then. Not often."

"Did they seem to be especially close?"

"Um, no. Not really."

"Did you ever get the feeling they were romantically involved?"

"No way. Uh-uh. They hardly talked to each other. Sam was a lot older. The kid was, you know, just a kid. None of us paid much attention to him."

"The defense says they were lovers."

"Uh-uh. No way. Sam was my roommate. I would have known. No way."

"Thank you," Dan said. "The defendant's attorney will now be asking you many of the same questions. Pay attention and answer them as truthfully as you can."

Time to make a fuss.

"Objection," Lee said. "The prosecutor has no business reminding the witness that if he isn't careful, the jury will realize how much coaching he's had."

"Objection, Your Honor!" Dan sounded genuinely angry. "I'd ask the Court to admonish Ms. Isaacs for her gratuitous remarks and instruct the jury to ignore them."

Judge Samuels nodded in agreement.

"Ms. Isaacs, please refrain from expressing your personal feelings concerning the witness' veracity, which are, of course, irrelevant. I am hereby instructing the jury to ignore your comments."

"Thank you, Your Honor," Dan said.

"And Mr. Andrews, please refrain from reminding your witnesses to pay attention and to answer the questions truthfully. All witnesses take an oath to tell the truth. It isn't necessary for you to remind them."

Lee smiled at the judge and thanked him. As soon as Dan sat down, she headed for the podium.

"Mr. Heller," she said, "which events are easier to remember—those that just happened, or those that happened a long time ago?"

"Um, those that just happened?"

"Very good. Now, when you first approached the DA for a deal, you were in the Boulder County jail facing charges of second-degree burglary?"

"Um, yeah."

"And that was back in December?"

"I think so, yeah."

"And the party where Sam's secret was discovered happened at the beginning of October?"

"I think so, yeah."

"So when you first talked to the DA, the party had happened about two months earlier?"

"Um, right."

"And in that first interview with the DA, which was taped, the DA asked if Jeremy was present at the party."

The witness glanced at Dan, who refused to make eye contact.

"I'm not sure."

Lee pointed to a portable CD player Phil had set up on the defense table.

"Do you need me to play the interview to refresh your memory?"

"Um no, I think you're right."

"So during that first interview in December, when the DA asked if Jeremy was present at the party, you said, 'I don't think so. I'm just not sure.'"

"Right, I wasn't sure."

A less experienced lawyer might have continued to belabor the difference, but Lee knew better. She spent the next hour discussing the witness' lengthy criminal history and the deal he'd made with the DA: eight years community corrections instead of prison. After that, she jumped around, asking about the witness' connections to the skinheads, his own hatred of homosexuals, how he survived by stealing, and what he knew about Sam, which wasn't much.

Finally, she closed her notebook. The rest would be easy.

"So the truth is, you and Sam weren't close?"

"Um, not really, no."

"Not like Casey, Rab, and Johnny, who were your real friends?"

"Yeah, I guess so."

"And yet you made a deal with the DA to rat them out?"

The witness began rocking back and forth.

"They'd already been arrested. They were going down anyway."

"Mr. Heller, if you'd been called to testify against Casey, Rab, and Johnny—your three 'real' friends—you would have described how they found the evidence that Sam was homosexual?"

"Yeah, so what?"

"You would have testified that the four of you were outraged that Sam was a homosexual and had kept it from you."

"Yeah." He stifled a yawn.

"You would have testified that the four of you began talking about having a boot party to kill the traitor."

"Uh-uh. Not me. Them. I just, you know, stuck around and listened."

"But you were there and knew what they were planning?"

"Um, I wasn't sure. I thought maybe they were just gonna fuck him up. You know, hurt him but not kill him."

"During that first interview with the DA, you said you thought they meant to kill him."

"Okay, yeah, but I wasn't like positive." His forehead was shiny with sweat.

Lee studied him for a moment.

"What if Casey, Rab, and Johnny come in and testify that you actually helped them plan Sam's murder?"

"That's a fucking lie! I never said a word. I just listened. The DA believed me."

"Maybe he shouldn't have."

"Objection!" Dan shouted.

"Fine," Lee said. "I'll withdraw the remark." Then turned back to the witness. "So you knew that the three men were going to murder your roommate."

"That's what they said. They might have been kidding."

"But you told the DA you believed them."

"Okay, yeah, I did."

Lee was half-turned toward the jurors.

"And even though you believed them, you didn't call the police?"

"Oh yeah, right. They would have found out and killed me."

"When you heard what happened, did you call the police then?"

"Jesus, how many times do I have to say it? I was afraid of them. You would have been too."

Lee was looking straight at the jury now.

"So it wasn't until you got charged with a felony home-invasion, and were facing up to twelve years in prison, that you were suddenly willing to help the DA bring the perpetrators to justice?"

"Yeah, after they were in jail."

"Mr. Heller, you had a week to warn your roommate before the murder."

"Yeah, well, I was mad. He lied to me."

Lee collected her notes from the podium, then looked up and said, "You could have saved his life."

"Yeah, well, he lied." He crossed his arms, tried to look belligerent.

She continued to stare at him.

Finally, the judge spoke.

"Any more questions, Ms. Isaacs?"

"No," she said. "I'm done."

Lee figured it would take all of Tuesday, Wednesday, and Thursday for the direct and cross-examination of the three co-defendants, but just in case, she instructed Carla to have Mary Matthews and Ethan Mitchell, the first two defense witnesses available starting Wednesday afternoon. You never wanted the jury, for even a second, to think you were unprepared.

Much of the timing, of course, would depend on how well Dan had prepped his witnesses. If Lee were Dan, she would order each of the co-defendants to admit everything, no matter how bad it sounded: Yes, I have an atrocious criminal history; yes, I agreed to a forty-eight year sentence in exchange for my testimony; yes, I hate homosexuals, Jews, all non-white people, and women who identify as feminists; yes, I planned to kill Sam Donnelly; yes, I helped kick Sam to death; yes, I was drunk but knew what I was doing; yes, after killing Sam, I went to a bar and bragged about it.

And that's exactly how it went with Casey and then Johnny. Since their arrest almost eight months earlier, both men had continued to shave their heads, anticipating the day they'd be welcomed by the white supremacists in prison. In the meantime, each had added a teardrop tattoo beneath his right eye to signify having killed someone. In their future home, it would lend them gravitas. On direct examination, both men readily acknowledged the crimes they'd committed, the harm they'd caused, their hatred of practically everyone, and their lack of remorse about the murder. In a strange and awful way, they came off as quite believable. Dan had outdone himself.

Lee's cross-examinations took hours but lacked the power and punch she'd hoped for. Both were "pretty sure" Jeremy had attended the party where they'd planned Sam's murder, but it didn't matter since "the kid knew what was gonna happen and was down with it." During the murder, he'd kicked the victim numerous times, shouted his encouragement, and later acted as the lookout. In the car on the way home, he'd "whooped and yelled with the rest of us."

Coaching sociopaths can be difficult, so Dan had kept it simple, advising them to agree with almost everything Lee suggested and to keep on insisting they were telling the truth.

Lee: "Eight months ago, you were facing a charge of first-degree murder?"

Johnny: "Right."

Lee: "A charge that carried a life sentence without the possibility of parole?"

Johnny: "Right."

Lee: "Which meant you'd spend the rest of your life in prison?"

Johnny: "Right."

Lee: "The evidence of your guilt was overwhelming?"

Johnny: "I guess so, yeah."

Lee: "You guess so? Your DNA was found at the murder scene, Sam's blood was on the tip of your boot, a snitch heard you planning the murder, and numerous witnesses overheard you bragging about it afterward."

Johnny: "Okay, yeah, you're right."

Lee: "So you really wanted a deal?"

Johnny: "Yeah, I did."

Lee: "Something less than life in prison?"

Johnny: "Right."

Lee: "But for a long time, the DA wouldn't offer you anything?"

Johnny: "Right."

Lee: "So you waited?"

Johnny: "Yeah, we did."

Lee: "And eventually the DA offered your lawyer a deal?"

Johnny: "Right."

Lee: "Second-degree murder with a stipulation to forty-eight years in prison?"

Johnny: "Right."

Lee: "Which was better than life without parole?"

Johnny: "Uh-huh, yeah."

Lee: "And so you said yes to the deal?"

Johnny: "We all did, yeah."

Lee: "And as part of the deal, you agreed to help the DA convict Mr. Matthews?"

Johnny: "Yeah, by telling the truth."

Lee: "And if you'd refused to help, there would be no deal?"

Johnny: "Right, there would be no deal."

Lee: "Now, before you got the deal, your lawyer had to give the DA an offer of proof of what you'd say at Mr. Matthews' trial?"

Johnny: "Yeah, which would be the truth."

Lee: "And the offer of proof spelled out all the ways you would say that Mr. Matthews was guilty?"

Johnny: "Right, the truth."

Lee: "And if you'd insisted Mr. Matthews was innocent, there would be no deal?"

Johnny: "Right, but it wouldn't be true."

Lee: "And without a deal, you'd end up doing life in prison?"

Johnny: "Right."

Lee: "So the deal required that you say exactly what your lawyer promised you'd say?"

Johnny: "Right, the truth."

Lee: "And when the deal papers said you had to be truthful, it meant you had to say what your lawyer promised you'd say?"

Johnny: "Yeah, right, the truth."

Lee: "Yeah, right, the truth. No further questions."

She sat down pretending to be satisfied, but wasn't. She'd cross-examined both witnesses on their extensive criminal history, on the various times they'd lied to victims, probation officers, police, and district attorneys, on their admiration of Nazis and other fascists, on each and every injury found during the victim's autopsy, and on their complete lack of remorse for what they'd done. She'd been thorough, dogged, and caustic, but somehow hadn't demolished them. After she was finished, they'd each had enough strength to scuttle away.

It was close to noon on Wednesday and Dan was looking pleased—two co-defendants down and one more waiting in the wings. The witnesses couldn't have been more despicable, but they'd accomplished what he'd hoped. The jurors hadn't liked the two men and were certainly skeptical of their motives, but they'd listened to their testimony. As far as Dan was concerned, he'd just put two more bent and rusty nails in the defendant's coffin.

Lee needed to do better with the final witness, but how? Dramatic accusations only happened on television. In court, they almost always backfired. Lee was an excellent attorney, which meant she never took a major risk unless she had to.

She was still thinking when Dan stood up and said, "The prosecution rests, Your Honor."

Out in the hallway, Lee caught up to Dan. She'd had to run to catch him.

"Hey," she said, "what happened to Rab?"

He pretended not to understand.

"Rab?"

"Your last witness against my client? The leader of the pack?"

"Ah yes, Rab." He shrugged. "Well, in our last conversation four hours ago, he said he didn't feel like testifying."

"I see. Did he say anything else?"

"Not much." Dan took off his suit jacket and draped it carefully over his arm. His blue pinstriped shirt, like all his clothes, looked fresh and crisp, as if it had never been worn before. "He said I had plenty of evidence to convict 'the little faggot,' so his testimony would only be redundant."

"Did he actually use the word 'redundant'?"

"He did. He's very smart. And scary."

"That's what I've heard. Did you threaten to revoke his deal?"

"Of course." Dan ran a hand through his gray, expertly cut hair.

"And how did he respond?"

"He said he didn't care, that with his propensity for violence, he would probably die in prison, whether he was doing life or forty-eight years. He guessed, however, that I wouldn't do anything."

"And will you?" she asked.

"I don't know. He's right. I don't really need him. If necessary, I might call him as a rebuttal witness after your client testifies. Or maybe I'll just let him be. He's kind of a creepy dude. So, who's your first witness? Mary Matthews?"

"I haven't decided yet."

"Well, FYI, I saw her husband wandering around the courthouse."

"Huh, I wasn't sure he'd make it."

Shit! What the hell was Leonard doing at the courthouse? Was Mary going to try to wriggle out of testifying? If so, Lee would threaten her with contempt. Would that be enough?

"Lee?" Dan said.

"Oh, I was just thinking about lunch. I'm starving."

"Tell me about it. My wife and I just started on the Paleo Diet. No more bread and pasta."

"Bummer," she said and then looked at her watch. "Well, I'd better go." She headed down the hallway to search for Leonard and Mary, America's foremost model parents, her stomach too knotted up to handle lunch anyway.

***

It took forty minutes to find Leonard and Mary hiding in one of the small attorney-client conference rooms on the first floor. Leonard had been talking to someone on his cell phone but closed it as soon as Lee walked in.

"Hi, folks," she said, sitting down across from them.

Leonard put his arm around Mary and pulled her close to him.

"My wife won't be testifying after all." Like his followers, he was wearing a black suit, but his was obviously expensive. His white hair had been carefully slicked back using some kind of gel.

"She has to. She's under subpoena."

"Doesn't matter," Leonard said. "I'm claiming spousal privilege to prevent her from testifying against me."

Mary's face looked pinched and tired, as if she hadn't slept. Her hair was uncombed and her pretty blue dress needed ironing.

"I'm sorry, Lee. I wanted to help, but Leonard just won't let me."

Lee counted to ten before speaking directly to Mary.

"Okay, so here's the deal. The spousal privilege doesn't apply unless Leonard has been charged with a crime. Since throwing a child out of your home for being gay isn't against the law, he hasn't been charged with anything. So there's no way he can legally prevent you from testifying. If you still refuse to cooperate, I'll ask Judge Samuels to hold you in contempt and to throw you in jail until you change your mind."

Mary turned to her husband and said, "I don't want to go to jail, Leonard."

Leonard glared at Lee.

"She's lying, Mary. No judge is going to throw an innocent, middle-class white woman in jail."

"I'm not lying," Lee said. "If I ask the judge to hold her in contempt, he will. Don't underestimate me, Leonard. I'll do everything I can to get your wife to testify. My client's future depends upon it."

Mary struggled away from her husband.

"Leonard, please. I told you I had to testify. I don't want to risk going to jail. I'm just going to tell the truth, that homosexuality is against our religion. We loved him, but we had to throw him out." She stared at her husband. "Or at least I loved him."

Lee stood up and said, "We have to go, Mary."

Mary stood up as well.

"I'm sorry, Leonard."

"There will be consequences, Mary."

"Oh, I know," she said wearily.

On their way upstairs, it took everything Lee had to keep her mouth shut. It wasn't her job to counsel witnesses to leave their husbands. Peggy had tried numerous times with Mary and failed. When the trial was over, she'd probably never see her baby sister again.

Carla was pacing back and forth in front of the courtroom. When she saw the two of them, she looked at Lee, who glanced briefly at the ceiling. Carla nodded her understanding.

"Well there you are," Carla said, taking Mary's arm. "I've been trying to contact you for hours. I'm so glad you got here in time." She made a motion for Lee to go inside. "We'll be fine until you call us."

As soon as Mary took the stand, Leonard entered the courtroom and stood in the doorway, making sure his wife could see him. After a couple of minutes, he finally sat down in the back row. Lee kept her questions short and to the point. At first, Mary spoke in a monotone, but eventually sat up straighter and answered the questions with feeling. Occasionally, she glanced toward the defense table, her face suffused with so much longing and regret, it was hard to watch. Jeremy, at least, was spared from seeing it. He was long gone, making love with Sam on a beach somewhere, or maybe sampling cookies at a popular bakery on Castro Street that Mark and Bobby raved about.

When Lee asked about Jeremy's upbringing, Mary said it was strict but loving.

Then Lee asked her to describe her son, hoping she wouldn't cry.

"He was a beautiful, gentle boy," Mary answered. "He never got in fights, was never disrespectful. He was kind and funny. He wasn't prejudiced against gays, but he didn't want to be one. He just was." She looked down for a moment and then up again, defiant. "I-I loved him very much. I still do."

When Lee asked her to describe the day they threw him out, she winced and then recounted how she and Leonard found their son kissing another boy, her husband's reaction, and then what happened afterward.

"Was that the last interaction you had with your son?" Lee finally asked.

Mary nodded, a tear rolling down her cheek.

"Yes." She sounded tired and defeated. "I know he had to go, but—but why so fast?" She was obviously addressing her husband, who was now walking out of the courtroom.

"Thank you," Lee said quickly. "No further questions."

Dan stood up and shrugged.

"Nothing from the People," he said, hoping to convey that the witness' testimony wasn't important enough to be subjected to prosecutorial questioning.

Lee guessed he wouldn't cross-examine any of her witnesses unless it was absolutely necessary.

After Mary left the courtroom, Lee checked to see how Jeremy was doing.

"You okay?"

"Not really," he admitted. "I wasn't even sure she'd come."

"Someday it's not going to hurt so much." She put a tentative hand on his shoulder.

"Are you sure?"

"No," Lee said. "I'm not."

The next two witnesses for the defense were Ethan Mitchell and Peggy O'Neill. Lee took her time with both of them, figuring Dan wouldn't question either one of them. Ethan testified about Jeremy's childhood, his non-violent character, his lack of prejudice and, finally, about the night he was thrown out of his home and took a bus to Denver. Ethan did so well that a number of jurors uncrossed their arms and looked a bit more receptive, which was all Lee could hope for. In a case like this, it was brick by brick till she'd constructed something credible and sturdy enough to be considered a reasonable doubt.

When Peggy first took the stand, Lee asked her to describe the Matthews household. For the next ten minutes, the witness painted a vivid picture of a family ruled by an autocratic father who had become increasingly irrational and controlling, especially concerning matters of religion.

"My sister is obviously under his thumb," Peggy concluded, "and I fear she'll never leave him."

As soon as Lee asked about her nephew, Peggy's demeanor softened. She vouched for Jeremy's non-violent character and his acceptance of different kinds of people.

"Unlike his father, he's never been hateful or bigoted."

When Lee asked about the night Jeremy came to see her, Peggy described a boy who was shivering with cold and emotionally devastated.

"He couldn't even make eye-contact."

At the end of her testimony, she said, "I didn't call the police because he wasn't missing. He'd been thrown out and didn't want to go back home. In hindsight, I should have called them anyway. The truth is, I kept hoping he'd come to his senses and live with me." She turned to the jury. "If you acquit him, he's going to stay with me and finish school in Boulder."

A few more jurors uncrossed their arms, which didn't mean they'd acquit the defendant, but it meant they were thinking. That the case was no longer a simple slam-dunk for the prosecution.

When Lee was finished, Dan waved a dismissive hand toward the witness.

"Again, nothing from the People." But then he changed his mind. "Actually, wait a minute, I think I will ask a couple of questions. Sorry, Judge."

As Dan walked to the podium, he regarded Peggy and said, "So let me get this straight: After he was tossed out of his home in Colorado Springs, you offered the defendant a place to live with the promise that you would take care of him?"

"Yes, but he—"

"But he turned you down?"

"Right," Peggy said. "Because he was too ashamed to stay."

"So, unlike most kids on the street," Dan continued, "the defendant actually had a safe, loving alternative?"

"But he didn't feel like he deserved it. He'd been thrown out for being gay, which he believed was a mortal sin. He hated himself and didn't feel that he deserved anything good."

"Are you saying he's not accountable for his choices?"

"Well of course he's accountable, but there were huge, extenuating circumstances." She was beginning to look frustrated.

"I hear what you're saying, Ms. O'Neill, but the bottom line is that your nephew chose to live on the streets and ended up becoming a skinhead."

"He didn't think he had a choice."

"But he did have a choice." Dan glanced at the jury. "Nobody pushed him off your couch. Nobody made him rip up your check for a thousand dollars. And because he chose to live on the streets, he risked becoming involved with dangerous people."

"He wasn't thinking clearly."

"Well, you obviously love him a lot. No further questions."

Thursday was a short day because the judge agreed to hold an emergency bond hearing on another case, which lasted from eight till eleven. At eleven-fifteen, Lee called her next witness, Mrs. Weissmann, who immediately charmed the jury with her dignity and keen intelligence. She was, as Carla predicted, everyone's dream grandmother, even for people who already had nice grandmothers.

The witness described Jeremy as one of the gentlest boys she'd ever met, someone she'd slowly come to trust. She testified that he'd visited her at least twice a week for months, that he'd shoveled her walkway, carried her groceries, and performed whatever chores she asked of him. His only reward was a plate of cookies and a glass of lemonade.

"I offered him money," she added, "but he refused to take it."

Without being reminded, she remembered to mention that Jeremy had dreamt of going to college and that she'd encouraged him. Finally, she described the day she saw the swastika on his arm and decided to tell him about her year in Auschwitz.

"He was very naïve and hadn't realized how badly the Nazis treated us. He was horrified by what I told him, and then . . . and then he was profoundly ashamed. During one of his last visits, a week or two before they took him away, he promised to have the tattoo removed as soon as he had the money. I believed him."

When Lee was done, Dan stood up and thanked Mrs. Weissmann for taking the time to testify.

After the lunch break, Lee advised Dan that her next witness would be Tim Reynolds, whom they all called Mr. Clean. As she'd expected, Dan demanded an immediate hearing outside the presence of the jury. While the guard waited in the hallway, Lee asked the court to allow her witness to describe Jeremy's on-going nightmares, refusal to eat, flat affect, and obvious distress, all of it culminating in a serious attempt to commit suicide. As soon as she finished speaking, Dan stood up, shaking his head.

"The defendant's suffering as well as his attempt to commit suicide is very sad but of course irrelevant. Ms. Isaacs is simply trying to garner sympathy from the jury. That's not allowed and she knows it."

Actually, besides garnering sympathy, the proposed testimony would help Lee argue in closing that her client's statements to the police had been influenced by grief; the statements, however, hadn't been mentioned yet, and Lee wanted to keep her options open.

After thinking about it, she said, "The information is relevant to bolster our theory that my client's behavior during and after the murder was the result of extreme grief."

It sounded good, but would the judge buy it?

Before the judge could respond, Dan jumped in again.

"If that's the case, Ms. Isaacs is offering evidence of the defendant's mental state, which is governed by the statute on impaired mental condition. As Ms. Isaacs well knows, the statute requires that she inform the court before trial of her intention to assert this defense, and then there's a whole procedure that follows, including ordering the defendant to submit to a court ordered examination."

Lee turned to Phil, who handed her a brief on the issue.

"Your Honor," she said, "we anticipated the prosecution's argument and have prepared a brief clarifying that evidence of the defendant's emotional distress which doesn't seek to negate the existence of a required culpable mental state isn't subject to the statute. I am not arguing that he wasn't capable of acting 'knowingly' or 'intentionally.' Instead, I am simply offering evidence of my client's grief and his attempt to kill himself as relevant to explain his behavior on the night of the murder and afterward. The prosecution's argument is a red herring, because it is totally inapplicable."

Dan pulled out his own brief and offered it to the judge.

"I, too, anticipated the issue and hereby submit a brief in opposition."

The Court then called a short recess. Lee remained where she was. After a moment, she closed her eyes, signaling her desire to be left alone. She needed the proposed testimony and was trying to think of how she could get it in later if the judge ruled against her. Jeremy sat quietly beside her, his arm pressed lightly against hers.

After twenty minutes, the judge returned and agreed to allow it. Lee nodded as if she'd had no doubt how the judge would rule.

When Mr. Clean explained to the jury that he'd been Jeremy's guard for the last eight months, the jurors all sat forward, clearly interested in his observations. His description of finding Jeremy after he'd slit his wrists was emotionally riveting. Dan couldn't afford not to question him.

On cross, he quickly drew out the guard's clear bias in favor of the defense and an admission that he had no actual knowledge of the facts of the case and thus didn't know whether the defendant was guilty or not. After that, Dan could have sat down but decided to emphasize what he would argue in closing.

"Mr. Reynolds, when you were in college, you didn't major in psychology, did you?"

"No. History."

"So you're not a doctor, a psychologist, or a psychiatrist?"

"No."

"You have a degree in history and, if I remember correctly from our interview, you'd like to go back to school and get a masters in criminology."

"Yes," the guard said, "you have a good memory."

Dan came around the podium and took a couple of steps forward.

"People feel suicidal for many reasons, don't they?"

"I guess so, yes."

"It's possible the defendant felt suicidal because he was scared of going to prison?"

"It's possible."

"Or because he was ashamed of being gay?"

"Yes, maybe."

"Or because his parents had forsaken him?"

"Yes, that's possible."

"Or because he felt lonely, misunderstood, and powerless?"

"Yes, that's possible, too."

Dan stared at the witness, daring him to disagree.

"Or because he felt guilty about helping his brothers murder a member of their gang and wished he'd behaved differently?"

After a number of seconds, the guard said, "I guess it's possible."

"Thank you, Mr. Reynolds. No further questions."

On re-direct, Lee asked, "Is it possible Jeremy felt suicidal due to intense grief?"

This time, the guard nodded vigorously.

"I think so, yes."

———

Because her next witness, Barry Simmons, hadn't arrived yet, Lee was forced to ask for another recess. The judge looked irritated, but he gave her thirty minutes. Earlier, Barry had called to say his ride had fallen through and that he would have to take the bus. While Carla searched for him, Lee waited outside the courtroom. Finally, at the last possible moment, she saw her investigator pulling Barry down the hallway. He was devouring a burrito from the first floor cafeteria.

"He hadn't eaten since yesterday morning," Carla explained.

"Thanks, Carla." Then Lee turned to Barry. "Are you ready?"

His mouth was full, but he nodded. He was wearing a brown cotton sweater and matching slacks that Carla had found at a thrift store in Denver.

After taking the stand, Barry sat up straight and answered all of Lee's initial questions without hesitation. With his new teeth and haircut, he looked like a respectable, middle-class man, someone the jurors could relate to. Occasionally, he'd reach up to cover his mouth and then realize he didn't have to. The look of joy on his face was almost worth the cost of his makeover. On direct, he described serving Jeremy and Sam on three different occasions at The Cave.

"How close did they seem?" Lee asked.

"Like real good friends. They sat with their heads together and they were smiling. I thought maybe they were relatives like me and my cousin Clark. They were totally at ease, you know?"

"Anything else?"

Barry pretended to think, although he'd been prepped to answer the question.

"Well, it struck me as kind of different. Most skinheads don't act like they like each other much. These guys did."

Because the prosecution knew that Barry had worked unofficially for his cousin, Lee asked her witness to explain it. She'd spent a lot of time tweaking his answer.

"Okay, so my cousin was desperate to keep his job and I was, in fact, a real bartender. So we didn't think too much about it. The owner paid for a bartender and he got one. Clark assured me that it was cool."

"Nothing further," Lee said. "Thanks."

On cross, Dan belabored the fact that Barry never guessed the defendant and Sam were gay, and certainly never thought they were lovers. Finally, he moved on.

"The tables in the back room are pretty small?" He'd obviously sent one of his investigators to the bar.

"Yeah, all the tables are. Not the booths."

Then Dan took out a photograph and asked Barry to identify it.

"That's the room they sat in," Barry said.

"And the tables are so little that, if two people sit there, they can't help sitting close."

"True, but they seemed very comfortable."

"Judge, I'd like to offer the photograph into evidence." Dan glanced at his notes. "I think it's our fifty-sixth exhibit, Your Honor."

"It is," Lee said. "And no objection."

After marking the photograph and handing it to the court reporter, Dan turned back to the witness, his expression much more serious now, signaling to the jury how he felt about the next set of questions.

"So, you and your cousin Clark were involved in a fraudulent scheme?"

"Fraudulent?" To his credit, Barry kept his eyes on the prosecutor. Lee had warned him not to look at her on cross, that he was on his own. That the jury would be carefully watching him.

"Yes, you pretended to be him and worked at the bar without the owner's permission."

"Okay, yeah, but it wasn't fraudulent. It was . . ."

"Deceptive?"

"Yeah, it was deceptive."

"And you did it more than once?"

"Six or seven times I think."

"And each time you were being deceptive."

"Okay."

Dan crossed his arms and looked sternly at the witness.

"Do you realize you could be charged with trespass and criminal impersonation?"

"That's what Ms. Isaacs told me."

"Ms. Isaacs told you that?"

"Yes, she said you might try to intimidate me by threatening to charge me, but it would be pure harassment."

Dan recovered like a pro.

"Well, you don't seem to be very intimidated. So your cousin Clark assured you it was cool?"

"Right."

"Is that the cousin Clark who is presently facing charges for vehicular homicide?"

"Yeah."

"Well, no wonder you trusted him. No further questions."

Lee could have objected to Dan's comment, but didn't. The point she'd been trying to make had been diluted enough. She glanced at the jury and wondered what they were thinking.

It was almost five o'clock. The judge banged his gavel, announcing the end of court for the day. Tired, rumpled-looking spectators stood up and stretched. Tomorrow, the defense would call Jeremy Matthews, who would tell his story to the twelve poker-faced jurors filing out of the room. Tonight, Lee, Carla, and Phil would drive to the detention center to prepare their client to be cross-examined by one of the wiliest prosecutors in the business.

After everyone left, it was so quiet. Lee looked around, marveling as she always did at this seemingly ordinary room where people's lives were determined, where they went on trial to justify or minimize their behavior, blame others, or simply beg for mercy. A room where judgments were pronounced and sentences handed down. A place where people squirmed, schemed, laughed, cried, sweated, shouted, or sat, calmly accepting their fate. And for the past thirty-five years, Lee's domain. Where she represented people accused of terrible things and did her best, whether they deserved it or not, to save them.

During her first month as a public defender, Lee had memorized the definition of a reasonable doubt. Since then, she'd recited it hundreds of times to hundreds of juries, never hurrying, acting as if the words were holy, the most important thing they might ever hear. If she had a mantra, it was this: Reasonable doubt means a doubt based upon reason and common sense which arises from a fair and rational consideration of all of the evidence, or the lack of evidence, in the case. It is a doubt which is not a vague, speculative, or imaginary doubt, but a doubt that would 'cause reasonable people to hesitate to act in matters of importance to themselves.

Amen.

CHAPTER SEVENTEEN

During a multi-day trial where the stakes are high, it's difficult for the lawyers involved not to succumb to trial psychosis—a state of mind where things seem to be going extraordinarily well even if they aren't—because they've invested so much of their energy, skill, and attention that the idea of losing becomes unimaginable. Lee understood the phenomenon well and was working hard to resist it. Dan, as far as she could tell, had succumbed on Tuesday or Wednesday and would be unreachable until after the verdict.

Still, after Jeremy's direct examination, Lee felt quite optimistic. For four tense hours, her client had managed to be totally present without being overly emotional or histrionic. The jurors were clearly affected by his description of Sam's murder. How could they not be? She ended her examination with a series of questions about her client's statements to the police, preempting Dan, who would have liked to be the first to bring them up.

She'd stepped away from the podium and walked halfway to the witness stand, as far as the judge would allow, and began by asking Jeremy about his state of mind after the murder. Jeremy thought for at least ten seconds, taking his time, the way Lee had recommended.

"Okay," he finally said. "So-so it was like I was stuck in a nightmare and I couldn't wake up. Part of me couldn't believe Sam was dead, and part of me knew he was and wanted to curl up next to him. When I got into the car, I felt kind of like an astronaut floating in space. Nothing seemed real. I felt so sad, I couldn't breathe."

Perfect, Lee thought, and then asked why he'd told Detective Roberts that Sam was just a faggot who deserved to die.

"It's what the others were shouting as they kicked him. I guess it just stuck in my head. Also, I hated myself for not saving him, so I was kind of talking about gays in general, that we were, you know, just faggots who deserved to die." He hesitated. "I-I don't feel that way anymore."

Lee smiled and then asked about kicking Sam.

"I wish I hadn't. I did it cause Rab told me to, so the others would think I was down with it. He was already dead, of course, so it didn't matter. But I still wish I hadn't."

"Jeremy," she continued, "you told Detective Roberts that you acted as the lookout. Was that true?"

"No. All I did was cry and puke, which was kind of embarrassing. I just said it 'cause that's what Rab told Casey and Johnny."

"Why do you think Rab told them that?"

"So the others would think I was helping."

"Last question: While you were speaking with the detective, was there a part of you that wanted to be punished?"

"Definitely. I didn't do anything to stop them. I-I didn't really even try. So I was kind of thinking I was just as guilty as the others. That if I couldn't kill myself, I should spend the rest of my life in prison." He looked directly at the jurors the way Lee suggested. "I don't believe that anymore."

"Thank you for testifying," Lee said. "No further questions."

During lunch, Lee allowed herself a five-minute daydream in which she and Jeremy were facing the judge while he read the not-guilty verdict: the drug-like rush, the wild relief, the eruption of joy behind them. The curiously short-lived happiness she'd feel. And then she opened her eyes and warned herself to stop, though her client had truly done better than all of them had hoped.

Dan's cross-examination ended at five o'clock, timed so that any redirect would have to wait till Monday. His tone throughout was disapproving but never mean. Like Lee, he began chronologically, recounting the story of how a young man who hated being gay had joined a group of homophobic skinheads and ended up participating in a murder. And how the young man, after the fact, had invented a different version where he and the victim were innocent, star-crossed lovers. A version belied by numerous witnesses and the young man's own confession. By four-thirty, many of the jurors who'd seemed sympathetic were now looking confused and unhappy.

At a quarter to five, Dan imitated Lee by walking halfway to the witness stand, but unlike his adversary, his action was meant to intimidate, not soothe.

"Mr. Matthews," he said, "if Sam had been the love of your life, you wouldn't have kicked him."

Jeremy looked exhausted but resolute.

"I wish I hadn't."

Lee's advice on cross: Answer the question with as few words as possible. Don't try to explain. Acknowledge whatever's true, even if it sounds bad.

"If he'd been the love of your life," Dan continued, "you would have run for help."

"I tried to but I fell."

"If he'd been the love of your life, you would have gotten to your feet and run some more."

"I should have."

"You would have run to the road and flagged somebody down."

"I know. I should have."

Dan's face registered both disapproval and disbelief.

"If Sam had been the love of your life, you would never have gotten back in the car with his murderers."

"I-I didn't know what else to do."

"You would have called the police as soon as you got back to Denver."

"I should have."

"You would have left the house as soon as the murderers were gone."

"I don't know why I didn't."

"You would have gone to the police and had those men arrested."

"I should have."

If Dan felt frustrated, he masked it well.

"But the truth is they were your brothers and you were just as guilty as they were."

Jeremy glanced down at his hands and said, "That's kind of how I felt." And then looked up again. "But-but I wasn't."

"Mr. Matthews, if Sam had been the love of your life, you wouldn't have told the police he was just a faggot who deserved to die."

"I didn't mean it."

"But that's what you said. Those were your exact words."

"Yes."

"And most importantly, if he'd been the love of your life, you wouldn't have acted as the lookout while the others kicked him."

"I-I didn't act as the lookout."

"But that's what you told the police."

"Yes."

Dan was looking incredulous now.

"Mr. Matthews, if you were innocent, you would have told the police what you're telling us now."

"Except I was in shock."

Dan took another step forward and lowered his voice to a stage whisper.

"You weren't in shock. You were simply telling the truth. Sam was never your boyfriend. He was just someone you knew, someone you killed. A faggot who deserved to die."

"No, he wasn't."

Dan pressed his lips together and nodded sadly.

"I agree. No further questions."

In case any of the jurors were looking, Lee smiled as if she were pleased. And in fact, it could have been much worse. Her client had done what they'd told him to. He hadn't argued, cried, or sounded defensive. Most important, he hadn't wilted during Dan's final assault; he'd held his ground. Was it enough? Lee thought it was, but wondered if she was still thinking clearly.

After everyone filed out of the courtroom, the defense team surrounded their client and praised him.

"You did great, buddy," Phil said.

"You think so?" Jeremy asked. His eyes were bloodshot and his face was very pale. He was beginning to lose weight again.

"Absolutely," Carla said, tousling his hair.

Jeremy asked Lee if she agreed with them.

"Yes," she told him. "Your answers on direct were excellent, and you held your own on cross. It went very well."

"Did the jurors believe me?" Not a shred of guile in the question.

"I don't know. But every one of them should have a reasonable doubt about your guilt. That's all we need."

"It-it would be nice, though, if they believed me."

Leroy stepped up with a pair of handcuffs.

"I don't know if it matters," he told Jeremy, "but I believed you. I didn't at first, but now I do."

"That's very encouraging," Lee said, smiling.

After their client had gone, Lee slumped in her chair at the defense table, too tired to pretend she wasn't. Her neck, which she'd managed to ignore for weeks, was killing her. Phil and Carla sank down beside her. Nobody was smiling anymore. After a moment, Phil tore off his tie and stuffed it in his pocket.

"It's like wearing a noose," he muttered.

Carla reached into her purse, pulled out her compact, opened it, and stared at herself in horror.

"Oh my God," she groaned. "Why didn't anyone . . . Oh never mind." She closed the mirror and sighed.

Lee pressed her aching neck and heard it crack. It's back, she thought and then began to chuckle.

"What's so funny?" Carla asked, already beginning to smile.

"My neck makes worrisome cracking sounds," Lee said.

Carla started to laugh.

"I have a pounding headache and a huge new floater in my left eye."

"Why are you both laughing?" Phil asked, looking puzzled. "My heartburn is so bad, I think I might have an ulcer. I was wondering if I should go to the emergency room." And then he started laughing too.

When they finally stopped, Carla pulled out a huge bottle of Tums from her purse and placed it on the table. Everyone took a handful and began eating. According to the clock on the wall, it was five-thirty.

"This is nice," Carla said, looking from Lee to Phil.

"I like the green ones," Phil murmured.

Lee smiled at them. It *was* nice, but their client's future hung in the balance. Time to get serious.

"Okay," she said, "let's talk. Phil, what do you think?"

"Well, it's close, but right now I think we can win."

"I agree," Carla said.

Lee thought so too, but was worried.

"What if Dan gets Rab to testify as a rebuttal witness?"

Phil sighed, then reached into his pocket, pulled out his tie, and pretended to hang himself with it.

"That's only true if Rab's a good witness," Carla said. "If he isn't, the jury could still acquit."

"Who represents Rab?" Lee asked her.

"Bradley Moore. He's not going to let you talk to his client."

"If I were him," Lee said, "I wouldn't let me talk to his client either. But I'd sure like to know before Monday if his client is going to cooperate."

"Oh happy day," Phil began singing.

"Because—?" Lee asked.

"Because Bradley owes me a ginormous favor. A few years ago, he begged me to take over a robbery case. He was doing too much blow at the time and wasn't prepared. We told the judge he couldn't try the case because of a conflict. I took it over and won it. If I ask nicely, I think he'd let you have a word with his client. He'd want to be there of course."

"That would be great. You sure you want to use up the favor this way?"

"Are you kidding? I owe you my career. Not only that, you let me be part of this team. It's been a long time since I defended an innocent person. It feels great. I was so burnt out trying sex cases I was beginning to wonder if I was on the wrong side—a truly sickening thought. But I'm jazzed again, ready to go back and champion all the killers, rapists, and thieves in Boulder County. So thank you."

"In which case you're welcome," Lee said, touched by his obvious sincerity. "All the killers, rapists, and thieves in Boulder County will be very lucky to have you."

Less than three hours later, Lee was standing in the lobby of the Boulder County Jail. Phil had called earlier and told her that Bradley would meet her there at eight, take it or leave it. She wolfed down an egg salad sandwich with a glass of water and three Advil, then changed into an elegant navy-blue pantsuit that fit her well. A simple white blouse, open at the neck, completed the outfit. Charlie complained bitterly as she hurried out the door, taking nothing but her car keys. Although it was pouring out, she didn't have time to find an umbrella.

The lobby was empty, but it had obviously been a busy day at the jail. All the ashtrays were full and the floor around the wastebasket was littered with crumpled pieces of paper. A broken cell phone, which looked as if someone had stomped on it, lay in a corner of the room. Although she was a few minutes late, she took the time to dry herself off in the bathroom. It never hurt to look as good as you could, especially when meeting a dangerous criminal for the first time.

Finally, she left the bathroom, walked across the lobby, and pressed the after-hours buzzer. Ten minutes later, she was being escorted down a long beige hallway toward the maximum unit where Bradley and his client waited in one of the day rooms.

Inside the room, Bradley was leaning against a blackboard covered with typical AA slogans, such as "Expect miracles," and "If it works, don't fix it." He was a competent, extremely arrogant lawyer who dyed his hair and wore large, expensive suits to hide his girth. His face was always tan, sometimes slightly orange. Because it was in her clients' best interests for her to get along with all her colleagues, including Bradley, she did. Dissemble or find another profession.

"Hi, Bradley," she said. "Thanks for letting me have a word with your client."

"So here's the deal. You may ask him if he's going to testify. I'd like to know as well. If you ask him anything else, I'll advise him not to answer."

Lee turned to Rab, who was sitting in a white plastic chair with his long legs splayed out in front of him. He had a strong square face, blue eyes, and a petulant mouth. Like a coiled snake, he didn't move, regarding her with curiosity. The jaguar tattoo on his neck was a startling emerald green.

"Hello," Lee said, putting out her hand for him to shake. "My name is Lee Isaacs. May I call you Rab?"

"Hmm," he said, as if it were a difficult question.

Lee waited, hand outstretched. A couple of seconds passed.

"Sure," he finally said and shook her hand. His grip was powerful. "People don't name their kids Lee anymore."

"Actually, they do."

"Really?" He scanned her up and down, apparently approving.

Bradley decided to intervene.

"So, she's going to ask if you'll be testifying for the prosecution on Monday. I hope you'll tell her yes. This will be an extremely short interview. I don't want—"

"Shut up, Bradley," his client said, and frowned at Lee. "So my little brother is a cocksucker?"

Lee decided to play it straight and breezy.

"I'm afraid so."

Rab burst out laughing. He had beautiful white teeth. Although he had a sense of humor and was obviously intelligent, something important was missing, something critical. A conscience, Lee thought. Which made him, at the very least, unpredictable.

"Have a seat," he told her, pointing to another plastic chair a few feet away from him.

Lee made a show of moving the chair at least four feet back and then sat down.

"You're a smart lady," he said. "I'll have to be careful."

"I was thinking the same thing."

Both of them smiled.

Bradley walked between them and said, "Rab, she wants to know if you're going to testify as a rebuttal witness. That means—"

"I know what a rebuttal witness is."

Bradley pointed to the black and white, industrial-sized clock on the wall.

"I don't have a lot of time, Rab. She needs to know if you're going to cooperate. Actually, so do I."

"Well, the truth is, I haven't made up my mind."

"Fine," Bradley said, "in which case, this interview is over."

Lee had nothing to lose. In a moment, she'd be walking down that long beige hallway out into the rain again. Without an umbrella and without any answers.

"That's up to your client, isn't it?"

"No," Bradley replied. "It's up to me."

"Beat it," Rab ordered.

"You heard him," Bradley said, jerking his head toward the door.

Lee bent sideways to look at Rab.

"I think he means you, Bradley."

"What?"

"I did," Rab said. "Beat it. I haven't had the pleasure of speaking to a smart foxy lady in months."

Bradley's face went from slightly orange to an angry red.

"Don't be fooled, Rab. She's an experienced attorney who represents someone you've agreed to testify against. She'll fuck you if she gets the chance."

"That seems highly unlikely," Lee said.

"Damn it, Rab, you're in enough trouble as it is. I am strongly advising you not to speak—"

Rab made a dismissive gesture with his arm.

"I can take care of myself, Bradley. Now beat it."

"Christ," Bradley muttered. "You can play whatever games you want, but the DA isn't fucking around. He's going to pull the deal if you refuse to testify."

"Don't get your undies in a twist," Rab told him. "I'm leaning toward cooperating."

"Oh," Bradley said, looking surprised. "Well, all right. Good. I'll come by on Sunday night."

"You do that. Now scram."

After Bradley left, the two of them stared at each other. The room was much too warm and smelled like an over-chlorinated swimming pool.

"Well, this is cozy," Rab said. He slowly clasped his hands, resting them on his lap.

Lee glanced around her. Besides the blackboard, there was a broken chair in the corner, and a pile of unwashed food trays stacked against the wall.

"Not really," she said.

"I've been confined in much worse places. Have you read all the pre-sentence reports written about me?"

"Of course."

"Then you know that I spent my childhood in dozens of crummy foster homes." His voice was very matter-of-fact.

"I can't imagine what that would be like."

"In a word, brutal." Then he brightened. "But, as a result, I've learned to transcend my physical surroundings."

"A handy skill given where you're headed."

He narrowed his eyes at her.

"Are you mocking me?"

"I wouldn't dare."

He seemed mollified. More silence. Lee sighed inwardly.

Suddenly, he looked intrigued.

"You're not afraid of me, are you?"

"No," she said carefully, "but I don't underestimate you."

He looked her up and down again, benignly . . . or perhaps not. But then he surprised her.

"You've trained as a martial artist?"

"How did you guess?"

"Please, it's obvious." He nodded to himself. "I trained for almost nine years in Wing Chun."

"A great system, especially for close contact fighting. Bruce Lee trained in Wing Chun before he developed his own style."

Rab's smile seemed almost genuine.

"My favorite movie in the world is *Enter the Dragon*."

"Mine too," Lee said, which happened to be the truth. She glanced at the thick metal door, which was locked from the outside. "My client will die if he goes to prison."

"Aw, no more foreplay?"

"Well, it's getting late and I need to know if you're going to testify against him."

Without any warning, Rab jumped to his feet, knocking his chair sideways. He'd moved so fast, it was almost a blur, but she'd watched his lower body and remained where she was, forcing herself to look unconcerned. He'd obviously expected a reaction and was now looking very surprised.

"Most people would have fallen over backward and then scurried to the other side of the room. You didn't even move. Why not?"

"You weren't serious. You were just testing me." She spoke calmly, as if her heart were beating normally. As if every muscle in her body weren't on high alert.

"How did you know?"

Years of experience, she might have answered, but it wouldn't have sufficed. She was not only being tested, but she also needed to get an A.

"Your feet," she said. "When you jumped up, your weight was in your heels. If you'd meant to lunge at me, you'd have landed on the balls of your feet, your body angled toward me."

"That's very perceptive." He leaned over, righted his chair, and then sat down again. "What would you have done if you thought I was serious?"

"I'd have rolled off the chair, picked it up, and used it as a shield, all the while shouting for the guards."

"A skilled response, except the guards can't always hear you. It depends where they are." His blue eyes appraised her. "What do you think would have happened in the meantime?"

"I guess we'll never know."

"I suppose not," he agreed, then placed his arms behind his head and stretched his legs out as far as they would go. Letting her know, if she were silly enough to believe him, that the test was over, that she could relax as well.

"So, the reason for my visit—"

"I hate faggots. They disgust me."

"You saved his life at least twice."

"Countless times, actually."

"Save him one more time." She spoke quietly and reasonably, without passion.

He glanced at the clock and yawned.

"I'm beginning to feel bored, Lee."

In a second, he would tell her to scram. She needed to surprise him again.

"What if I call you first?"

"As a witness for the defense?" He was smiling for real now.

"Yes."

He nodded approvingly, sat up straighter.

"Now that would be ballsy."

"Would you confirm my client's innocence?"

"Now why would I do that?"

Why would he? Appealing to his sense of right and wrong would be useless.

"Imagine the look on the DA's face," she finally said.

"Imagine the look on yours if I say he's guilty."

"But he's not guilty and you know it."

"Boohoo. A miscarriage of justice." He yawned again. "Well, this has been fun. We'll have to do it again sometime."

They stood up simultaneously. Rab was a couple of inches taller and almost a hundred pounds heavier. Lee made no move to leave. Nothing had been resolved, she still had no answers.

"Cheer up," he told her, "you gave it your best."

She took a deep breath, let it out, and said, "I think I'm going to call you first."

"Hmm. Have you ever played Russian roulette with a loaded gun?"

"No."

"I've played it half a dozen times. It's a gas. The rush is incredible. Drugs pale in comparison. Would you ever want to try it?"

Lee shook her head.

He turned his back to her, walked to the door, and began to knock on it.

"Then don't call me."

Monday morning arrived like an uninvited guest with piles of luggage. No sense shutting the door on her; she wasn't going to leave. Lee had slept poorly all weekend, spending most of her time smoothing out potential jury instructions and drafting four different closing arguments. The first assumed the best scenario, that Rab testified for the defense and saved his little brother; the second assumed he didn't testify at all; the third assumed he testified for the prosecution; and the fourth assumed the worst, that she played Russian roulette with a loaded gun and lost.

On Saturday morning, she'd sparred for almost an hour with Michael, who kept complaining she wasn't totally there, which was obvious, but she stubbornly disagreed. By the time they bowed out, she'd barely escaped a broken nose and another cracked rib. Or maybe the rib actually was cracked and she was simply refusing to acknowledge it. On Saturday night, she begged off dinner with Mark and Bobby.

"Too much work," she told them, but in truth she just didn't feel like talking. They would have wanted to discuss the case and the decision she had to make, but it wouldn't have helped. The decision would come from a deep and silent place. The trick, as usual, was to get there.

After an unusually long shower, Lee picked out her gray silk pantsuit and a rose-colored blouse. Without any hesitation, she chose a pair of sleek black boots with a two-inch heel that made her look tall and imposing. Today, absent any more surprises, she'd be delivering her closing argument. She made herself sit down and eat a large bowl of oatmeal, then brushed Charlie, and walked calmly out the door.

She drove south on Broadway and took a right on Canyon Boulevard, eventually pulling into the courthouse parking lot. Not even eight, and it was already warm out. Beyond the parking lot, a group of joggers were running along the creek path. And beyond the joggers, a stand of brilliant orange poppies that always seemed to bloom around Lee's birthday. Which—go on and say it—was in two days. *Yikes.*

She took a deep breath and regretted it. Okay, so her rib was probably cracked, but maybe only slightly. Perhaps the healing time would be faster than the usual two months. She twisted to the right and stopped. No, it wouldn't be. Ten minutes later, she'd unpacked her rolling briefcase and was dragging it toward the Justice Center.

Carla was standing outside the courtroom waiting for the rest of the defense team. She'd ditched her eyeglasses and her hair was red again.

"Hey, Lee," she called. "I brought you a cappuccino from Spruce Confections." Her smile was warm and tired.

"Thank you," Lee said. Good old Carla. What would she do without her? Find another investigator, she supposed, but no one else would be half as good, half as dedicated, or—she might as well admit this too—half as fun.

"Did you break another rib?" Carla asked, handing her the cappuccino.

All of Lee's kindly thoughts disappeared.

"What makes you think I broke a rib?"

"I don't know. It's kind of obvious if you're paying attention."

"Like how is it obvious?"

"Well, you're pulling your briefcase with your left hand, you're listing slightly to the right, and your other hand is holding your rib."

"Oh." Lee dropped her hand. "Well, I don't think it's that bad."

"Okay . . . if you say so. But when you fight with people, can't you wear something?"

"No," Lee said firmly. "And I'd appreciate if you wouldn't mention it to anyone."

Carla took a few steps back, placed her thumb and forefinger on her mouth, and turned them like a lock.

"Hey, guys," Phil called to them. He and Dan were neck and neck hurrying down the hallway. Dan looked smartly conservative in the tailored black suit he always chose for his closing arguments. Phil, on the other hand, was wearing a western-style leather blazer and fancy cowboy boots. He'd tamed his blonde flyaway hair with something that made it look wet.

Dan arrived with a grin.

"Well, well, the gang's all here. So, will you be putting the defendant on again?"

"Nope," Lee said, "he's done."

"Will you be resting then?"

"It depends."

"On what?" Dan, of course, knew. It was rare and delightful, a sudden double rainbow, when he didn't.

"On whether you're going to call Rab on rebuttal."

"You know I will. Thanks to your client's half-decent performance, I have to." He was trying to look sorry.

"Has he told you he'll testify?"

"No, but he's thinking about it. He's down in the basement holding cell. I told him I'd pull the deal if he refuses."

"What was his response?"

"That sticks and stones could break his bones but words could never hurt him."

"Sounds like he might refuse."

Dan shook his head and chuckled.

"I think he's having a grand time playing with all of us. By the way, he said you mentioned the possibility of calling him as a witness for the defense."

Carla and Phil both nodded. They'd talked to Lee on Saturday, but she sounded doubtful.

"Probably too risky," she'd said, and they'd agreed.

"Actually," Lee told them all now, "I'm seriously considering it."

Dan burst out laughing and said, "Yeah, right."

"No, I am." She thought for a couple of seconds before seeming to make up her mind. "But I'm willing to make a deal. I won't call him if you won't."

"Nice try, Lee."

"Then maybe I'd better call him."

Phil was looking worried now.

"Didn't he warn you not to?"

"He did," Lee admitted and rubbed her eyes. "How much time do we have?"

"Less than a minute," Dan said. "Hey, maybe you *should* call him."

"He's pimping you, Lee," Phil warned.

"Yes, I'm aware of that. And yet, I still don't know."

"Why do you think he'd help us?" Phil asked, not even caring that Dan was standing next to them.

"I'm not at all sure he will, but if I don't call him, I think he'll lose whatever respect he has for me."

"So call him then," Dan said, clearly enjoying himself.

"Maybe I will." She frowned. "Or maybe I won't."

The courtroom door opened and the judge's bailiff stuck his head out.

"Judge Samuels would like to begin. He wants to know whether the defense has any more witnesses."

"Carla?" Lee asked. "Do you have a quarter?"

Without a word, Carla fished in her purse, pulled one out, and handed it to Lee.

Both Phil and Dan looked incredulous. No one said a word as Lee flipped the quarter and then placed it on the top of her left hand. Her right hand immediately covered the coin. "Heads I call him," she proclaimed. "Tails I don't."

Phil wiped some sweat off his forehead.

"Lee, are you sure?"

Lee lifted her hand just enough to see the coin.

"Heads," she said, shrugging. "I guess I'll call him."

CHAPTER EIGHTEEN

Before returning to the courtroom, Lee made a quick detour down the hall to the women's bathroom. On her way out, she glanced in the mirror, stopped, and decided to comb her hair. Suddenly, she wanted to slow things down. Catch her breath. Let everyone wait for her. After putting her comb away, she leaned in closer to see if any new wrinkles were visible. None since the last time she checked, about a week and a half ago. Good. When she was fifty, she'd rarely inspected her skin because the rate of deterioration had been slow. Now it was speeding up, requiring vigilance and, what? Equanimity, she supposed. As she turned to leave, the word "dowager" came to mind. A hundred years ago, would Lee have qualified? Maybe not, because Paul hadn't left her a dime. So, just a well-heeled old widow then.

Carla was waiting outside the bathroom.

"There you are." She pointed to Lee's rolling briefcase. "Do you want any help with that?"

"No," Lee said, feeling cranky again.

"Didn't think so. You'd made up your mind already, hadn't you?"

"Of course. But did you see Dan's face?"

"Phil's too. I guess he still doesn't know you well enough."

Neither did Carla, really. But it wasn't for lack of trying.

They headed down the hallway. When they reached the courtroom, Lee stopped and put a hand on her investigator's shoulder.

"What?" Carla asked.

"Three things," Lee said quickly before she could change her mind. "First, we've worked together almost ten years and I just want to say how much I appreciate your faith in me. It never seems to waver. Second, you're a terrific investigator and I really enjoy working with you."

"Wow. Thanks. You're my favorite lawyer and I love working with you, too. And the third thing?"

"That whenever you've tried getting to know me, I haven't made it easy. I'm sorry. I don't know why, except I've always been a very private person. Still, you shouldn't give up."

"Never occurred to me, but thanks for saying it. So, does that mean you might go out drinking with me some night?"

"Absolutely not, but maybe we could meet now and then for coffee."

"I'd like that very much. Would it be up to me to make that happen?"

"At least to begin with. Well, shall we go in?"

"After you," Carla said, pushing the door open.

There were at least two hundred spectators in the room, but the judge, prosecutor, and jury were missing. Phil came up behind them, looking agitated.

"Where have you been?" he asked. "Dan told the judge you were calling Rab. It'll be a little while before they can bring him up. Are you sure about this?"

"Chill out, bro," Carla said. "She'd already made up her mind."

It took a moment to sink in.

"Oh," he finally said. "Ah, yes, of course." His shoulders sagged with relief. "So you think he'll come through then?"

Lee raised her hands, a gesture that was normally painless.

"I'm not at all sure. But if I don't call him, I think he'd feel so contemptuous, he'd testify for the prosecution."

"Just to fuck you?"

"Yup." She glanced toward the front of the room. "Where's Jeremy?"

"Leroy took him to the bathroom."

"All right, then." Lee squared her shoulders. "I guess I'll go set up." She dragged her rolling briefcase up the aisle toward the defense table, careful to stand up straight although it hurt more that way. A few minutes later, Leroy brought Jeremy to the table. Jeremy had showered and was wearing one of his last new shirts. Someone, probably Mr. Clean, had leant him a belt, which would of course be confiscated later.

"He's all yours," Leroy said, unlocking the cuffs. "He's a lot calmer than I'd be."

"What choice do I have?" Jeremy asked.

After Lee had arranged the table, Jeremy leaned in close to her.

"So you're going to call Rab?"

"I am," she said and waited for her client's reaction.

"Does he know I'm gay?"

"Yes. The others must have told him." She pulled out a new yellow pad and placed it directly in front of her.

"He really hates gays," Jeremy said.

"Do you think he'll help you anyway?"

"Maybe." His expression was an equal mix of hope and despair. "It'll depend on his mood."

Lee shook her head at the thought. What a strange and arbitrary world.

"Well, let's hope he's feeling benevolent."

"Yeah." Suddenly, his eyes were shining. "Hey, guess what? On Saturday night, I started praying again."

"That's wonderful, Jeremy. So you decided that an incomprehensible God was better than no God at all?"

"No. I decided that he's not incomprehensible, that he's kind and wants the best for everyone."

"Really? But in the Book of Job, he causes Job to suffer terribly just to test his faith."

"Yeah, well that's my father's God, not mine."

"I see." Should she leave it at that? Probably, but she was genuinely curious. "So what about suffering? Is everything that happens part of God's plan?"

"No, it can't be. I think that God is sad when bad things happen and wishes he could fix them, but-but mostly he can't."

"Well, that's definitely not the God in the Book of Job."

"No," Jeremy agreed.

"Can I ask an obvious question?"

"Sure."

"Why have a God if he isn't powerful enough to fix things? Why bother praying to him?"

Jeremy nodded as if it were a great question.

"For the company I guess. God is a really good listener and-and he has a sense of humor."

"That's probably essential. Actually, I kind of like your God. If I were going to believe in one, I think I'd pick yours."

"Really?" He had a sweet, lovely smile. In another few years, he'd be handsome—a nice advantage if he was free, and a dangerous handicap if he wasn't.

"Yes, I think so."

A moment later, Judge Samuels took the bench. Dan and Detective Bruno rushed in from the back of the room. Dan looked confident as usual, but his advisory witness was scowling.

As soon as Dan sat down, the judge announced he was calling in the jury.

Dan poured himself some water and said, "Mr. Seaman will be here shortly."

"Who's Mr. Seaman?" Jeremy whispered.

"Rab," Lee answered.

Jeremy's knees began bouncing up and down.

To distract him, she asked, "So how do you know God has a sense of humor?"

"I tell him jokes."

"Oh." Lee closed her eyes and saw it: Jeremy in his small dark cell, sitting on the edge of his cot, whispering jokes to God, and imagining His amused reaction. Dear Jeremy's God, she thought, please get him out of there.

The jurors filed in, looking relaxed and rested from the weekend. They took the same seats they'd occupied for the past two weeks, six in front, six in back. They greeted one another and made themselves comfortable.

"Ms. Isaacs," the judge said, "I understand you have one more witness?"

Lee stood up and answered, "Yes, Your Honor, Richard Seaman. He's the third co-defendant in the case. For the jurors' information, he's been referred to many times by his nickname, which is Rab."

"Thank you, Ms. Isaacs. That's helpful." The judge looked toward the entrance of the courtroom. "I think he's here."

Rab shuffled slowly up the aisle, clearly enjoying the attention. He wore the same dark blue uniform as the snitch and the other co-defendants. Somehow, despite the shackles and handcuffs, he managed to look dignified. The two guards escorting him were as big as professional football players. After he took the witness stand, the guards unlocked his handcuffs and with obvious reluctance, removed them. They left the shackles on, though, which was fine with Lee; she wasn't trying to convince anyone he wasn't dangerous.

"Wait a minute," Jeremy whispered, grabbing hold of Lee's hand. "How do you know this is right? Maybe it isn't."

She leaned down and said, "My gut says it is."

"Your gut? What's that? You mean your stomach?"

"No, it's different than my stomach. It's kind of behind it, in a much deeper place."

"Can you see it on an X-ray?" He was completely serious.

"No, it's something you imagine. But it's real."

"So, like, how do you find it?" He was still holding onto her hand.

"I close my eyes, get very still, and wait. Sometimes it takes a while, sometimes it's instantaneous. But eventually, it talks to me."

"And-and you trust it?"

"I have to."

"Okay." He let go of her hand.

Lee walked to the podium and greeted her witness by his formal name. Rab remained silent. After a long moment, he raised his right hand and made the shape of a gun with his thumb and index finger, pointing it at his temple. Lee nodded her understanding. And then he smiled, benignly or perhaps not. Lee took a deep breath, the pain in her left side actually steadying her.

"Mr. Seaman," she began, "you were charged with first-degree murder for the death of Sam Donnelly?"

"Yes." His voice was unexpectedly loud. A couple of jurors squirmed in their front row seats.

"Did you end up making a deal with the DA?"

"Yes."

"What were the terms of the deal?"

"Forty-eight years for my truthful testimony in the case against Jeremy Matthews." The best answer she could have hoped for. He was smiling again, waiting for her next few questions, the ones he might deign to answer honestly, depending on his mood.

"All right, good. So first of all, do you know my client Jeremy Matthews? And if so, how?"

"Well, I don't mean to be difficult, but is your client sitting at the defense table? I'm having a hard time seeing him. Could you possibly move the podium?"

"Sure," she said, pretending to believe him. "If it's blocking your view, I can move it."

Before she could, she heard a chair scrape back from the defense table. As she turned, she saw Jeremy slowly rising to his feet. For the first time ever, he didn't slouch. His face was expressionless. If he was frightened, he didn't show it.

"Ah," Rab said, rubbing his jaw. "Now I can see him. He's put on weight, but yes that's Jeremy. He lived with me and my roommates from the end of February 2011 until early October, when we were all arrested."

"All right then," the judge said. "The record will reflect that the witness has identified the defendant. You can sit down now, Mr. Matthews."

"Would that be okay?" Lee asked her witness.

"Of course. Thank you for asking."

"Not at all." She nodded toward Jeremy, who immediately sat down.

There was no sense procrastinating any longer. It was show time.

"Mr. Seaman, is my client Jeremy Matthews innocent of murdering Sam Donnelly?"

"Hmm," he said, scratching his ear.

Everyone in the courtroom waited as the seconds ticked by. Lee felt a trickle of sweat drip down the side of her blouse.

Finally, he stopped scratching.

"Actually, he is."

Lee moved quickly to the next question.

"Was my client at the party where you planned the murder?"

"No."

"Did he know beforehand that you and the others were planning to kill Sam?"

"No, he was very surprised. And dismayed."

Lee was almost rushing now.

"During the murder, did my client do anything to help kill Sam?"

"No."

"Did he act as the lookout?"

"Hardly. He couldn't even stand up. All he did was bawl and puke."

"Just a few more questions, Mr. Seaman. Did you tell the others he was acting as the lookout?"

Rab sighed and leaned back as if he were sitting in the most comfortable chair in the world.

"Casey and Johnny were beginning to think he wasn't down with it. I had to tell them something to chill them out."

"Why did you help him?"

"Hmm. That's an excellent question. Your client was so ridiculously unsuited for the street." He smiled at the jury. "Someone had to either help him or put him out of his misery. I decided to take him under my wing." And then he yawned, which meant he was getting bored and perhaps tired of being nice.

There were plenty of other questions she could have asked, but she had what she needed.

"Thank you, Mr. Seaman. No further questions."

Lee sat down, careful not to show how relieved she was. During the last ten minutes, the scene around her had gone from black and white to Technicolor. The jurors' faces and their clothing were suddenly red, orange, yellow, green, and blue. There was plenty of air to breathe, a future to contemplate.

On cross, Dan was careful not to ask any open-ended questions. He spent an hour on Rab's extensive criminal history, which was long and concerning, then spent an equal amount of time reviewing the offer of proof that Rab and his attorney had submitted to the prosecution. It was a textbook cross, which allowed no spontaneous comments from the witness. For his part, Rab betrayed little emotion and never lost his cool. Suddenly, at a quarter to eleven, Dan stopped. There was nothing more to be gained and the jurors were getting restless.

After Dan sat down, Lee rose to her feet and glanced at the jury.

"The defense rests, Your Honor."

There was a short recess and then Dan called Detective Roberts— a/k/a the Marlboro Man, although he'd left his big white hat at home today—to testify concerning the defendant's statements. Dan gave his witness a number of chances to elaborate on the defendant's admissions, but the detective refused. He remained scrupulously neutral, just as he had at the motions hearing. On cross, he answered all of Lee's questions exactly the way he did in April. At the end of his testimony, he winked at her, stood up, and stretched. A few of the female jurors watched him make his way out of the courtroom.

And then it was time for lunch. As Lee was leaving, one of the guards who'd escorted Rab in and out of the courtroom asked if she'd have a word with his prisoner. Lee immediately agreed. She took the elevator down to the basement holding cell, wondering what Rab wanted to tell her. She hoped his mood hadn't changed and that he wasn't already regretting his decision to help.

After being locked into a small glass cell with him, she waited. Rab was studying her closely and smiling.

"You're still not afraid of me."

"No." Then she waited some more.

After a number of seconds, he said, "You owe me."

"Big time. Is there something you want from me?" She hoped he'd be reasonable, that he'd ask for something she could ethically agree to do.

He began to pace, careful never to get too close to her.

"I thought about this all weekend."

"So you knew I'd call you?"

"Please, I challenged you." Finally, he stopped pacing and faced her. "I want a letter every month for the first ten years I'm in prison. I won't be writing back to you. I don't want a pen pal." He paused. "Make it from Ms. Lee Isaacs so the inmates will know you're a lady. Don't put anything on the envelope about being an attorney."

"Is there anything in particular you'd like me to write about?"

"Not really." He thought for a moment. "I'm interested in politics, current events, who's bombing who, and changes in the law. I did a huge amount of legal research on my cases and liked figuring out how the courts would rule."

"Okay," she said.

"Really? I thought you'd balk."

"Why would I? You saved my client's life." And mine too, she thought.

He put out his hand to shake. Without any hesitation, she took it.

"I can't make you keep it up if you get tired of it," he said. His expression was inscrutable.

"That's true, but I honor my agreements."

A guard knocked hard on the glass.

"We gotta take you, Rab."

"No problem," Rab answered. "We're done." He turned to Lee. "A paragraph or two is fine."

After unlocking the door, the guards watched their prisoner carefully while Lee exited the cell.

Before the door closed, she said, "You could have easily screwed me, but you didn't. Thank you." And then headed down a narrow hallway to the elevator.

Upstairs, she found a corner table in the cafeteria where, although she wasn't hungry, she forced herself to eat a bacon, lettuce, and tomato sandwich. She ate with her head down to discourage any would-be visitors. When she finished, she found an empty conference room to practice her closing argument, the one with the best scenario in which Rab ignored his demons and acted like a mensch.

⚜══════⚜

Toward the end of every jury trial, the parties and the judge confer in private about the instructions to be given to the jury. Usually, the conference is contentious, with both sides arguing about the admissibility of the others' proposed instructions. But the conference after lunch was remarkably civil, with no real disagreements. Given Rab's testimony, Lee's theory of defense instruction, which had seemed wildly speculative a few weeks earlier, was included without major revisions. Dan's face, for the first time, showed signs of fatigue.

As they headed back into the courtroom, Dan said, "You've done a remarkable job, Lee."

"Thank you."

"But even if they don't convict him, not everyone might agree to acquit him."

She pretended she'd never thought of this.

"And if they hang," she said, "things might not go so swimmingly for the defense the next time?"

"Exactly." Letting her know that if there was a hung jury, he intended to retry the case.

Suddenly, she wanted to poke his eyes out.

"Thanks for the warning, Dan, but absent a gross miscarriage of justice, I'm going to win."

"Maybe. Maybe not."

The closing arguments were tight, clear, and professional. Neither side resorted to passion, hyperbole, or begging. Dan's first argument coolly reviewed the elements of the offense and the evidence that supported a conviction. He reminded the jurors that the majority of the eyewitnesses including the snitch had testified under oath that Jeremy was guilty. He omitted any mention of Jeremy's confession and its implications, saving it for his second argument—the one Lee couldn't respond to.

Lee began her argument by saying, "Ladies and gentlemen, if there was ever a reasonable doubt case, this is it." And then, for the next hour and a half, went through the trial pointing out all the testimony that, taken together, necessitated a finding of "not guilty." She ended by recalling her opening statement in the case.

"So who is Jeremy Matthews? Is he a seventeen-year old monster who aided and abetted the brutal murder of the victim, or is he a boy who got in over his head and was unable to stop a group of older men from killing his beloved Sam? After listening to all of the evidence, the answer should be clear to you. But even if it isn't, the instructions still require you to acquit him. Why? Because, after hearing from all of the witnesses, it would be impossible not to have at least a reasonable doubt concerning his guilt." She paused, took a drink of water, and then as she almost always did, pulled out the instruction that defined a reasonable doubt and read it slowly to the jurors, making eye contact with as many of them as possible.

"And so, ladies and gentlemen, when you go back into the jury room to deliberate, that's the time to admit your doubts and vote for acquittal. If, out of fear or some other misplaced emotion, you vote to convict and then only later acknowledge your doubts, it will be too late. Jeremy Matthews will have been wrongfully convicted of a heinous crime and suffer the lifelong consequences. So please have the courage to fulfill your sworn duties and to find my client not guilty. Thank you."

In his second closing, Dan ended by reminding the jurors that their verdict had to be unanimous.

"Which doesn't mean that you shouldn't take your time, or that you shouldn't listen to everyone's point of view. Each person's judgment should be respected, and no one should be forced to surrender a strongly-held opinion just to satisfy the majority. Ultimately, however, because the defendant voluntarily confessed to the crime, the People of the State of Colorado expect a unanimous verdict of guilt. Thanks for your considerable time and attention. The American system of justice depends on people like you."

After nodding at each of the jurors, he finally sat down.

Lee closed her last manila file in the case and slipped it into her briefcase. As the jurors filed out of the room, Jeremy turned to her.

"So now what?"

"So now comes my least favorite part, the waiting."

"How long could it take?"

"Not that long. Tomorrow afternoon, I think, at the latest."

His knees started bouncing again.

"What if they can't agree on a verdict? The DA said it had to be unanimous."

I'll shoot myself, Lee thought.

"If they can't agree, the judge will urge them to try harder. If there are only one or two holdouts, the others can usually persuade them."

"And if they can't?"

"Then we do it all over again."

***

Lee spent the next morning pacing back and forth in her large, expensive office, past her classy furnishings, her ageless silk tree, and the Fritz Scholder painting of the purple horse whose expression continued to elude her. Yesterday, the jury had deliberated for an hour before being released. They'd returned this morning at eight. When the phone rang at a quarter past eleven, Lee stopped pacing and picked it up. The call was from Judge Samuel's bailiff.

"Do they have a verdict?" she asked.

"They have a question."

Lee groaned, then hung up and phoned Phil and Carla, who were sitting vigil in a Vic's coffee house on Broadway. Twenty minutes later, she and Dan were sitting across from Judge Samuels in his chambers. The court reporter had set up her machine behind them. Neither the jury nor the defendant was present.

The judge cleared his throat.

"At eleven-ten, the jury sent out this question: 'Can the defendant be convicted if he failed to contact the police after the murder occurred?'"

"The answer should be a simple no," Lee stated.

"I'm inclined to agree," the judge said. "Mr. Andrews?"

"No opposition from the People."

"In which case," the judge said, "I will write 'no' and send it back to the jury."

As soon as the conference ended, Lee walked out into the hallway where Phil and Carla were waiting.

"How bad is it?" they asked.

"Not very." She filled them in.

"Someone doesn't want to acquit him," Phil stated. "I bet it's one of the men."

"I hope it's not the bank manager," Lee said, "the one whose brother is gay."

Phil ripped off his tie and stuffed it into his pocket.

"More coffee and Tums?" he asked.

"Sure," Carla said. "Lee, why don't you come with us?"

Lee hesitated. The truth was, she was tired of pacing alone in her office.

"Oh come on," Phil said, grabbing her arm and making her rib hurt.

"I have work to do," she whined.

"Not today," Carla said, and grabbed her other arm.

She could have resisted, of course, but decided not to. The two people dragging her down the hallway had worked as hard as they could to help her win the case. The least she could do was be gracious. Besides, she was almost sixty. When older people acted churlish, the young rolled their eyes and pitied them, as if hardening of the arteries were to blame. Lee, of course, had been grumpy since the day she was born and forced to breathe on her own. Her parents hadn't minded and neither, thank God, had Paul. Well, to be honest, sometimes he did, but not often.

As they exited the building, the judge's bailiff caught up to them. His face was flushed from running.

"Lee, they have a verdict."

It was finally over.

"Have they called the detention center?" she asked.

"They'll be here in fifteen minutes."

The courtroom was filled with spectators who'd been waiting all morning. A number of them were now wearing rainbow pins in support of the defendant. As Lee and her team settled in, the media people were setting up cameras and crowding into any available seats. Mrs. Weissmann, whom Carla had picked up at seven, was sitting between Peggy and Mr. Clean in the row behind Phil and Carla. As soon as Jeremy arrived, the judge took his seat and everyone stopped talking. After both parties identified themselves for the record, the judge ordered the jurors brought in again.

A few minutes later, the jurors filed in, looking tired but satisfied.

"Do you have a verdict?" the judge asked.

The bank manager stood up, holding the verdict form.

"We do," he said.

The judge then motioned the bailiff to bring him the form. After glancing at it, the judge ordered the defendant to stand. The room was quiet. Lee and Jeremy rose to their feet and stood with their shoulders touching. Jeremy was breathing hard, so Lee took his hand and held onto it firmly.

"Concerning the charge of murder in the first degree," the judge intoned, "the jury finds the defendant—" He paused to smile. "Not guilty. Congratulations, Mr. Matthews."

"Thank you," Jeremy whispered, releasing her hand and kissing her cheek.

"You're welcome."

And then the room erupted. Peggy and Mr. Clean were hugging Jeremy. Carla and Mrs. Weissmann were crying. Phil was jumping up and down making strange hooting sounds. And a crowd of people had swarmed around Lee, trying to shake her hand. Her rib was killing her, but she didn't care. Eventually, the jury was dismissed with the admonition that they could talk to the parties if they wished but they certainly didn't have to. Without being told to, Carla slipped out to interview anyone who might be willing. And finally, the judge advised Jeremy that as soon as the detention center processed the verdict, he would be free to go. Peggy had to be pried away from her nephew.

"I'll be waiting at the bottom of the stairs," she told him. "And then we're going home."

Jeremy seemed the least fazed of everyone around him. Dry-eyed and calm, he thanked both Lee and Phil.

"I'll see you tomorrow night," he told them.

It took a couple of seconds to register.

"What's tomorrow night?" Lee asked.

"Your birthday party," Jeremy answered.

"Oops," Phil murmured. "That was supposed to be a surprise."

Before Lee could respond, Leroy walked up, grinning broadly.

"Come on," he told Jeremy. "The sooner we get back, the sooner you can be released. No handcuffs this time."

After Jeremy left the courtroom, Lee searched for Dan, but he'd already gone. She'd give him a week to digest the loss before calling him. Maybe two weeks. While she and Phil were packing up, Carla returned and told them what Lee had feared, that the foreman had been the holdout.

"Did you find out why?" Phil asked.

"Of course. Long story short: His brother stole his high school sweetheart, married her, and then came out. By that time, the foreman had married someone else. His brother never even apologized."

"Ah," Lee said. And then she remembered. "What's this about a birthday party?"

Carla glared at Phil, who raised his arms in self-defense.

"Hey, I'm not the one who squealed. Jeremy did."

"I hate parties," Lee told them.

"I know," Carla said, patting her on the arm, "but it's your sixtieth. Mark and Bobby wanted to throw you a party. They called and asked me to invite a couple of people."

"I wish somebody had run it by me. Who's going to be there?"

"Just Mark and Bobby, me and Phil, and Peggy and Jeremy. Oh, and Mr. Clean." She paused. "You have to come, Lee."

"I don't have to do anything."

Carla and Phil rolled their eyes at her.

"I'm going now," Lee told them, and began pulling her briefcase down the hall.

"See you tomorrow," they called.

Did she really have to be kind and gracious now? Is that what befitted her age? Maybe, but if seventy was the new sixty, and sixty was the new fifty, she had another ten years before she had to be nice and knuckle under. The thought made her smile. And in the meantime, she would be who she'd always been—herself.

When she reached the parking lot, she stopped to rest. In order to get her rolling briefcase into the 4Runner, she'd have to unpack the contents and place them one at a time in the back seat. For once, though, there wasn't a rush. When she'd finished, her side was throbbing. Slowly, she climbed into the front seat, found her keys, and held them in her fist. Goddamn it, she'd won!

"Yes!" she shouted, triumphant. "Yes, yes, yes!" After all was said and done, she was still a winner. Hold that thought, she told herself.

But she wouldn't hold it long. The next time was already looming.

CHAPTER NINETEEN

Ten years earlier, on her fiftieth birthday, Lee had woken up in an apartment on the west end of Provincetown, Massachusetts, one of the most charming gay meccas in America, where she and Paul spent a week together before visiting her dad in Boston. The Provincetown apartment, which belonged to an old lover of Paul's from college, was on the top floor of a house that had been recently renovated and now had skylights in every room. Outside the kitchen door, there was a circular metal staircase leading up to a widow's walk with a stunning view of the town and the bay.

After they'd risen and eaten breakfast, they hiked a few miles to Race Point, where they stared at an immense gray ocean that seemed to stretch forever. Behind them, the dunes lined the beach in both directions. As they stared, a number of seals poked their heads out of the water, splashed around, and then disappeared. And then it was so peaceful, they did something they'd never done before, something so unlike them, it was almost shocking. They'd meant to hike all morning and then rent bicycles and ride to Wellfleet. Instead, after sitting on the sand, they lay back and closed their eyes, and fell into a deep and dreamless sleep. A pale yellow sun warmed their faces and kept them comfortable. When they finally woke up, it was almost two-thirty in the afternoon. Lee couldn't remember ever feeling quite as rested or as happy as she did that day.

And now it was her sixtieth birthday and she was lying in bed alone. Well, not strictly alone. Charlie had jumped on her chest at six and woken her. Paul was gone, but she'd won her case and she was happy. Did it matter if she wasn't quite as happy as she'd been on her fiftieth? No, she decided, it didn't. Besides, since his death, hadn't she Photoshopped just a little of her life with Paul? Their relationship had been good—yes, really—but it hadn't been perfect. Whose was? Even her parents had quarreled a lot, although rarely after her mother's diagnosis.

Come to think of it, later that same day in Provincetown, they'd gone to the bar at The Crown & Anchor to hear someone named Bobby play the piano and sing songs that had been popular during the Second World War. The bar was packed with tanned, good-looking men who all seemed to know the words of the songs. Including Paul. It was obviously a gay thing and Lee felt completely left out. When she said she was bored, Paul told her to go but that he intended to stay. It was rare for them to feel so differently, to not be in sync. It made Lee feel dizzy. And to make matters worse, there were a number of men in the crowd who were clearly ogling her partner. So she stayed, but she didn't enjoy it. The rest of the week, though, was great.

Charlie was nuzzling her face, anxious for food and attention. She'd never gone back to Provincetown but had always wanted to, figuring they had time. It had obviously run out. Maybe, when she visited her father in two weeks, they could rent a car and drive down the Cape to Provincetown. Her dad hadn't been out of Braintree in years. As long as she found him a bridge game, he'd go. Last night, when she called to tell him she'd won, she also told him she would be coming more often now.

"You don't have to, kiddo."

"But I want to," she answered, feeling just a little bit hurt.

And then he surprised her.

"Okay good, but I'm still going to play bridge every day."

Finally, at a quarter to seven, Lee held her rib and climbed out of bed. She pulled on a black T-shirt and a pair of sweatpants that had once belonged to Paul. After she fed herself and Charlie, she would make a couple of phone calls, the first to Century Martial Arts Supply, to order a women's medium-size chest protector, and the second to an eye doctor she'd seen a few years ago. And that was it, she told herself—the extent of her concessions.

While she was eating her oatmeal and reading her mail, the phone rang. She assumed it was Mark and Bobby calling to remind her about tonight. After letting it ring for a while, she picked it up and said, "Jesus

Christ, I'll be there."

"Excuse me?"

"Who is this?" she demanded.

"Steve Roberts."

She put down her spoon and said, "Who?"

"Detective Steve Roberts. The, uh, detective who took your client's statements in the case you just won. After I testified on Monday, I came back in the afternoon and listened to your closing, which was terrific. No wonder you won. Congratulations."

"Thank you."

After a moment, he cleared his throat.

"So I was wondering if you were free on Saturday night?"

"Free?"

"Yes, to go out to dinner with me."

"I can't."

"You can't?" He sounded more confused than disappointed.

"No," she said, and then decided she could at least explain. "I've had this policy since I first became a criminal defense attorney that I'd never go out with cops or prosecutors. It's nothing personal. I just figured it would be easier." She picked up her spoon again and prepared to eat.

He was silent for a while.

"No exceptions?" he finally asked.

"No exceptions."

"Right. Well, okay then. Anyway, congratulations on your win and I'll see you around the courthouse."

She waited but he didn't hang up.

"Steve?"

"Yes?" he said eagerly.

"If you ever quit your day job, you could call me." Had she really said that?

"Well, I like what I do and I'm good at it, but if something changes, I'll certainly get ahold of you."

"Great," she said. "Good-bye."

She hung up the phone and went back to eating. Then, she glanced at the clock. It was a few minutes past seven. What kind of man called at seven in the morning to ask someone out on a date? Maybe he'd been working all night and decided to call before going to bed? Even so, it wasn't the usual way, which was to wait until the afternoon or early evening when the person you were calling would be fully awake and wouldn't be tempted to say something that might be construed as even vaguely encouraging.

When the phone rang again, she picked it up but said nothing.

"So I'm wondering if I gave up too easily," he said.

She closed her eyes and leaned back a little.

"Lee? Are you there?"

"I'm thinking about a conversation I had with Jeremy."

"The kid whose case you just won?"

"Yes. We were talking about relationships and admitting we were both a little fearful about starting any new ones. So, besides my legitimate never-date-the-enemy policy, I could also be a little scared about saying yes to going out with you."

"Well, if we're being honest, I felt nauseated before calling you and I'm a big tough detective. Actually, I still feel nauseated."

Lee opened her eyes and said, "Today's my birthday."

"Oh, well, happy birthday."

"Aren't you going to ask how old I am?"

"No, ma'am."

"How old are you?" she asked, finally smiling.

"Sixty-two."

"Have you ever been married?"

"Once, for twelve and a half years."

"What happened?" If he couldn't take being questioned, he shouldn't have asked her out.

"My wife left me for another woman."

"Ouch."

"It's okay. Now. In fact, we're pretty good friends."

"So how come you called so early?"

"Is it?" He paused. "Oops, I guess it is. I've been up since five. My cat woke me. Listen, do you like Italian food?"

"Sometimes, if I'm in the mood."

"Well, Dan said you did."

She stood up, carried her bowl to the kitchen sink, and began scraping its contents into the garbage disposal.

"How *is* Dan?" she asked.

"He's kind of depressed at the moment."

Suddenly, she had a thought.

"Did Dan suggest you call me?"

"Well, actually he did."

And then another thought, a nastier one.

"Before or after the verdict?"

"It was before the verdict, when he was pretty sure he'd win. So, uh, how about Carelli's at seven?"

Her no-dating-the-enemy policy had been set in stone for thirty-five years. During all that time, she'd never wanted to change it. Had never even been tempted. But what in the world lasted forever? Besides, taking chances was the only way to stay open to great surprises. And without an occasional great surprise, why try so hard to remain young?

"Okay, fine," she said, sounding a little too much like her father. *But I'm still going to play bridge every day.*

"Great. Shall I pick you up or meet you there?"

"Meet me."

"Yep, that's what I thought you'd say."

After she hung up the phone, Lee checked the clock again. Sometime in the next few hours, her client would be waking up in his own bedroom at his aunt's house, his whole long life in front of him. The thought made her very happy. Maybe someday he'd end up in Provincetown at the piano bar in The Crown & Anchor, standing in a crowd of beautiful men, all of them singing songs from World War Two. Or perhaps more likely, he'd end up in a church where he was welcome, standing among good liberal people, all of them singing songs in praise of an inclusive God. And that would be okay too. There were many kinds of bliss.

For Lee, it was winning cases and pushing her body to the limit. Because she couldn't spend the day in the dojo, she decided to hike instead, probably the Mesa Trail, seven miles from Boulder to Eldorado Springs and back again. Even with her rib, she'd be faster than anyone else on the trail. If she left by ten, she'd have plenty of time to hike and still be ready for her party, which she would attend and try graciously to enjoy.

In a couple of weeks, she'd call Dan and in the course of their conversation, concede how lucky she'd been, how easily she could have lost. They'd joke about the foreman whose brother was gay, about the witnesses Dan was forced to rely on, and how it all came down to whether Rab decided to screw her or the prosecution. Eventually, in a month or two, he'd forgive her.

And then one day, after she'd taken on another murder case, they would meet at Spruce Confections, where they'd each insist on paying. They'd have already figured out their strategy and what they hoped to accomplish, and then they'd laugh and lie and drink their cappuccinos and it would all begin again.

ACKNOWLEDGEMENTS

First of all, I'd like to thank Bruce Bortz, publisher of Bancroft Press, for loving my book and deciding to publish it. It's such a pleasure when a publisher shares the writer's aesthetics. It feels like kismet.

Second, I want to thank Alan Rinzler for editing my book and for encouraging me to look for a publisher who would truly appreciate it. Your editing and plot advice were invaluable.

My heartfelt thanks to Sawnie Morris, Curtis Ramsay, Molly Gierasch, Chris Ebner, Susie Schneider, Carol Terry, and Phyllis Cullen for reading the last drafts of my book and for cheering me on. Your words sustained me and kept me from losing my confidence, an easy thing for a writer to do; and without confidence, which is critical, there's no taking any chances.

Thanks also to Peggy Jessel, my legal expert on juvenile procedure. I hope everything in your life has gotten better. You're a wonderful person and you deserve to be happy.

Special thanks to Kat Duff and Jamie Ash, my soul sisters in Taos, who let me read the book to them and were always willing to discuss the story. Your love, enthusiasm, and support have kept me going as a writer.

Two excellent private investigators worked with me when I was a practicing criminal defense attorney: Eli Klein and Patti Mazal. Neither of them was the prototype for Carla, who sprouted full-grown from my writer's brain, but just like Carla, they were incredibly talented, tenacious, and dedicated. And so much fun to work with.

My second biggest thank you goes to my dear friend Daniela Kuper, who gently prodded me to write another draft when I thought the book was done. Your constant reassurance and love are priceless. Thank you so much, sweetheart.

And finally, I wish to thank Leslie Haase, my beautiful and talented partner, for spending the last twenty years of her life with me. And for understanding my periodic need to disappear and write.

Twenty years? Yikes.

ABOUT THE AUTHOR

Jeanne Winer was an attorney in Colorado for thirty-five years, specializing in criminal defense. During that time, she represented thousands of people accused of murder, kidnapping, sexual assault, robbery, drug offenses, and other serious crimes.

A long-time political activist, she received the Dan Bradley Award from The National LGBT Bar Association for her trial work in *Romer v. Evans*, a landmark civil rights case that preceded and paved the way for the *Obergefell* decision in 2015, which legalized same-sex marriage throughout the United States.

Her first novel, *The Furthest City Light*, won a Golden Crown Literary award for best debut fiction. *Her Kind of Case* is her second novel.

Like the heroine in her book, Winer is a martial artist who holds a third-degree black belt in Tae Kwon Do. She lives mainly in Boulder, Colorado, with her partner and cat, but spends a number of months each year writing in Taos, New Mexico.